THE MAJORITY

ALSO BY ELIZABETH L. SILVER

FICTION

The Execution of Noa P. Singleton

NONFICTION

The Tincture of Time:
A Parent's Memoir of (Medical) Uncertainty

THE MAJORITY

ELIZABETH L. SILVER

RIVERHEAD BOOKS

New York

2023

RIVERHEAD BOOKS
An imprint of Penguin Random House LLC
penguinrandomhouse.com

LIBRARY OF CONGRESS CATALOGING-IN-PUBLICATION DATA
Names: Silver, Elizabeth L., 1978– author.
Title: The majority / Elizabeth L. Silver.
Description: New York: Riverhead Books, 2023.
Identifiers: LCCN 2022044475 (print) | LCCN 2022044476 (ebook) |
ISBN 9780593331088 (hardcover) | ISBN 9780593331101 (ebook)
Classification: LCC PS3619.I5475 M35 2023 (print) |
LCC PS3619.I5475 (ebook) | DDC 813/.6—dc23/eng/20220929
LC record available at https://lccn.loc.gov/2022044475
LC ebook record available at https://lccn.loc.gov/2022044476

Printed in the United States of America
1st Printing

Book design by Amanda Dewey

For Avital and Levi, always

I ask no favor for my sex. All I ask of our brethren is that they take their feet off our necks.

● SARAH GRIMKÉ, 1792–1873

Laws are a dead letter without courts to expound and define their true meaning and operation.

● ALEXANDER HAMILTON, 1755–1804

THE MAJORITY

Half of the United States is waiting for me to die. The other half stands by, candles in hand, praying for me to hang on. At least that's what they tell me. At least that's what they say. But people never really want what they think they want.

Every Monday, Tuesday, and Wednesday from October through April, the main doors of the Supreme Court open at eight. There are only fifty seats available for the general public, and by nine thirty a.m., those eager visitors who waited outside for hours will have secured most of them. Sometimes, when nobody's there, I walk into the main courtroom to sit in the back of the gallery. The perspective is different, almost more ominous. From there, I can see four marble columns standing tall before deep mahogany curtains edged in gold. When I was younger, I used to stare at the curtains in pictures and later in person, sometimes wanting to hide in them. Now I know better than to hide.

On the days we have argument, a court crier pushes the buzzer, warning the crowd that there are five minutes to prepare and take a seat. The nine of us wait in the robing room backstage, where no one can visit, beginning the process of coming out into the courtroom. We have a private pregame ritual, a rotating handshake among all nine of us, as if to say, yes, we are all in this together. Everyone takes part in this tradition, now between six men and three women who sometimes like each other and sometimes hate each other when the robe is on, and tolerate each other when it's off.

The court crier opens his mouth.

"Oyez, oyez, oyez."

We walk out of the robing room to take our places behind our specific chairs at the bench. Mine is marked with a tiny gold plaque carved with the initials S.O.B. I take my seat. The chief justice glances to either side and picks up his gavel, slamming the wood with a single pound. It pierces the silence as I scan the gallery. My eyes are old, though. They don't always see what's in front of them. My hair has faded from the yellow, stubborn blond of my youth and I've lost some of my height; though having started at five feet eleven inches, I'm still taller than most of the men who have surrounded me for decades.

As arguments open, all eyes are on me, wondering what I'm thinking. But it's my own eyes, still a clear, light blue, that are the first to reveal the truth. If you look closely enough, you might have to reconsider everything you know about me, everything you thought you knew about the first female Supreme Court justice of the United States of America, the Honorable Justice Sylvia Olin Bernstein.

The first time I sat in that chair, I felt an unnecessary distance from a breathing life, as if I were meant to be protected by an older code. Outside, people waved signs of praise, of hate, of hope that the Contemptuous S.O.B. might make a change.

I hated the name.

"Just call me bitch," I wanted to say. "I'm nobody's son."

You see, everyone thinks that I broke the rules, but I didn't. Not really. I just oiled them up a bit for everyone else. But biographers want to present me like that: pretty but rough, demanding but kind, a model for how to get to the top as a woman and be remembered in history with elegance and idealism. This is the true story, though: I wouldn't be here if I'd had the luck of my cousin Mariana, or if I'd fought the fight like my friend Linda. Still, history chooses whom to crown an iconoclast, whether they deserve it or not. History is only as good as the historians, and I'm no longer trusting them to tell my story.

Part One

BROOKLYN

1949

CHAPTER 1

I was twelve years old when one half of my father's twin cousins came to live with us. It was nearly four full years after the end of the war and it took nearly all that time for her to emigrate from Germany to the United States. Over one thousand days; two hundred longer than she and her family had been in the camps. After the liberation, she moved to Munich and lived there among a small handful of survivors until America welcomed her to its shores. She settled in Brooklyn with us. The rest of my father's family lived in internment camps, awaiting passage to somewhere that wasn't Continental Europe. Somewhere like Great Britain or Australia, Canada or Israel; maybe even Argentina. We were simply the first to come through for Mariana. Had London called a month earlier, my life might have turned out very differently. Would I have found the law? I might have become a secretary to a businessman, a wife and mother, maybe a teacher? It's hard to imagine.

It was spring of 1949 when my father brought Mariana home, trailing behind him in the doorway like a stray dog. We lived in a tiny two-bedroom apartment off Kings Highway in the old Midwood section of Brooklyn. Together as a team, my parents owned the deli downstairs, drawing a few looks from the religious communities:

Marty, a man raised in a black hat and *tzitzit*, with his wife, Susan Henrikson-*cum*-Olin, whose thick blond strands baffled the kosher crowds, but didn't stop them from coming to eat.

Though my mother was born Christian and spent the first twenty-two years of her life in church, she met my father while waiting in line for a newspaper and coffee in Prospect Park. A week later, she shunned pork and crucifixes and began wearing a *Chai* pendant around her neck. What she bequeathed to me, in addition to her hair color, eye color, and height, was her quiet providence, something that nobody in Midwood quite understood. After all, everyone around her— the black-hats and *sheytl*-wearing *Chasids*, the *tallis*-touting academics, the soon-to-be-awakening feminists—had one thing in common: they knew that she didn't need to fight to live. Her life was not centered around survival. Survival, on the other hand, was something that trickled down to me from my father's side the day my cousin Mariana arrived.

Mariana's presence shifted the dynamic in our family. In a matter of days, my mother was no longer the gatekeeper to my life. It happened almost immediately. The minute one person enters, another's role shifts, and it can take a lifetime to understand what that means.

"Sylvia," said my father upon their entrance, "I want you to come here and meet your cousin." His face was solemn, his hands still.

I was sprawled out on the couch reading *Life* magazine. Jimmy Stewart was smiling in a slant against the flash of the camera. When I looked up, my mother was standing behind the couch, frozen, almost as if she knew what was about to come next.

"I want you to meet your cousin," he said again. "Mariana—"

"Olin*ovsky*," Mariana said, intentionally completing the name with an emphasis on the third and fourth syllables.

My father nodded, his head dropping up and down mechanically, saying the two names distinctly in my direction. Ours first, "Olin," and then Mariana's, "Olinovsky," two, three, four times, until I understood the difference in the names—that there was and wasn't one.

"Hello," I said, waving from the couch. I didn't bother to stand up.

Mariana nodded with her mouth closed tight, sealed with an invisible lock around the lips. She carried a single bag half-filled with a few belongings. When she walked, you could barely hear her. Her footsteps were silent, her movements invisible, unnoticeable.

"She's been traveling for quite some time," he said to me. "And she's very tired. Why don't you help me make the bed?"

I looked around. We lived in a small two-bedroom apartment, sharing three hundred square feet between the three of us before Mariana arrived. On a good day, each corner was piled high with bags and belongings. On a bad day, you couldn't find any corners.

"Sylvie," said my father again. His voice was hurried. "Your *room*. Sheets. Now, please."

Mariana stood emotionless at the front door, still, stalled in thought before turning away, clutching her bag close to her chest. My mother tried to take it from her, help her, comfort her, but she refused.

"This couch is fine," said Mariana. Her accent was deep. The *th* sound seemed to convert seamlessly to a *d* at times, with all *s*'s landing as *z*'s. *Dis couch iz fine. I von't be here long. Thank you for—*

"Please, Mariana," my father said, smiling. It was the kind of smile that a man knew would get him what he wanted. "We're family. Never thank me again. Okay?"

My mother echoed.

"Please, Mariana——" she said.

It could have been for anything, though.

Please be kind. Please stop. Please rest. Please don't talk to my daughter about what you went through.

But Mariana placed one hand out, just in front of my mother's face, stopping her from finishing her thought. A single hand that seemed to materialize out of nowhere.

My mother, never questioning anyone's authority—at least not outwardly—paused. "I'm sorry?" she said, confused. At first, she stumbled over her words. "D . . . did I say something? I'm . . . I'm sorry."

Five seconds ticked the clock forward as they shared a kind and appreciative glance. What they exchanged in that look, I'll never fully know. But looking back, it seems they traded places in that moment, shifted their roles, creating a triangle between the three women in the room.

"It's okay," said Mariana, reluctantly. Everything in our home seemed to come as a surprise to her. The softness of the carpet beneath her shoes, the heat inside the building, the internal questioning of those around her. "Thank you," she added.

It was as if she didn't know how to say those two words. Or perhaps she had forgotten. Words lost from language can rust, and it often takes restoration to get them back to their proper use and luster. *Thank you* was only a small part of that loss.

That first night, Mariana slept on the couch, unwilling to take my bed or my parents'. My mother didn't push.

"I'm fine out here," she said to us repeatedly. "*Proszę. Bitte.*" Please.

My father glanced at my mother, whose head dipped down, and then together, my mother and I spread sheets across the couch, tucking them loosely around the corners. I walked to my bedroom to gather an extra pillow and brought it out to Mariana. In the minute I was gone, she had moved from her stance by the doorway to sitting on the edge of the couch, exhausted, her eyes closed. I left her there, slumped over the arm of the couch, her forearm supporting her head like a pillow, two lines engraved between her brows.

Later that night, I tiptoed out of my room to use the bathroom. The only way to get to the toilet was to pass the couch. I looked down the hall to my parents' room. The light was off. I continued toward the main room, stopping in front of Mariana, who was asleep but still sitting up on the couch over the sheets, the makeshift bed partially made, her body stiff against the cushions as if it were no longer made to rest. Though unconscious, she was still fully dressed, her arms now placed closely beside her belly, between the pillow and her bag, like puzzle pieces fitting.

I couldn't help myself. I stood over her, waiting for something to happen. I don't know what I was expecting, but I couldn't look away. A thin strip of moonlight reflected the light from the kitchen, slashing her in the face, just under the eyes. It lit the rest of the room in pale yellows, enough so that I could see how bony and frail she was, even years following what I would soon learn was the end of her starvation at Auschwitz. A pulse beat quickly in her wrist. Her feet, still wrapped with socks and shoes, were resting on the floor as if she was prepared to run.

Then, my parents' door opened and my mother emerged as if she was already a ghost. She was standing on the other end of the room with two hands placed on her hips.

"Sylvia," she whispered, furious. I stepped back and stubbed my toe on the edge of the coffee table. Footsteps filled the room as my mother walked toward me, grabbing me.

"Stop staring. Go back to your room."

I tried to ignore the pain in my toe, but stumbled again as I waited for it to subside.

"I taught you better than to spy on our guests," she said quietly, helping me up and leading me back toward my room. "You have school in the morning. And Mariana is exhausted. Please don't bother her."

A strand of loose hair had fallen into my mother's eyes. I could see that she was looking straight ahead at me, disappointed. Her disappointment is something I still carry with me around my wrists like handcuffs.

"It takes time for someone to be comfortable in a new place," she said. "Especially after what she went through."

"Is she leaving?" I asked.

My mother glanced at the sleeping Mariana.

"No," she said, placing a hand over her chest. "I don't think so."

We looked to each other without speaking, until she decided to break the silence.

"Please, Sylvie, just give her some time. You don't know that she will want to share her experiences with anyone. Please, don't bother her."

A loud thump sounded in the living room. We turned toward the couch.

"She's not bothering me," said Mariana, her voice coming out of the silence. She tried to push herself up from the couch and leaned on one foot more than the other as she sat up.

"Mariana," said my mother, shocked. She turned around, tapping her chest with the heel of her palm. She didn't surprise easily. "I thought you were asleep."

Mariana still tried to push herself up, but couldn't, her body slumped into the couch like an anchor.

"I didn't mean to frighten you," she said, rubbing her eyes.

Her voice didn't match her words, somehow. It was flat, almost unaffected by me, by my mother, by what we said. She didn't care what we thought, how we felt, whether we were frightened. Fear was nothing to us, I would learn. Not the way she knew it.

My mother walked toward Mariana and placed a hand on her shoulder, hoping to make peace. Always an outward hand, never an outward word, always stopping me from making that first move. Before I could say anything, Mariana flinched, jumping back an inch.

"Did you want to talk to me?" she said, directly to me—not my mother.

"I, uhh," I stuttered, looking back and forth between the two of them. "I don't know?"

My mother's cheeks turned red with embarrassment.

"What is it? Yes or no?" said Mariana, matter-of-fact.

I didn't wait.

"No," I said, without thought, without pause. I glanced at my mother, who looked down, and then back to Mariana.

"Then please stop watching me," said Mariana. "I don't want to be animal in a zoo."

My body pulsed with shame all the way to my toes, but I couldn't help myself. I was drawn to her. Why did she clutch her hands together so much? What did it mean to be a twin and lose half of yourself before the age of twenty?

"Sylvia, please," said my mother. "Let her rest."

"You want to ask me questions, ask me questions," Mariana said, patting the open space beside her on the couch. "Nobody has talked to me about it here."

Mariana didn't look to my mother, instead focusing her attention on me.

"I'll go to sleep soon, Mom," I said. "I'm going to stay with Mariana for a bit."

My mother waited by the threshold of the door, her eyes shifting between us, once, twice, three times, before responding. She always did that. She always waited, contemplating each thought, each choice of words, before speaking.

"Okay then. Good night," she said to both of us, reluctantly. "Don't stay up too late."

Just as her door closed, Mariana awakened, as if she had waited four years to speak, four years to come alive again. And my mother vanished as quickly as she had appeared, back into her room, back into the darkness, where I'd struggle to find her for the rest of my life.

"You want to know about my sister," Mariana said, as if that fact had traveled here with her like her suitcase. "Do you want to know what happened to her?"

I sat up straight, my spine tingling. I didn't look back to see if my mother reappeared, her eyes jutting down, her brow disapproving; yet I could imagine that her lips were warm and open, reminding me that she loved me still, no matter how much she disapproved of whatever I was doing.

"Your . . . twin?" I said.

She nodded.

"Your other cousin," she said. "You had more cousins. Many, many more."

"Uh-huh," I said, feeling half of my body sawed away. I never had a brother or a sister. I don't know if my parents tried to have more children, and if they had, nobody told me.

"Aviva was my older sister by three minutes," said Mariana, adjusting herself on the couch. "At ten, she was already a painter. People came from around Germany to see her paint. And two years later, she was killed by a man pretending to be a doctor as he, how they say? Practiced . . ." She stalled, searching for the right word on the ceiling, before saying, "Experiment. Yes, experimented," she declared, continuing. "Experimented *on* her. On her *body*."

I wrapped my arms around myself.

"He used her body to determine if eye color can be transferred with a needle and saline solution. That was the scientific question for Dr. Mengele."

She said that name as if I should know it.

"I was in one room, while they were doing things to Aviva in another to test their experiment with the needles and the eye color. Her eyes were as blue as yours," she said to me. "Mine were brown. That was the main difference between us. Her eyes were light blue, so light."

I blinked three times quickly to keep my eyes from drying. I always thought I got my blue eyes from my mother's side. The *goyim*.

"At the end of each day, we were together in a single bed. She told me after the first night that her arms tingled like each hair was being removed individually from her head to her ankles. A few days later, she could no longer go to the toilet. She developed a pain in her belly and then she began losing her eyesight, just as was predicted as a side effect of the experiments. Her vision came together like a . . . like a . . ." She thought, looking up at the ceiling. "Like a melting candle. Four weeks later, she couldn't see anymore. She was blind."

I tried to look away, but couldn't. Her eyes and ears reddened, her cheeks steamed, but she never cried. Not once.

She told me that Aviva was kept in an all-glass room. People could see in, she said, but Aviva could not see out. Not for the entire time she was in there. Two days after she went blind, her right eye started itching. She scratched at it, pulling at the skin on either side to try and get to the center. Blood hardened under her nails, but she didn't notice. Eventually the eye became infected, but it didn't matter because she couldn't see out of it anyway. Her face broke out into a rash and started rotting all over her cheek. The skin tore. She went crazy.

I had to pee and my chest hurt as Mariana continued. But still she didn't look away from me; her gaze was as powerful as a gun pointed at my head. She told me that for an entire two days, Aviva screamed out. She screamed in four languages. German, Hebrew, Polish, and English. She told me that before the war, Aviva was a famous child prodigy back home. And that when she was ten, they put one of her paintings on display in the *Germanisches Nationalmuseum*. It was probably burned with the rest of the Jewish art, which was why Mengele wanted to use her in his experiments. To see if he could transfer her vision, her view of the world, into someone else. If that was possible, then they could ultimately take all the visions, all the strengths of the Jewish people and place them in the body of an Aryan man. They wanted to put Aviva's blueness into Mariana's eyes, but lost interest when her eyes fogged over. While Mariana never saw the needle, they took Aviva out behind the medical barracks and shot her in the back of the head. She said Mengele's officers didn't want to be bothered with her sister's screams or hear her cry out or watch her scratch her "good" eye anymore, the one that wasn't infected.

Then Mariana yelled BANG with all the power her small body could take and it sounded as if an actual gun had just gone off inside our apartment. My mother would surely wake up. The apartment wasn't that big. I could hear the flush of the toilet and the squeaking of the pipes each time someone brushed her teeth.

I shook my head nervously. It felt like a bug was crawling under the outer lid of my right eye.

Mariana took a breath and regained her focus before continuing.

"You know what Mengele later wrote about the experiment?" she said.

I waited for the answer for nearly a minute as the memory warmed Mariana.

"'*Es ist nicht möglich, eine künstlerische Vision vom Körper einer Frau semitischen Ursprungs auf einen Mann mit arischem Ursprungs zu übertragen. Ergebnis: Die künstlerische Vision kommt wahrscheinlich von mehr als dem eigentlichen Auge.*'"

"'It is not possible to transfer artistic vision from the body of a woman of Semitic origin to a man of Aryan descent. Outcome: artistic vision likely comes from more than the actual eye itself.'"

Mariana looked away from me when she finished translating, but for the first time, I couldn't turn anywhere else. My right hand reached up to my face and I started to rub my eye, slowly at first, pulling down the corner of the eyelid with my index finger.

Mariana pulled my hand from my face.

"Don't give in to it," she said, handing me a token of tenderness under her breath like smuggled contraband, before picking up exactly where she had left off. "After the war, one of Aviva's paintings was found hanging in Mengele's house."

My eyes dropped to Mariana's right hand, which was tightened into a fist, dry from the cold. Flecks of skin flaked off around her knuckles. Barely twenty, but with the hands and gestures of someone at least forty. My mother's forever age. Mariana yawned. Inside, I noticed that she had very few teeth in the back. And her mouth, rotting from the inside, released a putrid odor.

"So, all of this is to say that I do not want to be looked at when I'm sleeping," said Mariana. "Do you understand?"

It was less of a question than a demand.

"Yes," I said. I nodded on instinct.

"Good," she said, her shoulder touching mine, sisterlike, picking up her left leg with her hands and pulling it onto the couch with the rest of her. As we touched, the electric current from her shoulder transferred to mine, and I couldn't help but join her.

Some people can pinpoint the exact moment that changes them, that rams them in a new direction. A person, a calling, a siren shifting the tracks. Mariana pulling me toward her, luring me in, was that precise moment when my life really began.

CHAPTER 2

After a few months in New York, Mariana etched a place into the landscape of the city. She began to breathe with greater ease, leaving the apartment with more frequency, even finding friends of her own. It wasn't hard for her. Even if she never told them anything about her past, she spoke with nearly everyone she encountered, spreading a bit of her desires, her not-so-hidden stories, and her goals among them like confetti. Anyone who picked up a single piece of her felt special, without truly knowing why. They just wanted to be in her company, the company of this beautiful woman with the thin brown hair and forced smile.

Mariana discovered cabaret clubs in Greenwich Village and jazz at Minton's. She went to readings at the New York Public Library and met other survivors in New York at gatherings, where they found renewed strength in numbers. She learned to eat more food, so that her body was able to take on additional weight. The empty spaces on her face filled out nicely. A soft pillow grew under her chin and she liked to play with it as if it helped her think. The harsh lines of her cheekbones softened, the deep lines around her mouth and eyes relaxed, and she started to look more her age. She was only eight years older than me. Not old enough to be either of my parents, but old enough to teach me about them. She walked the sidewalks of Prospect Park in the days and evenings, smoking cigarettes and wearing a long coat as if it were the biggest luxury in the world. She walked through ponds and gardens, museums and libraries. She even walked into a court-house and began watching a trial.

"They're open to the public," she said to me one day when I came home from school. My mother was making dinner for us, listening from a few feet away. "I'm watching two right now. One, a boring case about custody, which I have no idea why is even in the system, and another fascinating one about a murder. An old man shot an old lady while she was in the bath and it turns out it was the husband and he's claiming self-defense because he thought she was a burglar." She paused, her eyes wild with fire. "In the *bathtub*? A burglar coming at him in the bathtub? That's preposterous. It's pretty black-and-white, if you ask me."

She was picking up casual English from television shows, repeating lines she'd heard in person. I was still studying fractions in school, but our education was at the same place. It took me over twenty years to realize, but this was the only time we were really the same. After all, she had been my age then when her schooling had stopped. She had been my age when her mother was taken away. She had been my age when taken to the camps.

Meanwhile my mother was always nearby, hearing our exchanges, skeptical from the beginning, staying mostly silent when Mariana was around, as if their voices couldn't be heard simultaneously, as if they weren't able to coexist in that apartment.

"Do you really think you should be going to these things?" she asked, as if Mariana were walking into a drug den.

"What? The trials?" said Mariana, nearly laughing. (Always on the verge, but never fully on the right side of joy.) "Of course I should.

They're not hiding anything *here*. I come from a family of the law. My parents would have wanted me to know about how it really works here," she said to my mother, before turning her attention back to me. "So with the bathtub murder, I think the jury's going to decide tomorrow and I'm going to go back and watch."

My eyes widened. "Really?"

"Want to go with me?"

"She's in school, Mariana," said my mother, annoyed. "She can't just leave her classes on a whim to go walk around the city with you."

Mariana shrugged and walked away without responding, her foot dragging in her ever-present tall laced boots. I hadn't noticed it when she first came to us, but now her uneven gait was more prominent. My mother hated that Mariana would walk away mid-conversation like this. The message was that Mariana didn't have time for any more words. Especially from my mother.

I never told my mother that I skipped school to go with Mariana to watch the jury announce its verdict the next day. It was a Friday and the weekend desperation coated every person we passed on the subway, on the streets, on the steps leading into the courthouse. Outside the courthouse, a vendor was selling roasted peanuts out of a cart. Mariana's long hand dropped into her pockets and she pulled out a couple of nickels to buy two bags.

"You know what I think, Sylvie," she said to me, crunching on a hot nut. "I think that these peanuts are the best food in this city. You don't see animals running around storing sauerkraut for the winter," she said, laughing to herself. "It's nuts. Only nuts."

I chewed on a few. My teeth nearly broke with each bite, but I didn't want to disappoint her.

She placed an arm around me and led me toward a bench at the edge of the block, just a building away from the courthouse.

"Aren't we going to go inside?" I asked.

She didn't answer.

I looked over to the stairs, the windows, the marble, and ached to see it up close.

"You know that back in Warsaw, both my mother and father were doctors of law," she said. "Lawyers."

I didn't say anything, but I hadn't known before she mentioned it to my mother the other day. My father knew almost nothing about them before he sponsored Mariana to live with us, apart from the fact that we shared a sprinkling of blood with grandparents a generation earlier. They weren't religious, I knew. They were assimilated. They would have expected to be safe there. They were wrong.

"Before they died, before the books burned," Mariana said, "my mother told me to look at the letters—to look at what makes the laws—for clues about what comes next."

I nodded. The sun was still high, even though we needed light jackets in the early fall. When I looked at her, the rays hit my eyes, making me squint.

"In Germany, they made laws that permitted man to exterminate another," she said. "To kill anyone they wanted. They made it the law that some people were better, more important than others. And the better people could make all the rules for the others."

My mother once told me that wheels go forward in motion, rarely the other way around. The only time they go in reverse is when you're trying to figure out how to turn around and go the right way. And even then, it's only temporary. I've always wanted that to be true. I've always longed for my mother's optimism, buried somewhere in her years between subservience and hope. I didn't say anything about her that day, though. I just listened to Mariana at that moment, watching her mouth curl around certain letters and close around others. I had already noticed that she bit down on her lips when she wasn't truly sure about what she was saying.

Mariana pulled out a small black book. In it were pages filled with her words, her thoughts, I would later discover. But she didn't let me see inside. Not yet. We sat beside each other on the bench, ogling the people walking around us, watching the leaves blow from the wind as she fingered the spine of her book and then flipped to the deckled edges to strum them like guitar strings, quickly and with syncopated rhythm.

"What's that?" I asked.

She looked through her handwritten notes. "Aha," she said loudly, finding a specific page. "Yes, here it is." She was excited. "Life, liberty, and *property*. This is where everything here begins for your laws. Not this silly pursuit of happiness. What is happiness anyway?" Mariana nearly coughed over the word as if it hurt to say.

"*Haaaapy-ness*," I said, trying it on.

"Happi-nessssss," she said again, laughing. "It's like candy. You want it, but you don't need it."

Her words rushed together quicker than I could keep up. Even in English, her thoughts ran like a river.

"Happiness is a ridiculous word, Sylvie. Do you understand?" she said, bringing the conversation back on point. "This is from your laws, not ours. This is what my mother and father were always talking about. They wanted to move *here*. They had plans. They wanted to come here before things got worse, but . . ." She didn't finish.

She closed the book in her hands and turned to me. A few people walked by us, but they were smudges, foggy background strokes in a painting. She chewed on the right corner of her inner lip and looked around, grinning with fury.

"They changed the laws about us in Germany and then Poland.

That's how it started. That's how all of it started. And most of you don't even know what *it* is that started. You are walking around, going to watch trials about bathtub murders as if that is a big deal. That's nothing. An accidental shooting in a bathroom?" Her voice levitated above me, high, churlish, laughing with abandon.

"I don't think it's nothing," I said. "I don't—"

"No," she said again, quickly. "It's different here. The laws here are different. My mother and father told me that. They studied. They knew things could change in Germany, but not here," she said, as if skipping on a broken record. "Not here."

I waited, rubbing my hands together.

"Speak," she said, raising her voice. It wasn't quite yelling, but it felt that way. "Say something. Don't just sit there listening all the time."

"I'm confused," I said to her. "I thought . . . I thought you *liked* going to the trials. You told my mother that's why you—"

"It's not about the trials," she said, placing her hands on her head, defeated. "It's about how the laws in this country work. Why else do you think we wanted to come to America?"

"Because," I said nervously, my eyebrows jumping, hopeful. "Because *we* were here."

She smiled with her eyes, but her hands were still busy searching. They were always busy, moving, doing something. Her top half never stopped moving; it was the bottom half that slowed her down. But that would take another decade.

"Yes," she said, almost annoyed. "You were here, too."

My eye began to itch again. It happened when she raised her voice, every time she seemed to be angry, every time I was insecure; like an ant had crawled its way into my eye, and I would be desperate to peel my eyelid back and scratch it. It took me years to touch my eye and scratch an itch in its surrounding area without feeling sick.

I thought I understood but I was wrong.

"My mother said we don't always need change," I said to her. "But if you want to do anything, then you need to stay quiet and play the game and then once you are *in* the game properly, you can do things the way you want."

"Your mother's a fool," she said, locking eyes with me.

I turned away.

"I see her sitting by, quietly. Born a Jew or not, she would have been one of the first burned in the ovens."

My gloved hands ran to their partners, each finger fitting with its pair until they formed a large double fist. I opened my mouth to respond, but nothing came out. One of the roasted nuts was tearing the flesh at the back of my throat, stealing my voice. I never thought I was like my mother. I wasn't sure I should keep my head down the way she wanted me to. But in that moment, I said nothing to Mariana. I said nothing when she threw away my mother as easily as she threw away a burnt peanut that spoiled the bunch.

The first in the ovens.

"I'm not going to apologize for that," she said.

I pictured my mother flat on a board, her eyes closed, her beautiful blond hair shaved to her scalp as flames consumed her. My entire body convulsed from the inside out, my arms and shoulders waving in the wind like the blue flame of a *Shabbat* candle, untouchable, shapeless.

"What's this?" said Mariana, mimicking me. "Shrug? You shrug when I speak? You shrug when I speak about my sister? When I speak about your mother like this?"

"I wasn't shrugging," I said, yelling. "And my mother isn't a fool."

My voice shivered. It hurt to speak, but I liked the way it felt. Nerves crawled all over my skin and back up to my eye. Mariana looked back at me; she was composed again. She grabbed my fingers, pulling them away from my eyes.

"Right," she said, nodding. "Good, I'm glad to see you have *something* in there."

I have something in there, I wanted to say. I feel things. I felt things when you walked into our home. I felt things when I watched you fill with anger, with fuel, with need.

"You know, Mariana, laws change," I said. "They changed the laws in Germany, like you said. They can change them to hurt, but they can also change them to help, too. Right?"

I glanced away momentarily at the courthouse, the large doors shut.

"Are we going to go inside and watch the trial?" I asked.

She shook her head, no. Then she wrapped her arm around my shoulders, squeezing me toward her.

"I shouldn't have said that about your mother," she said. Then she stood and walked away from me, limping ever so slightly on her left side. She didn't bother waiting. She just assumed I would follow. I almost always did back then.

"Come," she said, surprised, returning to me, taking my hand, and pulling me toward the subway. "Let's get home before sundown. Maybe we'll have *Shabbes* dinner together."

I don't think I ever forgave her, though. I moved on; we moved on, but forgiveness is an unpolished gem. You have to examine it to see if it's real.

CHAPTER 3

On the way back from the city, Mariana and I didn't speak for an hour, walking through Central Park, our hands in our pockets, our boots covered with dirt, a few stray leaves dropping to our shoulders and hats. There was nothing more to say.

The subway was crowded in the afternoon. Scores of men in black-and-white suits were standing on the podium waiting for the train. Less populous than the suits, though, were the red-lipped ladies with their black heels and ankle straps, their wavy hair glued to one side of their faces like a water slide, the look of dying hope in their eyes. Mariana looked like all the others waiting for the train.

"Don't move," she said to me. "Stay beside me the whole time."

"I've been on the subway before," I said, slightly annoyed.

Her eyes skated upward.

"This is my city, Mariana," I said, as if I had to remind her.

It was dark in the station and heated with bodies. When the train's light warned of its arrival, Mariana grabbed my hand and pulled me to the front of the crowd.

"Let's get a seat."

We walked onto the train car before the dozens that followed us, and were lucky to get a standing room spot near a pole and a single empty seat.

"You sit," she said to me.

I shook my head.

"We're not doing this, Sylvie," she said, wrapping her fingers around the pole. She pushed me down onto the seat with her open hand just as the lights snapped off, the train stopped short, and bodies fell on each other like dominoes, one after the other.

"Mariana!" I yelled.

When the lights came back on half a minute later, all that was left where she'd stood was the wavy line of her moist fingerprints on the silver pole.

"Mariana?" I shouted. "Mariana!"

"I'm fine," I heard from below. "*Sha*."

She was on the floor, lying on one side, her legs splayed, struggling to get back in place. I reached down to help her, but she threw my hands off.

"I'm fine," she said again, forcing it on me.

Still, she was on the ground and sweating visibly. Droplets over her lip, wet marks under her arms, a sock slipped down her leg around the calf. There I noticed it for the first time, the skin distorted, dusty white where it should have been pink.

A man at least as old as my father (maybe more), moved beside me, inching his way toward her.

"Miss," he said, addressing her. "Are you okay?"

She refused to turn to him.

"Miss? You had quite a fall there. You should bring it up with the New York transit system," he said, reaching down to help her.

"And say what?" she practically shouted. "I'm fine. Nothing to see. Nothing to look at."

She pushed herself to her feet but her left foot wobbled, unable to hold her weight. The man grabbed her arm to catch her, his grip tight, and her arm twisted beneath his hands.

"Get away from me!" she yelled, tugging her arm away.

It didn't take long for dozens of eyes to peer our way.

The man backed away, his two hands up in the air.

"Sorry," he said. "Just trying to help."

She dropped her hand from the pole and wiped it against her damp shirt.

"I'm . . ." she said, struggling to speak. "I didn't mean to shout like that."

Her accent was still present, but fading quickly.

I stood beside her, placing my arm around her shoulders, but she pushed me away, too. Touch was not something she was ready for.

"I'm a doctor," said the man, handing her one of his business cards. He was short, a sort of thumbtack in shoes. At only five foot four, his chest was so wide, it made him look like a square.

"I noticed you had difficulty standing on your foot after the train stopped. If you would like someone to take a look, please come to my office. I'm in Brooklyn, so if you are in the area, please pay us a visit. Don't worry about payment."

The card was tan and thick and the stitching was visible in the veins of the paper.

Tony Discanti, D.O. General Practice of Medicine. Brooklyn Heights.

I'd never known Mariana to hesitate about anything. Maybe this was the beginning for her, or maybe it was the beginning of my ability to see things differently, but after staring at it, she finally took the card.

"Thank you . . . doct—" she said, fumbling over the word *doctor*, ultimately deciding to use his first name. "Thank you, *Tony*, but I'm feeling perfectly fine. I don't need any help."

She grabbed my arm and pulled me away from him to sit at the opposite side of the car.

"Here is better," she said to me.

I don't want to be animal in a zoo, I could hear her say.

The train came into a station. We were still in Manhattan.

"Let's get off here," she said.

"What about getting home in time for *Shabbat*?"

She grabbed my hand so tight, I could feel her bones against mine through our gloves. Looking back at Tony the doctor, she squeezed my hand even harder and urged, "Let's go now!"

CHAPTER 4

Some memories are preserved in pure form. Others are more elusive, and in recollection imbued with invented detail. When I recall conversations with my mother, they rise from a scaffolding of facts in my mind, but are colored with meaning that I've no doubt imposed.

I remember that night because Mariana brought me home after nightfall. We missed the prayers over the challah and the candles and the wine, and my mother refused to speak to me until my father and Mariana were both asleep; my father in their bedroom and Mariana still on our couch.

I was sitting in bed catching up for the day of missed school when my mother knocked on my door. I can remember the color of my blanket—a deep burgundy, frayed around the edges. I remember that I was wearing dungarees and folded white socks with lace around the cuffs, and that I had bitten my fingernails down to their quicks.

"Can I come in?"

Her blond hair was beginning to turn a little around the temples. A rake of gray lined the spaces beside her forehead. When she sat beside me on my bed, I wanted to apologize. I wanted to tell her that I was sorry for missing *Shabbat* and skipping school, but I never got the chance.

"I got you something," she said.

I put down my biology textbook.

"It was just published last week." She handed me a small brown bag from Shakespeare & Co. "I was in the city today, too, and I saw it."

She didn't acknowledge anything else about our both being in the city that day. I opened the bag and pulled out a thick book with large yellow letters. *A Tree Grows in Brooklyn.*

"It's a novel about a young girl from right around here," my mother said, smiling, "obviously." She looked comfortable and content. "She's very smart, just like you, and works very hard. She focuses on her education because she knows it will change her life. This was thirty, forty years ago, Sylvie, and some things have come a long way since then, but they still have a long way to go. I think you would really love it."

From a foot away, I imagined I could hear my mother's heart beating. Her internal metronome was always too fast, unsteady, as if her body's clock were rushed. That unsteady ticking has followed me my entire life, whenever I get close to another soul. The ticktock of their lives slipping away from mine.

"Read it," she said, gesturing to the book. "And then we'll talk."

I flipped through the pages. The book looked sweet, but I was more interested in the news. I was more interested in talking to Mariana. I wanted to learn more about what had happened in Europe, not a story from around the corner.

"This is meant to be a distraction from Mariana's story," I whispered. "Isn't it?" I paused. "I know what happened there."

She nodded.

"I've been speaking to Mariana about it," I said, pushing.

Again, she nodded. "I know you have, Sylvie," she said, leaning toward me, pulling the blankets up around me as if I were still a little girl. She paused, thinking, gathering her thoughts properly before speaking again. "I wasn't sure I wanted you to know everything. You're so young. You don't need to know *everything* wrong with the world. Not yet."

She kissed me on the cheek and stood. A wavy vein wandered down her forehead.

I sat up against the blanket.

"I'm not that young."

"Look, Sylvie," she said, leaning in. "I'm going to tell you something about how things work. The system we live in is malleable, it's flexible. It can be moved, changed, sculpted into something else. But you must know how to work with it. You've learned about art in school, right?" She didn't wait for my response. "Michelangelo didn't sculpt the *David* without first knowing how to work with clay. You *can* make the world a different place if you want, but you must do it by learning the rules. Learn how to work with clay and then sculpt it as you see fit. Do you understand?"

"Yes," I said. But I didn't.

"Change the system from the inside out if you want it to last. Otherwise, it's temporary. You're just putting paint on a canvas that fades with time. A sculpture is permanent." She paused, and I could see she was thinking. "There's almost more of us than them, so it's just a matter of time before things are going to change for us," she said, seeming to switch the subject, though I wasn't quite sure what she was trying to tell me. "Not yet, but they will."

Not *yet*.

Three letters so filled with possibility. Something that has yet to happen, someone whom I have yet to meet, a family I have yet to disappoint. A word pulling life forward, pulling me forward to the me I have yet to discover.

"Go to sleep now, but make time to read the novel. I'd really like to talk to you about it when you're finished. Okay?"

"Okay," I said to her, and placed it in the space beside my pillow. A few minutes later, after she left my room, I got up and put the book on my shelf, closed.

Two nights later, my mother came to my bedroom again, breathy, emphatic, pointed. She held another brown paper bag from Shakespeare & Co., and told me she needed to speak with me about something. It seemed urgent.

She made me promise to say nothing to anyone. She made me promise to keep this a secret. Secrets, she told me, are a precious commodity. Everyone wants them, but nobody knows how to protect them. This time I pulled my knees into my chest to make room for her. She removed fifteen different envelopes from the paper bag, allowing me the space and time to read the name on each. All but one was addressed to my mother vis-à-vis my father—"Mrs. Marty Olin," not "Mrs. Susan Olin," or even "Susan H. Olin."

I can still picture her fingers today, dry around the knuckles, with deep valleys between the second and third knots. Once she let me trace my fingertips over the hills and valleys until I tickled her and she burst out into laughter. But not that night. That night she wasn't laughing. That night she didn't let me touch her. She handed me the envelopes and told me that inside were several bank statements—*her* bank statements. She told me that they were technically in her name and that my father didn't know about them and didn't need to know about them. That the money came from little pouches of the weekly allowance he gave her for personal needs over time. A haircut, extra clothing, lunches with her friends. She saved all of it for me to use for college in case there was no money left anywhere else. My father was never a great businessman. My mother always took care of the books.

I remember sitting on the bed and flipping through those bank statements. My father's name was on them, but at the same time it wasn't. I didn't have the words to ask why. I wouldn't have known that her own name on any of those checks would have been illegal in most banks and most states at the time. But it was.

She placed her hand on her chest, trying to take a deep breath, and she struggled. Sometimes to this day, I can hear the air going into her body, but I can't always hear it go out. It was a harsh sound, blocked, a drain clogged. Three days later, she was diagnosed with cancer. She would be dead in less than a month.

"Did you read the book yet?" she asked. "*A Tree Grows in Brooklyn?*"

I hadn't.

"Yes, Mama," I said. "I did."

It was my first lie. Since then, I can't count all of the ways I've failed her.

Right after she left my room, I heard her enter the bathroom. She turned on the faucet and let it run for a long time as if to keep me from hearing her sob. Then I heard a shuffling of feet, some words exchanged with my father, and finally a deep quiet. She never told me about the cancer. She didn't see why her final weeks with us should be focused on death.

The night she died, I read the book in a single sitting.

CHAPTER 5

My mother was buried in a Jewish cemetery in a commercial area of Brooklyn. It was a simple ceremony. My father spoke, I spoke, my mother's brother spoke. I hardly knew him, so his voice wasn't reassuring or calming. My mother's parents didn't want her to have a Jewish burial, so they sat nearby in chairs, immobile, stoic. When my mother converted to Judaism a month prior to marrying my father, her family stopped speaking with her. It's not that they disowned her for the decision, but that they couldn't quite wrap their heads around why someone would want to convert to Judaism at the height of Hitler's rise. *People are fleeing Europe* because *they are Jewish*, they told my mother as they begged her to reconsider. She didn't flinch. She said, *People are fleeing Europe not because they are Jewish, but because of Adolf Hitler. And if it's not Europe, it's Russia. If it's not Russia, it will be somewhere else. It's always been like this.*

They couldn't bear to see their only daughter choosing what they believed would be a difficult life. They came to my parents' wedding and stood beside the *chuppah* with my father's brother, his only living relative, and watched as their child married into what they knew with certainty would be a life of pain.

Surprisingly, this was one area my mother wasn't shy about discussing. A life of pain, she once told me, is one in which you are not pursuing your desires. A life of pain is one in which you are limited by your biology. She loved how Judaism inspired her to think for herself, to speak for herself, how the women in the Bible were just as, if not more, powerful than the men. She just thought women's power was accomplished in a different way. Not by disruption, but rather by fitting in at first through quiet acceptance by the masses, and then shifting mindsets from within. Like how she got my father to cook more: She started making meals for him, but once a week burned his favorite dish so that he came up with the idea that he would start cooking that one on his own. After enough time, he was doing half of the cooking and half of the cleaning. She winked at me after he "came up with the idea," and sat down on the couch to read a book while he put on the apron. *From the inside out.* It was the little victories that only she appreciated that pushed her forward.

My father, though he shaved his beard and stopped wearing a *kippah* when he married my mother, considered the funeral and burial to be a strict interpretation of the Bible, and so he followed it with orthodoxy. Women were not counted in the *minyan*, the ten-person collective required to say the prayers over the dead. And my father, a traditionalist, adhered to this belief, even if he didn't observe Orthodox Judaism at home. He didn't pray at synagogue more than a handful of times each year, but when he did, it was with reverence to the oldest traditions. I still know to this day that my mother would have been devastated that women were not counted to make a *minyan* at her funeral, horrified to know that the community she embraced with more passion than had she been born a Jew refused to count her daughter as she mourned. But rules aren't always followed the way intended, especially when chosen haphazardly.

Shiva was held at our house, and each element of tradition was kept tightly intact. My father's shirt was torn at the lapel half an inch, his dress was black, and he sat, reclined, in an open spot on the floor beneath everyone else. Someone I didn't recognize doled out drinks and food to everyone else who came by, consoling them in their grief. The incomprehensible, unconscionable grief of a husband burying his wife, of a child burying her mother.

On the first night, our apartment was filled with mourners: people who came to the funeral and burial, neighbors we'd met a handful of times, frequent customers, friends from my mother's past. Mariana sat with me the entire time, never shedding a tear. I don't think she had any left. Her body was long dry, a hardened coral. Maybe she thought us lucky that we were able to bury my mother, her body heavy with envy. But she never told me.

Kaddish was spoken shortly after the rabbi arrived. The mourners came swiftly, paid their respects, and left. For seven days, people stopped by, offering their sympathies. For seven nights, save *Shabbat*, a rabbi visited to lead a *minyan* to say the Mourner's *Kaddish*, the prayer for the dead. Ten men gathered around the couch and mumbled Hebrew words I knew well. But I was never welcomed to join. You didn't need to be religious to observe *shiva*. It was universal, for every member, practicing Jew or not.

Mariana and I watched from the side of the room, mouthing the words. *Yitgadal v'yitkadash sh'mei raba.* My father glanced over at us from time to time.

"What can I do?" he said quietly with a sympathetic shrug, and then continued with the prayer.

In order to be counted among the ten, you had to be an adult in the Jewish eye, someone who had been called to the Torah, someone who was a man already. I'd never had a Bat Mitzvah. Mariana hadn't had one, either. *Bat* Mitzvahs, for girls, didn't really exist then. Only *Bar* Mitzvahs, for boys.

By the sixth night, the mourners had thinned. "What should we do about *minyan*?" my father asked the rabbi. He was counting, and in the room was my father, the rabbi, six friends of my father's, Mariana, and me. Eight men, two women.

"I know I haven't had a Bar Mitzvah, but you can count me," I said to the rabbi. "I know the prayers. So does Mariana. Then we'll have ten."

The rabbi turned his gaze back to my father and shook his head.

"Men," he said to my father alone, reiterating the rules. "We need ten *men* to say the prayers."

They looked around, thinking, rubbing their temples, their beards, their noses.

"What about the neighbor?" said someone. "He's a nice man. There's a *mezuzah* on the door."

"He shops at the deli," my father added. "Sometimes buys kosher meat."

"We can see if he's home?"

"Marty . . ." Mariana said, her voice muffled.

I hope he didn't hear her. I hope he didn't choose to ignore her. But I'll never know.

"Good," said the rabbi.

My father walked toward the door. "I'll go and find out."

I heard him knock on the neighbor's door.

Words exchanged, a little laugh, a little sigh. We heard a few more footsteps and a door close and then my father reappeared in the doorway of our apartment.

"This is Rick," he said. "He and his son Ari offered to complete the *minyan* for us."

Ari couldn't have been much older than thirteen, maybe four-teen. They definitely weren't religious, but they were Jews who, it seemed, had been Bar Mitzvahed, and that was enough to make the *minyan*. The rabbi bowed his head ever so slightly to them and then ran his fingers through his beard.

Rick stared at Ari when they joined the men on the couch. An eyebrow raised, a subtle sign. *This is a story I'll definitely tell the guys later.*

"*Yitgadal v'yitkadash sh'mei raba*," said the rabbi, beginning the prayer again in Hebrew.

The nine men joined him, and just like that, the group of ten was complete. Ten men, mostly strangers, chanting in unison with the rabbi, as if they belonged at my mother's funeral more than I did.

I unraveled my fist. It was wet. I didn't need to look at Mariana to feel her fury on my shoulder, to feel her hand on my back.

"*This*," she said into my ear, "is *scheiße*. You think half of these men knew your mother? No. Not a single one of them."

I folded my arms, mouthing the prayer. I didn't care if they didn't include me. It didn't matter if they heard me. I was going to say each and every word aloud. I was going to recite the *kaddish*. I was going to be a part of the *minyan* whether they counted me or not.

"*Yitgadal v'yitkadash sh'mei raba . . . b'alma di-v'ra chirutei, v'yamlich malchutei . . .*" I began.

"Stop it, Sylvia," whispered Mariana.

I didn't listen, continuing.

"*B'chayeichon uvyomeichon uvchayei d'chol beit yisrael . . .*"

"Stop," she said again, this time louder.

I nudged her away.

"*Ba'agala uvizman kariv, v'im'ru . . .*"

"Sylvia!"

And all eleven of us chanted, "Amen."

"Sylv—"

"What?" I turned to her, almost screaming. "What?"

It was then I realized I had been crying. It was then I realized how loud I was, how very unlike my mother I was already becoming.

The rabbi glared at me.

Mariana folded her arms. She walked toward the group of men.

"This is sham," she said to everyone. "God wishing the dead well. Ten holy men sitting around making prayers to a God that doesn't exist for a body that is gone."

"Mariana," said my father, holding a prayer book tightly in his hands. Shame draped his eyes like the sheets covering all the mirrors in the house.

"Rabbi," she said, walking up to him, reaching out. He flinched when her hand dangled but two, three inches from his face. Contact would be impermissible, especially to this rabbi. "Tell me something. Why is it that Susan's own daughter cannot properly mourn her while two strangers can?"

The rabbi fingered a stray hair in his beard without replying. He couldn't address her. He wouldn't address her.

"What about her own parents?" she insisted. "They're also not counted in this?"

My father looked to Mariana and whispered, stating the obvious. "They're not Jewish."

"So they can't mourn her with *this* prayer?"

The rabbi continued mumbling the prayer as if Mariana wasn't speaking.

"You're holding *minyan* here for a woman who wasn't even born Jewish, did you know that?" she said to him directly. "Susan would have hated that her own daughter, who knows the prayers probably better than you, has no place here. Did you also know that there was an argument about whether to bury her in the Jewish cemetery? Is any of this too much for you to accept?"

"That's enough," my father said, raising his voice for the first time since my mother died. The issue was with her parents this time, not anyone else. After all, she had converted and had every right to a Jewish burial. He'd fought hard for that with both her parents, fearing that they'd be separated in death just as much as they'd been forced to be in life. That, of course, had nothing to do with the rabbi or *shiva*. But it seemed the fight was out of him now. Sweat consumed much of his shirt under his arms and around his chest. His pores were wide and large and angry. The burial was not the real issue anyway.

"Mari," said my father. "This isn't the time or place."

"Then when *is* the time or place?" she demanded, waiting for a response that never came. "A funeral is just a funeral, Marty. When you're dead, you're dead. It doesn't matter what people do after. You're dead!"

He walked away from the group and grabbed her hand, pulling her into the hallway.

"Stop pulling my arm," I heard her say. "You're just as useless as the rest. Refuse to stand up to authority. Refuse to speak up when you see something wrong."

"Mariana, it's my wife's—"

"Don't touch me!" she screamed, peeling his hand off her wrist. White fingerprints faded around her forearm, second by second. Ghosts leaving her body, one by one.

The door to my room slammed shut. She was inside and it was clear that nobody knew when she'd come out. My father merely walked back to the men, picked up his prayer book, and continued with the prayers. The ten men completed *kaddish,* and without asking permission, I went back down the hallway, where the door to my own bedroom was just as closed to me as the wails of *kaddish.* This was as holy as a handful of words, as meaningful as words in a language I didn't speak.

"Mariana?" I knocked. "Can I come in?"

The door opened a crack.

I sat beside her on my bed. We were quiet, the two of us, unsure of what—if anything—to say, but certain that for the first time in her stay here, we finally understood each other.

"I'm sorry about your mother," she said eventually.

I nodded.

"I want to tell you it gets easier over time, but it doesn't," she said. "Not really. Not when you get to mourn her or you don't. When you get to bury her or you don't."

I wiped my nose. A dribble of mucus had escaped when I was trying not to cry.

"Do you think if you had gotten to say goodbye to your mother, you'd feel better by now?" I asked.

"No," she said. "Death is death."

There was a rustle outside my bedroom. The front door was closing and opening as the mourners left.

Mourning, it seemed, was a sacred observance, a privilege for some. One reserved for those who made the laws thousands of years ago. It took me decades to realize it, but Mariana was right about almost everything. I never told her that. I regret it. It consumes me with sadness and rage and yet I'm grateful that it forces me to remember those I've wronged. Regret does that. It defines part of our experience and yet we strive to live a life without it. It's impossible, though, to live life not wanting to change at least one part of your past. I have three great regrets in my life, and this is one of them. Not telling Mariana everything that came after this moment. Not telling her that she was right about so much.

"They must be finished," she said, as we watched the snowflakes fall down the windowsill. "Do you want to go out there now and do it right?"

CHAPTER 6

It was two weeks since she died. A week since *shiva* ended. This was the hardest part, a few weeks after, once regular life resumes, when routine reminds you what you've lost.

Mariana didn't know where I was taking her, but I needed her with me when I approached him. The same way she brought me to court, this time I brought her to another place of judgment.

We stood before the synagogue my father had attended when he was a child. It sat at the corner of a small intersection off Prospect Park and now resembled a storefront or defunct elementary school. I had never gone to *shul* without my mother or father, and over time we rarely went at all. In all her time with us, Mariana never once asked to go and pray, to open a *siddur* and say the *Shema*. And I never asked for myself or for her. It was actually only my mother who had recited the *Shema* daily. Once she dipped her body in the pure waters of the *mikvah*, she subsumed her life entirely in a new direction. It took me most of my life to realize how much strength that took, how much independent thought it must have required to leave everything she believed in, everything she knew, to start a new way of thinking.

The old synagogue looked small from the outside, so when I walked in, I was surprised to find the interior bright and airy. Men in black coats and hats passed down hallways in formation like a line of ants, and disappeared into the sanctuary. I followed them.

I opened the second set of doors—ornate and adorned with golden designs—and walked into the sanctuary, where I could have sworn my name was being whispered in the robotic *davening* of the men.

Sylvie . . . Sylvie . . . Sylvie . . .

The voices billowed in the dead space between us, coming alive. My fingers began to shake.

Sylvie . . . Sylvie . . . Sylvie . . .

"Wait," Mariana said.

She stood by the door, refusing to enter, just like the day at the courthouse with me, where she hesitated, unable to actually walk inside.

In just a few weeks, she had already begun to take on some of my mother's roles. She wouldn't let me go anywhere on my own. She reminded me to keep up with my homework, even during *shiva*. She sometimes put food together for me, though she didn't know how to cook. But she almost never touched me, not even when she climbed into my bed to sleep beside me, never holding my hand, never embracing me, refusing to let her skin connect. It was only recently I learned that it is called "skin hunger," where your body is deprived of the necessary human touch. After my mother died, my entire body's skin was so deeply hungry that I longed for accidental touches on the playground or the subway. Mariana's own sense of touch must have been confused entirely, both needing touch but fearful of it. I don't know how the body recovers from that.

"You can't go inside," she said, her arm outstretched like she was handing me a rope.

Wooden benches surrounded the *bima* at the center. The arc was the crown of the sanctuary, with decorative golden leaves scattered beside it. Three Torah scrolls rested there, the center of holy life, the center of Jewish law.

"Sylvie," she said, whispering loudly. "Come back."

I shook my head.

No, I wasn't going to wait by the entrance.

No, I wasn't going to hesitate.

"Shhhh," I said to Mariana. "It's a holy place."

"We don't need to be here," she said.

I turned away from her. I was standing on the ground floor, which was reserved only for men. Upstairs was the gallery for women, where if they chose, they came to pray.

Deep near the ark, though, a few men were praying silently. One glanced up from his prayer book and looked at me briefly before turning his attention back to the book. I was a sound, an annoyance that buzzed around the room, but nothing so big that I would stop him from completing his obligation of daily prayer.

"*That's* why you wanted to come here?" Mariana said behind me. "To look at the men's section of a synagogue? Sylvie, they were all burned. The men *and* the women's sections."

The men in black hats looked up, startled by the sound of Mariana's voice, but quickly returned to their prayer books.

A door opened from the rear of the sanctuary, somewhere near the ark. The rabbi from *shiva* walked toward me. The men standing in prayer nodded to him in deference and he nodded back, running his hands through his beard.

I walked down the aisle around the ark and directly to him. Mariana didn't follow me.

"Rabbi," I said.

My mother was still as dead as she was when we buried her. When *they* buried her.

Before I could say anything else, the rabbi gently pointed to the top section of seats, where a woman was standing, holding her own prayer book. She was wearing a wig. It was dark and silken and dropped to her shoulders without natural curl. A cluster of girls and women surrounded her.

"For you," he mouthed, and turned around to walk to the men.

"I'm nearly thirteen," I said to him. He stopped where he was. My voice was nervous but steady. A decibel louder than it was when I spoke to Mariana. "I will soon be old enough to satisfy my obligation of prayer. *Then* could I be counted in a *minyan*?" I said.

The rabbi turned around, but refused eye contact.

I walked over to him and pulled some papers from my bag. There were five pages in full, written to the edge of the margins on the front and back. Underlines and letters in all capitals, blue and black ink. Every night for the past two weeks when my father went to sleep, I read through my mother's books about religion, about who can practice and why. Books that explained the Torah, books she'd studied to become a Jew herself. And when the sun decided to rise each morning, I placed them beside the copy of *A Tree Grows in Brooklyn* under my pillow.

But now the pages dangled in my hands, rattling between us like a white handkerchief. He wouldn't have to touch me to take them. He wouldn't have to even consider accidentally rubbing skin with me to read what I had written.

"Here," I said. "These are for you."

He didn't take them. Instead, he paused, glancing up again at the women's section and then the black-hatted men, and then back to me. I was wearing a dress that showed the bottom tips of my knees.

"Show me where it says that women are not required to pray," I said to the rabbi. "Show me in the Torah where it discounts the presence of a girl. Where is the rule written down?"

He ran his fingers again through his beard. "Walk with me," he said.

"I'd prefer to stay in here to talk."

He opened an arm and led me away from the men to the edge of the sanctuary, not far from Mariana, whose eyes were glazed watching us.

"Here is quieter," he said, clasping his hands at the center. "Your father is a good man. I know you both are going through a difficult time. How can I help?"

I looked through the papers in my hands.

"I understand that girls—women—are not obligated to pray and therefore aren't counted in a *minyan* or for a Bar Mitzvah, but I've started to read about what the rabbis say. Our obligations are to nurture. Our obligations are for the home. And since we are distracted by that, we aren't needed to pray."

He nodded, smiling—proud, even. In another world, he'd pat me on the head and say something about my good homework ethic. Or that I'd give a good speech at my Bar Mitzvah one day. Or Bat.

"And what a holy obligation that is," he said. "The *most* important one of all."

"But you are teaching people that *we* don't count in the eyes of God," I said to him.

"Am I?" he said gently.

He looked at the prayer sections.

"Does it actually say that anywhere in the Torah?" I asked again.

His eyes still surveyed his sanctuary, awed by its fullness, its majesty despite everything, before turning back to me without words.

"It's an interpretation only, isn't it?" I said. "*Your* interpretation."

In one direction, his eyes were still connected to their prayer books. In the other, twenty feet away, was Mariana, refusing to enter the sanctuary, her invisible rope still extended to me.

The rabbi looked into my eyes and softened. He rubbed his beard again, twisting it with his left hand. "You are very young and curious," he said to me. "That is a good thing. But Jewish law is Jewish law. A *minyan* is composed of ten men. It is the obligation of man to pray. It is the obligation of woman to produce children."

"And when she is finished producing children?" I asked. "If she even wants them."

"She *may* pray," said the rabbi, "but she has no obligation to do so. Public prayer requires attendance. Women are given this beautiful exemption because their obligations lie elsewhere. An exemption is when she is given a way out of—"

"I know what an exemption is," I said, again holding out the papers to him. "*This* is exclusion, not exemption. And exclusion is based on custom. Custom is not written down in any book," I said. "Is it?"

He held out his index finger and waved it near his temple as if I were onto something. Or maybe he was just humoring me.

"Is it?" I repeated, though more of a declaration this time than a question. I was right. I knew I was right.

"These are great conversations to have," he said, his voice curling up at the tip of each sentence. "To study. To learn." He paused again. "Very good."

His voice was slow but not lethargic. A sort of high-melodic baritone, climbing into a space with no final stair, a story without an ending, a joke without a punch line.

"Very good," he said again, and then pantomimed tapping me on the shoulder without actually touching me, and turned away. He didn't take the pages. He walked back through the same small door, hidden in the rear of the sanctuary. It closed with a quiet thump.

"Sylvie," Mariana whispered from nearby.

The papers were tight in my fingers. Mariana had walked into the sanctuary for the first time. I didn't even see her enter.

"You can't change him," she said. "You can't change his mind."

With one hand over mine, she walked me foot by foot, arm by arm out of the sanctuary until we reached the entryway to the building, where the rabbi's wife, the *rebbetzin*, the same older woman in the dark wig, was waiting for us, holding our coats in her hands.

"He didn't even listen," I said, once the dry air finally collapsed in my throat.

"He heard you," said the *rebbetzin*. "He may not have listened, but he heard every word you said."

Mariana stood silent, immobile before the two of us.

"I'm so sorry about your mother," the *rebbetzin* said to me. Her face was filled with empathy. "Come here." She wrapped her thick arms around me slowly. Inside her embrace, a confounding sort of safety washed over me. It was the first embrace I'd received from anyone since my mother had tucked me into bed the day before she died.

Eventually, I stepped back when I heard footsteps. The rabbi was listening from a good distance. I didn't need to turn around to know. I held the papers back out to her, and the *rebbetzin* took them from my hand.

"I'll pass these on to him," she said.

CHAPTER 7

The night after the incident with the rabbi, Mariana came into my room and slept beside me in my bed, a space between us to keep her distance. She was propping her foot on a pillow each night and wincing in pain when she had to get up to use the bathroom or walk to the kitchen.

For days, I passed the synagogue as swiftly as I passed my father at home, silent, acknowledging without fully seeing, knowing that there was something behind the face that I needed to see. But each time I thought about it, I moved on, going somewhere else, somewhere new, somewhere with joy and voices, and people who didn't know that my mother was dead.

Over time, I stopped talking with my father about my day because he stopped talking about it with me. I stopped asking Mariana about how she was feeling because she stopped asking me. Not the other way around. Never the other way around.

Weeks passed. I had my first birthday without my mother. My father brought home a cake that tasted like paper. Then Mariana made me a new one, and together they sang me happy birthday in a minor key and each went back to their respective days; my father tending to the deli, and Mariana sketching away in her notepads, trying to become her sister.

I was thirteen now. I took a science test and a literature test. I had my first kiss and it was smelly and sweet at the same time. We kissed near a doctor's office that was sandwiched between an elementary school and a pharmacy. The sidewalk in front of it was still filled with leaves, while the panels on either side were swept clean for pedestrians. After the kiss, I opened my eyes and saw the letter *E* misshapen on the storefront window. I walked toward it, examining the familiar name. Letters were painted in silver on the bottom of the window on the first floor of the building. *Tony Discanti, D.O. General Practice of Medicine.* All of the *e*'s were slightly warped in the exact same way. I told the boy I needed to go and do something, and that I would be able to walk home alone, so he left. I never saw him after that. I don't even remember his name.

Later that night, I found Dr. Discanti's card in the seams of Mariana's notebook when she was sleeping. It was worn and creased as if she'd been playing with it. The next day, I went back to his office. The leaves that had been raked away were replaced by a new collection, and they crunched beneath my feet.

It was quiet inside, quieter than I would ever see it for the next fifty years. There were five chairs in the waiting room, four of them empty. An older woman sat at the front desk.

"Do you need something, sweetheart?" she asked when I walked in.

I stumbled over my words.

"Yes," I said, nodding. "How do I get an appointment here?"

She handed me some forms on a clipboard. "Fill these out. But first, let me check our books to see if we have any openings."

She licked her forefinger and turned a large page.

"Uh-huh," she mumbled. "Uh-huh."

A door opened behind her and Tony Discanti walked out of it, looking at a few forms. He ran his open hand through his hair and then put the clipboard in the basket on the door before disappearing into another room. He looked almost the same as he had on the subway, only perhaps more sure of himself.

"We've got an opening tomorrow at two fifteen p.m.," said the receptionist. I looked down at her desk, where the calendar was partially displayed. The first few hours of Tuesdays and Wednesdays were completely blacked out. "Is this for you? You'll need to bring a parent with you."

"No," I said, thinking. I bit the corner of my lip. "It's . . . it's for my mother."

CHAPTER 8

"Please don't be angry with me," I said to Mariana when we stopped in front of the doctor's office the next day.

She faced the building.

"I made an appointment for you."

Her eyebrows jumped. "In there?"

As she read the sign, the color in her face remained exactly the same. White, pale, scraped with scars around the temples and chin, but unsurprised. I was waiting for pushback, I was waiting for her to yell at me, tell me that I was overstepping, but she didn't. She merely turned to me. Her face was still strong, but she didn't seem as tall as she had before. I was growing. We were nearly the same height.

"Why?" she said. There was no anger behind it. Just a simple question. Fair and easy. "Why *now*?"

"Because you are always limping," I said.

No embellishment, no garnish on my body language or my speech.

"Because you don't take off your shoes or socks in front of anyone," I continued. "Because when I look at you, it hurts to walk."

She inhaled before replying. "Okay," she said simply. "Then let's go in."

I signed us in at the front desk and the receptionist gave Mariana forms to fill out. We waited no more than fifteen minutes before a nurse called us back.

"Mariana Olinovsky," she called out, butchering Mariana's name, placing emphasis on all the wrong vowels.

We were taken to a small examining room in the corner of the office, and within a few minutes, Dr. Tony Discanti walked in. He was reading a chart when he opened the door.

"I see we have Mariana Olin—" He read from the chart, tripping over her name. "Olinooff—"

"Olinovsky," said Mariana, correcting him.

When he looked up, recognition soothed his face.

"Oli-*nahf*-skee," he said, correcting himself, searching his memory to place her. "You," he finally said, settling on a memory, hopefully the right one. "We've met before, right? From . . . ?"

"From the subway," I said. "You gave her your card. Said you could help."

"Right," he said, looking at me and then her again and me and then her. "Of course. Yes."

"Dr. Discanti," I said. "Can you please look at her foot?"

Mariana's eyes grazed me with confusion, fury, and love at the same time.

"Yes," he said, nervous, almost giddy to see her again. "Of course. Please, Miss Olinovsky. Can you sit on the exam table and remove your boots and socks?"

Mariana didn't move. Her body didn't budge, but her eyes continued to trail between Dr. Discanti and me as if she were reading us line after line. I'll never know what the reason was or why she chose this time to change, but that's the thing about change. It comes when we least expect it.

She began to unlace her boots, one then the other, until at last, her feet were exposed. I covered my mouth instantly. The left foot was double the size it should have been, double the size of her right foot and ankle, deep red and powdery white from dry skin. Her ankle was pink and swelling.

Dr. Discanti picked it up and began to examine it as if this were the tenth foot he had examined that day by noon.

"Does this hurt?" he asked, pushing down on the top of her left foot.

She winced when he so much as touched it, let alone palpated.

"How about this?"

He moved it in another direction.

"Ouch!" she squealed, and then looked to me, horrified, and then back to Dr. Discanti.

"I'm sorry, Miss Olinovsky," he said. His face was caring. "I just need to see what's going on here."

He tried a few more moves, shifting her foot, touching the skin in ways that were clearly supposed to elicit some form of response, and in each and every one of them, Mariana held in her pain, biting her lips and staring ahead at the half-dying fern in the window.

"Are you nearly finished?" she asked.

He nodded and placed her leg back on the exam table, while searching for the right words. I was a part of the wall decor, trying to camouflage myself between a diploma and a picture of two seals kissing.

"Your foot is warm to the touch, and swollen," he said eventually.

She nodded, unimpressed.

"Has it been like this since the fall in the subway?"

"Yes," she said. "It was like this before, though."

"Did it get worse since the subway?"

She nodded again, this time saying yes.

"It looks like you likely sprained your ankle," he said, delivering the news without fanfare or emotion. "Your leg is also swollen and it looks like you may even have a small fracture. I think we should probably get it imaged. I'll refer you to an orthopedic surgeon who can——"

"No," she said, placing one hand up to him, stopping him instantly. "It's just my foot, my leg," she added, uninterested, and then turned away.

"I see." His face was stoic, but unable to hide concern.

"It's not terrible pain," said Mariana, putting on her sock and beginning to get dressed again. "The boots help."

It was hot inside the office. I rolled up my sleeves.

"If it's a break, though, and not properly set, this could heal improperly and create long-term problems," Dr. Discanti said.

Mariana looked to me and then him, and pushed her boot onto her right foot and began to lace it, ignoring him as if he were speaking a language she didn't know, had no time to learn, no desire to understand.

"Miss Olinovsky," he said, "I am not a surgeon, so I can't help you directly, but your ankle and leg are quite swollen. This is really something you should follow up with a surgeon about. I have some recommendations and referrals. There are many options for injuries like this——"

"This isn't an injury," she said. "It's my leg. It's just my body."

Mariana looked away and grabbed the left boot.

"When was the last time you saw a doctor?" he asked her.

She didn't respond.

"I'd like to help you, but——"

"She was in the camps," I said to him, trying to stop Mariana from fleeing. "In Auschwitz. During the war."

He nodded slowly, the color in his face draining, the steadiness of his hands vanishing. There were many refugees who would eventually come to New York from Europe, but not at this point. It had only been a few years. America hadn't opened its doors wide enough.

"I see," he said, turning his attention to her.

She closed her eyes the minute he looked her way.

"Did you come here directly after the war?"

Mariana swallowed. I could see her counting backward in her head, tapping her fingers against one another. It wasn't meant to be a betrayal. She didn't keep it a secret. At least, I didn't think she was keeping it a secret.

"Six months," she said. "I've been here for six months."

"And before that?"

"I was in Germany. Waiting. To come here."

He nodded. "I see."

"And before that I was in Auschwitz," she said. "It's been this way for years."

She placed one hand on my back and I nearly jumped.

"That's it," she said. She never mentioned Dr. Mengele or her sister, or her parents or coming here.

"It's been like *this* for years?" he said, worried. "Or did the swelling start after the subway incident?"

She looked to me like I had the answer. I know she seemed to be in pain before the subway, but it had gotten much worse since then.

"If you fractured it years ago, we don't know if it fractured again. It's possible that the subway fall could have re-aggravated it. Or you reinjured it or have a secondary injury around it. I really think you should see an orthopedic surgeon to make sure your bones can be set and you can heal appropriate—"

"We have to go now," she said. "Thank you for seeing me. I will pay you for this visit. I may need some time, but I will pay you." She turned to me. "Let's go, Sylvie." Her voice cracked when she used my name.

"But—"

"Let's go," she repeated, again, her voice cracking.

He had turned off a switch that had taken six months to turn on. And it was my fault.

I followed her down the street, into the subway, up the stairs, and toward our building. We walked together in silence—her walk filled with noticeably more pain, more pronounced in how she placed one foot in front of the other. But she pulled me with her as quickly as she could past the elementary school, the corner bakery, our deli. She was out of breath. It must have taken so much effort to walk around hiding her pain. In this, she was exactly like my mother. In this, she hid her life, concealed it so that I could do nothing to help.

All women couldn't be like this, I thought, hoped—just masking their pain and their needs from others.

"I'm sorry," I said when we were just a block from our apartment. Since my mother died, it was the longest we'd been together *without* speaking, *without* eye contact. "I'm really sorry."

She took the back of her sleeve, wiped her mouth, and stopped in front of our stoop, staring at the three little stairs she needed to climb to walk inside. She tried to walk up the stairs, but her foot wobbled and she grabbed hold of the handrail.

"Please answer me," I said. "I'm sorry for—"

"For what?" she said. Her voice was flat, deflated. "For caring? No, Sylvie. There's nothing to be angry with you about. I know why you did it."

I could hear the sound of the ten men chanting the Mourner's *Kaddish* in unison: *Yitgadal v'yitkadash sh'mei raba.*

"Really?" I asked.

Her body slumped forward and her shoulders rose, shrugging.

"Are you shrugging at *me* now?" I said, nearly laughing.

"No," she said, looking around as if she wasn't quite sure where to go. Upstairs. Up three short stairs to the door and then twenty-five stairs to a walk-up where she slept half the time on a couch and half the time beside me like a sister. Or dozens of back steps to a park, where she'd see children and families who reminded her that hers were gone. Or to school, where she wasn't enrolled because she was too old for elementary school and not educated enough for high school or college.

"No," she added, thinking. "I'm just uncomfortable. That's all."

She rubbed the bottom of her chin. Her fingernails were bitten. One of them looked like it had recently bled. In my head, I kissed them, but affection wasn't what Mariana wanted. It wasn't what she needed. She sat down on the stoop, pulled out her notebook, and started writing.

I sat beside her.

"Can I ever see what you're writing in there?" I asked.

For the first time that day, she showed me her teeth. Though a few were missing in the back, she had the smile of a movie star.

"One day maybe I'll show you," she said. "It's nothing special. Just some thoughts, some drawings."

"Drawings?" I perked up. "Like Aviva?"

This time she smiled with her whole face. "Like Aviva. But nowhere near as good. She was the artist. I was actually a dancer. How is that for bad luck?"

I glanced at her feet. Her bad foot looked heavy, weighed down by an anchor, forcing her to stay exactly where she was: sitting on the stoop in Brooklyn beside our family deli.

"I'd just call it irony," I said. "Besides, I think we can both say it's worse than bad luck."

She laughed and, for the second time that day, tapped the side of my body with hers, the two of us one body for a brief moment.

"You're funny," she said. "Joking about *this* already."

"I didn't think I was actually joking."

"People like *that* man aren't going to help you," she said, glancing up at the clouds. "Certainly not doctors. Not doctors like him."

I waited for her to continue.

"What will *he* do?" she said. "Give me medicines? Cut it off? Both? I'm not stupid, Sylvia."

"No. That's not what I was trying to do."

"What *were* you trying to do, then?" she said.

I pulled off my jacket, one arm at a time, thinking.

"I want you to answer," she insisted. "Don't just sit there quietly inside your head. Answer me. Be different from your mother. Speak out."

With each word, each cut, it felt like she had died again.

"I'm sorry," Mariana said quickly.

"You meant it," I said, my voice hardening. "Didn't you?"

"I honestly don't know what I meant," she said. "Except that I shouldn't say that about her."

She pushed herself up on the stoop an extra step so that she was higher than me.

"This foot, this . . . walk reminds me of what happened. I need it. I need it to hurt. Do you understand?"

I backed away.

"Do you understand me, Sylvia?"

"Yes," I said.

My hands were up. My voice was loud, but not too loud. Never yelling, never shouting.

"I understand, Mariana," I said, even though I didn't. Not then.

It was the first time I noticed the hedged lines across her cheeks and the fan of anxiety beside her lips. Mariana and I were less than a decade apart in age. When we met, we locked together at that moment at the same level of education. Six months later, we would find ourselves in very different places. I was close to going to high school. With the help of my mother's money, I would eventually go on to college, law school. She would stay in my father's apartment the entire time, until eventually it became hers.

"What are you going to do now?" I asked her, still sitting on the stoop. "What if that doctor was right? And you need surgery? What if he was trying to help you? What if he is actually good?"

"Don't give me any of that *farkakte* stuff about hope," she said. There was a snarl around her lips that stung. "People being good at heart. I used to think that *before*. I thought about everything in life like that *before* we were taken away. Before Aviva was killed."

The hand was up again, right to my face, right in front of my eyes, and for the first time, I realized it was more of a shield for her than a signal for anyone else. She didn't want us to see in.

"You know, one of the reasons my parents wanted to come here is because there are judges who are Jewish."

"Not the rabbis?"

She shook her head.

"Cardozo is the name of one of them," she said. "And Brandeis is another. I don't understand what they say in their writings, but they were Jewish. And famous judges. That, I know."

I recorded their names in my memory. I didn't need a notepad with me. The pages in my mind were already beginning to fill without my even holding a pen.

"So what am I going to do, you ask," she said, once she'd gathered her thoughts. "What am I going to do? What am I going to do? I can't answer that. I just want to get through each day. What are *you* going to do?" She sat forward and placed one hand on my shoulder. "You're going to go to school. You'll become a lawyer, like my parents. You'll make sure they never change the laws on us here."

I laughed. "No pressure here."

"Do you have another choice?" She didn't laugh; she didn't even smile. "Do you, Sylvie?"

There was no answer that would be right for her. Not at that time. Not later.

"I still have to go to high school, Mariana," I said. "And college. I have no idea what I want to do after that."

She turned to me, her eyes dry. She didn't know about the money. She couldn't have. The envelope was safely under my bed, along with a handful of photographs, the copy of *A Tree Grows in Brooklyn*, and a few LPs. I checked on it each night before going to sleep to make sure it was still there, but every once in a while, I had a pang of terror that I'd lost it. Or worse, that someone else had found it.

"I saw what you did with the rabbi, Sylvie," said Mariana, not missing a beat. "I see how you tracked down this doctor because you wanted to help. You are able to do something here. You are strong. You are smart. You won't sit back, waiting for something bad to happen to us. Right? You will make sure *this* can never happen here. Promise me."

This, she kept saying, her lips moist. There were so many versions of *this*, I had lost track of which was most important to her. In that moment, I wanted to tell her that she could follow her parents' paths here, too, not just me. Become doctors of law like they were. But I didn't. Only certain histories get to be rewritten. Others get lost. I knew that even then. The ones that come to light only do so through sheer luck, through timing, through the hands of the right biographer. Had Mariana been born later, would she have become a judge? Would she have become a famous artist? A mother?

"Right now, Sylvie," she said, pointing to her leg, "I just need to decide what to do about this. Maybe Tony the doctor's right. Maybe I need to see another doctor."

"A surgeon? Do you want me to help? Come with you? I'll be there with you every step of the way," I said.

She shrugged, leaning on my shoulders.

"Shrugging?" I said to her. "That's all *you're* doing now? Shrugging?"

"And you have a problem with that?" She laughed. "No, Sylvie. You can come with me when you can come with me, but you need to focus."

I cleared my throat. A few kids walked by us, kicking around a soccer ball. Downstairs, though, inside the deli, my father would be weighing pounds of pastrami and portioning turkey breast on the meat slicer. Outside on the stoop, though, Mariana was giving up. Or rather, I was giving in.

CHAPTER 9

Mariana's story would be written without a map, while I drafted mine with a cartographer's eye. I would bring home friends for dinner and boyfriends for *Shabbat*. I would write for my school's newspaper under the name Sydney Olin, and later edit its headlines, determining what student would write what article, whose voice would dictate the news of the day. I would refuse public speaking and hide behind the printed word, never coming out from behind the desk to personify the truth behind it. I would read *A Tree Grows in Brooklyn* every year on my mother's *yahrzeit*, the anniversary of her death, and visit her grave three times a year: on her birthday, her *yahrtzeit*, and my birthday. For two straight years in high school, I would learn piano from the Russian woman who lived down the hall, but abandon it when I no longer cared. Mariana would pick up a paintbrush and splatter paint across a canvas, trying to reincarnate her sister's masterpiece probably still hanging in the *Germanisches Nationalmuseum* in Nuremberg. Every once in a while, I thought about stopping by the synagogue to see the rabbi, to ask him about my pages, to see if he'd read my words, but I never did. I would take the train into Manhattan and see my first Broadway show, *Guys and Dolls.* The music was nice, but the story bothered me. I preferred opera, like my father, where I could forget myself in the music, despite the ridiculous plots. I'd visit my mother's parents in Connecticut and think about college.

I would eventually attend Brooklyn College, and live at home while I studied English literature, psychology, political science, journalism, and history. My father didn't tell me that he'd sold part of the deli to help pay for the tuition, so I was able to hold on to my mother's secret money. I took a journalism class in college for about five minutes where they focused on the importance of headlines; though, I couldn't help but think that a headline wasn't enough language to really convey the full story behind it. So I tried literature, which was interesting, but I wanted to do more than read and talk about books. So I took a class on psychology, but realized how much we were being used as guinea pigs, and then I kept going, trying out new courses, new outlets, new possibilities for what to do after college. I began to study German, so that I could learn the source of what had happened to us in Europe. I didn't tell Mariana about it, not at first. Even though she spoke the language, she avoided almost anything in German, but I wanted to understand the people who seemed to hate us so much. If you understand someone, you can connect in a way to change them. You must find common ground in order to have that evolution, though, so I continued to practice, reading Goethe and Arendt and Brecht, slipping in and out of classes and office hours with teachers and professors who I hoped would guide me in the right direction.

But it wasn't enough. I wanted to see history come alive, so I went home to Mariana and asked her if she wanted to return to a live trial with me. It had been years, so I was surprised when she said no. She was already wearing her painting overalls and was in the process of working on a small canvas. Her shoes were off for once, and her feet were wet: colorful footsteps interrupting the white expanse of rolled canvas. She still walked with a limp. My father would often mumble about Mariana's canvases taking up too much space, but he never had the energy to do anything about it.

Soon, Mariana would stretch even larger canvases across our living room—36-by-36 and 48-by-48—in order to re-create her childhood in blacks and reds and blues. She still spoke with me about her parents, but less so as I showed less of an interest. I studied cooking and needlepoint and Freud. I dated a Jewish boy named Ezekiel and a Christian boy named Earl and gave my virginity to an atheist named Leo, who also gave his to me, and I introduced none of them to Mariana or my father. Mariana went on a date with Dr. Tony Discanti after two years of friendship, and my father sank deeper and deeper into a spiral of solitude. Sometimes it was about the deli, sometimes about my mother, sometimes about himself. He was worried about money, he was worried about Mariana, he was worried about me, maybe. I didn't know. He never said. But I didn't think about it. I was gone, mostly, in school and then college and with friends and boyfriends, so much that the apartment over the deli became nothing more than a place for me to rest.

So it was at the end of each day, from high school to college, from Hebrew school to the LSAT, I would come home every night and sleep in the same bed I'd slept in when Mariana walked into our home a decade before. Only now she was sleeping in a bed next to mine, a slumber party that never ended. Until it did. Because parties always come to an end.

CHAPTER 10

One day as I was walking home from college through the park, I stumbled upon the rabbi from *shiva*. I was twenty-two years old.

"Rabbi," I said, stopping him halfway between a playground and the sidewalk. He was focused, walking directly through the park in a diagonal line to the *shul*. I knew where it was. I had walked across this park nearly every day on my way home from school, from college, from outings with friends or dates, secretly hoping to see him. I never had. Not in the years following my mother's death, not in the time I spent in the neighborhood (which was rare these days), studying late at the library, walking arm in arm with Earl or Leo or Ezekiel.

"Rabbi," I said again, louder. There was no need to rush. He looked up. We were both alone. It was spring.

He was older now, too, the ratio of brown and gray in his hair reversed. I was taller than him by at least two inches, and showing more of my legs in a shorter skirt than I had ten years earlier. My head wasn't covered.

"It's Sylvia Olin," I said to him. He stared at me without recognition. "Marty Olin's daughter," I added as a reminder. I didn't bring up Mariana. He wouldn't remember her anyway. Though he had given sermon after sermon about the Holocaust, he had never taken the time to get to know *her*.

His hand kept to his beard and he twirled the strands around his fingers over and over, thinking, until finding the right memory.

"Yes," he said eventually, teasing out the word. "It's good to see you." I wasn't sure if he meant it.

I didn't shift my body, nor turn my face. Over the years, my body had grown steady, strong. I didn't move if I didn't feel the need; I didn't cower if I wasn't sure. And now I was towering over him. But he wasn't shifting, his body as firmly placed on the ground as mine.

"And you," I said.

I hadn't seen him since I was twelve. But this was no time for catch-up. I just wanted to know.

"Did you ever read my papers?" I asked.

He cocked his head to one side, confused.

"Papers?"

But he knew what I was talking about. I have no doubt he knew.

"My mother had just died when I came to see you many, many years ago. You didn't count me in the *minyan* because I was—"

"Yes," he said, realizing. "Yes of course. Martin Olin's only child."

"Right," I said.

He leaned closer to me. "Your father prayed to me for years, many years, worried about your soul. Worried about where you would be in a year, in two years, in three."

The wind swept a few leaves toward us.

"Did he?" I said.

The rabbi nodded.

"What else did he say?"

He shrugged. "What's he to say? He's your father. He wants what's best for you."

"Which is . . . or was?"

"What is best for you," he said again, holding out his hands in equal measure in front of himself. "A good husband. A good match. A prosperous future."

I shook my head. "Like his? Like the one he had that you never accepted?"

He looked away, toward his synagogue. "Miss Olin, I have to get going now."

"I'm going to become a lawyer," I said to him. "I was admitted to law school. Harvard."

The rabbi stopped and looked up without a shift in response, without a blink of an eye, as if it didn't matter.

"*Mazel tov.*"

"Thank you," I said, and he walked away. He didn't turn back. He scurried along the path of the park directly toward his *shul*. His laws hadn't changed in five millennia. There would be no reason to think they'd change now. And for me there were now other laws to worry about. I went home and began to prepare.

CHAPTER 11

It was only a few weeks until I moved out of Brooklyn. I had begun to pack and clean in order to make space for Mariana to take over my room. I pulled the special bank envelope from under my bed and counted the remaining cash. After my mother died, I withdrew most of the money and hid it there. Based on my savings, there was enough for tuition and only one year of living expenses. So that he wouldn't worry, I told my father that I had gotten a scholarship. It was true. I had earned a small amount for school. He assumed it was a full scholarship, and I didn't correct him.

In Boston, I would share a small apartment with another student, off campus. The law school had been exclusively male until nine years earlier, and they hadn't integrated women residentially on campus, so they put me in touch with another first-year law student—a woman named Linda Audre Loving—and helped us find an apartment to share not far from campus.

The fall breeze was cooler than I had anticipated the day we traveled to Cambridge, Massachusetts. I'd never been so far north. Mariana and my father insisted on taking the train up to Boston to help me move. Though she'd had several surgeries on her leg by that point, it still caused her great (and, she claimed, necessary) pain.

The apartment was small, but not smaller than I was used to after sharing a room with Mariana. It was on the second floor of a prewar building that hadn't been updated. A large window faced the street, through which you could see a new parking lot. Orange carpet bled everywhere, complementing delicate carvings in the dark brown wood, the only original remnant that seemed worth preserving. There were water stains on the ceiling, and I could hear the neighbors both above and below. But the two bedrooms were furnished—each with a small bed, desk, and chair—and even though it smelled like mold, it was the first time I'd had my own room in ten years. It was perfect.

Mariana and I sat together on the stoop of my new home, our shoulders touching like sisters, our hands conjoined like those of mother and child.

"We're not going to go through these silly goodbyes," she said. "Goodbyes are for friends. Goodbyes are for strangers. Not us."

"Right," I said, trying to smile.

"Look." I motioned. "My dad's staring out the window as if he's trying to eavesdrop."

"So he is," she said, not even bothering to check. "Tell me, Sylvie, who is your roommate? What do you know of her? Is she Jewish?"

"I have no idea," I said. "Just that her name is Linda. She's from Baltimore."

She smiled. "Be good to her, whoever she is."

An hour later, they were on the train returning home to New York, and I was alone. I pulled out an envelope that had been mailed to me weeks earlier, with the handwritten letter from Dean

James Macklowe offering to help arrange my housing. It was Macklowe who had suggested I share the apartment with Linda Loving, one of the first Black women admitted to Harvard Law. Those were his words; he made a point of writing that down, along with the point of me being one of the first Jewish women admitted. I didn't realize then how rare it was to get a handwritten note from a professor, let alone a dean, and I assumed Linda had received the same. I assumed a lot of things back then.

I wasn't sure when Linda was arriving, and while I waited, I picked up the orientation schedule and the list of five hundred new students, searching for my name among the others.

Sylvia Olin.

First year.

Brooklyn College, Class of 1959, *summa cum laude.*

Brooklyn, New York.

DOB: October 27, 1936

I flipped through more documents: a map of the campus, a list of all mandatory courses for first-year law students, and a welcome note from the administration, again signed by James Macklowe—the second document I'd received from him. It would not be the last.

Part Two

CAMBRIDGE, MASSACHUSETTS

1959

CHAPTER 1

James Macklowe was the dean of student affairs at Harvard Law from 1950, the year that boasted the introduction of women law students, until 1965, when he left.

He once told me not to worry so very much about some Supreme Court decisions. The judiciary is one third of a system, and individually the justices are just one ninth of that system. Though they held power, it wasn't that much power, he said. That was then. Then, I nodded and silently agreed, nervous in his company. Then, I was his student, his subordinate. Then, I was about to become a lawyer, an advocate, and I was so far from wearing the robe that I assumed he was right. I assumed they were all right. It's taken me nearly all my life to realize that we were both wrong. Though one person alone cannot create a nation, it is very easy for one person to destroy that nation; and it's the names of the destroyers—not creators—we remember most in history. I am neither creator nor destroyer. I am merely an arbiter.

Linda Loving and I spilled into the large lecture hall with more than one hundred other aspiring lawyers, herding in packs. Dean Macklowe stood at the front behind a small dais filled with papers, a heavy textbook in his hand and an expression of superlative pride smudging his face.

Macklowe had recently turned forty-three. The youngest dean on staff, he had also become the school's youngest tenured professor at a mere thirty-two. Every Tuesday and Thursday he taught constitutional law to first-years. Linda and I were two of the nine total women in our entire class of over five hundred, but the only ones in Macklowe's class. The other seven women were spread evenly among the three different sections.

"Constitutional law is the *real* reason you are all here, isn't it?" said Macklowe, holding up a copy of the document. "The foundation for all things: country, life, progress. This short document reflects the rights instilled in our world. Our civil liberties, our personal privacy, our future. The right to carry arms, the right to speak when we wish, to assemble, write, print, opine publicly or privately," he said. "We are in a time of exciting change, my friends. A transformative time like no other."

His voice was a constant pivot, always searching for the right volume, the right inflection. He wore a tightly fitted suit and stylish glasses, making him appear detached and approachable at the same time. His hairline was preternaturally low, and thick dark curls swirled out of place near his eyes. He represented the idealized future of every student in front of him and he knew it.

"We've reprinted our textbooks for the first time in five years. Since our last text on constitutional law, we've desegregated schools in *Brown v. Board of Education of Topeka.* The Supreme Court has voted to end segregation on public buses, and the Reverend Martin Luther King Jr. has risen to become a beacon of strength and inspiration not just for an entire community of people, but for all of us. The president of the United States has even sent in the National Guard to a high school in Little Rock, Arkansas, to desegregate our schools. All of this is happening in America *right now*. This is our country in life, in revolution, breathing and evolving. But the inequality . . ." he said, holding on to that last word, dangling it before us with his pointer finger, as if aiming at me and Linda directly, "between Black and white men has become even more pronounced."

Around the room were scores of young white men in tight jackets, skinny ties, and thick black glasses, writing down every word he was saying. Their faces were mostly pale; their skin dotted with freckles and often splashed with red from the occasional blush. A few were tanned a shade or two darker from a summer spent at the Cape or the shore, though I couldn't be sure. I'd never been to either. There were Black men at Harvard Law that year, too, and in the years earlier, but none in Macklowe's section. Besides, he used that moment to point to me and Linda—not any of the men.

"This is our Constitution amending and growing, evolving with time, and becoming *modern*," Macklowe said, holding that note, wavering on the word *modern*, as if he were an operatic tenor. "What does it mean for the rest of you? What does it mean moving forward—to take what is written in this book and extend it to life?"

"He's proselytizing a bit, don't you think?" said Linda, leaning over to me in the middle of class. She was sitting to my left, her hair pulled into a high bun like a ballerina's. She wore dark lipstick and dressed like she was the instructor—in full professional attire.

I couldn't take my eyes off Macklowe as he spoke, though. As a result, my notebook was empty.

"It's an historic time, and you are the people who will be controlling it," he continued. "At least some of you. Think about it. Women have access to birth control in a single pill."

A trickle of laughter waved through the crowd.

"We have our tenth class of women here at Harvard Law. With nine women in it," he said, almost giddy. "Look around in this class. Look around the campus. Find ways to be a part of the evolution of law as it is happening. You are part of it all. Please, do not take this opportunity for granted."

My body warmed from the heat of 125 sets of eyes falling on me and Linda, until Macklowe took back the floor.

"Now," he said. "I want each of you to take a look to your left."

Linda was settled in her seat, looking to her left at a boy with a tie and glasses, who also looked to his left. I was on the aisle. Linda was to my left.

"Now, turn to your right," said Macklowe, continuing.

Because nobody was to my right, I looked to the back of the class to a student standing near the door, holding a stack of papers, who seemed sort of aimless.

"One of the people beside you will run this country one day," said Macklowe. "Become a law partner, a senator, a CEO, a federal prosecutor."

Linda looked at me.

"The other person will not make it past first year," he said.

There was a tense silence as students took in his meaning.

"I know that might sound jarring, but it's simply the truth. You are at the oldest continually operating law school in the country. This is no small accomplishment and you should all feel pride in being here—every one of you. But it's a high burden. You will be tested in class and out of it. Your work in this class matters, your summer positions down the line will matter, the people you meet will matter. When I call on you, you will be prepared and stand and answer. It is not meant to be stressful, though it may be for some, and that stress may help propel you forward. Rather, it is a contract we will make with one another. I agree to stand up here and teach you, engage in discourse of the law with you, and you agree to learn, to be prepared, and to maintain the proper decorum that brought you here. At the end of the day, I am rooting for your success," he said. "We are nothing without your success, so please, if you need any help at all, my door is always open."

The room filled with murmured noise, suppressed idealism from each of the students hoping for a private meeting with Macklowe.

"Now, I'd like you all to meet my research assistant for this semester," said Macklowe, holding a hand out to the aimless student I had noticed earlier. He was white, pale, and gawky, and from his position, it was hard to tell if he was tall or short. "Mr. Joseph Bernstein. Mr. Bernstein is a second-year and he will be coming around now to pass out the course syllabus." Macklowe motioned for him to walk down the wide stairs of the dais.

My first impression of Joe Bernstein wasn't exceptional, not like it was with Linda or Macklowe. His hands were fidgeting, and though he was pooling a stack of syllabi in his hands, his fingers were climbing to the top button on his shirt as if he needed to unbutton it. He counted the syllabi and passed them out to the top row of students, and then walked down to the next row in the lecture hall to do the same. But no sooner had he begun than he tripped on a step, and came crashing down from the back of the lecture hall to the front, where Macklowe was standing at the lecture dais. Collectively, we all heard his body land heavily between the steps, his legs twisting painfully as dozens of syllabi sprawled across the floor like a spilled deck of cards.

But Dean Macklowe merely tilted his face toward Joe without

bothering to help him or even ask how he was. Instead, he pivoted back to us and opened his mouth halfway, letting a millimeter of a grin slip our way.

"The stairs might have won today," he said, glancing at Joseph Bernstein, "but we still have students who need to know the readings. Time is of the essence."

Joe sat up quickly as if nothing had happened.

Linda covered her face. "My god, that's embarrassing."

Then he touched his left eyebrow and winced.

"I feel bad for him," I said under my breath.

"While Mr. Bernstein nurses his injuries, let's get back to work," said Macklowe, back to the text in his hand. "Where were we?"

Joe picked himself up and began to walk around the room again, passing out the course syllabus row by row. I didn't quite catch the next few minutes of Macklowe's lecture, as I was focused on Joe walking with his head down, limping, until he reached my row.

When he passed me a syllabus, our hands grazed and my body tensed.

"Thanks," I said, taking the syllabus. It was three pages and stapled three times on the long-edge side like a book.

He nodded, counting out another ten, and he then asked me to pass them on.

I took the papers, but nobody was looking at him anymore. Nobody else thanked him. Nobody asked how he was, and in that moment, I felt sympathy and the need to somehow heal his wounds, physical or otherwise. I watched his index finger, moistened with a quick lick, count out another ten packets, pass them to another row, move on, and do it again. And then, I felt momentarily calm.

"You okay?" I whispered before he got too far away.

His eyes shifted left to right as he counted people and papers. Ten, he marked, moving on. Either he didn't hear me or he chose against answering.

"Mr. Bernstein," I asked again, slightly louder than before. "Are you okay?"

He turned to me and said, "Fine." His teeth were mismatched, the front two turning into each other like magnets in mid-pull, and his pants were torn at the knee where he'd skinned it. A smear of red was visible beneath the material.

Linda tapped my shoulder. "Syl."

I didn't look at her, but she did it again.

"Syl," she said.

I turned to her, confused. Moments later, her face froze.

"What?" I said.

She dropped her hand from my shoulder and looked away to her textbook.

"Linda," I said, whispering.

I looked up, and Dean Macklowe was walking right up to me, standing in front of me, his face registering something between anger and disappointment.

"I would hate to get in the middle of this riveting conversation," said Macklowe, "but seeing as I'm here, I might as well. Why don't you tell me about it?" He opened his arms as if asking me to dance. "Could you stand, please?"

The pleats of my skirt fell into place as I rose to my feet. My ankles and toes were blistered from the heels I was wearing. They had been my mother's. My father had given them to me when I moved to Boston. The only other pair I owned were a gift from Mariana, and I had worn them so frequently they were now too ragged for the first day of class.

"Thank you, Miss . . . ?"

"Olin," I said. "Sylvia Olin."

"Miss Olin," he said. "As one of nine women in this class, and one of two in this section, you hold a particularly special role. I certainly hope this is not an indication of how you'll act in my class in the future." He glanced next at Linda. "Or you."

When Macklowe's eyes connected with mine, though, it was as if the next thirty years flashed in fifteen seconds. A ballet turned into a waltz, which turned into a tug-of-war. I didn't see it then, but weeks later I'd realize that I was taller than him by at least two inches. And the taller person is always supposed to lead in dance.

"Of course not," I said. "I apologize."

Linda said the same and I could hear the frustration in her voice. It was subtle, but there.

"Good," he said, walking back to the podium. "Good to know."

Linda ducked her head ever so slightly.

"Sorry," I whispered to her.

Macklowe then continued as if he'd never stopped, while I searched for Joseph Bernstein, who had moved back to the last row of class. He was writing in a notebook, his face turned away from everyone like he was trying to hide.

"Now, please open your textbooks to page two fifty-three," said Macklowe. "*Brown v. Board of Education of Topeka.*"

I sat up to readjust my seat while he presented the case to the class. My skirt folded under me and I needed to get comfortable. But as I sat down again, I noticed Macklowe looking my way, and again we locked eyes. He wasn't staring at the body of students before him; he was looking at me. It was at once mystifying and illuminating, a spotlight with dust filtering through, and at that moment, I understood what it felt like to be in the light of his gaze. And I liked it.

CHAPTER 2

Linda Loving came to Boston from Baltimore via Cleveland. Her mother was widowed from the war long before Mariana made her way to us in Brooklyn. When Linda was only eight, her mother started a successful dress company in Baltimore, built it into a six-store empire around the Eastern Seaboard, and then got remarried in Cleveland to a white man whom Linda never really liked. Her mother had twins with him when Linda was sixteen, and for this reason, Linda both loved and hated Ohio, frequently wanting to be with her mother, but almost always wanting to escape her stepfather more than anything else. The stepdad left as soon as the kids turned one, for no reason other than the pathetic non-reason he left in a note: "Sorry, I can't." They never found out why, or rather, Linda's mother never told her. They moved back to Baltimore, where Linda helped raise her brothers for a few years, until she left for college; but without Linda or the husband to help at home, her mother's clothing company took a hit. She had to close down all but one of the stores and was never able to grow the company back to its full fleet.

Seeing the writing on the wall, her mother cashed out. She sold the business while it was still worth something, and moved to DC.

She turned her attention to politics and the civil rights movement, raised money for candidates she believed in, dated frequently, and went back to school for business administration. At the end of the day (and many marriage proposals later), though, she refused to marry a third time.

Because the age gap was wide with her brothers, the twins never felt like Linda's siblings, not fully. Her skin was shades darker than theirs; one of them passed for white and the other fit in almost everywhere and nowhere at once. But Linda didn't look like them, and this made her love her mother even more, a woman who mirrored her in beauty and ambition alike. This, Linda confessed to me later, is how her mother got ahead when everyone was trying to hold a strike against her. Beauty, attraction, no matter what, gets people to look at you, she said to me, blowing a perfect ring of smoke toward the window. And if they look at you, they listen. They may not understand you, they may be misguided, they may be wrong, but they are at the very least hearing you, and over time, hearing turns into listening.

Linda came to school already deep in a relationship with a guy named Ray Blayne, who both heard and listened to her. He was nothing like the ex-stepdad. They had gone to both high school and college together, and shared a future plan spread out like a tape measure across the entire floor of her life. She had a photo of him in her room in which he sported a too-skinny mustache and cheekbones that were rounded like baseballs. He looked cute enough, but not nearly as attractive as she was. That was all I knew about him—what I could see—and all I really knew about her relationship for a while, too.

We had been roommates long enough that we shared meals, stories, and homework, but whenever Ray called she vanished into her room, as if her romantic relationship were off-limits between us. The longest boyfriend I'd ever had was Leo, and that had lasted no more than a month. Ezekiel and Earl were a handful of dates each. I never even introduced them to anyone who mattered. There was never any conversation about what would happen if I moved out of New York.

A few weeks after Joe Bernstein's fall, I found Linda hiding in a stall in the women's bathroom.

"Hey," I said, tapping on the door. "You all right?"

Her high heels were visible below. She was smoking; ribbons of smoke traveled between the stall door and its metal hinge. And through that crack I could see that her face was wet, her makeup smudged.

"Linda?"

She opened the stall, wiped the space under her eyes, and pulled another cigarette from her purse. She and Ray had broken up. It was mutual, she said, but that made it no less painful.

"Do you want to talk about it?" I asked, leaning on the door.

Her thumb turned the metal grate of the lighter, trying for fire, but it didn't light. I took it and lit the cigarette for her.

"Well, he went to dental school. I came here."

"And?" I said, handing the lighter back.

"Somehow we decided to make it through college together, but this—*this*—is apparently too much."

"What's too much?" I asked. "The distance?"

"Sure," she said, inhaling. "We'll call it that."

She stood from the toilet seat and came out of the stall. We slumped together against the wall near the window, beside the sink and towel dispensers. The one women's bathroom on campus was an old men's bathroom that had been converted. None of the other buildings had women's bathrooms, so we were expected to use this one no matter where we were.

She pulled out a new cigarette.

"Want one?" she offered. It dangled between her fingers toward me.

"Okay," I said.

"Did I ever tell you that we—Ray and I—were the only two Black kids from our high school who went on to grad school?" she continued, getting comfortable on the bathroom floor beside me. "People made a big deal of it in college. The next year there were twenty."

I shook my head. "No, you didn't."

"I don't want it to be a big deal," she said. "I want it to be the goddamn norm."

Her eyes were still wet. She lit my cigarette, and then handed it to me. "Here."

Even though I'd never so much as held a cigarette, I took it and I inhaled, feeling the smoke enter my lungs, burning my throat and calming me at the same time.

"You going to be okay?" I asked, trying not to let on how green I felt. I was mesmerized by the orange glow incinerating the paper between my fingers.

"Eventually, I will be. Obviously," she said, nodding. "I mean, this is just one part of my life. Not my life, just one part of it. Ray Blayne doesn't get to decide my mood. Not all the way from San Francisco."

She inhaled deeply, and then let another ribbon of smoke tunnel out between her lips as she held back tears.

"That's where he lives. Did I tell you that? San Francisco. Well, just outside."

I shook my head. "Let me grab you a tissue."

"It's fine, Syl," she said.

But her eyes were wet and her nose was running, so I reached over into the stall and grabbed a roll of toilet paper to hand her.

"The thing is, I don't know why I'm so upset," she said, tearing off three squares. She blew her nose.

"You can be upset."

"Yeah, but I shouldn't," she said, coughing slightly on the inhale. "Not about this. *I* was the one who told him I didn't want to get married. *I* was the one who told him I wanted to focus on my career, on being *here*, being one of the Nine."

"The Nine," I cheered.

"The Nine," she echoed, almost as if she regretted it, and at the exact moment, the burning cherry at the end of her cigarette dropped onto the stack of toilet paper rolls that was sitting nearby. In less than the time it takes to blink, it began to light. We watched, mesmerized, as the stack began to smolder. Small pieces of lacy paper folded into each other, the ash spreading and glowing, until there was actual flame. And once there were flames, they moved quickly.

"Sylvia!" she yelled.

"Jesus Christ."

"Shit!"

The flames reached for the stack of paper towels.

"Shit, shit, shit!" she said. "Water!"

"Water," I echoed. "The sink!"

There was no smoke detector, no alarm sounding for help. And the sinks—made of one hot and one cold faucet—were too small to get enough water.

The fire continued, and we kept trying to fill up little handfuls of water from the tiny faucets, but the water wasn't putting it out fast enough, so we emptied our purses and filled each with water, dumping it onto the burning toilet rolls and the hand towels, and the patch of wall near the door, until at last the flames subsided.

"It's out," she cried, bursting into laughter. "It's out!"

We slumped down on the tile floor, now sprayed with a thin layer of smoky residue, our hearts beating fast and in sync.

I looked at the contents of Linda's purse spread all over the floor, drenched. Three lipstick tubes, one makeup bag, a notepad, a pen, a copy of the Constitution. There was also an old wallet with plastic envelopes of pictures of her mother, the twin brothers, and the boyfriend who was now no longer. In mine, there had only been a notepad, pen, keys, and a photo of my mother.

"Want to burn the picture of Ray now, while we're at it?" I said.

"Want to burn down the school in addition?" she said.

"Let's first see how this year turns out," I said.

Linda held out her hand and pretended to hold a glass of champagne to toast my invisible glass. "Touché, my friend." She nodded, exhausted.

Nobody had ever called me friend like that before. "Sylvia," "Sylvie," "sweetheart," but not "friend" alone.

"Why thank you," I said, grinning, sweating, catching my breath, and happier than I'd been in years.

After the fire, Linda and I started studying together. We tested each other on the law ("What happens in *Marbury v. Madison*?"), took turns buying food (mainly pasta, occasionally fish), and walked in on each other on the toilet and on the phone (though usually she was the one being called). Linda's writing was praised in our Legal Research and Writing class. The grading and submissions were blind, and without fail, she repeatedly scored the top grade in our section. We shared a typewriter, and I sometimes looked over her sample briefs to see what she was doing right. Nevertheless, I bested her in

Constitutional Law, and we got about the same grades in Criminal Law and Torts. By the end of the first semester, we were not just the top performing women in our year, but among the top students overall.

When I now think of all the ways I failed Linda, though, I flinch at the memories.

CHAPTER 3

By the time spring semester rolled around, Linda had expanded her friend group and I studied alone most nights in the reading room of the law library. I headed there late one Thursday night to prepare for Ladies' Day in Macklowe's class, the one day each term in class when he would call on the women specifically. I found my usual seat, and as soon as I pulled out my con law book, a voice wafted through the green lamps on the table.

"Olin comma Sylvia?"

I looked up.

"Joseph Bernstein," I said, recognizing him instantly. From my vantage point, he seemed tall, though I would later realize I had almost half a foot on him. His brown hair was parted on the side and smoothed back with gel. A few strands were out of place, sticking out. "From Dean Macklowe's class."

He leaned over to shake my hand, offering his. I took it reluctantly. It was moist, slightly sweaty. Then, he pulled out the chair across from me.

"May I?" he asked.

I hesitated. I hadn't seen him since first semester. We'd gotten a new TA for the second.

"Sure," I said.

He removed his glasses and smoothed out the divots on either side of his nose where the pads had just imprinted into his skin. I thought he looked a lot older than he should for a law student, even if he was just a year ahead of me.

"Joe," he said. "You can call me Joe."

"You can call me Sylvia," I said.

He sat.

"I came to Macklowe's new section after class last week to find you, but you had already left. Then I called your apartment and your roommate said you like to study here. I took a chance." He smiled. I don't think he had any idea that he was actually sort of charming.

"You spoke to my roommate?" I asked.

"Yeah," he said, looking confused. "Linda, right? She's also in your section with Macklowe. She told me you were here."

"I can't quite tell if I should be worried or flattered," I said.

His brows came together and then flattened.

"Flattered, obviously," he said, smiling all the way. "Now that I'm not assisting your section, I've been wanting to speak with you, but you never stick around long enough after class. I didn't want to scare you or anything," he stumbled on, fumbling around with his hands. "I'm sorry. I hope this isn't too weird."

The cut inside his eyebrow from his fall in class had healed poorly. I didn't know it then, but it would turn into a scar that I would brush over with my fingers every night in bed for years.

"Life is long," he added. "I kind of want to spend it with someone interesting. Someone I can speak with about all this stuff that we're learning. You seem like someone interesting."

I couldn't help but laugh.

"Oh, you're not joking." I said.

He shook his head, no. "Why would I joke about that?"

"First *real* conversation we have out of class, and you bring up marriage?"

"Not with you, necessarily," he said, quickly covering. "Not with you, of course."

"Now you insult me?"

"No, no, no," he said, hands up, defensive, sort of cute. "You're twisting my words."

"Am I?" I said. "I guess I'm in the right profession, then."

He dropped his hands to the table and they landed with a delicate tap. He was kindhearted, sweet.

"So you came to Harvard Law to find your wife like some women go to college to find a husband?" I said. "Is that it?"

"I guess so." He laughed, taking it in. "What does that make me?"

I considered my words carefully.

"Perhaps a unicorn. Perhaps a madman. Perhaps a liar. I'm not entirely sure which one yet, but I'm weighing them all equally."

"All three?" he said, his brows raised.

"Not a possibility."

He smiled. Maybe he wasn't as ill-equipped for flirting as I thought he was. Or maybe his lack of skill was what he used to flirt.

"I want to be with someone whose brain is even more beautiful than her face," he said, nearly choking on his words. "And we're in the library, so I was drawn to yours."

"My what?" I laughed. "My *brain*?"

It was sort of sweet, his saying things he thought I would want to hear. Saying things that would, over time, become cliché and boring, but at the time were sort of surprising. After all, none of my previous boyfriends had commented on any part of my body they couldn't see or touch.

"You're very kind, Joe," I said. "And I would love to continue this conversation, but I really can't tonight. I have plans with my room-mate later and I have to stay on top of my work. My internship starts in a few days."

"It's not the summer yet," he said. "You're not supposed to start until you've finished first year."

"I petitioned to get started early so I could add it to my sched-ule. It's just one afternoon a week. I'm more than ready to be in the courtroom."

He didn't respond, but brought his hand to his cheeks and scratched.

"It's just a few months early," I said as if I owed him an expla-nation.

He nodded and his eyes mixed with admiration and envy at the same time.

"Where is it?" he eventually asked.

"The public defender."

"Really? I didn't think they were allowing women to do that," he said, seemingly confused, his face turning pink. "Not that I agree with that policy. That's not what I mean—"

"It's okay," I said. "It's actually one of the first years women have been allowed in the program, provided we don't actually go into the prisons to meet with the clients. I wrote up a memo and presented it to the administration, and they went for it, with the caveat that it can't impact my current course load, which it won't. I won't let it. Besides, it's only once a week."

"I'm impressed, Olin," he said. "And that's sort of difficult to do here."

He cleared his throat. I don't know why, but I cleared mine right after.

"Well, the truth is, twenty-five places turned me down for a summer internship," I said. "I was worried I wouldn't get one at all, so I started looking early, and turned out I was right to be worried. My thought was that if I already had a foot in the door, then they'd take me for the summer. The Middlesex Public Defender's Office and the administration were actually open to it. So now I want to get in before they change their minds."

"Set a goal, make it happen, and voilà. Nicely done, Olin."

I laughed quietly as he smiled. He couldn't fathom all the steps I still needed to take to get to his position. He didn't seem entitled about it, just unaware of all the privileges that being male brought him.

"I'm finishing up my research for Macklowe this term," he said, "and then I'm going to work at Ropes and Gray in Boston. Internship starts second week of summer."

"See? You have your summer plans lined up early, too."

"But I'm a second-year," he said. "And I'm still waiting to hear back."

"That's a really great job," I said, glancing back to my papers.

"I'm Macklowe's research assistant through the end of the year. It's only first semester we TA the Con Law class. Then, he gets a new one over the summer."

"I see," I said.

"Macklowe's going to write me a letter of recommendation like he does for all his assistants, and then I'll get the right job, and ta-da." He grinned. "Embarrassing falls and such make it all worth it."

"I wasn't going to bring it up," I said.

"Hard not to," he said.

His left hand curved into a privacy cone as he leaned in to whisper to me.

"Rumor has it that Macklowe wants to leave Harvard for public office. Run for congress or something. So whatever happens in class doesn't really matter anyway. I'll have him on my résumé and a letter from him. That's all I need."

"I wasn't that aware of his reputation."

"There it is," he said, as if punctuating that part of the conversation, eager to move on to the next. "You know, you were the only person that entire day who asked how I was."

"It *was* a terrible fall," I said.

I liked the way his lips came together when he used the letter *w*, and the way he said his *r*'s, sometimes with a guttural shiver. It made me listen, forced me to hear what he was saying.

"Not to change the subject," he said, "but I want to add something to the record. I think you also have a beautiful face."

CHAPTER 4

You ready for the bullshit that is Ladies' Day?" said Linda.

I had just walked in the door and she was standing at the stove, boiling pasta. It was her night to cook. I had made sandwiches the night before.

"No hello, how are you?" I said. "No, how was the library tonight? No, put some better outfit together so you don't go out looking like a slob?"

"I save those for the right occasion," she said, smiling, looking at my outfit with only a modicum of distaste. I had five dresses that I rotated in various iterations. Linda liked only one of them. Meanwhile, her closet overflowed with clothing I wished I could have worn. Colors, thick heels, fitted sweaters. Even if I'd had her style, though, the clothes would have fit me poorly. She did try to dress me better from time to time, help me buy makeup, redo my hair, but it never took. My shapeless body was a twig.

"Can you believe it was only fifty years ago that the Supreme Court upheld a law basically telling women that they can't work because they get pregnant?" she said, focused.

"Yup," I said.

"Of course Macklowe would choose *this* case for the day we're called on," she said, cutting up onions.

"Of course he would," I echoed.

We were in midterms. The spring semester was halfway over. We'd discussed every assigned reading together over dinner, passing our thoughts across the table as casually as the salt and pepper shakers, helping each other prepare, testing each other on the facts, the analysis, the outcomes.

"*Muller v. Oregon*. 1908," I said, moving on to the case of the day. "What's the issue? Go."

Linda looked up and put on her best in-class student voice.

"This case is about women wanting to work longer than ten hours a day to improve their economic conditions. The law prevented it purely because, and now I'm paraphrasing," she said, changing her voice, dropping volume, adding sarcasm, "apparently, we can't get and stay pregnant if we work. And look out, world, because if that happens, goodbye humanity."

She paused, snapping back into her best student-presentation voice.

"That's what they argued."

"And won," I added without pause.

She smirked and then poured the cut onions into a heated skillet on the stove.

I recalled a particular line from the majority opinion in the case, and added, "Justice Brewer stated, and I quote, that 'woman has always been dependent upon man.'"

Linda rolled her eyes.

"What else?" I continued, still remembering the immortal language. "Right. Just that, and again, I'm still quoting, 'her physical structure and a proper discharge of her maternal functions justify legislation to protect her from the greed as well as the passion of man.' Closed quote."

I may have overemphasized the phrase *passion of man.*

Linda laughed and pushed the fried onions around in the skillet, thinking, while I started setting the table.

"Jesus, Syl, does Macklowe really think that teaching old law that perpetuates this nonsense is good education? Why read *this* case?"

I picked up a few cloth napkins to add to the place settings at the table.

"Well, we read *Dred Scott*, don't we? We have to learn the bad case law to know how it changes," I said, remembering how I'd read *Mein Kampf* in my German class in college, when everyone else thought I should have only been reading *Anne Frank*. To me it made sense to read both.

"Yeah, but they're not teaching this as *bad* law," said Linda. "You know Macklowe is going to make it seem like this was some landmark case that actually *helped* women, when the truth is that the Supreme Court said our well-being as women is of public interest purely to perpetuate humanity. She changed her voice again to quote the opinion. "'Since healthy mothers are essential to offspring, the physical well-being of women in general is the object of public interest to preserve the strength and vigor of the race.'"

This was all from memory, nearly word for word.

"We are vessels to them," she added. "Nothing more."

"It was fifty years ago, Linda," I said. "And it's no longer good law. It was overruled in 1923. The focus was about contractual and economic independence—"

"Under the guise of looking at women as precious flowers who can't make decisions on their own."

"Be that as it may," I said, "it is clearly not the truth and it is actually no longer the law."

I took two plates from the cabinets and she grabbed two glasses.

"At least we can both say now that we're probably ready for class," I said. I was hungry. I hated the case, but was equally fascinated by it. And I enjoyed talking about it before being interrogated on a public stage.

"But you're not answering the question, Syl."

"I am," I said.

Linda turned off the stove and poured the contents of the pot into a bowl. Then she turned to me as if expecting some sort of explanation.

"In context, and context matters," I said, "it did *both* good and bad for women, don't you think? It provided women with some protection while simultaneously putting them in a protected class. But even if we look purely at the bad components—which I'll give you, it is ninety-nine percent bad—at least it's no longer controlling law."

She cocked her head at me, opened a bottle of wine, and poured.

"Be that as it may, fifty years isn't that long ago."

"You're right," I said, tapping my fingertips against each other, thinking. "You're right."

I picked up my glass of wine, as did Linda, and we clinked them together.

"We're definitely ready for Macklowe's questions," she said, smiling without a curl in her lip or furrow in her brow. It was a smile I didn't recognize.

"You know, Mariana says our sole job is to repopulate the earth," I said, thinking of my cousin's strong voice, missing her dinners and the way she could take over a room. "Repopulation, no matter what. I imagine she might think this was actually a good law."

"*That's* your response?" said Linda, stunned.

It was hot and my armpits were starting to drip. I put down the glass of wine, untouched.

"It's true. She thinks she's a failure of a human being because she can't replace her sister and her parents and the other six million killed in Europe," I said. "Even if she had ten children, she'd never feel right."

Linda's hand tapped her chest and didn't stop.

"What?" I said, looking to her.

"No offense to your cousin or anything, but that's the most absurd thing I've ever heard," she added. "She can't actually believe that. One person can't replace two. Let alone six million."

I remembered Mariana outside the courthouse, flipping through her notebooks, trying to read the law as she understood it with her seventh-grade education. The law, literature, even the Bible can mean something different to each person based on their lived experience. Given her past, would this really have been so absurd for her to think?

"Not to be the bearer of reality here, but this little case isn't about six million people. This case is about one. And how *one* female person isn't a real person with economic agency, with the agency to make her own contracts, which leads to economic freedom and marital freedom and on and on from there. So, take from that what you will."

"Okay," I said. "I will, and I do. And that case is from 1908. Think about it. What's the big difference between *Muller* in 1908 and *Adkins*, which overruled it, in 1923?" I paused for effect.

"The passage of the Nineteenth Amendment in 1920," Linda answered.

"Exactly," I said. "And then again, in 1923, the Equal Rights Amendment was first proposed—"

"And then dropped," she reminded me.

"True, and yet in 1950, women were welcomed into Harvard Law, and now in 1960, there are nine women here," I said, opening my arms to take a dramatic bow. "It may take a while, but eventually we get there."

I'd never spoken this way with Mariana, at least not so clearly about something we were both learning, about something we both cared about, and I certainly never spoke about these subjects with friends from college.

I loved it; I devoured it. I needed it.

"But *I* still can't vote in most of this country," she added under her breath, hidden between her uncomfortable laughs, which were only sort of loud this time.

I don't think I fully heard her words at the time, but when I think back to that conversation, I'm sure she said it.

"Can I ask you a question?" she said, changing the subject quickly. "I had an interesting phone call earlier with our favorite legal stooge."

I bit the inside of my cheek, confused. Then, her smile dropped, and she finished her glass of wine. The mood changed, like we were no longer riffing about the law or history or Mariana.

"Are you dating Joe Bernstein?"

CHAPTER 5

It was a humid day in Boston on the first day of my internship. The Middlesex Public Defender's Office was located on the second floor of an old office building downtown, three blocks from the courthouse. Moist air funneled into town all the way from the harbor and stretched into the hallways of the courthouse, where I met my new boss for the first time. I had never stepped foot in the office building.

"Harvard Law, eh?" He glanced at my worn heels. "All right, let's go. We've got docket in about ten minutes." He was rushing into court and took me along for the ride.

"Ten minutes?"

"Moves pretty fast around here," he said. "You'll get used to it."

The first case I sat in on was what the public defender called a rote case of domestic squabbles. "They come and go so frequently," my boss whispered, "that there's not a whole lot we can do. The women recant, they need their husbands to support them, you know how it goes."

I nodded like I knew. I'm sure Linda wouldn't have done that. Definitely not Mariana.

"We've got trial coming up in a few days. They'd like to dismiss the case, and quite frankly," he said, leaning into me with a whisper, "so would I."

"Why?" I asked.

"They're so personal," he said, pausing. "I hate these cases. Look, it's marriage. Let them figure it out for themselves, for Christ's sake. Right?"

But within five minutes, I was face-to-face with our client, Devin McCartney. A cursory review of the police report, which I'd skimmed in passing, showed how the victim, Amy McCartney, had been found by her youngest child, bruised, lacerated, and unconscious on the kitchen floor of their newly rented apartment, pants pulled to her ankles and tied together around the calves. A pool of mucus-thick blood was dripping from her torn vagina, out of which stood minia-ture razors of broken glass. Two feet away from Amy, the police found a Corona bottle, jaggedly broken at the neck. The sharp, ragged edges of the bottle were covered with not only Amy's but also Devin's resi-due. And the edges of the Corona bottle matched up with the edges of the glass debris in Amy's vagina. It didn't take long to place the pieces together to form the narrative of the domestic assault. I had ten minutes. I could have done it in three. The story was clear: Man marries woman. Man beats woman. Man rapes woman. Man believes he owns woman by virtue of the law. Man makes the money. Woman stays silent. Repeat.

I'd studied these cases in class. I'd read these cases in the news. Mariana told me about how she'd seen these cases in New York a de-cade earlier, though she was more focused on the theatrics, the cho-reography of it all, trying to learn the language and the routine and the procedure.

"I think we can dispose of this quickly," the public defender said to me and Devin. "Amy isn't going to testify."

I looked around. "Where is she now?"

"*Not* testifying," said the defender.

Devin and the defender turned their attention to me. An angry pulse seemed to beat from Devin's body while we stood outside the courtroom discussing strategy.

"She's not?" I asked.

"That bitch better not come close to the witness stand," said Devin, his voice hoarse and pressured.

The public defender placed his hand on Devin's shoulder, calming him instantly with a touch.

"How often does the victim choose not to testify?" I said. "Shouldn't she take the stand?"

I saw Devin from the corner of my eye. He was blond and attractive in a flashy movie star kind of way, and when he caught me staring, he smiled back like he was in a magazine photo shoot. He'd do the same for the twelve jurors later, no doubt.

"Are you sure you don't want to walk over to the prosecutor's office and get a job there?" said the defender, pulling me aside. "*Devin* is our client. We are working on behalf of *Devin*."

"The prosecutor's office wasn't hiring women," I said, turning around to face him.

"You certainly think on your toes, sweetheart, but try to keep the jokes out here," the defender said to me, placing a hand on my back and steering me into the courtroom. "Now, the first day for anyone is like being thrown in the trenches," he said. "We all get through it. Just sit and watch. You'll be great."

An hour later, Devin's case was called, and the defender, Devin, and I approached the bench when called upon.

"Your Honor," said the defender. "I've got an upstanding member of the community in hot water here and for no real reason. There is no evidence against him, no witnesses, no testimony that can confirm any of what his wife is even alleging. Some doctored photos that don't even match up with her statement? He's never been convicted of a crime before and he owns the best little pizza parlor in all of Boston."

The judge hid a smile behind his hand as if he knew exactly what the defender was talking about. Neutrality would obviously be displayed, but his neutrality was a wink to the idea of fairness. This wasn't the way it read in our textbooks. It was coming alive for me, all the little details between the parties that were off the record—the knowing gestures, the nods and smiles, the glad-handing. I wasn't exactly sure how the record could capture what was happening.

The defender continued. "Your Honor, you have far more important matters to deal with than allowing an accidental call to the police to turn into something that could clog our justice system for the next year or even two. I know you have serious crimes to adjudicate. Let's call this duck what it is. The wife doesn't even want to press charges. They have three children and he provides for them *well*. I've written all this up in my Motion to Dismiss, so we are respectfully requesting that you grant our motion."

The judge looked over a thin brief in his hands—three typed pages stapled at the top. The paper was torn. It was sloppy. Not even the worst student in my class would have considered turning in a paper half as bad.

"This it?" the judge asked.

The defender nodded. "Yes, Your Honor."

"Mr. Prosecutor," the judge called out, while eyeing the motion. "Please approach the bench."

The prosecutor proceeded to the bench wearing the same suit as the defender, same haircut, same vocal inflection, all dropping the "or" in "honor" like they were on a team.

"Your Honor, with all due respect to the court and my esteemed colleagues," he said softly, matter-of-fact, "we are not prepared to dismiss this case. There is evidence supporting assault. This is not the first time the defendant's attacked someone, let alone his wife. We have evidence that shows he has attacked other men, as well. This evidence is offered purely as proof of his MO, not to be considered prejudicial."

I waited behind the defender the entire time as Devin waited at the defense table. He was wearing a tweed sports coat and brown pants, which were ripped at the bottoms near the heel. His large hands were jittery, fidgeting in and out of his pockets, and they were covered with scars: a trapezoid over the outer part of his right thumb, a cloud-shaped mark on a middle knuckle. He could probably squeeze my head like a grape if he wanted.

While the two attorneys spoke with the judge, Devin's eyes darted around nervously, and I followed them as they landed on a woman I was certain was Amy McCartney. Nervous, plaintive, demure, she was dressed in a frilly pink blouse with her hair twisted into a low bun. The bruises had long since healed, as had the cuts, making room for fear in her eyes. I couldn't tell if she was more terrified of losing her husband or of going home with him.

"This is a domestic squabble, Your Honor, pure and simple," the defender pushed, his voice elevating in volume. "One person's word against another's, consensual sex gone aggressively physical. Nothing more."

I thought I could see Amy's eyes, flooded with conflict, tear at their edges when she heard; caught between what she needed to survive and what she needed to be safe. That was the central problem, though. Not that this was a domestic squabble and that she had been injured, or that she may have wanted this case to go away, but rather that she needed it to. She needed him to come home to her. I didn't realize it so clearly at the time, but it took only a few months of practice years later for me to recognize the look.

"Your Honor," I heard myself say, staring at Amy.

"Yes?" he said, confused. "Miss——?"

"Olin."

I turned toward the bench.

"She's my intern," said the defender, tossing me away.

"Come here," said the judge, interested.

I walked up to the bench.

"Your name?"

"Sylvia Olin," I said. "I'm a law student at——"

"Miss Olin, then. Tell me what you're thinking," he said.

Nowhere in the trials I'd witnessed or studied had a judge asked a law student her opinion in the middle of court. They didn't care. They wouldn't care what we thought, or what I thought, certainly. But he seemed to either genuinely be interested or he was humoring everyone around me.

"What does the evidence reflect?" he asked.

Amy McCartney was inside the courtroom. She must have wanted to speak but couldn't.

"This case cannot and should not be dismissed, Your Honor," I said, without thinking it through.

At the time, it was pure instinct, a gut reaction mired in the overreach of youth. But I continued even though I knew I shouldn't.

"The victim is inside this courtroom, and it's clear that she wants to testify. And with that testimony, at the very least, you have——"

"Excuse me, Your Honor," the defender said. "I need a moment with my law student here."

He slammed his hand on my shoulder and pulled me away.

"Are you kidding me?" His voice was heavy, explosive. "Harvard?!"

I looked back to the gallery, searching for Amy McCartney's face, but it was gone, and the door exiting the courtroom was swinging back and forth.

"Sit down," he said to me, directing me to the chair behind the defendant's table. His face was as red as the inside of his mouth. "Do not say another word."

I sat on command. My defender turned around and looked to the judge, who was flipping through papers on his desk. Devin Mc-Cartney was sitting at the defendant's table, his fists balled beside his thighs, hanging, prepared, loaded. And for the first time that afternoon, my hands shook.

"Your Honor, I'm so sorry," said the defender, walking back to the bench. "She's a student."

The judge looked away from the defender and toward me.

"Come back up here for a moment, young lady."

I stood from the chair and walked up to the bench, each step growing heavier with the weight of error. It was not the same as walking inside the synagogue toward the rabbi; this time, I wasn't holding a week's worth of research in my hands. This time, I had already failed, but I couldn't let on that I knew I'd made a mistake because it wasn't about my mistake, but rather about intimidation from Devin and the entire system on Amy.

This was exactly what Mariana was talking about when she said she wanted me to become a lawyer. Lawyers can't speak purely with their hearts; they need facts and research, and the good ones integrate both fact and emotion. I hadn't quite learned this yet. Not fully. It would take another few years.

"Yes, Your Honor," I said, facing him.

"Miss Olin, is it?" said the judge, as I took my place before the bench. The defender was standing beside me.

"You are representing the defendant, are you not?"

He paused, investigating the space behind me, and then came back to my face.

"Yes, Your Honor," I said.

"And yet you have spoken on behalf of the State, potentially harming your own client."

"Yes, Your Honor," I said on impulse. "I suppose that's what I did."

"You *suppose*?" he asked, sitting back in his chair, crossing his arms on his chest. "I'm confused."

When a person of power repeats your words and then calmly adds, "I'm confused," he's never really confused. He's using that time for effect; he's using that time to push your own language against you. He is most certainly not confused. In all my years on the bench, I've used that line at least thirteen times. I remember each one vividly, and each time, it yielded results.

"Please," he said, uncrossing his arms. "Explain your reasoning."

My chest burned. I imagined my body as Amy's—the cutting of my flesh, the searing pain of a sharp object inside me, forceful and unwanted. A hand, open and rough against my mouth. Thick tape, the strip of a belt. A shattered beer bottle stabbing me again and again and again and—

"Miss Olin," he demanded. "I'm asking you a question."

I pictured Mariana in her cell, naked and on the ground, poked and prodded, violated.

I pictured Mariana's parents wearing black robes and white collars and wigs.

I pictured the man in the courtroom in Brooklyn who killed his wife in the bathtub, cuffed and taken away.

"Miss Olin, I'm ordering you to answer my questions," said the judge, filling with anger. "You are disrespecting the court, and you are disrespecting me. If you can't answer, I'm going to hold you in contempt of court, law student or not."

"Speak up," said my defender.

But I never went into that courtroom in Brooklyn. I never actually saw what happened. And I wasn't in Germany twenty years earlier either. I didn't actually see firsthand what happened to Mariana or her sister. I was standing in judgment without bearing true witness, as if the law was a proper stand-in for ethics, as if it was a dictate for morality. I didn't know how to explain the inconsistencies, so I said nothing. I knew that I needed the time to gather the research. I needed the days to practice what I would say. I needed to think clearly, but nothing in that moment was clear, except how quickly I had spoken improperly, and how long I'd waited to respond, as if my momentary lapse of judgment had stopped me from correcting a past wrong.

"Miss Olin, it's a simple question. Please answer, or I repeat, you will be in contempt of court."

Your Honor, I tried to say, I wanted to say, I needed to say—but I was silent.

I hated my impetuousness, my inexperience, and I deserved everything that happened next.

Then, the judge slammed his gavel.

I was cuffed for contempt of court and taken away to a small cell in a nearby building. I knew what contempt of court was. In *Perry Mason*, the lawyers were always shouting out and abusing the rule of law, and were constantly arrested for it. In law school, I learned that that was a dramatic ploy on TV; it almost never happens.

But still, it happened to me.

They placed me in a small holding cell with two other women: one, a middle-aged white teacher who refused to tell me why she was there, and another white woman just a few years older than me, dressed in all white.

Three hours later, I was bailed out by someone the bailiff called "Black lady, real pretty," and nothing else.

He walked me through a series of rooms, where I was returned my belongings, filled out some paperwork, and waited for Linda.

"I have to say, Olin," she said, when I was finally allowed to see her, "between the two of us, I never thought it would be you who would need to be bailed out of jail."

CHAPTER 6

The Cloak Room was an old hangout for judges that, twenty-five years earlier, had been converted into a law school bar frequented by second- and third-years, and sometimes by professors. It was hidden in the basement of a restaurant on the main drag in town. Linda swore that drinking here was a rite of passage for all law students. They'd only recently opened their doors to Jews and women, so Linda and I weren't long welcome, but still she insisted we stop there before heading home.

She opened the door forcefully, with a confidence I envied then, and still envy now. Smoke filled the air. An old jukebox crooned in the corner. I was afraid that anyone who looked my way would know. They'd smell the jail on me, the contempt.

"You do realize I'm about to get kicked out of school," I said to her.

"You're not going to get kicked out." Her mouth was set in a line.

"You don't know that," I said, nervous.

The place was crawling with spies—lawyers and judges and professors—and no doubt police, too. They had to have known. What I'd done was painted on my fingertips.

"How am I going to tell Mariana?" I said.

Linda looked at her watch as if she were waiting for someone.

"Well, if that's your only concern," she said, distracted, "don't tell her."

"That's not my only concern," I said. I bit my fingernails and some of the ink rubbed off on my face.

"Relax," she said, wiping at my cheek as if I were her toddler. "Have a drink, have a smoke, don't think about the PD. You'll deal with that later."

A chill rushed through me. *Later*, I thought. If there was a later.

Linda was inspecting the men at the bar, as if trying to settle on one. I glanced at the bartender, who was sort of cute with straggly hair parted on the side. He wore a plaid button-down shirt with a green apron. He didn't seem to fit in this crowd either. I liked that about him.

"Don't look too surprised or anything," said Linda, "but Joe Bernstein is sitting over in the corner with . . ." she said, squinting to see better, "Dean Macklowe."

She turned to me, inspected my face, and then turned away just as quickly.

"Stop stressing. It's giving you wrinkles."

I relaxed my brow, though I didn't feel relaxed at all.

"Let's go to them," she said. Her voice was full, no cracks, no slips in volume.

"No," I said, showing her my fingertips. I rubbed what ink was left on my peacoat and hid my fingers in my pockets.

But her eyes were singularly focused on their table.

"Come on," said Linda, smiling. "You aren't going to get anywhere just sitting around and watching."

"Please don't say anything about what just happened," I said, as she grabbed my hand and pulled me toward them.

"Nice to see you again," said Joe, blushing when I looked his way. He stood up awkwardly to greet us.

"You, too," I said quickly, dropping my eyes.

"Join us," said Macklowe, moving over in the booth. Linda slid in beside him while I sat down next to Joe on the other side.

"Can I get you a drink?" asked Joe. "Both of you?"

Linda's eyes volleyed between us.

"I'll have a beer," she said.

"Same," I said.

"Bernstein, go get the girls some drinks," said Macklowe.

"Of course," said Joe, inching his way around me. Our bodies touched for the second time. His back brushed against the side of mine, just near my waist, and I clenched beside him. He was wearing the same pants from day one in class, only now they were sewn back together with a ragged seam. I wondered if he'd stitched it himself.

"So, Loving," said Macklowe, looking directly at Linda. "You know that I'm rewriting next year's Constitutional Law textbook right now to incorporate all of the recent changes in civil rights. I read *Stride Toward Freedom* and I've been thinking of incorporating some of Dr. Martin Luther King's writings into class."

"Is that so?" Linda said, and for a brief moment, it sounded like she was humoring him. Not the other way around.

"Indeed," he said. "I've heard him speak more than once. In fact, I even went down to Montgomery to hear him preach in person."

I knew she'd heard things like this before. Many times. Around campus, anyone moderately involved with civil rights would reach out to Linda or to the one Black male student in our class, to try to demonstrate that they were on the right side of history. The same thing had happened to me in college whenever the subject of the Holocaust would come up, or the latest attack on a synagogue or Jewish deli.

"Anyway, I'd like to hear your thoughts on Kennedy and what he hopes to do to further integrate our schools and society, if he wins."

Linda was wearing a short skirt and Macklowe's forefinger touched her skin briefly as he gesticulated.

"Yes," Linda said politely, as Joe came back to the table, his hands full. "I'd be honored."

The whole time, I couldn't take my eyes off Dean Macklowe. He seemed different up close, still powerful and filled with pride, but sincere in wanting to know Linda. I couldn't tell if she liked being in his spotlight. In class, when he questioned students directly, people were either prepared and reveled in it, or unprepared and hated it. Linda was both. She was prepared and yet she hated it, she'd told me after Ladies' Day. But this was the Cloak Room, not class. He wasn't teaching us when he sat beside us; he was drinking with us and chatting with us, and almost, I could have sworn, trying to relate to us.

"I'm not terribly concerned about whether or not Kennedy will live up to the promise," Linda said. "Promise can mean different things for different people."

"Perhaps," he said, "but I certainly want him to have a chance."

He placed a hand on Linda's thigh.

"Excuse me," she said, bending over to pick up her purse on the floor, and when she moved, his hand dropped.

I tried to catch her eye, but she didn't glance my way. She just nodded and smiled to Macklowe and continued the conversation. I looked to Joe, who didn't seem to notice what Macklowe had done.

"Let's discuss this further, Miss Loving. I've got to head out now, but I'll look forward to it," he said.

Then he pushed himself up from the table and Linda stood and smiled, letting him out of the booth. "You know my office hours. I hope you'll come by." He waited before adding, "All of you," and then nodded with a kind and hopeful grin. It was a gesture so slight that you'd have to look for it to see it, but Linda was not smiling back at him. He gathered his briefcase, his coat, and his glasses and walked toward the door.

"Holy shit, that's incredible, Linda," said Joe. "He actually wants to work *with* you."

"There is no way that man saw Dr. King in person," she said. "No way."

She straightened herself on the bench and adjusted her skirt to pull it down an inch.

"Why would he lie about that?" said Joe.

"Exactly," I said, smiling, not at Linda, but at Joe. He held my gaze and matched my smile.

"I think you may have just gotten a golden ticket," said Joe.

I didn't like that Macklowe had put his hand on her leg, and I wasn't sure what she thought about it, either, but it didn't seem like she wanted to talk about it.

"Dean Macklowe isn't lying," Joe continued. "I've worked with him for nearly a year and he's exceptional. One of the brightest legal minds out there. Everyone knows it, and everyone wants to work with him, take his classes. You ladies don't know how lucky you are that you're in his section. He's going to be on the bench one day, I'm sure of it."

"Is that so?" said Linda. "And here I thought he was all politician."

Joe dropped his smile slowly, a bit confused, a bit envious.

He was right, though. Macklowe could make Linda's career if he wanted to.

"So, are you going to take him up on his offer?" I asked.

"He only wants to use me to show the world he believes in school integration. I'm the Black woman he's going to put on a serving plate to do it," said Linda.

"He's trying to teach the next generation of lawyers by showing them how to be great, how they can help us make the country be stronger, better, more progressive," Joe said defensively.

"No," she said. "He's teaching everyone the way it's supposed to be. Not the way it is. He needs to be honest about the way it is first before shining me up and putting me in his display case."

"You may not want to believe it," said Joe, "but Dean Macklowe can make your career. And he wants to help *you*. This is a *good* thing, an enviable thing, I swear."

"Linda, he's right. This is an incredible opportunity," I said, echoing Joe. "You're one of the *Nine* this year. Think about it. What that means, what that could do."

"I'm sick of 'the Nine' this, and 'the Nine' that," Linda said, and downed the rest of her beer. "It's bullshit. They're just putting a number on us. When was the last time anyone did that and it worked out well? Want me to call Mariana for you?"

I didn't respond. I didn't know what to say.

Joe looked confused.

"Can I get you another drink?" he asked us, clearly trying to break up the conversation.

"Yes," said Linda. "I'll have another one of these." She held out her bottle.

Joe nodded. "Syl?" he said.

I shook my head, no, and he left.

When he disappeared back into the bar, Linda turned to me.

"What?" I said, unsure where she was going.

"*You* know," she said, angling her gaze toward Joe.

"What about Macklowe's offer? You're just going to change the subject? Just like that?" I said, thinking about her comment about Mariana, thinking about Macklowe's hand on her thigh, thinking about Joe.

"Just like that," she said, eyeing Joe again. "So?"

I remembered the first night in the library with Joe. I'd never felt that excited about anyone before.

"First, Joe calls our apartment to find you, and now this?"

"This?" I said. "What *this*?"

"You know, I wasn't sure if I should have told him where you were that night. I mean, on the one hand, it was kind of creepy, but on the other hand, it was also kind of sweet in that Hollywood kind of way, and I'm still not sure which one yet," she said, looking him over. "So I thought we'd test it out."

"Happy to be your guinea pig," I said.

"He seems pretty harmless."

"Honestly, I'm not sure what to think about him," I said. "Not just yet."

It wasn't entirely true, but I wasn't ready to admit to Linda what I was feeling until it was clearer to me.

"You may not be sure about most things in life, but you'll be sure about him as time goes on. Ray and I knew from day one we were dating."

"We'll see."

"No matter what, though, don't get too serious with him," she said. "He's just a boy. Focus on school. That will last. That will hold your hand. They can't take that away from you."

"You sound like Mariana now."

"Well," said Linda, smiling, "I take back what I said before. She's obviously brilliant."

CHAPTER 7

With the black residue of fingerprint ink still on my hands, I said good night to Linda and went home with Joe Bernstein. He lived alone in a studio apartment on campus. We sat on his bed, the light from the windows highlighting our shapes, our bodies, our hair and freckles and fat. He took my hand as his lips pulled up at the corners, and he kissed me, first on my mouth and then my ears and my neck. There were three buttons on the front of my shirt and he began to undo them one by one, until he reached my bra. I unlatched the back of it, placing it on the foot of the bed. He seemed nervous, but joyful, and for the first time all day, I felt like I was in control of everything around me. I pushed him onto the mattress, undoing his tie and removing his shirt. He kissed my neck and my shoulders while I pulled at his belt and we climbed into that oversize bed and got to know every inch of each other's bodies. We never even turned down the lights.

After, we held each other for over an hour, quiet, our bodies slippery with sweat. As he stroked my hair, I traced the outline of his lips.

"I thought of you for months after we first met. Then when I finally worked up the courage to ask you out, I was hesitant," he said. "It might not have seemed that way in the library, but it took me weeks to find you. You were cute, but you also have this cowlick across your forehead that is slightly blonder than the rest and I wasn't sure you were Jewish."

"Well, my mother wasn't," I said. "But she converted and wanted to raise me Jewish."

"Okay," he said, kissing me again. "We won't tell my parents that."

The following morning, he made me breakfast—eggs, toast, oatmeal, and orange juice—and brought it to me in bed before dawn. I wasn't hungry, though I couldn't tell him that, so I sipped on some orange juice. It was sweet and filled with pulp and I loved the heaviness of the texture.

I thought I had shaken off the previous day, but it was finally landing with its full weight. I felt an urge to tell him about the flash of the camera in my face when I was booked, or the darkness of the ink on my fingers when I was printed, or how that was the least terrifying part of my day. Even standing beside Devin McCartney wasn't the scariest part. It was my reaction to it all, my reticence, my impetuousness followed by my deafening silence.

Joe's apartment was spare but not empty. At twenty-four he seemed to have a life, a history, but not too much baggage. A handful of pictures hung on the walls—a framed photograph of him with a group of boys who looked like him, all wearing the same suit, white bow ties, brown vests, their hair cut short around the ears. Another image of Joe with his parents, sitting on an oversize couch. His grandparents, perhaps, aged but preserved. Magazines were stacked on the floor; law textbooks gathered dust in a different corner.

He pointed to a particular photograph hidden behind a few of the others.

"That's my mother," he said, placing a hand on my shoulder.

Joe looked like her—lithe in appearance. Perhaps she was clumsy as well, awkwardly insistent to the point of charming. Behind her was some unframed artwork and what looked like an impressive home library: books from floor to ceiling, crowned with a sliding wooden ladder. I imagined Joe climbing the ladder as a young boy.

"She's stunning," I said to him.

"She was our age here," he said. "She had just married my father."

He looked at the image as if it were a painting in the Louvre.

"She died in childbirth," he added.

"Oh," I said, my hands rushing to my cheeks. "I'm so sorry."

"I don't tell a lot of people," he said. "Most people think my step-mom is my real mom. Which isn't entirely untrue. She raised me. She *is* my mom."

"But," I said, encouraging him to go on.

"But," he said, lacing his fingers between mine, "I never got to meet her, my mother. My birth mother."

I listened.

"She was a model and had hoped to become a painter one day. She learned so much about art from modeling for painters that she wanted to paint for herself."

"What sort of modeling did she do?"

"Everything," he said. "In the early magazines, she was apparently one of the favorite models of the Upper East Side in 1935. And then she got pregnant with me."

"I had a cousin who was also an artist," I said, when the timing seemed right. "I never met her either. She was killed in the concentration camps, but apparently, she had an extraordinary gift. Could have been a force. A child prodigy."

He closed his eyes and then opened them again many seconds

later. Maybe he was imagining her, or the painting, or what his mother would have become had she survived his birth.

"My mother died when I was twelve," I finally said to him. "Cancer. My father didn't handle it all that well. My cousin, Mariana, helped raise me while he sort of disappeared into a cocoon and didn't speak with anyone for years."

I paused, tapping the inside of my teeth with my tongue.

"Then I went to college and he just stayed inside of it alone. I wish for his sake at some point that he had met someone. Like your dad did."

"It works for some people," he said, smiling halfway. "I don't know what my father would have done had my mother died when I was twelve. He might have been the same way."

"Maybe," I said. "Timing in death is just as important as it is in life. Isn't it?"

He closed his eyes again, agreeing. The light through the window flashed in my eyes and I remembered it all: my mug shot, the fingerprint ink, the judge's gavel. My first lecture in Austin Hall. Mariana's face from across the dining table. The inside of the jail cell. The cemetery where my mother lay.

I sat up quickly and the empty glass of orange juice that was to my side toppled to the floor.

"Are you okay?" he asked, ignoring it.

"Yes," I said. "I'm fine."

He took my hands in his and kissed each one on the palm, on my wrists, and all the way up to my shoulders.

"I know you're fine. And I know you know you're going to be fine, too. Just remember, you're in a great place. You've got the public defender and hopefully I'll have Ropes and Gray when my job with Macklowe is over. Just waiting on the letter of recommendation."

"Right," I said.

I was fairly certain I no longer had the public defender as my law school clinic or a summer internship after what had happened, but Joe pulled me closer to him and I didn't want to disappoint him.

"And maybe *this* can help get us through it all together, right? It's nice to have someone to do this with."

His breath warmed my face and he kissed me, and I waited a brief moment before kissing him back.

"It *is* nice," I said eventually.

Four days later, a letter from the administration was waiting for me in my apartment mailbox. In that time, I had left several messages with the public defender, but he never returned any of my calls.

I opened the envelope immediately.

> *Dear Miss Olin,*
>
> *We're contacting you regarding your incident with the Middlesex Public Defender's Office. It is pertinent that we discuss this matter in person. Please contact my office to schedule an appointment.*
>
> *Sincerely,*
> *James Macklowe*

And there it was.

My appointment would be in two days.

Nothing had happened yet, and everything was about to.

CHAPTER 8

The door was ajar when I arrived.

"Hello?" I knocked lightly. "Dean Macklowe?"

There was a muted silence inside. Warm gin, thick carpet, slight body odor.

"It's Sylvia Olin," I said. My voice was breathy, even a bit flimsy. "Hello?"

A few papers rustled out of my line of vision as I peeked farther inside, until he finally seemed to notice I was there.

"Of course, Miss Olin," he said, looking up. "Come in."

His hair was disheveled like he'd just awakened from a nap. In nearly two semesters of classes, I'd never seen a single hair of his out of place. His part was always crisp, a single peach line dividing two hemispheres. This time, a few stray hairs gave the part a zigzag that, had he realized, I'm sure would have bothered him.

"Our meeting is scheduled for now, yes?" I said. "Or am I coming at the wrong time?"

"No, you're right on time," he said, waving. "Take a seat."

I pulled out the chair farthest from his desk and sat down, look-ing at his photos. The first, pushed forward for everyone to see, was of a younger Macklowe posing formally with Abraham Pindgarden, the Supreme Court justice whom he was known to idolize. Several times a semester, Macklowe would mention that he had clerked for Pindgarden, even if it had no clear connection to the conversation. Pindgarden had been on the bench for only a year when Macklowe clerked for him, so it was widely understood that they had learned the ropes together.

Macklowe must have spotted me ogling his photos, and then he picked one to show me. The frame that held it was small and rust-colored, and garnished with bronze leaves on the top two corners. The photo was of two children: a girl, maybe six or seven, and a baby boy, each wearing bathing suits. The little girl has blond hair cut short around the face, parted in the center, just like her father's. She is smiling while the baby looks away from the camera lens.

"My daughter and my son," he said to me.

"How old is she?" I asked. "Your daughter."

"About six years old in the picture," he said, placing his hand on my shoulder. "She's eight now. And he's almost two."

"Where was this?" I asked.

"The Cape," he said. "My family has a home there. We've gone every summer since before I can remember. I'm happy the kids are going to get the same experience," he said.

In the photo, his daughter is wearing a striped bathing suit and the sun is shining like I suspected it shone on girls who vacationed at places like Cape Cod.

He put the frame back on his desk and took the open seat across from me.

"But that's not why you're here, is it?" he said. "From what I understand, you're here because of an hour in jail. Is that right?"

"An afternoon, actually," I said, embarrassed and ashamed.

He leaned forward across the desk as if we were friends, conspirators.

"Between you and me, the administration here can be a bit dictatorial, like they're taking cues from Stalin, so why don't you tell me what happened and we'll see what we can do about it."

The muscles in his face were hard at work, particularly around his jaw; demonstrative evidence that yes, he was listening. He was attentive. The professor everyone loved. And I was grateful to be speaking with him and not anyone else.

"It's not much of a story," I said.

I had prepared for this meeting. I had taken notes and practiced.

I told him about the domestic violence case. I mentioned Amy McCartney and her silence and that I realized I obviously shouldn't have spoken for the victim, but that it was a momentary lapse of judgment that would most certainly not happen again. It wasn't that I didn't know how the job worked, but that I didn't think it through. I was impetuous, and I was sorry.

"Miss Olin, I know I shouldn't need to state such elementary facts of the law to one of my students here, but in this practice, we are innocent until proven guilty," he said, standing. "We don't make decisions based on a gut. We make decisions based on fact, evidence, testimony, rules of law, precedent."

"I understand, Dean Macklowe," I said defensively. "It won't happen again."

He walked around his desk two or three times, humming the whole time, circling me.

"I actually reached out to the public defender I was working with to explain, but I haven't been able to get in touch," I added. "We never got to debrief after the event, and he didn't come to the jail that day.

In fact, I haven't had any contact with him since then. He just let me go to jail. But I would like to have a second chance, because—"

"Let me ask you something, Miss Olin," he said, stopping me. "Did you really want to work for the public defender? Because you put out a very compelling argument to allow for this experiment, which clearly failed."

The sun was hitting his face as he spoke. Dry wrinkles surrounded his temples and when he turned his head, I noticed two large chicken pox scars on the back of his neck. That's what I focused on. Not the sweat collecting in my palms, nor my heart rate increasing when I should have had a clear answer to give him, but only his skin and how its slight imperfections stood out in the light, and how he had used the word *failed*.

"What type of law do you want to practice following graduation?" he asked, as if one thing had to do with the other. "Please don't mention Germany as you did in your application, but I'd be very interested in what practical path you see for yourself when you finish here . . . if you finish here."

Had he really remembered my admissions essay? Over a year later?

"Broadly speaking, I want to work in civil rights however I can," I said, thinking it through before speaking. "I can't tell you exactly what position I'd like to have, and though I realize that many of my esteemed peers come here wanting to be partners at law firms or senators or district attorneys, I'm not naive enough to assume that by mere virtue of my admission here, I will get there, or that those positions are what I even want. I want to learn the law and use it as much as is possible to give women better opportunities at home and at work, no matter how it takes me there."

"Go on," he said, and his eyes lit up when he smiled at me, an energy that was contagious.

I gathered my thoughts, aware of the empty space waiting for me to fill it.

"You speak in class about all the changes we are experiencing right now. For Black men. For women. The textbooks are literally being reprinted as we speak. I'd like to see them continue to be reprinted as all women achieve the equality you so clearly speak about in class."

"Well," he said. "I thought you did a fantastic job with *Muller* and *Adkins* on Ladies' Day."

"Thank you," I said, and I meant it. "Though I'm not sure why you put Linda and me on a separate day. Wouldn't it benefit the male students just as much as the female students to have us questioned together?"

I waited for his response, and when he had none, I pulled the Con Law textbook from my bag and began flipping through pages.

"What are you looking for?" he asked, coming around to my side of the desk and placing one hand on my back.

I leaned back into my chair so that he had no choice but to remove his hand.

"*Brown v. Board of Education*," I said.

The truth was, even though he taught *Brown* in class, I couldn't tell how he felt about it. Publicly, he supported it, but professors were often saying one thing publicly and doing another privately. And I didn't want an answer he could rationalize away.

"Page three fifty-six," he said instinctively, as I eventually landed upon it. Then I looked up to him.

"I have no doubt that the nine justices on the Supreme Court knew that they were actually making new law, changing history when they decided this case," I said, just getting started. "Do you?"

"I can't speak for them," he said firmly, "and, clearly, neither should you, but it is a prime example of the evolution of the American common law," he said. "Though we inherited it, we have in turn created something unique and magnificent. We allow the law to grow, to breathe, to evolve over time with new changes to society, new conflicts that inherently arise within that society, from—"

"From the need of the people and the judges who see fit," I said conclusively.

He nodded. "Yes."

Then he waited.

"It's an extraordinary system, Miss Olin. To be able to change with a changing society, the common law is, quite simply, humane. And it's only one part of our ecosystem of laws. There is legislation, of course, and the Constitution, but each of these collectively work as a backbone of society."

"Including and especially the dissents," I said.

"Yes," he said, uncrossing his legs. "People study a dissent and sometimes even use it to make new law, to correct a past error or injustice. And that is a great thing. Think about it. In this country, we not only respect—"

"But we *publish* the other side's opinion, the one that did not have a majority of votes. This is what gives me hope," I said. "This is one of the reasons I wanted to become a lawyer."

He looked down at the book in my hand and smiled.

"Hand me the textbook," he said, taking it from me. He flipped through the pages quickly, as if he knew exactly where to stop. I wasn't quite sure how we had moved on from my arrest so quickly, but I didn't question it.

"Read this," he said, pointing to a different page in the text. "*Plessy v. Ferguson.* 1896."

"The case that established the principle of 'separate but equal'?"

"Yes," he said. "Now, take a look at its dissenting opinion."

I read the underlined passage quickly.

> *What can more certainly arouse race hate, what more certainly create and perpetuate a feeling of distrust between these races, than state enactments, which, in fact, proceed on the ground that colored citizens are so inferior and degraded that they cannot be allowed to sit in public coaches occupied by white citizens? That, as all will admit, is the real meaning of such legislation.*

"Those are the words of a *dissenting* justice in 1896," he said, "*disagreeing* with the separation of children in schools and every other element of life, making it clear that he does not agree that separate is equal. In fact, he believed it was definitively *not* equal. And yet we had that doctrine until just a few years ago, when the court unanimously reversed itself on school segregation in *Brown*."

Macklowe's tone was gentle but authoritative, and laced with intellectual kindness, like he knew the people who were being written about on paper. I didn't get that experience from any of my other professors. They felt cold and unreachable. In Macklowe's office, I was in a seminar. I wanted so much to speak with him about the law that I'd nearly forgotten about his hand on my back earlier.

"May I?" he asked, taking the textbook back. He flipped through the pages again, settling upon one in the back. The edges of his mouth tipped downward in smile.

"Now listen to this from another opinion," he said.

> *To separate children in schools from others of similar age and qualifications solely because of their race generates a feeling of inferiority as to their*

status in the community that may affect their hearts and minds in a way
unlikely ever to be undone. . . .

He handed me the book so that I could finish it on my own. I read:

We conclude that in the field of public education the doctrine of "sepa-
rate but equal" has no place. Separate education facilities are inherently
unequal.

I stopped and looked up.

"That's the *majority* opinion of *Brown v. Board of Education.*"

"It is indeed," he said. "Taking similar ideas, and even some language, from the *Plessy* dissent."

He stood and began to pace his office, walking the short distance
from the table to the door to the desk and back again.

"Think about a dissent this way," he said, looking away from me.
"When in life is the opposition, or the quote-unquote minority opinion, ever given the time of day?"

He looked to me, excited, eager, his eyes coming to life.

"The answer is almost never," he said. "Never."

I wanted to say in school, in social discussions, in the media and
opinion pages across the newspapers, but he didn't give me the
chance.

"In this exquisite system, which isn't perfect, of course, we have
provided valuable real estate within the law and the judiciary to hear
voices that may not be the leading voices," he continued. "That is
something to value, to treasure and revere. And the reality is that in
the future, perhaps other people—the courts or lawyers—will read
some of the dissents and apply that language to a majority opinion
and create their own laws. In that sense, the dissent becomes—"

"The majority," I said, smiling.

"Exactly," he said, placing his hands on my shoulders again in victory.

I turned my chair to him and his hands dropped to his sides. I hadn't visited for his office hours before. I hadn't spent hours with him at the Cloak Room like others did, or outside class following lecture. I liked him. I saw exactly what Joe meant when he said that his job with Macklowe was the difference between surviving and thriving here.

He walked away from the chair.

"This type of thinking from my students gets me excited," he said, looking over at me. "Very excited."

I wanted to say, me, too, but I didn't.

"May I take a look again?" I asked, reaching out for the textbook.

He handed it to me and I searched through the pages, looking for the Constitution in full. The Fourteenth Amendment. *Equal Protection.*

I began to read.

"It says: '*No state shall make or enforce any law which shall abridge the privileges or immunities of citizens of the United States; nor shall any state deprive any person of life, liberty, or property, without due process of law; nor deny to any person within its jurisdiction the equal protection of the laws.*'"

When Mariana first presented this language to me as a child, it was boring and uninteresting. Language that just wanted to knot itself together. She was fascinated with it, but I didn't fully engage. Rather, it seemed it was her parents' interest, a distant passion that began to rub off on me only as the years progressed. Now as an adult, though, it looked different, somehow nuanced, filled in with shadows and interpretation and color.

"If *Brown* used Equal Protection to argue that separate is not equal for children of different races in school, wouldn't that also be true for the sexes?" I said. "Shouldn't it?"

He chuckled, this time choppy and loud, unashamed. I know it wasn't that what I said seemed funny. Maybe it was just incomprehensible.

"The Fourteenth Amendment was established and written following the civil war to free the slaves," he said. "It was to help Black men."

"I know," I said to him, "but laws change. They evolve, as you say. What one law means for one time can change to mean something else years later."

He nodded slowly.

"Our country is not the same country as it was when the Constitution was written, let alone the same country as when the Fourteenth Amendment was passed. Isn't that right?"

"Yes," he said, the word slow and sticky.

I continued. "So it would make sense that Equal Protection would apply to all people, then. The Constitution doesn't say for men *only*. Right?"

Again, he nodded in agreement. He could have been the Orthodox rabbi, running his fingers through his beard, contemplating the old book, unwilling to revise his view of it.

"It does not expressly say 'not for women.' True, but—"

"Wasn't that the basis for the suffragettes in 1923 when they proposed the Equal Rights Amendment?"

"Miss Olin, that proposal was after the ratification of the Nineteenth—"

"But if you think about it, Dean Macklowe," I said, cutting him off, "with that in mind, I imagine—and I suspect you may agree based on the interpretation of the Constitution we are learning in your class—that I'd have far more opportunities for employment this summer if this amendment were applied to women, too." I needed to finish; I had to finish. I might not have any other opportunity. "Certainly, you would agree, based on the concept of stare decisis and on the evolving scales of justice that you discuss in your class. Wouldn't you?"

He turned away from me and started flipping through some papers on his desk.

"Dean Macklowe?"

He didn't reply immediately, but then again, he often failed to reply on demand. That, I'd learned by this point. No matter how much attention he paid to you.

"Sir?"

From a distance, I could see that he was holding a paper with letterhead from the Middlesex Public Defender's Office. My hands started shaking. In all this time, I had almost forgotten the reason I was here. It wasn't just office hours to discuss the law. It was an appeal for my summer internship, my future, maybe even my place here in school.

He held on to it briefly, waiting, before eventually turning to me.

"Miss Olin, I have a thought," he said, walking directly to me. There was less than the thickness of a dictionary between us. I could smell his breath, see the silver fillings in his back teeth, spot a speck of perspiration on his shirt below his armpit.

"Here's what we're going to do," he said triumphantly, patting me on the leg. His hand lingered about two or three seconds, just above the knee, below the thigh, where Joe had touched me three nights earlier.

"I'm going to tear up this letter from the judge and the office of the public defender. It never happened. It was your first day. They

136

didn't give you an orientation. It wasn't an internship. It's not even the summer. You can pretend you didn't understand. This was the first year the clinic even has women, et cetera, et cetera. I can work on getting the arrest record expunged."

"But I don't want to pretend I didn't understand," I said. "I understand the law. I understood the law. I made a mistake. I was impetuous, which is something an attorney is not. An attorney, a judge, any person who takes oath of office must be measured, reasoned, articulate, and for that brief moment, I was not and I realize it. It was completely out of character for me and I have learned from that moment. It won't happen again."

"Oh," he said, in passing. "I know that. I'm not worried about it. You're a woman, you're emotional. It happens. We shouldn't let that stop you from being one of my nine. Right? You've come too far."

He tapped on my knee three short times and then ripped up the letter from the public defender like it was a fierce political demonstration of sorts, and left the pieces on his desk. There were eight of them in jagged, uneven squares.

"So Sylvia," he continued. "How would you like to be my research assistant for the summer? My current one will be leaving at the end of the year, and I haven't found the right candidate to succeed him just yet. You seem like a perfect fit. This might solve your little problem." A swab of mischief dabbed his eye. "And mine."

He'd never called me by my first name before. I liked it.

"What do you think?"

Joe finished this position months earlier, and no matter how poorly Macklowe treated him in class, Joe loved the job and wanted it to continue throughout the year. But Dean Macklowe hired one student per semester, one per summer, and wouldn't change that rule for anyone.

"Truly, Olin, I'd hate to see one of my nine girls be tossed to the curb because of a conscience, albeit professionally misplaced," he added. "I have no doubt you learned from this incident, and I'm afraid that it's unlikely for you to be able to find a new internship in such short time, and without something on your résumé for this summer . . ." He placed his hands on his mouth and fumbled around a bit, thinking without conclusion.

The door was closed. I didn't hear any footsteps outside.

"Yes," I said quickly. "Yes, thank you."

"Wonderful," he said, walking away from me, leaving me standing near the chair. "Just wonderful," he repeated, his voice softer, more subdued. "I'm really glad we had this conversation. You have a strong, competent mind. I'll see you back here first week of summer, starting at nine a.m. We'll work through September until the next semester begins. I'll write up an official offer, and send you all the information so you have it for your records."

And that's when I felt the muscles in my neck pull my head up and down, distinct, separate from my mind. Then the corner of my eye itched, just below the upper lid.

Leave it alone, I heard Mariana say in my head. *Don't scratch it. It will go away.*

But it didn't. It had returned when I least needed it, least wanted it.

"Do you have any questions?" said Macklowe.

I bit the inside of my lip. I was dry, dehydrated. If I left and didn't return, I wasn't sure I'd have another shot. I forced a smile.

"No, sir," I said, placing my handbag on my shoulder. "Thank you for this incredible opportunity. I really appreciate your help."

CHAPTER 9

An hour later, I stood slightly dazed inside my half-empty apartment. I was dying to talk to Linda. I wanted to tell her that I'd visited with Macklowe and that he offered me a summer internship. I wanted to tell her that it had been one of the most intellectually stimulating moments of my life until it became one of the most confusing. But Linda wasn't home, so I retreated to my bedroom and fell onto the bed, replaying everything that had just happened. My shoes were still tight around my ankles and my hair pulled back. When I removed the hair tie holding my hair in a low ponytail, my scalp loosened.

You're a woman. You're emotional, it happens, I heard, and my smile started to drop.

I tossed off my shoes and sat up to undress, but in my haste the skirt zipper caught on my blouse. Frustrated, I twisted and pushed and pulled, tearing the fabric.

But the voice—his voice—returned.

I'd hate to see one of my nine girls be tossed to the curb.

I ripped off my ruined skirt with both hands and threw it on the floor beside the garbage can. I found an old nightgown and gravitated to the telephone in the kitchen. I hadn't heard Mariana's voice in nearly a month. After five long rings, she answered.

When I tried to say her name, my voice vanished.

"Sylvie?" she eventually said. Her voice was softer than I remembered it. "Is that you?"

I waited before responding.

"Sylvie," she said again, her voice dropping in volume. "What's wrong?"

I lowered myself into the kitchen chair and ran my fingers up and down the yellow phone cord.

"I know you better than you know yourself," she said to me. Her voice was maternal, right when I needed it to be.

"How is your leg?" I asked, wanting to return the favor.

"*Now* you speak," she said, her austerity returning. "My ankle is fine, my leg is fine, it's all fine. It's not bothering me today. I walk, I bike, I dance. That's that."

I tried to picture her dancing now at thirty-one. She dated, most seriously Dr. Discanti, but she never wanted to commit. He had stayed around throughout the years, but she always kept him at an arm's length, and he accepted this as best he could. She would go out with other men from time to time, whether he knew it or not. After I moved out she no longer volunteered this information to me, though it didn't interfere with our closeness. At least I didn't think so at the time. I was wrong about so much then.

"Don't play games with me, *bubbeleh*," she said. "You got the college, but I got the knowledge. I know exactly what you're up to. Don't pretend I don't. So now tell me. What's going on at *Harvard Law?*"

No matter when, no matter where, and no matter how old she got, she never tired of putting joyful emphasis on those two words.

"How's my dad?" I asked, changing the subject.

"He's fine," she said. "Goes to work and comes home. Same."

"You know he doesn't call me," I said.

"Well, you don't call him."

"I know," I said, realizing. "I know."

"Or me," she said. "Not much."

I cleared my throat. "I know. It's just so busy here."

"I'm sure it is," she said. "But it's okay. I don't mind. You're doing what you need to do. You're doing what you should do. Stay focused. That's all. Just stay focused."

I picked a frayed cuticle on my right index finger and listened to the static on the other line.

"Is he home?" I asked. Maybe I would tell him about Macklowe's job offer.

I could hear a slight buzz of movement on the other end.

"No," she said. "He's still at the deli."

"Right."

"So, Sylvie," she said. I moved the phone to my other ear and listened to her voice. Her accent was diminishing, but still present. A faint memory of where she came from. "What's the real reason I get this call today?"

I didn't have an accent to remind me of where I came from. I didn't have anything.

"Nothing," I said. "I just wanted to hear your voice."

I never heard back from the public defender, but I continued on with the rest of the semester almost as if the whole experience hadn't ever happened. I didn't speak with Linda or Joe about any of it, including my meeting with Macklowe. When I was in class with Macklowe, we interacted as if I were just another student. I started seeing Joe several times a week, but mostly my life rotated among the library, my apartment, and class. I told Joe that the public defender was better slated for second-year clinic, and he didn't ask more about it.

CHAPTER 10

You can keep the extra food," said Linda, as I walked into our apartment after second semester ended. "I bought it for the apartment, not for me." It was a week after finals, and she was packing furiously.

"What's going on?" I asked.

Linda wasn't wearing makeup, which was rare. Her lips were faded with no tint of red, her eyes naked. She was pulling out garment after garment and stuffing them in suitcases, removing dishes from the cabinets and stuffing them in boxes without wrapping them first.

"Linda . . ."

She looked down at the floor, almost as if she were avoiding me. She didn't have a summer internship lined up. Months earlier, we had applied together and been rejected together. She never wanted to talk about it, and I didn't push.

"Talk to me," I said.

She didn't respond for at least a minute. It didn't seem like a large amount of time, but then again, a lot of things can happen in one minute. The decision to defend someone's life, drop an atomic bomb, make love.

"Does this have something to do with Ray?"

"No," she said, tripping over that word, almost laughing. "God no."

"What is it, then?" I said, practically begging.

"Well," she said thinking, waiting. "You remember back in the first week of school when Dean Macklowe said to look to the person on your right and then look at the person on your left?"

"Yes," I said. I wanted to fall over. I knew where this was going.

"You're looking at the person on your proverbial left. She won't make it till graduation. She won't even make it to second year."

"Stop," I said. "How is that even possible?"

She held my eyes for an extra beat, as if I was supposed to know.

"I don't understand," I said. "You're at the top of our class."

"I *was* at the top of our class first semester," she said, tossing her arms in the air. "Not anymore."

She walked directly into her room, and I followed her. Inside, she continued emptying her drawers into a suitcase.

"What happened?"

"I failed," she said to me after half of the suitcase was filled. "I failed out. Okay? That's it. They're kicking me out."

"That's not possible. We've done everything together. Studied together, taken tests together."

"*You* didn't fail," she said. "Don't look too sad."

"Linda," I said, hurt. "You couldn't have failed."

"Well, I did."

"What class?" I said, nervous.

"Con Law," she said, after stalling a little too long.

"Macklowe's class?" I said, surprised. "Are you kidding me? He loves you."

I could see her fist—clenched and tipped with red paint on her nails, laid against her chest—rise a millimeter and fall back a millimeter, rise and fall, completely even with her breath. It was slowing down, her anger subsiding, her nerves calming.

"Did something happen?" I asked.

She turned to me. "No."

I should have known then that there was more to the story. She never answered questions that quickly. Yes, she was always outspoken, but she never answered anyone without deliberate thought first. That's what made her such a great law student, and I know that's what made her so successful later, too.

"Maybe Joe can talk to him," I said. "I know that he cares about—"

"Sylvia," she said, stopping me.

"I can try to talk to him, as well, since I'm—"

"Just leave it." She breathed in slowly, calming herself. "When you fail, you are kicked out. It's not like there's anything you can do after the fact."

Sadness masked her face so that I couldn't read what was beneath.

"Sure there is," I said, thinking of Macklowe and how open he was to helping his students. "There is always something to do. Talk to the administration. I'm sure they'll give you another chance. They have to. One class shouldn't get you kicked out."

"You think I didn't already do all that?" she said, exhausted. "That's it. It's over, okay? Please, just let it be."

She sat beside her suitcase on the floor and stared at the beautiful clothing surrounding her. I walked over and placed my hand on hers, kneeling beside her. Neither of us removed it at first and then the moment passed and she tossed my hand aside, so I sat down beside her and felt her body shaking.

"Are you going to be okay?" I said eventually.

That was it. Six little words. Six stupid, useless words that yielded nothing. *Are you going to be okay?* A meaningless question, echoing in a vacuum. Maybe I could have gotten her to speak further about what happened if I tried another way, but I didn't.

"You *are* going to be okay," I said, switching two words to turn it from a question to a statement, probably only diminishing the chance of real communication.

"You know, Syl, I thought I wanted this legal career, and the truth is I don't think I do," she said. "It just took me being here to realize it. It's not so unique. It happens every year. *Look to your left. Look to your right.*"

It was so quiet I could hear her fingertips press against the bags under her eyes. I could hear her breath syncopated with my heartbeat, her toes digging into the worn carpet.

"That's arbitrary and you know it," I said.

"Maybe it is, but it's not worth it. It's just not," she said, exhausted.

"You don't actually believe that. Do you?"

She turned around. Her lips were dry and her bottom lip was starting to split ever so slightly.

"Who cares if you don't go to Harvard anymore?" I said. "You're a phenomenal law student. Go to another school. Stick with it and you'll still graduate a lawyer and go off and do whatever you want. Make money. Change the world."

"That's so idealistic, so naive," she said. "So naive. Change the world?" she echoed, forcing an uncomfortable laugh. Her tongue dipped down to wet her lip, and she started to smile, but then it went away as quickly as it came. "What world are you trying to change, Syl?"

"The world for women," I said on instinct. "Isn't that why we're here? Why we're *both* here?"

"Speak for yourself," she said.

"I am," I said. "I thought we were both here for the same reason.

That stupid 1908 case. Your mom. Mariana. Germany. It *can* be different. It *will* be different. But not without people like us fighting for it, changing the laws—"

"The rules aren't exactly the same for you and me," she said, turning from me.

Then she looked back to the bed, exhausted, like she needed to sleep. But it had been stripped clean.

"Come," I said, picking up the sheets from the floor. "You're paid up through the summer on this place, so let's stop with this crazy rush of an exit. Let's sit down and figure this out together. There has to be a solution."

She wiped her nose with the back of her hand and looked at me for the first time that day without pretense, without cover, and said nothing.

"Here," I said, opening the fitted sheet and handing her one side of it. "Let's make your bed and talk, because you're not going anywhere."

Reluctantly, she took the other end of the sheet in her hands, and together, we fit it over her mattress.

"You know what they call the worst student in medical school?" I said as I picked up the flat sheet. "The guy who failed almost every class so they nearly kicked him out, telling him he'd never amount to anything?"

"No," said Linda, taking the other end of the sheet and placing it on top of the mattress.

"They call him doctor," I said.

"Yeah, yeah, yeah," she said, tucking in the corners on her side. "I've heard that one before."

"And they'll call you counselor, too. Or whatever else. Just don't give up yet. Please," I said.

I walked around the bed and took her hand, and this time she kept it there. Her face softened.

"You belong here," I said. "You earned your spot. I really don't believe they'll so easily take it away from you."

Linda cleared her throat and then lay on the newly made bed, still silent. I joined her, and our shoulders touched as we looked up at the ceiling. There was a large crack in the shape of Florida poking out from the closet door.

"Your room is bigger than I initially thought," I said to her, inspecting the space. "Much bigger than mine."

"Yeah," she said, a smile escaping. "It's got some problems, but it's about fifteen square feet larger. I measured it one night when you were out with Joe." She let out a slight grin. "I was actually sort of surprised you chose the other room first."

"I didn't really choose it," I said, remembering that first day in September. "Mariana walked through it and thought I should give the larger room to whomever I was going to be living with. She thought it would start things off on the right foot, and I agreed. Looks like she was right. Besides, I didn't really have my own room since I was twelve, so any size was fine with me."

Linda placed her arms under her head as if she were stargazing. I did the same, and together, we spotted a few constellations of stains and paint chips that, in retrospect, were probably mold.

"I have no problem begging, Linda, and I'm happy to get all greedy on you, too," I said, turning to her. "Yes, you're brilliant. And yes, you'll probably be the first woman on the Supreme Court, so it really wouldn't behoove you to just give up so easily here. But if you want to know the hidden truth? It's that I really don't want to be here without you. And I realize that sounds horribly selfish, but it's true. Apart from Mariana, I've never really had any good girlfriends before. And she's my cousin."

"*That's* what you think this is?" she said, shooting back with a straight face for a second too long.

I didn't say anything back. Maybe I should have. Maybe I should have known how to read her better.

"You should see your face right now, Syl," she said, all smiles. "I'm just playing with you."

"Oh?" I said, confused, forcing a laugh. "Look, I'm not suggesting you should stay here because of me, obviously. That's ridiculous. I'm just saying—you've already paid your rent up through the summer, so before you definitely close the book on law school, think about it. I'm working for Macklowe this summer. I can talk to him. I really think he can help. I imagine he would want to."

"I know I don't want to go back," she said calmly. "Please don't talk to Macklowe or anyone else for me, Syl."

"If that's what you want, I won't," I said, biting my tongue.

She studied my face before saying anything else, clearly trying to decipher my motives from every angle.

"Okay," she said. "I'll stay in the apartment through the summer, but only until I figure out what to do next."

I put my arm around her, hopeful, relieved. "We'll get through this together."

She didn't say it back. In fact, she never told me what she was feeling in that moment, though I suppose I never really asked.

I wish I had.

CHAPTER 11

James Macklowe lived in a large brownstone in Brookline, Massachusetts, about twenty minutes from Harvard's campus. He'd inherited the building from his parents when he turned eighteen, along with family money, and now I'd been invited to a private dinner to kick off the summer job. Joe, who had been to the Macklowe brownstone before, came this time as my date.

Mrs. Macklowe answered the door wearing an orange cocktail dress that dropped mid-knee, along with a short double strand of pearls; precisely the uniform I imagined for a woman like her married to a man like him.

"You *must* be Sylvia," she said. Her deep voice echoed in the grand space. "Welcome to our home. James has told me so much about you."

I walked inside and removed my coat. Was I to call him *James* now?

"Here, let me take those for you," she said, gesturing to our jackets.

"Thank you, ma'am," Joe said.

"It's nice to see you again, Joe. What luck does James have, to have not one but two great research assistants one after the other?"

The house was spotless. An old Georgian laced with antiques and original artwork in ornate frames on nearly every wall.

Her eyes scanned me from head to toe. "James says you're Jewish, too, like Mr. Bernstein. But you don't look Jewish." She paused, as if reevaluating her thinking. "Funny."

Joe grabbed my hand and squeezed, as Mrs. Macklowe sighed and then opened her arms again.

"Come," she said. "I want to introduce you to our family." The girl from the photo in Dean Macklowe's office jumped to her side. "This is our daughter, Alexandra. Simon, the baby, is upstairs sleeping. But Alexandra has heard a great deal about you from James."

I looked to Alexandra. She was missing one tooth in the front and its neighbor was mid-growth.

"Nice to meet you, Alexandra," I said. "I've seen your picture in your father's office. I can't wait to see you in the courtroom one day."

Mrs. Macklowe let out an unruly cry in jest.

"Say thank you, Alexandra," her mother insisted, and Alexandra echoed her in propriety. *Thank you.* It was a scene that years later would have bored me endlessly. The dutiful wife, the adorable child, the successful, moneyed husband.

Joe kneeled down to Alexandra and pulled out a flower from his coat. A single daisy.

"For you," he said, handing it to her.

"Thank you, Mr. Bernstein," she gushed, taking it and hugging him.

"She has a thing for Joe," Macklowe whispered to me as he walked into the room.

Macklowe was dressed casually—khaki pants and a button-down shirt, open at the collar, no tie. It was the first time I'd seen him out of a suit and he looked uncomfortable, almost naked.

What followed was a dinner party of formal precision: china, cream colored and edged with fleurs-de-lis, crystal wineglasses and crystal water glasses. Conversation about weather, fashion, a few bits of gossip. Once the last of the dishes were cleared, Dean Macklowe led me toward the living room, while Joe stayed behind with Mrs. Macklowe in the kitchen.

In the sterile living room was a circular table filled with decanters and glasses that must have been worth at least a year's tuition. Macklowe gulped a large helping of sherry and poured another glass for himself, before glancing at me.

"You didn't want any, did you?"

I shook my head. He proceeded to open the bottle of red that we had brought. A Merlot that the man at the store said was fine.

"Sit, Sylvia," he said. His voice was soft and inviting. He nodded to a nearby chair, but I didn't sit.

"I'm sure Joe must have told you, but I like to get to know the students I work with. I find it important in our process."

I nodded yes. He handed me a glass and then sat in a large leather chair, spreading his hands across each of the arms.

"Sit, sit," he said. "You're making me nervous."

I sat on the ottoman and crossed my legs.

"You know, Sylvia, it was fate when you came to my office with your little problem."

I didn't want to think about the public defender's office. I just wanted to watch him drink, hear him speak. I was grateful for the job. I was grateful not to have fallen victim to my own poor judgment that day.

"I'd like our time together to be more productive even than what it was with Joe. He was helping me with some research for a law review article I was publishing, but I'd like to move things in a new direction with you."

I held the wine in my hand and looked at him, curious.

"Please," he said, opening his arms to the chair beside him. "You're making me nervous on the ottoman like that. Relax, make yourself at home."

I moved to the chair, and perched upright, very much not relaxed.

"Things are changing. Ten years ago, there were none of you. This year there are nine. Maybe next year there will be eighteen. And the year after that thirty-six. You see where this is going."

I nodded, agreeing, hopeful. I wanted to remind him that there were only eight of us left; Linda was gone. But I didn't.

"I'd like to see that, too," I said.

"Right," he said, slapping the arm of the chair with his fist. "Exactly. That's why I'm running for DA next year. I'll announce soon, but I'm letting you in on the secret early. I'd like you to help me with the campaign, and in particular with the votes for all the women who seem to be going for people like Kennedy. It will entail some speechwriting, some research, some information gathering. Do you follow?" he said.

"I think so," I said to him, without giving him the plaudits he probably wanted from this private announcement. It wasn't really shocking. First stop, hold a position of power in the courts—city or district attorney—then state attorney general. Next step, get appointed by the governor for a position as a judge in the state, or better yet, by the president for the US Court of Appeals. Final step, the Supreme Court. You had to start somewhere, and someone like Macklowe would have had it all planned out from the beginning. This was just the first step.

If I could have told him then that dreaming of the position was the last thing that gets you there, he never would have believed me. Sitting on the bench is something you can't consciously imagine. If you do, you lose sight of the reasons you might actually arrive.

"So no cite checks?" I said, looking back at him. "No legal research?"

"Well, we do have to maintain some appearances," he laughed. "But mostly I'd like you to come with me to a few local events at some private clubs and professional organizations where I'll be speaking to both men and women in factories and in schools. There are certainly more women who want to practice law now, I imagine, so you'll be helpful there. And there are people who want to follow the changes being made in Washington. Because I agree with them, Sylvia, in case you haven't gleaned this from our conversations—limited as they may have been so far—I quite agree with them." He looked at me and then to a family portrait that was on the wall, and back at me again. "Clearly."

I sipped my wine. "Clearly?"

"I have a daughter," he said, whispering. "Times are changing for her. I want her to have opportunities like you have. Do you understand?"

I could hear Joe and Mrs. Macklowe finishing up in the kitchen.

"You want to give your daughter the best possible future," I said. "That, I understand."

Dean Macklowe leaned over and nearly placed a hand on my knee, but stopped himself short when he saw Joe approaching.

"Well, there's no best," he said. "But there are ways of getting to better."

CHAPTER 12

For three months, I walked into Macklowe's office with a list of assignments, crossing them off one by one; making calls in his district; and doing a final review of the article he planned to publish in the *Harvard Law Review* about a possible equal rights amendment, based on research I presented. I would speak with him occasionally, but our paths rarely crossed in person as much as they did on paper.

After applying to everything from assistants to CEOs to assistants to judges to assistants to retail giants and restaurateurs, Linda eventually got a job at *The Boston Globe* over the summer, working as an assistant to the editor who covered the legal beat. She never fully unpacked her suitcase, as if she were ready to move out at any time, but she got dressed every morning and left for work in an office filled with life. While I was doing cite checks in a windowless office, Linda was actually in the courts, learning about them from an entirely different angle, writing about them. Even though she hated it, she brought coffee to the editors who needed it, and filed papers for the secretaries who didn't show up, and then every once in a while, she would get sent out to cover a small story when no one else could. It was usually something that didn't make the paper, but she got the practice and saw the routine and structure of the newsroom. "Next week, I'm going to help my editor cover a copyright case," she said, more excited than she'd ever been about actual copyright law. "My editor wants me to bring him black tea, not coffee," she once said, sort of happy about it. "Can you believe it? Tea? How's that going to caffeinate anyone?" She would tell me about the stories she was working on, and they changed practically daily, while I was working on the exact same note for three months. Each day she came home, her face was softer, more at peace, and more joyful than the day before.

Meanwhile, I saw Joe twice a week, once for dinner out and once at his place, where he routinely cooked a five-course meal. He recounted stories of his summer job at a small law firm, and was excited about how it was going to lead to a full-time position there. He'd never heard from Ropes & Gray as he'd hoped; Macklowe hadn't written the letter for him, and Joe had gotten this small firm job on his own. It suited him. Linda, Joe, and I ate together occasionally, but most of the time, it was Linda and me at home.

I went home to Brooklyn a few times, but I never told Mariana that my summer was being spent helping Macklowe reach the next rung on a ladder that he already knew how to climb.

The reality is that I was barely doing any legal work. I was drafting speech after speech for Dean Macklowe in which I wrote things like, "My dedication to changing the fabric of our country is in line with John F. Kennedy's civil rights policies, so if you are planning to vote for him, vote for me." And "Progress is forward movement in context." Then I would leave the typed drafts on his desk, where he'd review them the next morning. I don't even think that Macklowe liked Kennedy, or planned to vote for him, either, but he was piggybacking onto the message to help himself. So instead of learning about the law from him, I would find lines crossed through all of my words, and notes in the margins like:

Make this sound like me.

Make it sound stronger.

Use my voice, not yours.

The Fourth of July came and went, as did the onset of the heat in August as everyone started to get ready to return to school. People read novels, bathed in the sun at the beach, while I lived alone inside a windowless room.

It was near the end of the summer when I found an article from *The Boston Globe* hidden in the stack of my assignments. On page three, it read, AMY MCCARTNEY IN JAIL ON FIRST DEGREE MURDER, her mug shot printed below, sensationalized as if she were Bonnie Parker.

I walked into Macklowe's office, holding that morning's newspaper out to him.

"Ahhh, yes." He was grinning like he had just let me in on an exclusive secret. "I thought you might be interested. That's *the* case, isn't it?" he said, as energized as he was in our first meeting together. "The one that led you to all this *glamour*," he said, teasing out the word.

"Yes," I said. "I mean, not the exact case, but she is the victim." I waited before correcting myself. "*Was* the victim."

I skimmed the article while he watched. Amy McCartney's husband had attacked her for the third time that month. In response, she had pushed him out the window of the apartment building they shared with their three children. They lived on the third floor. He died five days later, after living on a ventilator with twelve broken bones, a collapsed lung, and a punctured spleen.

"I read the indictment," he said. "I'm guessing the defense will claim it was self-defense. How would you advise her this time if she were your client?"

She was in jail? She *killed* him?

"Don't think too hard, Olin," he said. "I asked you a question and I need a response."

I picked up the newspaper and scanned the words again.

Hospital. Fourth offense. Police called. Torn vagina.

"I think that this is a tragic situation with an outcome that serves justice to nobody," I said.

"True," he said quickly, unimpressed. "But now you're *her* lawyer. What do you say?"

Amy McCartney's hair was darker than I remembered it and cut short around her face. A bruise dripped down over her right eye and her brow was split in half. She wasn't avoiding the camera. It was almost as if she wanted the camera to see her when nobody else would.

"Well, I hope that her defense team is presenting her entire narrative because *how* she is represented matters just as much as *what* happened," I said, thinking. "If her attorneys present her story as a violent angry woman who snapped with revenge, then she'll likely be locked away forever. But if they present her story as a tortured victim who had been hospitalized time and time again due to her husband's repeatedly documented assaults, they'd have no other option but to see that she was defending herself here. And not only that, she was defending herself and the lives of her young children. I imagine there is evidence of a repeated pattern of abuse that would have ended either way with one of them dead. And at the end of the day, it will depend on the right attorney taking the time to understand and tell her narrative to properly defend her."

He unfolded his arms and listened.

"And what if the story was reversed?" he asked. "And Devin killed Amy?"

"The approach would be the same for Devin McCartney as it

would be for Amy McCartney. And if I had a second chance last term, I would have presented his narrative at the time, too." I stalled, thinking. "But I'm going to go out on a limb and assume that their narratives are somewhat different."

"So you want to throw out the law in lieu of, what . . . *story*? *Assumption*?"

I couldn't tell if he was mocking or teaching me.

"I never said anything about throwing out the law, James," I said, using his first name without thinking. "It's not just the rule of law that commands, but also the narrative of life that is key. How we merge the two determines a fair, reasonable, and right outcome."

He stood up over me and cleared his throat.

"Miss Olin, please remember that, at least for now, I am your teacher," he said, his tone a warning. "And if you are to become an attorney, you will have a responsibility to speak appropriately, with deference to the court and those around you—have a certain demeanor, if you will. The minute decorum breaks down, so too does the law. I know that you understand this possibly better than any of my previous research assistants, if you understand what I'm saying."

Demeanor, I thought. *Decorum*. Just another couple of lousy words for emotion.

His words echoed within these walls again. *It's because you're a woman*, et cetera, et cetera.

"But beyond this question of decorum, you will need to look at the facts and the evidence and whatever narrative is presented, and question it," he said, shaking it off. "You must hear all the facts and either defend or dismantle them. And in doing so, you question them more than your own experiences dictate. Question your own gut, question what evidence you see before you even with your own eyes, and know the exact answers for everything before you ask."

"And what exactly is the lesson here?" I asked. "What am I questioning? That women are treated poorly by society? I don't need to learn about that from this case—be it from the judge and his paltry dismissal of her prior case all the way to this reporter's one-day write-up. It's thin demonstrative evidence that probably repeats in courtrooms and newspapers in every county. There is a larger story here, no doubt, that nobody is eager to hear. And if someone did, I imagine both she and her abusive husband would be in far better places than they are now. Not to mention their three children, as I'm sure the newspaper left that part out. They have, what, eight hundred words to complete the story?"

"Don't make this about you," he said. "Or all women. This is about the law. You must look at each case individually. And only at its facts. And what you have in front of you is one journalist's coverage which may or may not be accurate, which may or may not be slanted."

"Which is why it's more important than ever to present the best narrative for the client in court, and my fear here is that this client likely won't have that, given the options of who is representing her. Considering there aren't a terribly large number of women in the courtroom these days, again, I'm going to go out on a limb and say her attorneys are probably men. And probably, they'll present her facts and her story the way it happened from their perspective. So, yes, I'm talking about the law, facts, evidence, the totality of the circumstances, but it still needs to be presented to a judge and jury in a certain way. And without the proper marriage between the law and narrative, there is systemic breakdown, and I suspect that is what will happen here. A systemic breakdown from the very first case that led to death. And, yes, Dean Macklowe, if I could go back and do it again, I would have said that."

I dropped the newspaper on the floor. Immediately, he walked over to me, bent down, and picked it up.

"Here," he said. "Keep it."

"I can get a copy myself. Linda Loving is working for the paper now," I said, hoping somehow that dropping her name would spark a memory of his other star student.

"I heard," he said. But it clearly didn't matter. I couldn't tell what he was thinking.

He folded the newspaper and placed it on his desk, and I saw him differently. Or maybe for the first time.

"Perhaps your demeanor will be helpful in this field after all," he said, thinking, attempting an uncomfortable kindness that didn't match the conversation. "Do you want me to make a phone call to the public defender's office again? By now they're certain to have forgotten your green missteps and we could get you an externship during the fall of next year."

His voice was almost paternal, but his words didn't match them, as if he were playing a game. He was twenty years my senior, three inches shorter than me, and until now, always seemed larger. But he wasn't. He was just working, teaching, seeing the world from his experience, without considering another.

"Why are you offering all this to me, and not any of your previous RAs?"

"You're referring to Bernstein, aren't you?" he said. "Look, Sylvia. I realize you two are dating, but I'm going to tell you something that only the people who care about you will say. Joe Bernstein is at Harvard now, but in a few years, he won't be. And what's more, he wouldn't be. He's a nice enough guy, a stand-up student, hard worker. He was perfect for the job last year as it was more clerical; he did my research for me, and had no problem sitting inside the library all day checking cites. But he isn't going to make us proud. He isn't going to become partner at a law firm or run a business or even teach at a law school, and he's certainly not going to be entrusted with a government position." He paused for no more than two breaths before continuing. "Shall we just agree that he's suited for other things?"

My throat cleared instead of my eyes. "Why are you saying this?"

He sat on the large chair in his office and crossed his legs, leaning back comfortably.

"Because I care about you, Sylvia. I *respect* you." The second-to-last word of his sentence was punctuated with a bullet. "I would tell my own daughter this if she were in your position, which I hope she will be one day." He glanced at the family photo framed on his desk for a fraction of a second before returning his gaze to me. "Times are changing. Believe me, they're going to be hard enough for you as is. Think about your future. Think about what *you* want and *you* need. Don't make them harder weighed down with someone like Joe Bernstein."

CHAPTER 13

Joe was already in the kitchen making his specialty when I got to his place. Penne alla vodka was on the stovetop and he was sautéing mushrooms and green beans beside it.

"He kept you late tonight," he said to me. A glass of red wine was in one hand, while his other was mixing vegetables. I walked over to him and kissed his cheek. He handed me the glass. "This is for you."

"Thanks," I said, taking it.

The heat from the stove had turned him into something swollen and sweaty. He poured the pasta into a strainer in the sink, and ribbons of steam circled up to his face, fogging his glasses. He was now cooking every night to de-stress, and I got to enjoy the occasional fruits of his labor.

I walked to the couch with the wine. My feet ached and my stomach was unsettled. Joe picked up on this and started rubbing my back, my shoulders, kneading out the stress. I reached around to touch his face, his eyelashes, his mouth, where the fine lines were starting to spread. I kissed him, testing his lips against mine once again.

He tasted like red sauce.

I wasn't quite sure what I wanted, but I knew Macklowe was wrong.

I kissed Joe again.

"What are we doing here?" I said, rubbing his earlobe between my fingers.

"What do you mean what are we doing here? Dinner." He winked.

"I'm serious, Joe," I said.

"We're in a relationship," he said, confused. One side of his mouth was smiling. "We're as far into it as you want it to be. Because I'm all in."

I smiled without hesitation, without thought.

"I'm falling in love with you, Sylvia Olin," he said, wrapping his arms around my waist.

At the time I wasn't sure I would ever fall in love, and if I did, I never imagined it would be with someone like Joe Bernstein. And yet, here I was falling in love with Joe Bernstein.

"You don't have to say it back," he said, kissing me, and in that moment, I didn't think about anything else except that I knew that I wanted him, too.

Think about what you want and you need, I heard. *Don't make it harder weighed down with someone like Joe Bernstein.*

"Come," Joe said, pulling me back to the stove in the kitchen. Then he took the spoon and dipped it in the sauce, offering it to me.

"It's good," I said, though the acid of the tomato made my stomach flip.

"My mom's recipe. Been perfecting it for years." He dipped the spoon again and tried it himself, proud.

I took the spoon from his hands and placed it on the table. Then, I touched his face, drawing circles around the high bones of his cheeks.

"*This* is really good," I said, kissing him. "Just as it is."

"So you're saying it's not a good time to bring up the fact that I want a lot of kids one day? Maybe four or five? Maybe even a baker's dozen?"

"Probably not," I said, and the doorbell rang. "I'll get it."

When I opened the door, Linda was on the other side.

"Can we talk?" she said. Her face was solemn. But before she could say a word, I vomited all over the hallway.

Y ou're pregnant, aren't you?" said Linda, as we sat down in Joe's bedroom.

It was the first I'd even thought of it.

"I honestly have no idea," I said. Through the partially open door, I could see Joe cleaning up my vomit in the other room on his hands and knees, scrubbing.

"And the nine became eight, and the eight became seven," she said, dropping her hand to her side, sort of prophetic, sort of singsongy, like a radio jingle.

"No, I don't think so," I said, feeling myself want to vomit again.

She stared at me.

"I'm not pregnant, Linda," I said. "At least I don't think I'm pregnant."

"You're pregnant," she said. "I've seen this before. On my mother, twice on my aunt, once on a friend from high school."

I played with the skin under my chin, feeling around for something different, something she saw that I couldn't.

"Do you want it?" she asked.

I wanted to finish my internship. I wanted to graduate from law school. I wanted to fulfill Mariana's plans, and my plans, to teach law, to make sure that nothing that had happened in Germany would ever happen here. I wanted to become what my mother should have become, if she had been born at a different time. I wanted equity for girls and women, and the abolition of Ladies' Day in law school, and a Supreme Court made up of nine women. But I had no idea how to get any of it just yet. I didn't have Macklowe's ladder to climb. I didn't even know what my ladder would be, but I knew I wanted to climb.

"I don't know," I said.

"Bullshit, Syl," she said, smiling with a fierce kindness I wish I had. "You know. Everyone knows what they want deep down."

I rubbed my stomach, wanting to vomit again to avoid answering the question.

"It's both the easiest and hardest question in the world to answer," she said.

I ran my hands through my hair as she sat forward.

"Fine," she said. "I'll tell you what I want. I want to make a difference in the world. I want to shift the conversation about the law, about society, about civil rights, and quite frankly, if I can't do that through the law, that's okay. I'll do it another way. I'm not even sure that the law is the best, most effective way to make change anyway. I don't want to be one of the only Black students at Harvard. I don't want people like Macklowe talking to me about Dr. King just because of the color of my skin. I don't want it to always be hard, but maybe it will always be hard. And if it will, then perhaps I can help make it slightly easier so that next time there are nineteen students in law school and then nine hundred bylines by women in the newspapers. *Brown* isn't the only way things can change. There are other ways, too. Nobody sees the people who write the goddamn laws. We see the people enforcing the laws. We see the people talking about the laws.

We see the people breaking the laws. And who is seen matters. How they are seen and how they are presented."

"Right," I said, agreeing.

"And you know what else I know?" she continued. "I don't want to get married. I *don't* want children," she said, thinking. "And the reason I really know that is not because of that ridiculous 1908 case we talked about or my mother or any of my old friends. It's because I nearly had one."

She took a breath before continuing further. I wasn't sure if I was meant to respond in that moment, but I didn't. I listened.

"It was a few years ago in college, when Ray and I were dating. I got pregnant and then I had a miscarriage. One day I was filling out my application for law school and the next day blood filled my pantyhose," she said. "I was happy about it. It hurt for a bit, but it didn't hurt much after that. Ray was devastated. I wasn't. There you go."

"I'm so sorry, Linda," I said, sad, but for reasons I couldn't exact. "I didn't know."

"Of course you didn't know. Why would it have come up before?" she said, matter-of-fact. "But I'm glad it happened. It helped me realize exactly what I want and what I need early on."

"Is that why you two broke up?"

She waited to respond, as if she were replaying a conversation in her head, and then she finally answered.

"No."

"Okay," I said, nodding.

"So what do you want, Syl?" she said again, pushing.

I knew the end goal, but not the game to get there. To this day, I still wish I were more like Linda: clear, fast-thinking, charismatic. She had figured out what made her happy when her original goal didn't. She didn't sit on it, wait on it, think too hard about it; she just took control and ran.

"I think I may want to marry him," I said, feeling pulled to Joe in the other room.

It wasn't untrue.

"Really?" said Linda.

"Yeah," I said, discovering this as I spoke.

Joe was nearly finished cleaning the floor. I knew Linda didn't approve, but I didn't care. It was okay to want both Joe and the law. They completed each other; they fed off of each other, each making the other stronger.

"I like Joe," said Linda, hesitant. "I do."

I laughed.

"No, seriously, Syl, I do. He's sweet and very loving. He's smart and he cooks and most importantly, he loves you, clearly," she said, looking behind me to see where he was. Then she lowered her voice. "But here's the thing. You can talk about Joe all you want. How he's different, doesn't seem like the others, thinks he can be a so-called equal partner in life, but that is such a fantasy. It doesn't exist. Men like Joe don't exist."

"Men like Joe don't exist?" I mimicked. "Come on, Linda."

"He wants kids, right?" she said. "So many kids, I bet he wants ten goddamn kids. But he can't actually carry the kids, or give birth to the kids, can he? You'll have the kids. And when that happens, he won't be cooking and cleaning at the end of the day. You will."

"That's not fair."

"That whole 1908 case about women being another type of person, it's not just bad law. It's *the* law. So if that's the world we live in, what happens to a man like Joe Bernstein, then? He can be different from all the others, but until everyone else is different, too, he'll become just like them."

"I don't know," I said. "I understand what you're saying, Linda. I do. Believe me. It's not like I don't think about it. But it's also entirely possible that men can evolve, just as women can if we don't coddle them into being a certain kind of species, a special protected class, to whom we as a society give special rights," I said, feeling my decision growing stronger with each word. "Joe and I are both going to be lawyers. We will have similar jobs. There's also an argument for having a supportive partner while pursuing your dreams. And if Joe cleaning up my vomit on his disgusting green carpet isn't illustrative evidence of that kind of support, I'm not sure what is."

She smiled. I could tell how hard she was trying to be a good friend.

"And I want that," I said, touching my stomach and looking down. "And I think I want *this*, too."

"You think?"

"I *know*," I said, raising my voice and then catching myself so that Joe wouldn't come running in. "I know I do."

"Well," she said, nodding reluctantly. "I guess I'm glad to hear you say that because I came here to tell you that I'm moving to New York."

I grabbed my stomach and stood up from the bed. "Are you trying to get me to throw up again?"

"No," she said with a smile, placing her hand on my knee briefly, bringing me back down. "A few weeks ago, I interviewed for a job at *The New York Times*, and I just found out that I got it."

My chest hurt the minute she said *New York*.

"I wanted to tell you in person," she added. "I mean, I'm going to be an assistant to an assistant and I'm fairly certain there's no upward movement, but I'm going to see where it goes. My boss at the *Globe* made the call for me. Wondered why the hell I was ever in law school to begin with when this obviously suits me better."

"And what do you think?" I asked.

She grinned. We both knew she wouldn't be an assistant long.

CHAPTER 14

A month later, I married Joe Bernstein in a small ceremony at his family's home on Long Island. I wore a white dress that dropped just below my knees. About two dozen small pearls standing in as buttons traced my vertebrae all the way to my neck, making it difficult to sit comfortably. The rest of the dress was silk with two swaths of lace over the shoulders. I wore flats so that I could kiss Joe easily under the *chuppah*. I let my hair down, parted to the side, and added a bit of curl to the bottom.

Joe wore a tan suit with a narrow blue tie that fell a little short of its proper placement. That was part of his charm. On first glance, everything seemed in place, but when you looked a little closer, something was off. That something off reminded me that he was vulnerable and imperfect, like me.

I put a single lily in his lapel and held on to my own small bouquet of lilies, which were tied together by green and brown ribbon.

Mariana and my father were there, along with Linda and a handful of other students from our class, but mostly it was Joe's family. He insisted that Dean Macklowe attend the wedding, because we had both worked for him. "Think of how it will make us look," he said, excited and ambitious, hopeful. I agreed for him, unsure exactly how it would make us look, but we didn't belabor the point. It wasn't worth it.

Minutes before I walked down the aisle of the beachfront property, Joe and I locked eyes, and in that split second, I saw a glimpse of the future. Of laughter and arguments and silence. Words climbing with anger and resentment. Appeasement. Regret. Joy. Compromise.

And then we blinked and time skewed and reversed and skipped and stopped. I was twelve years old, standing in front of my own mother, wearing all black, covered with goose bumps, as she left me forever. The clock ticked loudly until I heard Mariana's voice, and the crispness of it brought me out of the memory.

"Let's talk," she said. She was wearing a long blue dress that covered her legs all the way to the ground. "Now," she insisted. She grabbed my hand and brought me into the nearest room.

Clutching Mariana's hand, I thought of Tony Discanti waiting for her out in their seats. I had seen them together earlier. He was thinner now, and balder on top, but he still looked the way I remembered him from our first meeting: kind and good. And his eyes told me everything I needed to know about his feelings for Mariana. He was the earth and she the sun: he revolved around her.

I thought I had that with Joe. At least I hoped I did, wedding or not.

"I'm really happy for you," said Mariana, touching my dress where the baby's heartbeat called. "I just wish you had told me before today."

Her cheeks were red. She wasn't trying to hide her joy. I wasn't showing yet, but I felt chastised that I hadn't told her myself.

"Listen to me, Sylvie, and listen to yourself. You really want this?" she asked again. "For you?"

"Yes, of course I want this," I said, taking her hand in mine. Her eyes were somehow darker than I remember when I was a child. *Artistic vision cannot be transferred from the eyes of a Jewish woman to an Aryan man*, but something does transfer between people over time. The way they see, the way they look, the way they want to look. It all changes.

"Good," she said, almost relieved. "I'm glad. Your baby will have a good home, then. You will be safe here."

The string quartet started playing.

"Come with me," I said, pulling her to my side. "Stand beside me at the *chuppah*."

I walked down the aisle with Mariana on one side and my father on the other. Joe and I took our place before the rabbi. We circled each other seven times. We both stomped on a delicate glass. We danced the *hora* for ten minutes and spent one of them up in a chair being thrust into the spotlight by the few guests in attendance. We ate cake at the sweetheart table. My father was too shy to give a speech, so Joe and I decided to step in on his behalf. Joe was always ready to play any part at any time, which is something I loved about him. We spoke before a crowd. We made promises and sealed vows and danced with a symbolic handkerchief between our fingers. Twenty minutes later, we danced in a corner to "Cheek to Cheek" by Ella Fitzgerald, while the rest of our guests swayed center stage.

But at the ceremony, it was only us. Under the *chuppah*, a simple wooden pole topped with Joe's *tallis*, our temples touched in melodic rhythm, and we kissed. *I promise to love and support you*, he said to me before I echoed him. *I promise to love our children and travel the world beside you*, I said to him before he echoed me. *I promise to be your partner in this world so that everything that happens to me happens to you,* he said. And I said the same. *I promise to compromise and sacrifice for you and our family,* I said. And so did he.

The beginnings of marriages are always full of promise, aren't they?

CHAPTER 15

The baby was delivered three weeks early, via cesarean. It was April 28, one week before second-year final exams, and when she arrived early, I missed them entirely.

She was tiny and surprisingly alert, with splashes of red all over her chest like a Jackson Pollock painting. Her fingers, pink and small and hairless, wrinkled up and down the bones like gloves that hadn't yet found the right owner. When they brought her to me, and her soft skin pressed against my chin, her nose touched my nose, and it felt like we were one body. We named her Aviva Susan Bernstein.

She looks like you," said Joe, touching her nose. She had my mother's upturn at the end of her nose, as well as her long lashes and oversize ears, but really, I could have sworn she looked like Joe. Exactly like Joe.

"She has no hair," I said.

"No babies have hair, Syl," he said, smiling. His eyes were bright with love. Mine were puffy and exhausted.

"All babies have *some* hair," I insisted, my voice a bit too loud, making her cry. "Right?"

"Shhhhh," he said softly. "Shhhh, sweet child."

"Shhhh, Aviva," I whispered in her ear. "Ahhh-veee-vahhh," I said. "You've had a big day."

Her mouth opened wide and her eyes shut into two half-moons. She wouldn't stop crying.

"May I?" asked Joe, as if he were a stranger. He took Aviva from my hands and held her over his shoulder, and she stopped crying almost instantly. I had just held her in my body for nearly nine months, carried her from place to place, massaged her with my palms, applied creams to my belly, listened to soothing sounds. I had protected her from the weather and from foods and drinks and stopped moving when I was supposed to, but I couldn't calm her. He could.

"Aviva, Aviva, Aviva," he chanted. The bottom half of my body was still numb and blood was still trickling out, but he was the one who soothed her with his goddamn chanting.

"Let me try again," I said, my arms outstretched, wanting Aviva back.

Joe nestled into her neck, shushing her, whispering to her, and then transferred her to me limb by limb. When it was complete, he raised a fist in triumph, quiet, serene.

"Look, her eyes . . ." he said, practically squealing as she opened them. But I couldn't tell the color. Not yet. Did he see something I didn't?

But no sooner could she see me than she started crying again, and I finally noticed—she had one green eye and the other blue. Later on, the doctors predicted both would turn brown, but they never changed.

"Let me," said Joe, reaching out, his hands trying to take her.

"No," I said.

I pulled down my hospital gown and tried to attach her to my right nipple, which had darkened in the previous few hours.

I was so engorged that her head was smaller than my breast. I didn't know how she would latch.

"It's not working," I said to Joe. "She hates me."

"Stop," he said.

"You wanna try?" I snapped, and then squeezed two fingers around my right nipple, forcing it into her mouth, practically suffocating her. "Take it," I said to her, not even trying to whisper. "Come on, take it."

Her mouth was closed.

"Just take the goddamn nipple already," I whispered, pushing her into me.

And then Joe leaned over to us and massaged her slowly with the palm of his hand, and she calmed. Just like that.

"There, there . . ." he said, removing my nipple from her mouth. She cried again. Then, he guided my nipple back into her mouth, his hand on her arm, and on impact, again she stopped crying.

"Are you kidding me with this?" I said.

Joe laughed.

"Keep your hand there," I said. "The whole time. Don't move it even if she moves. No matter what," I said, until at last she latched. "Aha!" I cried, relieved. "Yes!"

"Shhhhh," said Joe, leaning closer to Aviva to keep her calm. "Your mother doesn't get excited easily. This might be the first time in our entire relationship, so if this is what it takes . . ."

He stayed beside me, massaging my shoulders as I hunched over, holding her, wiggling my feet as the sensation returned to them, singing to Aviva until her cries subsided and night fell. Joe went home after visiting hours were over and was back in the morning for three days until Mariana eventually took his place. He had to study for finals, and shortly thereafter, the bar exam.

I never got to finish my second year.

CHAPTER 16

Joe and I barely spoke in the weeks following Aviva's birth, wandering in and out of different lanes as if we no longer knew how to drive. I stayed in bed for what may have been days or weeks; I can't remember.

Those first few weeks of Aviva's life were spent with a pen in my hand, still studying, trying to retain everything from that semester. Joe was studying for the bar exam, absent from our daily routine as if Aviva were just a visitor, someone who only temporarily disrupted his evenings.

The sun would rise and set, rise and set. Or rather, it seemed to be continually setting. Aviva and I slept only in the mornings, never bearing witness to the start of a new day. In the evenings, when Joe would come home and pick her up, she would instantly stop crying.

I love you, he would mouth, to both of us, but really more to her. Almost always just to her.

I would hear him singing to her, serenading her with the toreador song from *Carmen*, as he warmed the milk.

Hi Aviva Bernstein, how are you today? I fought a bull, I fought a bull. Yes, it was the meanest bull in town. Aviva, how are you today?

He'd taken to writing his own lyrics into the libretto, finding it his own form of creative expression, the way he let loose when school was causing him grief. But as I listened to him croon, all I could think was that he *wasn't* a composer when it came to Aviva. He didn't make her, create her, build her.

Hi Aviva Bernstein, how are you today? he would continue, daily. She squealed with joy every time he sang. Every note, every breath. She loved it and I hated it. And then I hated him for making me hate *Carmen*, one of the few operas I didn't hate. And then I hated myself for thinking so negatively about him. And *Carmen*.

Would she love him more because she saw him less than she saw me? Was the excitement of momentary intimacy the prize that would clinch her long-term affection? Was the joyful wonder of his eyes what she needed to sleep?

We'll honor and obey each other, he had said to me when he proposed.

We'll change the world as a team, he had professed while we were in bed together on our honeymoon in Maine less than a year earlier.

I wanted to be beside him. I wanted to complete school, and practice law however I could at this point, but the administration hadn't responded to my requests to retake my exams. They hadn't even acknowledged them. And Joe had not asked about my plans either.

Every day in those weeks, I would stand from the bed and walk to the bathroom, where the mirror fired back at me. My eyes were sunken, my cheeks blotchy. My ears seemed to protrude more than usual from my head. I was a Picasso painting on the outside, my face distorted and dripping in various pieces down my cheeks, and probably no different inside.

Hi Aviva Bernstein, how are you today?

His voice would travel under the door and lodge its way in my consciousness.

I fought a bull. I fought a bull.

I wanted to kill that goddamned bull.

I would shower to escape his voice, and when I did, the water stabbed me, little stalactites dropping all at once. A cave crumbling, leaving me inside. From beneath the water, I could hear Aviva start to cry again in her crib. I wouldn't move; instead I would allow the shards to prick my back, turning it into the night sky. Joe was with her. She was fine. The water eventually would turn warm and then hot and then warm again, hiding Aviva's wails in the next room. I would wash my hair, my fingers catching in the tangles, and then my face, which had sprung new pastures of acne. Unwanted adolescence reappeared everywhere: on my cheeks, my chest, my back. I would wash my body and my hands would shrivel in the heated moisture. When I looked closer at them minutes later, a towel running up and down my legs, I saw my fingers. The extra skin hanging on, the glove refusing to fit. We were the same, Aviva and I, our bodies reflections of each other. I left the shower, dried myself, and walked out to the bedroom, where Joe and Aviva were waiting. She was sucking on his forefinger, momentarily quiet.

"I think she wants you," he would say, kissing her head and then mine, and then leaving.

So I would climb into bed beside her and my body would shift into her. I would tell myself how much I wanted to love her, I did love her. Unlike me, she wasn't grotesque. She was gorgeous, this little child wholly entrusted to me. I loved running my fingers along her shoulders and elbows and knees. Aviva, this blue-eyed green-eyed thing, this blond doll, this child, this monster, this babe, this perfection, this beauty, this bliss, this love, this weight, this confusion, this body in my body in my home in my life in my heart in my head in my gut in my arms. I whispered in her ear, my voice wet with hope.

"What on earth do I do with you?"

CHAPTER 17

After Aviva was born, I didn't have a summer internship because the plan was for me to take care of the baby those months and return for my third year. But then Aviva came early, I missed my finals, and the administration didn't know how to handle it. They'd never had this problem before. They said they'd convene and get back to me with a decision shortly.

For six weeks, I waited by the phone. It sat on Joe's desk beside stacks of papers, textbooks, his offer of employment pending bar results, and a copy of our wedding photo. His bar exam materials sat here, too, beside a pair of scissors and stacks of handwritten notes. I read over a question and knew the answer. Then I read over another and another and another, and knew them all. I sat down and completed one hundred multiple choice answers. But still no call. I left personal messages for Macklowe, and general ones with his office, asking for a makeup test date. Macklowe sent flowers and a stuffed animal—a little dog we named Remi—but said nothing about school in the note, and he never responded to my calls.

As I nursed Aviva and studied, my hair was in my way, so I tried to pull it back, but it was dirty and unwashed and fell limp on the sides of my shoulders. In the previous months, it had been ripped, singed, knotted, and bitten. I didn't have the time to clean it, let alone brush it, so I picked up the scissors and began to cut.

Then, the phone rang.

CHAPTER 18

Your hair," said Joe, when he came home later that evening after studying for the bar exam at school all day. "What happened?"

He placed a hand on my neck, where my hair was now missing.

I pulled away, annoyed. "Thanks."

"No," he said, reaching out. "I mean, you look beautiful, but . . . why?"

He rushed over to me and played around with my new short hair.

I took his hand down. His voice didn't match his words. The timing was off.

"Is everything okay with Aviva?" he said, looking toward her sleeping peacefully under a blanket in the crib.

"Yes," I said, nodding. "She's fine."

"Macklowe called," I said, filling the space.

"Finally!"

"He said that there's a problem and he wants me to come in to discuss."

"That's not cryptic at all," he said, his eyes widening. "But at least now things can get back on track. Right?"

"I'm not entirely sure that means they'll accept my proposal," I said, frustrated. Did he not hear me when I said there was a problem? "I have no idea what that means for the fall semester. If I'll be allowed back in."

"Well, when do you meet?" he asked, focused on my hair instead of my face.

"Next week," I said.

He bit his bottom lip. "Why so long? School starts in a month."

"He's on vacation," I said, growing angrier. "Aviva is already three months old. They've had three months to think about this. I don't know why he couldn't just tell me what the problem was over the phone so I could start working on fixing whatever it is before I see him."

Joe held my gaze without answering, returning to my face, my eyes. It was clear he wasn't listening—not completely. He'd been at school until ten every night for the past month, while half of his peers were studying at home. He could have studied at home, too. The exam was in two weeks. And now his focus was on the wrong thing.

"You don't know what the problem is yet, Syl," he said. "Whatever it is, it's a problem you can tackle. *We* can tackle."

"Stop it," I said.

"What?"

"Stop saying *we*. This isn't your problem. It's mine. Not ours. *Mine.*"

"Sylvia," he said, his voice trying to calm me. "It sounds like Macklowe wants to help you. Right? He's helped you before. Why else would he call you in?"

"I don't want his help anymore. Not this time. I shouldn't need his help for this. I didn't do anything wrong. I did the work on my own. I didn't miss a single class that entire year. He of all people should understand this."

"I'm sure he does," said Joe.

"No," I said, thinking back to the past year, as my professors and peers watched my belly grow, as they laughed when I rushed to the bathroom, sometimes more than once a class. Instead of asking me about the cases I presented in class or the work I did on law review, they were asking me about my changing body.

"He doesn't," I said.

Joe sat down delicately, taking my arms in his. There were blond hairs everywhere around me—on the couch, the floor, my shoulders. A sizable cut from the scissors straddled the knuckle over my right ring finger, now clotted and dried. I didn't even notice it earlier. Now all I could see were small nicks and cuts everywhere on my hands.

"Sylvia, you can reach out for help every once in a while. That's how the world works."

"Don't tell me how the world works, Joe," I said, nearly shouting. "You don't know how the world works for me."

"Sorry," he said, "I didn't mean it like that."

I was exhausted. My feet were swollen. My hands started to sting where the skin was torn, and I noticed little fingerprints of blood on the coffee table.

"Sit here," he said. "Don't move."

He ran to the bathroom and came back with half a dozen cold wipes and a large bowl of warm water. With love, he massaged and washed my hands until it was dark outside. He brushed aside the cut hairs and they glided to the floor like little dandelions. Then he cleaned those up, too.

"What do you need from me?" he asked.

His voice was as soothing as the water.

A pounding started in my head and then shook down my body. My mouth was dry, my throat hoarse, I licked my lips in circles.

"Aviva is only three months old," he said, thinking. "The plan was for you to stay with her this summer, and—"

"Don't, Joe," I said, my voice quiet, my body tired.

"What?" he said, protesting.

My stomach was curling.

"The plan is faulty," I said. "Clearly."

I looked beneath my pants; a red line connected the two sides of my abdomen in a crescent. Depending on the perspective, it was either smiling or frowning.

"What can I do, Syl?" he said. "Tell me."

"I can't tell if I should be angry with you or if I should love you more," I said to him. "And I don't know what to do about it."

His face turned white and then red and then pink and white again. The beat of a fast-moving heart.

"Okay," he said, confused and nervous.

"I'm not envious of *this*," I said, looking around. "I'm proud of you, and I'm not envious of the bar exam exactly, or your job. But I am confused. And frustrated. And I don't want to read and research and present a fully formed argument to you as to why. I'm just angry. That's all. I'm angry and I don't know what else to say."

I could tell how nervous he was. I could tell he didn't know what to say because his nostrils flared and his hands stuck to his sides like a nutcracker's.

"Sylvie . . ."

"Don't *Sylvie* me," I snapped. I didn't mean to, but I did. "Why aren't *you* home right now with Aviva?" I went on. "Why aren't you home with her part of the time while I go back to school part of the time? Wasn't that part of the deal? *Everything that happens to me happens to you.*"

He swallowed and looked up at me, empty.

"Because I have the bar exam. There is no flexibility there. And I have a job lined up and we have a baby now and need to pay our bills. We can't live in campus housing anymore once the bar is over," he said. "I'm sorry. But it's the reality."

His eyes were glossy.

"Sylvia," he said, taking my hands in his. "I can't let us not have a home, not eat. Especially right now."

"Is *this* what you want?" I asked. "Is *this* what you wanted? Always?"

"No," he said, shaking his head. "But it is what it is."

"Please . . ."

"What do you want me to say, Syl?"

"That we'll fix this," I said. "We'll fix this *specifically*."

"We'll fix this," he said, but it felt hollow, an echo in a tunnel. "We are in this *together*. We will figure it out."

We will figure it out. Five words that people without foresight drop like loose change. Without a plan, just figuring it out means nothing. The loose change is gone and you're broke.

"But how?" I said.

There was no way for me to work and him to stay with Aviva when he had just graduated from law school. Even if I was able to graduate and work, he'd make ten times what I would and we both knew that.

"I'm not sure how," he said. "I don't know the best option here. I don't know what would be best——"

"For me or you?"

"For *us*," he said, urging.

But as he said *us*, he was far away, and it seemed as though "us" was me and Aviva and he was himself. Macklowe was right. *There's no best, but there are ways of getting to better.*

Lately, I'd started hearing more of Macklowe in my head as I waited for his phone call. Maybe this is exactly what he was talking about when he warned me to think about my future. *Don't make it harder weighed down with someone like Joe Bernstein.*

"If anyone shouldn't have graduated, it's me," said Joe, taking Macklowe's place in my thoughts. "I think we both know that. That would be the better scenario."

"Would it?" I said, curious.

He placed his hands on his hips and cocked his head to the side. "Yes, of course it would."

I believed him. I don't know why I did, but when he spoke, he was honest and clear, and pure.

"I hope you know that."

"I do," I said. "But . . ."

"Shhh . . ." he said, pretending to move the hair that no longer fell down my neck and back and shoulders, and kissed the open skin on the back of my neck.

"I really do like the hair," he said. "It's so unlike you, and yet it suits you."

When he said those few words, neither of us had any idea how much like me my new hair really was, how much it would come to define me in a world made for people so very unlike me.

"I love it," he added.

It was the first smile I'd cracked in weeks. Then, he leaned over to me and kissed behind my ear. That was the second.

Maybe Macklowe was wrong. Maybe there were ways of getting there.

Then Joe kissed the space beneath the edge of my new hairline, and down my neck and my shoulders and then down my right arm and my left.

"Joe," I said quietly, looking over to the crib. "Aviva."

"Shhh," he said, turning me around to face the bookshelves, away from her. I didn't move anymore. I didn't stand. I didn't do anything, but lay flat as he apologized all over my body for the first time since Aviva was born.

CHAPTER 19

I walked to campus, pushing the stroller, watching the world come alive around me. Students were walking around with their satchels hanging across their chests, their arms overflowing with books, smiles on their faces, completely ignorant of what could happen to them. There were also professors, mostly men, wearing full suits and carrying briefcases. Some women pushed carriages around in high heels and pointy sunglasses. I watched a couple of young girls laugh at something and then walk on, as if it were just another day. The air became thicker, more dense, and I struggled to let it in the more I watched the students stroll through campus.

When I arrived at his building, I pulled the stroller up three stories, step-by-step, making sure it was still and quiet so that Aviva would stay asleep, until I arrived at Macklowe's office.

"Come in, come in," Macklowe said. "It's good to see you, Olin." He held the door for me while I backed in, pulling Aviva's stroller with me. She was sleeping, her soft face silent, her lashes folded into each other, her fingers muzzled with socks.

"Look at you," he said, smiling full, almost proud. "You're a mother now."

"Yes," I said. "And thank you for the gift. Aviva loved it."

"Oh good, I'm glad," he said. "Alexandra loved her stuffed dog, too. Her mother said that she never went anywhere without it."

"Right," I said, returning his smile. He glanced at Aviva and then back at me.

"I'm eager to hear about what the committee said, Dean Macklowe," I began. "Will I be able to start in the fall? I'm more than ready to return."

He sat down and crossed his legs.

"I understand that," he said. "But it's a little more complicated than I had initially thought. Half of the committee thinks it unfair to the rest of the students to just let you simply take the exams later, make them up as if nothing happened. They've had students take their exams with burst appendices, broken legs, black eyes, nausea. Those problems haven't been excused in the past, they say, so why should yours now?"

I tried not to respond immediately. I tried not to be impetuous and use the wrong "decorum," et cetera, et cetera.

"Because this is none of those things," I said, surprising myself.

"Is that so?" he pondered, and I didn't rush to respond. "Be that as it may, that's still only part of the story. The committee worries that the student body will rise up against them, and that everyone who does poorly will demand a redo. Of course you can see the slippery slope here."

"But I didn't do poorly," I said, growing frustrated. "I was unable to take the exams because I was giving birth."

"A week earlier," he said, correcting me. "You weren't giving birth *at the time of the exams.*"

"No," I said. "You're right. It was just a few days earlier, but Aviva was premature. She and I were still in the hospital for observation and treatment when the exams took place."

"Again, be that as it may," he said, "you were also enrolled in law school. You had two responsibilities, and it was clear that you couldn't do both. There was a conflict."

I began rocking the carriage, pushing it back and forth with my hands, so as not to say anything I shouldn't, and hope that Aviva stayed sleeping.

"That said, in my experience, students who take leaves of absences, regardless of the reason, fail to return to school, or if they do, they often fail to return to their prior level of performance. But your work was good—*is* good," he said, clarifying. "You were by far the best research assistant I ever had. I don't want you to fail to return."

"I appreciate your support," I said. "So what are my options now?"

"You don't have many," he said. "The committee isn't inclined to let you waltz back in and register for next year, having left the last incomplete. There is a system here that ensures the best education, the best outcome for our students. Simply registering for your third year without the second being complete interferes with that."

"Dean Macklowe, not permitting me to reregister when I was expelled for unclear reasons could be construed as problematic," I said, my voice as calm as it was when I was putting Aviva to bed. "In a recent article authored by Justice Pindgarden himself, he even spoke about the importance of women in the law, and on the bench."

"Please, go ahead," he said. "Tell me how much of an advocate for women Justice Pindgarden is. I'm sure you know that much more than I do." His voice was slowly climbing, the edges of his mouth turning down in a twisted smile. He knew he was right about everything he did.

"You are violating my right to equal protection of the law by taking away my admission to this school," I said.

"I think we've pretty well established that there is no Equal Rights Amendment, regardless of its merit. We've had this conversation before, haven't we? There is no equal protection clause for women, or lawyers or students, for that matter." He took a breath. "The Equal Protection clause applies to Black men after slavery."

"Why can't it be applied here?" I said. "What have I done to have my protections removed?"

My voice was still calm, deep, controlled. I continued to chew the inside of my cheek.

"Just so we're clear, Olin, you are not *entitled* to this degree. Nor this education."

"I realize I'm not entitled to it, nor anything else. But I did earn admission, pay my tuition, and for no legitimate reason, I was stripped of that admission because—"

"I wouldn't say there was no legitimate reason," he said, looking to Aviva and raising his voice, nearly waking her.

She twitched in her slumber, and I prayed that she would stay silent. I wanted to pick her up and kiss her, embrace her, soothe her sleep, but I couldn't. Not then, not on so many occasions when I should have.

"Dean Macklowe, in class, in your home, in your office hours, you've preached about the changes we're making. Progress, you've called it. Well, isn't *this* part of it? Do you expect that the nine women you so gallantly and publicly welcomed into Harvard Law only remain provided we don't have children? Are *you* prepared to stop having children to pursue your career?"

Aviva was nearly awake. I picked her up and placed her against my shoulder, tapping her back, and she quickly succumbed to my soft touch, soothed.

"Do you want *her* to?" I asked, gesturing to the photograph of Alexandra on his desk. "It might not be clear now, Dean Macklowe, but having children can make me a better attorney, a stronger advocate for my clients."

He turned his head toward Alexandra's photo but said nothing.

"Your most frequent motivation in teaching us and in giving speeches and in conversation is that you are hopeful for your daughter. I want the same future for mine."

He looked at me for a second or two, thinking.

"Right," he said, rubbing his cheek in circles, as he turned his head to the stroller.

"*Aviva*," I said. "Her name is Aviva. She's three months old. I'm fairly certain she looks somewhat like your daughter, Alexandra, did at three months."

He looked around the room, his fingers tapping his lips, thinking.

"You want to pride yourself on admitting women at this school, Dean Macklowe," I said. "You started with nine my year and now you're down to seven. Surely that's not because we can't cut it. Perhaps the blame lies elsewhere."

He leaned forward. "I think you may want to calm down, Olin."

"My voice hasn't raised a decibel since I entered this office," I said. "We both know that."

He unlatched his hands from each other. Around the office were the obligatory stacks of books and diplomas and certificates, but this time also, there were campaign posters that I'd helped curate, commemorative only, for a campaign that failed almost as soon as it started. This time, he was standing on one side of his desk and I was on the other.

"Dean Macklowe?"

"Look," he said, almost changing the timbre of his voice. "I can go back to the committee and try to convince them to give you a second chance, but it's going to take some finessing," he continued, teasing the words. "While the committee has not permitted you to retake your final examinations, perhaps I can convince them to allow you to simply repeat those classes next year."

I pushed the stroller back and forth. Aviva's right fingers were breaking free from the sock covering them and making their way to her mouth.

"Actually, we can probably call this a third chance between you and me, but nobody's counting." He laughed. He was proud of himself.

Aviva's body was starting to squirm.

"But some of my classes are yearlong and others are only spring courses. I won't be able to take those for almost a year."

He crossed his hands together and slipped his fingers into one another.

"Yes," he said, his voice pacifying. "I really don't know if this will be workable, and it's just an idea, and really, it might not work. If that's the case, I'm very sorry. You'll be out of options here. But if the committee agrees, and you have to redo the full second year, then so be it. But you will be remarkably lucky if so. You'll still graduate, you'll just graduate a year later. That's not a terribly concerning issue, especially given your current situation."

He folded his arms and smiled. A warmth spread through his face.

"Just so we're clear, I can't promise anything, especially under the circumstances."

My stomach ached and I placed my hands on it to stop whatever was happening beneath the skin. I made a fist and squeezed tightly, just as I did when the rabbi finished the Mourner's *Kaddish* ten years earlier. I took one more chance. I waited at least three seconds to respond, promising myself to present as calm, civil, competent, to make him forget he had just urged me to calm down; to not have the wrong demeanor.

I heard my mother's voice for the first time in years. *If you want to do anything, then you need to stay quiet and play the game and then once you are in the game properly, you can do things the way you want.*

I needed to get back in the game.

"Look, Olin, if you're not okay with it—"

"No," I said, gathering my thoughts. I didn't know how I was even going to pay for an extra year of school. I'd get another job doing anything at all. I'd heard through the grapevine that there was a new system that allowed students to take out loans from the government to pay for school. Maybe I could apply. I just needed to get back in the classroom.

"And tuition for the extra year?" I asked.

"Of course you'd have to pay, but it's just one extra year, not three," he said as if it were spare change for him. "And you're married now, so you have a husband to help with that. Don't you?"

I nodded, scared to speak lest my nerves break through my voice. He probably couldn't smell the water spilling from beneath my arms, under my breasts and between them.

"Shall I go to the committee with this and try?" he asked.

He held out his hand to me and it hovered above his desk for a good ten seconds, until I took it.

"Yes," I said, shaking his hand. Then he placed that hand on my back and tapped three short times.

"I'm glad that's settled," he said.

After I closed the door behind me, I hurried home with Aviva. I wanted to shower, but what would I be washing off?

After all, he never really touched me.

CHAPTER 20

It was Mariana's voice I heard first, and then the door opening.

"Hello?" she said, walking in as confident as if she lived here. She dropped her bag on the kitchen table and came directly to me.

I was on the couch, looking over Joe's old study manuals for the bar exam, with Aviva on my shoulder, digging and twisting her face around near my armpit, and it was delicate and sweet. Mariana's face, though, was emotionless, as she reached out for Aviva.

"Thank you for coming back," I said.

I wiped a lacy fleck of saliva from Aviva's lips and kissed them. *I love you*, I said to her. My right hand climbed to her head and cradled it, gently massaging the soft, fuzzy hair. Then, I handed her off to Mariana.

"I can't be here forever," she said, patting the baby, "but I'll stay until you find a real babysitter."

"Thank you," I repeated. "Thank you."

"It—this, law school, everything—it can't all be for nothing," she said to me, strong. She held on to Aviva as tightly as she held on to me.

I made a face at her.

"Yes, it *is* a lot of pressure," she said, reminding me. "And it's good to have that pressure. Far worse than nobody counting on you at all. So stop complaining."

She shushed Aviva and held her to her heart, humming sweetly. From the minute Mariana started to sing, Aviva's smiling didn't let up. Mariana's long brown hair, brittle from root to tip and starting to turn gray, fell against Aviva's head. Her voice, loud and melodious, cut against Aviva's intermittent laughs, and I was reminded of my baby's namesake, the first Aviva, Mariana's other half.

Mariana's voice was the first thing I heard when I woke up the next morning as she sang an old Yiddish melody.

Zolst zayn lebn . . . zolst zayn lebn.

It was a deep ribbon alto, low as a man's. She was resting on the cot two feet from me, holding Aviva, making baby faces, singing to her in little Yiddish melodies I never heard growing up from my convert mother. "*Zolst Zayn Lebn.*" "You Should Live and Be Well." Her finger was tracing the circumference of Aviva's cheeks, delicately transferring the softness from skin to skin.

I rubbed my eyes and yawned, grateful to have her back in my room. She told me how happy she was that I'd named my daughter after her sister. She couldn't stop talking about how much she looked like her Aviva, as she squeezed Aviva's thighs, her cheeks, her arms. But I'd never met her sister. If she looked like Mariana's Aviva, then she would look like Mariana, too. I thought it was too early to tell who Aviva really looked like. Her one blue eye was clearly the same blue handed down to me from my mother—not my father, not from Mariana's side.

Perhaps it was the exhaustion, but Mariana now looked fiercely maternal and exquisitely aged, the way a book matures with time, becoming both more weathered and more valuable. And she was still exactly who I needed at that moment.

"Is it okay for me to go now?" I asked. "I don't want to be late to class."

Mariana's face was wet in reply. In twelve years, I'd never seen her cry. Not at my mother's funeral, not when I left for college, nor at my college graduation or after her many surgeries. Not even when she held Aviva for the first time.

Watching her hold my baby, I could picture Mariana holding her twin sister's hand, their hair shaved to their scalps, their young skin, thin as paper, hanging off their bones, nearing death, incomplete without the other.

"Go on, then," she said. "Though I don't know how you can stand to be away from this little one."

"That's not fair, Mariana."

"What do you want me to say, Sylvia?" she said, tired. "You're happy doing this, right? Going back right now so early? For what? For . . . the same classes? To do the same thing over again?"

I didn't want the laugh to come out as loud as it did. I didn't want to frighten Aviva with it, but I couldn't help myself.

"*Happy?*"

"Yes," she said. "Happy."

"*Happy?*" I teased, putting on her accent. "What's with this silly pursuit of happiness? It's just like candy. You want it. You don't *need* it."

She grinned, remembering. "I did say that, didn't I?"

"Not only did you say that, but you led me to believe that it was your mantra."

She rolled her eyes playfully. "Well, you can't believe everything you hear."

"But when you're twelve, you probably should, especially when it's coming from an adult you trust!" I said, frustrated.

"Twelve, thirteen," she mumbled. "You were practically thirteen, then. Anyway, it doesn't matter. What matters is that I'm here now. And I'm going to help."

I reached for Aviva, supporting her under her back. She was calm and happy and warm. Her head steadied against me and gently lay against my chest, our hands entwined.

"I'm sorry," I whispered to her, kissing her *kepi*. "I won't be gone long. I promise."

CHAPTER 21

My first day back in school felt like picking up where I'd left off. I didn't take notes, as I had already completed the classes, so I tried to audit new courses that I had missed the previous year. Sometimes in class, I stared at a photograph of a smiling Aviva that I kept in my purse. When I was called on, I stood and answered, and when I wasn't, I listened. A month into the semester, still deep in the machinery of school, Mariana had to go back home to Brooklyn. She'd gotten a great opportunity from an art gallery. Joe had begun his job already, and we took turns at home with Aviva for a few days each until we found a temporary babysitter.

Five weeks in, sitting in lecture, my belly rumbled. My organs seemed to shift in a way I'd only felt once before, and as soon as class ended, I ran down the hall to the nearest bathroom, the men's, where I vomited into the toilet. When I could breathe again, I looked up and saw Macklowe standing beside me. He was a bit blurry, but his face was falling into shape as he handed me his handkerchief.

"Thank you," I said.

"You're in the men's room," he said. It wasn't exactly a question, nor was it a reprimand.

"Are you okay?" he asked. His concern sounded genuine.

"I'm okay," I said. "I'm fine."

He handed me a wet paper towel, and reached down to help me up.

"You should go to a doctor," he said. "You don't look right."

I looked at my reflection in the mirror. I was tired. I hated being tired. This was what my mother had looked like close to the end. And then I retched again.

"Here," Macklowe said, handing me a clump of toilet paper to use as a towel.

I took it and wiped myself off.

"May I have a few moments to collect myself?"

"Of course," he said.

He didn't say another word after that. He washed his hands and walked out of the bathroom and back to his office.

I slumped over the sink. I didn't like what I had seen in the mirror. I wasn't my mother. I wasn't Mariana. And I wasn't myself. I splashed some water on my cheeks and when I looked up again, no one was there.

It's because you're a woman, I heard, even though he had already left.

Then, two male students walked into the bathroom and stopped near the door when they saw me.

"Ummm," one of them said, feigning confusion and shock. "Excuse me? This is the *men's* room."

I wiped my face dry and turned to them.

"Excuse you," I said, tossing the toilet paper and walking straight out of the building.

I caught a bus to the nearest ER and waited for three hours, missing my next class. When I was finally called back, the nurse instructed me to pee in a cup. Sitting in the stirrups, I felt my breasts and wondered if they were again growing. But they were still leaking milk.

I was still nursing. This wasn't possible. This wasn't supposed to happen.

"Mrs. Bernstein, you could have just made an appointment with your ob-gyn," the doctor said. "You didn't need to come to the ER in the middle of the day."

"I know," I said. "But I couldn't wait."

CHAPTER 22

The following week, I told Joe that I was going to visit Mariana for the day in New York, that she had an important doctor's appointment she wanted me to take her to. He stayed home with Aviva, and I took the first train of the day, at four thirty a.m. By the time I arrived in Brooklyn, it was already well into morning.

Linda was waiting for me outside the subway station in Prospect Park, wearing heels and burgundy lipstick and carrying a large bag over her shoulder. She had gotten into journalism school at Columbia, and she'd never looked so happy and confident. In my entire career, I don't think I ever felt that content. Not even at the end.

"Ready?" she said.

I took her arm and we walked together through the park, avoiding my father's deli. Mariana was usually painting in the back of the apartment then, so she wouldn't see us if we walked by at that hour, but I didn't want to take any chances. This was the only time that worked, and it had to work.

"It's this way," I said. "Come."

Dr. Tony Discanti's office looked exactly the same as it had over ten years earlier, only now a few more of the letters on the window were starting to fade. The *D* in D.O. had now nearly been wiped away from years of snow and sleet, and he hadn't bothered to fix it. Not then for only two letters and not now for eight.

Inside the office, the decor hadn't changed, either. Seven empty chairs were huddled around the perimeter and the same old art hung on the walls. A door opened beside the receptionist's window and Tony Discanti appeared.

"Come on back," he said.

It was just past ten in the morning. In two hours, the office would be open for afternoon patients. It was a Tuesday, one of the mornings that the office schedule, I remembered from when I was a child, was completely blacked out. I'd figured it out several years back, but never brought it up with him until a week earlier when I called.

Dr. Discanti had thinned down a bit since he and Mariana had gotten together, but his typical jubilance was missing, as was the new-patient paperwork. He barely looked me in the eye as he led me toward a small examination room in the back of his office, which may even have been the same one I'd sat in with Mariana years earlier.

"Thank you for this," I said.

"Take a seat," he said, bowing his head, his face neither angry nor encouraging. "How far along are you?" he asked, without emotion.

I looked to Linda as if she knew, and she nodded as if she had all the answers.

"I think around seven weeks," I said. "Maybe eight."

"All right," he said, gloving up.

He took my temperature. It was within normal range. Then he glanced at Linda from head to toe without response, not too dissimilar to the way he'd examined Mariana when he first spotted her on the subway.

"This is my friend Linda," I said to him.

"Nice to meet you," she said awkwardly.

He started to speak, but stopped himself, and then turned away from both of us.

"Does Mariana know you do this?" I asked.

He shook his head and turned his back to me as he prepared something in a corner. His hands were busy. The clock on the wall ticked loudly.

"So then neither of us will share," I said. "I don't want her to know. Okay?"

"I gathered that," he said, pausing. I could see he was thinking before speaking, deliberating his words before letting them loose. "But she'd be supportive."

"No," I said, quickly. "She wouldn't. I'm sure of it."

His brow twitched and he looked confused, like I had just told him she was cheating on him, which she very well may have been. He waited a few seconds too many, his face ashen. But then his color returned and he seemed to regain himself.

"Okay," he said finally, his voice calm. "If that's what you want, I won't."

"Thank you."

"Okay," he said. "Now Sylvia, I want you to lie down. You'll feel a little pain but it will be short-lived. Do you have any questions?"

I lay on my back while looking up at the ceiling, counting the holes in the acoustic tiles, and walked out one hour later with a handful of pills. That was it. Linda had stayed with me the entire time. We had a slice of pizza together after, and then she helped me back on the train, and I was headed home to my apartment in Boston.

On the train ride home, I only bled a little.

By the following morning, I was nursing Aviva as Joe prepared breakfast. I pulled open my shirt and Aviva latched onto me within seconds. No guiding, no questioning, no curiosity; just the animalistic need of a baby for milk. Maybe it was being away for the day, but I needed this time with her in bed. I loved giving Aviva something that no one else could. I loved the way she would sigh every third minute when enjoying herself, when she would reach around with her free arm and massage the open skin on my abandoned breast, when she would tap along the ribs above my chest like each bone was a piano key. I didn't realize it then, and it took me far too long to realize it through her adulthood, but these were the times I needed her, too.

As Dean Macklowe expected, it took me an extra year, but I repeated my spring courses and scored the top grades in the class. Eventually, I graduated and was ranked first in my class. I took out student loans in one of the first few years they existed, as all of my mother's money had been used for the previous years, and it took me five times as long to pay it back. My first job out of school was as a clerk for a judge on the First Circuit Court of Appeals. From there, I went on to the Federal Public Defender's Office, where I worked for fewer than three years before moving to New York.

By the time Aviva turned three, James Macklowe had spent two years as the District Attorney of Suffolk County, and when she turned six, he was appointed to the Federal Court of Appeals. I suspected Macklowe was unsatisfied there, but it was suspicion only. He penned opinion after opinion in favor of integration and in favor of working rights for women, so I was pleased he was on the bench, as were most of the women I knew. Pindgarden had taught him well. During my clerkship, I read many cases about wrongful termination, custody disputes, theft, rape, murder, squatting, legislative oversight, police misconduct, and more. The judge I worked for ruled from his seat in court as if he was entitled to the position. I knew then that if I ever graced the robe, I would never take it for granted, nor would I have my clerks do the research alone. I would be as involved with the research as I was in the oral argument as I was in the writing.

But you know that already if you're reading this.

What you don't know is that Aviva learned to walk at eighteen months, talk at about twenty, read at five years old, and cook at eight. By the time she was making grilled cheese, I'd begun working at the ACLU in Manhattan and occasionally teaching constitutional law at Fordham in the evenings. Joe was hired at a small firm that specialized in tax law. I loved nothing more than meeting him for lunch in Washington Square Park and surprising him with fresh fruit and vegetables from the farmers market, which he and Aviva could use to cook dinner. We lived together, worked together, slept together, tore our challah on Friday nights together, prayed together, and loved together. *Everything that happens to me happens to you*, we both said and we both believed. We spent a lot of time on Long Island with his family because he wanted it that way and I couldn't refuse. If he laughed, I laughed, and if he cried, I cried, no matter what was happening around us. Usually we spent the high holidays with his family and Passover with mine, and we invited Linda to our weekly *Shabbat* dinners, which he cooked specifically for her and for Aviva, who both loved his pasta far more than I did. Aviva played Sarah (not Adelaide) in *Guys and Dolls* in middle school and failed to make honor roll by .02 on her GPA. She never told me this. It was Joe who explained that she was scared to tell me about her GPA or honor roll or the fact that she wanted to drop some of her extracurricular activities—especially piano and yearbook. I didn't let her. I spent my days taking on cases that dealt with anti-Semitism and women being denied liberties as a result of their gender: there was a case about a professor who was refused tenure when she became a mother, a case about a dancer who was kicked out of teaching dance when she wore a leotard tight around her belly at eight months, and a case about reproductive rights just after *Roe* became law.

Aviva turned twelve the year *Roe v. Wade* was decided. I sat her down and explained to her what it meant. She didn't quite understand it, but I know she remembered the conversation. We didn't speak much about it after that, though Mariana did pull her aside to have a conversation that day, too. I wasn't sure what Mariana had said, though something told me she was undoing everything I'd just tried to say. Joe and I never spoke about *Roe* once. Not when it came out, not when cases trying to overturn it flooded the ACLU afterward, not even before. I didn't want to know how he felt. Assumption was safer for the longevity of our marriage.

I started a new program with the ACLU called the Seneca Falls Project, named after the Seneca Falls Convention of 1848, the birthplace, they say, of women's rights. We took on twenty cases in our first year alone, growing in four years to become the primary legal center for women's rights, regardless of where they fell on the spectrum. And Linda covered many of them in the papers.

Linda became a reporter first for *The Washington Post*, covering local politics and eventually national legal news, and then moved back to *The New York Times*, where she covered law and politics, primarily. She wrote features about the Voting Rights Act of 1965, the assassinations of Dr. King and Bobby Kennedy, the continued marches for justice; she wrote about cocaine on Wall Street; she wrote about the rotating Supreme Court, and the rising gender equity among law school graduates that, nevertheless, always seemed to stop somewhere around the age of thirty or thirty-five. Sometimes she picked up a feature and wrote about Mariana's art, and race and religion and romance and technology and marriage and health care, and even covered Macklowe's appointment to the Federal Court of Appeals. She slept with beautiful men and women over the years, bringing a few of them into my life, but mostly leaving them out. Her brothers ended up in college, but dropped out to start a clothing business. It was T-shirts, mainly. Linda's mother helped them get started, but stayed out of the business as she was too busy with her own political work. Linda wore the T-shirts from time to time. She was proud when she put one of them on to go out to dinner or a movie, setting a fashion statement that was several decades yet in the future. She didn't want to be held down to any neighborhood, let alone any person, and dated someone new every year or so. Pangs of envy sliced through me at times, as she traveled the country and the world, describing it in exquisite detail for all of her readers, first in the pages of the newspaper or a magazine, and eventually, years later, in a book.

From the inside out, my mother's voice returned to me, when Linda's name appeared on page ten, then page six, then page one of *The New York Times.*

From the outside in, I could see Linda saying with a smile, winking at me from the pages, as she eventually became the newspaper's most popular and respected columnist.

Once Linda moved back to New York, we saw each other weekly for lunch and dinner. She would come with me to Aviva's school recitals, and later I would meet the men and women she wanted me to meet. I nursed her when she had kidney stones. I never missed a single byline. Aviva loved it when Linda and Mariana stayed over at the same time, as if she were surrounded by a trio of mothers—each showering her with love, each mothering her in her own way.

Still, for Aviva, it was always Joe who made her world spin, and most of the time, she made his spin, too. Every once in a while, she would confide in me about her friends and her fears. I loved when she told me about her heart, even if she shared it with me on occasion only. I could feel those confidences, rare as they were, beat inside me for years.

Aviva sang songs and wrote plays that her friends came over to perform. Sometimes I saw them and sometimes Joe recorded them for me and played them late at night once she'd gone to sleep. She started fighting with me like every other preteen fights with her mother, and I was told it was only a phase. I had never gotten to that phase with my mother, so I didn't quite know how to broach it, instead deferring to Joe for everything. Occasionally, I was let in to visit Aviva's bubble, but I always felt like I was just visiting.

Meanwhile Joe worked his way into the depths of tax law and grew his small firm into a larger one, with offices in three additional cities. And Mariana continued to paint in the back of the apartment over the deli, canvases she rarely let me see. Eventually she took over the entire apartment, when my father left it to her in his will. He died a few years after we moved to New York, unexpectedly, after a short bout with pneumonia. He never found a new partner in life, never came out of his apartment to do much except work at the deli and go to synagogue for daily *minyan*, and I understood. When he married my mother, she redefined his life, and when she died, he never quite knew how to rebuild it without her. He was buried next to her in the Jewish cemetery. His headstone read, "MARTY OLIN, beloved father, husband, and grandfather," and was etched with Hebrew lettering. It was simple and never without a stone or two accompanying it.

I admit that we weren't close and I haven't had much to say about him. My biographers have pushed for more when the topic of my father comes up, but they back down easily when I push back. I think they are happy to believe a father's influence on a daughter is less profound than a mother's, though one need only look at Joe and Aviva to see that this simply isn't true.

But that first full day away from Aviva, the day I left Dr. Discanti's office in Brooklyn, something inside me changed. When I came home, I slipped in between the sheets with Joe and Aviva. Her lips were starting to turn upward into a natural smile, and she was still beautifully bald. When she saw me in bed beside her, she began to laugh, and so did I under a halo of moonlight. Joe's arms were around us both. He didn't ask about my day and I didn't ask about his. And when the phone rang, I didn't bother picking it up.

Zolst zayn leben . . . I sang, hearing Mariana's voice in mine.

In bed, Joe leaned over to kiss me. I kissed him back and then he answered the phone.

"It's Mariana," he said, holding the receiver out to me. "Says she needs to talk to you. Says its urgent."

But Aviva began to finger my hand, drawing little circles into my palm. She looked at me and opened her mouth in a slight grin. While I was gone, a single tooth had cut through on the bottom, and it looked like a bit of hair was growing in on her head, rounding out the peach fuzz. It was coming in so light it didn't look real. She was really starting to look like my mother.

"Tell her I'll call her back," I said, smiling at Aviva. "I can't talk now."

Part Three

NEW YORK CITY

1973

CHAPTER 1

My daughter once asked me if it's hard to admit my mistakes. Looking back, I'm sure I know which ones she's thinking about. But I don't think we can look to our mistakes without viewing the long-term outcomes. The truth is, sometimes we get things right at the end but go about them the wrong way. What's good at one time isn't *always* good. If you look into the mires of history, it always works that way. Progress and regression. A little bit forward and a little bit back in order to charge ahead, like a zipper caught on a thread. Eventually it may work again, but there will be a lot of damage in the process. Reconciling this is one of the most difficult things I've had to do, both on the bench and off.

I stared at the legal brief on my desk, fanning the file with my thumb, barely able to contain my excitement. *Alma Álvarez v. Finger Lakes Independent School District.*

I had spent four years at the ACLU, in large part launching and working on the Seneca Falls Project, and I'd been waiting for a case like this almost the entire time. By then, I had taken three cases to trial, and six more to the Courts of Appeals, but I had not yet been granted cert for a single case to the Supreme Court. I remember telling Joe ages ago that I wouldn't move on until I had brought a case all the way to the top. But there was something different about Alma Álvarez and her story, I could feel it.

It was the end of summer of 1973 in New York City. Joe had recently made partner at his law firm, albeit a small one, but one that carried with it enough gravitas and benefits to sustain my work at a nonprofit. We lived in a small rental apartment not far from the Flatiron Building, which we'd found four years earlier when we arrived from Boston. Aviva was entering seventh grade at the local public school and busy with chess and soccer and her friends. We were a three-headed Jewish mythological creature looking three separate ways at once.

The day we'd first moved into that Manhattan apartment I'd promised Joe that we'd give it a year and then move out to Long Island to be near his family, to a home with green wallpaper and a pink-tiled kitchen. But I think he knew from day one that we'd never move again. Four years later we still had the same routine we'd started with, walking to work, walking Aviva to school, and curating a caseload of civil rights cases that ran the gamut from free speech to landlord-tenant to hate crimes to cases like this one.

But now Alma Álvarez looked at me from my desk as if she knew me. Alma, a graduate of SUNY Binghamton, had been working as a high school math teacher at a public school when she got pregnant. The short version of the story doesn't take a tremendous amount of imagination. She was fired from her job when she got pregnant and her doctor put her on bed rest. She sued and lost. Then she appealed and lost again. Then she found us.

Pregnancy discrimination was everywhere and nobody cared.

There were no laws on the books in 1973 to protect pregnant women, so one by one, women had babies and left the workforce. Or they chose not to have children, like Linda. A few women seemed able to balance both career and children, but not in every field. I was trying to do this myself, but performing mediocrely. Aviva preferred Joe by a landslide, and I still hadn't helped women as much as I had promised Mariana and myself I would when I graduated law school ten years earlier. Or even three years earlier when I started the Seneca Falls Project. Sure, women were making waves on the pages of the newspapers, but it wouldn't matter if those loud waves didn't make their way into the courts or Congress. Though I knew I wasn't completely alone, I often felt it. My life revolved around home, the office, Linda's apartment in Manhattan, and Mariana's in Brooklyn.

My colleague Stan Diamond, the branch director, often helped with these cases. He was fifteen years my senior and proud of the ginger mustache that traveled down the sides of his lips, mixed in with Irish freckles. He had chosen to work at the ACLU for gay rights, namely on behalf of his sister, and had been at the organization since he graduated from law school before I even knew what civil liberties meant. He was a lifer.

I enjoyed Stan's company, but I didn't always want him helping on my cases. From time to time, he would leave briefs on my desk, asking if they were the right fit for the project. By this point we had many to choose from, as word had spread about our work. We couldn't take on all of the requests we received for representation, no matter how much we wanted to, but we took on the cases we could and applied for cert where we could, and were frequently turned down by the high court. But we continued on, believing the next case that crossed my desk would be our *Roe*. There was a new approach I'd wanted to argue, and Alma's case seemed to have the right set of facts to try. I was reading over her file for the third time that day when Stan burst into my office.

"Loving is in the building," he said, blushing with excitement. "Why didn't you tell me she was coming today? I would have worn my better suit."

I didn't want to lose my thought, so I scribbled down a few notes on my legal pad: *Title VII, passed in 1964, covers sex discrimination, but it's not enough here. Because it covers sex discrimination, it should prohibit discrimination in pregnancy as well, related to all matters surrounding childbirth both before and immediately thereafter, but it doesn't. At least not codified.*

"Tell me she's single this time," he said, his face dropping into an almost sweet, almost pitiful expression. Linda didn't always tell me about the people she dated, not since law school. Sometimes I could tell if she was really interested in someone, but those moments were fleeting. I did know, though, that she liked Stan as a friend and as a source. And that was it.

"She's not interested, Stan," I said. "And you're not her type."

He leaned against my desk.

"What? She doesn't like mustaches? Redheads? Lawyers?"

"Exactly," I said, smiling.

Stan shrugged everything away. Nothing got to him.

Linda was getting great assignments at the *Times.* And her pieces gained traction. But she still lost out on major bylines to someone by the name of Luke or Paul or Peter. *Does it have to be a bloody apostle?* she once said to me.

I glanced at my watch. It was three o'clock on a Tuesday.

"I've got to get Aviva," I said. I put down the papers, spilled a few drops of coffee on them, and stuffed the file in my briefcase to read later at home.

Linda appeared in the doorway of my office. "Syl, hi. Hello, Stan."

"Linda, hi, I'm sorry but I have to go. I can't be late for Aviva twice in one week."

The last time I picked her up, I was fifteen minutes late and she refused to speak with me for at least a day. The one before that, I was on time, but everyone else had been picked up early, so I was still late in her eyes. She'd barely spoken to me for the rest of the week.

"She'll understand," said Linda. "Want me to come with you?"

"No," I said. "But come for dinner tonight. Maybe she won't stay mad at me if you're there."

She picked up a few files on my desk and quickly ogled them.

"So, Loving, can I help you with something specific today?" said Stan, doing his best to charm her.

He blushed as the phone rang.

"Dammit," he said. "Be right back."

Linda eyed his back as he closed the door behind him. Stan and I shared a secretary, who was often off work, so we took turns taking calls for each other. Today was his turn.

"What are you really doing here?" I asked her. "You usually call first."

"I was in the area," she said, as she rubbed her cheek with her thumb.

"Okay," I said, waiting for more.

"I saw Ray Blayne," she said, very matter-of-fact.

"Ray-from-college Ray Blayne?"

"Uh-huh," she said, nervous. "He lives in Harlem now."

"Wow," I said slowly. "What does he want?"

"I don't know," she said. "He's married, though. To a white woman he met in dental school. They have four kids."

"I see," I said, thinking. "And again, what does—"

"We've been *seeing* each other, just as friends," she said, cutting me off before I could say anything else. "Please don't say anything. I just wanted to talk to you about it."

I twisted my wedding ring around my finger in circles.

"How long?" I asked.

She cleared her throat. "Not long."

"And just friends, really?" I said.

Behind Linda, though, I could see Stan writing something down on a piece of paper and hurrying toward me. Linda wasn't answering.

"Alma Álvarez is on the phone for you," he said, walking into my office and handing me a paper with a number scribbled on it.

"Now?" I said. "She's on the phone now?"

"Who's Alma Álvarez?" Linda asked, changing her tone.

I glanced at the file in my briefcase.

"A possible case," I said to her quickly, wanting to get back to Ray.

"A good one," Stan said.

Linda pulled out her notebook and a pen instantly, as if the past two minutes never happened.

"Not yet," I said to her, lifting a hand.

"Why not? Sounds like a story."

"I need to talk to her first. All I know right now is that she's a thirty-year-old former teacher and coach and was fired from her job because she got pregnant. The entire female student population at her school was also collateral damage because once they fired her, the school had no more phys ed for girls. They hired a male teacher to cover her, who incidentally, and, of course, won't coach the girls, and then the school decided not to hire her back. Said they'd filled the spot."

"With the new teacher?" said Stan.

"You got it," I said.

"Sounds like it has your name written all over it," said Linda. "I can do a profile on her."

"Yes, you can," added Stan.

"Please, wait," I said. "I haven't even spoken to her yet."

"So speak with her and then call me," said Linda, grinning at Stan. "With Syl working on this case, I can see the headline: *One of the Harvard Nine Fighting for Women's Rights.*"

"It's a specific form of sex discrimination against pregnant people," I said, correcting, "that, I think, is now illegal based on Title—"

"Shhh," she said, this time putting a hand out to me, stopping me. "My friend, even your initials make it a good story."

"But now, she's on line three," said Stan.

I shook my head as the red button on the phone blinked at me, and I waved them out of the room. "A little privacy, please?"

Stan left first, as Linda stalled.

"Can you wait? I want to finish our conversation," I called out to her. "Ray? You were telling me something."

"There's nothing to finish," she said with a nod, as if she had thought through her decision and realized she'd made a mistake. "Truly."

Alma and I spoke for nearly an hour. When I finally got off the phone, Linda was gone. I was also late in picking up Aviva. By the time I made it to school, she was sitting outside on a park bench, alone, flipping through a math textbook. She'd grown to be nearly my shoulder height by her twelfth birthday. Her hair was blond, like mine, but thick and curly like Joe's. Her vision was imperfect, not terrible. The doctor had prescribed glasses, which Aviva mostly refused to wear. But her poor vision wasn't the reason she didn't look up when I approached. She didn't want to see me.

"I'm so, so sorry, Veev," I said as I came near.

She was wearing a narrow belt around her waist. Her legs were longer than her torso. Her skin was clear but there was evidence of makeup that had been removed before my arrival. A few smudges of pink lipstick, and beige foundation had stained her collar. It was the fourth time this month alone. She wasn't even trying to hide it anymore.

The truth is that my colleagues at work felt easier to handle than the unknowable child at home. The people at work had been taught how to push, how to argue. Aviva just complained a lot. She wished aloud that I were Mariana, that I were Linda, that I were any one of her friends' mothers who were either baking cookies at home or burning their bras in the streets. Nothing in between. She didn't discriminate or see one path as better than the other. She just knew that she didn't love mine.

"Let's just go home," she said, leading the way.

I would have given anything for my mother to pick me up from school—even late. But on the six blocks home, my child and I didn't speak once. I had no idea what to say. And I suppose neither did she.

CHAPTER 2

A few days later, Aviva walked into my bedroom holding a copy of *The Village Voice*, squealing with excitement. Inside was a feature written about Mariana.

The article was small, hidden inside a listing of several gallery shows for the week. Nevertheless, it included a photo of Mariana, wearing overalls covered in paint, standing in front of a large canvas stretched from floor to ceiling. It reminded me a bit of the photo of Joe's mother in his dorm room in law school; black-and-white frame, the daguerreotype aesthetic, the model displaying her own work. Mariana's canvas was partially painted and I couldn't yet tell what it was supposed to be. Even in black and white, the colors appeared faded and her face was emotionless.

In recent years, Mariana's life had flourished—both personally and artistically. She was painting more and getting noticed. She had broken up with Dr. Discanti years earlier when she couldn't give him a child. (She always phrased it that way: *I couldn't give him a child*—not that she couldn't give herself one or that he couldn't give her one.) She got back together with him a few months later when he claimed it didn't matter, and then they promptly broke up again. Over the years, they were on and off so many times, it was unclear what they were to each other, except that they loved each other, pure and simple. I saw him on occasion. Once at a Passover Seder they cohosted when they were together; another time at the grocery store when he walked by me as if he didn't know me; once when Mariana brought him over to our apartment for Aviva's birthday party. Each time, their relationship was different, as if their union were one of indecision. But I think in reality, their frequent changes were the only consistency she had. And he knew that and loved her enough to play along.

Aviva pointed to the article, excited. "Obviously, we're going to her gallery opening, Mom."

I took the magazine from her hand and glanced at it again.

"Obviously," I said, smiling, proud.

When my father died, Mariana turned his bedroom into her art studio, stretching canvases across the room. She stopped painting only during that brief time when I needed her help with Aviva as a baby. When Aviva had questions about school, it was Joe she went to for help, and when she had questions about life, it was Mariana, not I, who comforted her. Mariana held her when she didn't get to play Laurie in her sixth grade's production of *Oklahoma!*; Mariana comforted her when she had a bad haircut. I was the one who took Aviva to the doctor and held her at night when she was a scared of the dark, and it was I who taught her to read and sing, and play piano. But eventually she stopped running toward me altogether. I don't know when it happened. Maybe it was six, maybe it was eight?

"Of course we are going," I said to her. "But you'll need to make sure you finish all your homework and Bat Mitzvah prep first. It will be on a school night."

She followed the newspaper in my hand, without replying. Her front teeth fell into her bottom lip, a nervous tic that was becoming permanent. Whenever she wanted to avoid something—a conversation, responsibility, work—she slit her mouth in two.

"Ah-vee-vah," I said, sighing, trying to pull her back in as if she were a kite.

She looked up from the newspaper. "What?"

"I want to make sure you heard me," I said, feeling my face flush.

"I heard you—"

"About finishing all your homework first."

"The show isn't tomorrow, Mom," she said, rolling her eyes and pointing to the specific date below the listing. "It's next week. I have plenty of time."

"Of course," I said, nodding, the sides of my mouth swinging upward without the rest of my face, until I remembered Alma Álvarez. "Wait . . . *next* Thursday?"

She nodded, looking at me, annoyed.

"I can't go."

Aviva stared, trying to hold herself in.

"I can go *this* Thursday, but not next Thursday. *Next* Thursday, I'm supposed to go up to Seneca Falls to meet with a client."

"Reschedule it," she said, matter-of-fact. "You're the lawyer. Isn't that part of the power? Choosing the meetings?"

I tried not to let her thinking—so different, so vastly uninformed—bother me.

"It's not about power, Aviva. And it's not that simple," I said. "She's a schoolteacher and has limited time to meet. I need to work around her schedule. She's rearranged things for us to meet. That is a day there is no school. And there are several important court deadlines coming up, so we can't push it off any—"

"It's Mariana's first art show, Mom," she said, focused and pure. "Dad's already cleared his schedule for it."

I waited and looked at my watch. It was after six.

"Where is Dad, anyway?"

"He's on one of his walks."

"Again?"

She shrugged.

"Look, Mom, I know you're not trying to get out of this—"

"Of course I'm not," I said, defensive. "There's nowhere else I would *want* to be, but of all people, Mariana will understand why I can't. For this, especially. She would have told us earlier about the date if she cared that much. Trust me, Mariana's the reason I need to put this first."

"You sure about that?" she said, bending down to pick up the newspaper. "You can tell yourself whatever you want, but I don't think Mariana would be okay with you missing her first—and maybe only— art show in her entire life. She's, like, fifty. When is this going to happen again?"

"She's forty-five, Aviva," I said. "And I don't know. But if it's happening now, I can only imagine it will happen again."

"That's cold, Mom," she said, and walked away from me as every other preteen girl has ever walked away from her mother at some point in time. "You could have a bit more feeling, don't you think? I mean, she practically raised you."

I sighed. "She didn't raise me, Aviva."

"Oh, right," she added, looking directly at me. "It's me she raised."

A strand of curls dropped into her eyes and she brushed it away. She was breathing heavily and wearing purple on her nails. I don't know why I hadn't noticed that before. She was nervous, that was all. Not rude. Just nervous around me. I scratched my eye, something I hadn't done in years.

"I'll be there, Aviva," I said. "You know I will. I'll make it work. It's not an issue."

"Good," she said.

But I couldn't look at her. If I did, I'd have to accept her anger and I didn't want to say something I'd regret, so I stared at the floor, the fuzzy orange carpet. The dark spot on the table, singed at the corner where a candle had fallen from a menorah. I stared at the *ketubah* from our wedding, hanging on the wall, framed. I stared at the emaciated line of light reaching out to me from under the door. Aviva spent hours behind that door, shut out from the world, or perhaps just shutting me out. When she was a young child and first spoke back to me, I was terrified that she'd hate me one day. But Joe didn't understand. *Why?* he would say. *Why is it that you think she'll hate you?*

Because that's what stories like this show—in the books, in the movies—and I never got to that point with my own mother. Would I have become closer with my mother had she lived through my teenage years? Or did I pull away from Aviva because I didn't know what to do?

"And while we're at it, I might as well tell you: I don't want to have a Bat Mitzvah," she breathed. "I'm . . . *not* going to have one."

She didn't falter, she didn't look away. Had she practiced telling me this? In front of a mirror? To a friend?

"I know it's a big deal to you," she added, "but it's just not a big deal to me."

Don't say anything yet, I thought to myself. Don't call her rude. Just let her talk.

"Okay?" she added, and it was clear she was waiting for my response. Would I ignore her or erupt? Would I give her fuel for her contempt?

"I'm confused," I said to her eventually.

I was most certainly not confused.

"Aviva, can you explain?"

She looked away. "I don't think there's anything to explain. I just don't want to have one."

"Have you stopped studying?" I asked. "Have you stopped practicing?"

She stalled, looking for the right words.

"No," she said. "Not completely."

"I don't understand what that means. 'Not completely.' Either you have or you haven't. Which is it?"

She looked away.

"If you care so much about all this stuff, why don't you have one?" she said.

"We both know I couldn't," I said. "Girls didn't have them back then. It was a different time," I said.

"Right," she said quietly, muttering under her breath. "A different time."

She looked toward the window. Outside, people were walking around. Outside, a different life was unfolding. Outside, her friends were joining their mothers in the streets, protesting, and she wouldn't even read a book for me.

"I can't force you to do anything," I said. "But I'm not entirely sure you see what is so important about this milestone. Try to help me understand your reticence."

"My *reticence*," she said, taking a loose strand of hair from her face and twirling it around her right forefinger. "Well, for starters, it's a boy thing. None of my friends are having them. And Dad said I didn't have to."

CHAPTER 3

Alma Álvarez lived twenty minutes east of Seneca Falls, New York, in a small community nestled in the Finger Lakes, a five-and-a-half-hour drive from the city. I drove upstate by myself, leaving at three that morning to make sure I got there by nine, and I would be able to get home by six that night to make Mariana's art show. I had rented a 1974 Oldsmobile Cutlass with no working air-conditioning for the day. The ACLU budget wasn't that large and I didn't want to waste money on, quite simply, air. By the time I arrived on Fall Street, I looked like I more easily might have run the 265 miles on the interstate. My cheeks were red and my clothing soaked in sweat. It was the first time I'd stepped foot in Seneca Falls. The town seemed to whisper to me as I entered, the trees rustling in an exaggerated show of fall colors.

Alma lived in a two-bedroom house on a dirt road with her husband, Edmond, and their fifteen-month-old son, Hector. The house looked even smaller than the two-bedroom apartment of my childhood. It was in foreclosure, with about thirty days remaining until they had to move out, and boxes were stacked on the porch. They had no place to go, so for the short term, the three were going to live at his parents' two-bedroom apartment nearby.

Alma and Edmond had met at SUNY Binghamton, a few short hours away, where they were both studying to become teachers. He was a walk-on on the baseball team, warming the bench for the entirety of his college career, save one mid-season game in which he scored a home run for the team, bringing them into the finals. They ultimately lost the season, but Edmond's pride in that one hit carried him all the way to graduation. He would never become a professional baseball player, not even close, but he was a favorite coach of high schoolers in his small New York hometown, with a population of less than ten thousand. Alma studied political science and education, and quickly got a job teaching tenth-grade science and coaching the girls in soccer and softball at the school her husband had attended as a child. It wasn't exactly what she wanted to do with her life, but she liked it enough. The school was near Edmond's parents, and they'd have help if and when they had a family. Six years out of school and Alma and Edmond had managed to make a nice life for themselves. They loved their new home and had hoped to stay indefinitely.

Soon after Alma became pregnant, though, she developed complications and was forced to be on bed rest for the duration of her pregnancy, unable to stand on her feet in the colorful classroom she redesigned in August each year. Instead of giving her a substitute teacher, the district fired her before baby Hector (named for Alma's paternal grandfather) was born. She and Ed worked through their savings as Alma held on to the hope that she'd eventually be rehired, and when she wasn't, they sued. She took on a side job in retail as they scraped together enough money to keep their house for a bit longer, but it didn't last. Shortly after Hector's first birthday, they were in foreclosure.

When I arrived, Alma and Edmond welcomed me into the house, showing me around the room where she would prepare for her classes each day and where Hector had taken his first steps. Alma wore wide dungarees with a striped shirt that hugged around the midline, pulled together by a thin gold belt. A green butterfly was pinned on the top right of her shirt. She wasn't particularly tall or short; a sort of average height and build that doesn't get you noticed at first. But the longer you looked at her, the prettier she became.

Edmond, too, had taken time to dress neatly, in a blue button-down shirt and belted khaki pants. His combed brown hair high-lighted a spare gray here and there. The longer I looked at him, he didn't change or become more familiar. He looked like so many other men in button-downs and khaki pants. He was wearing glasses with dark shades turned up at the top.

We walked to a nearby park with a sandbox where Hector could play while we talked. Edmond drew circles with his finger in the sand, little characters and letters to help Hector learn. When Hector ran back and forth to the sandbox, Edmond never stood, never got up to physi-cally follow his son around, instead observing only from a distance.

"The trial court basically laughed at me," said Alma.

She waited as if she expected me to respond, but I learned long ago not to interrupt clients even in silence because they always have more to say.

"That must have felt terrible," I said when the time was right. "I'm sorry."

She eyed Hector from a distance, poised, as Edmond dipped his attention in and out of the conversation.

"Edmond," I said, shifting the discussion, "you have short-term disability insurance at the school for when or if you become ill or get injured either on or off the job. Right?"

Edmond nodded without taking his eyes off of Hector. "Uh-huh."

"He does," said Alma. "He got a sub and was paid when he was out in rehab for his ankle."

"That's what I suspected," I said, as Alma again glanced back to Hector by the slides. "Alma, you also have this same short-term disability insurance at the school, as well, but it isn't being applied for you for your pregnancy."

"Right," she said.

"There is a growing body of case law that is trying to argue that pregnancy could and *should* be included in the list of conditions that are covered for short-term disability insurance, so that you can continue to get paid and retain your job while you are dealing with pregnancy or specific pregnancy-related complications. A few cases like this have stalled before they've gotten to the high court, but because you and your husband are both teachers at the same school, had this same insurance, and he was able to use it for his ankle and you were not for your pregnancy, I think there is a strong equal protection case here where we can set a precedent and make a big change for women everywhere."

I tried to keep my voice calm and steady—I wanted to convey my excitement but not scare her. Alma was listening with interest, but frowning ever so slightly.

"I plan to argue that pregnancy should be covered as a short-term disability for the sake of this insurance coverage. If it were, then I'll argue that it could have protected your job. The fact that it doesn't apply here means that the law is not being applied equally to you both. Quite simply, we can argue that you were being discriminated against for being a woman."

"When I broke my ankle, I took off for a few weeks for rehab and then couldn't coach the baseball team for two months," said Edmond. "They used my short-term disability insurance when I took off for the surgery and didn't dock my pay or fire me."

"But that's different from pregnancy," said Alma, confused. "*That's an injury.*" Lines deepened across her forehead.

"Is it?" I said. "Think about it as both—that it is and it isn't. It's not entirely different within the law, and from the perspective of the nine men who will be listening to the case, it may be a way for them to understand."

Hector waved to his parents from across the grass, and the lines in Alma's forehead vanished.

"Mrs. Bernstein," she said, coming back to me. "I worked for that school district for six years. I gave the kids everything. After my regular classes, I also coached the girls in soccer, softball, and sometimes even track and field. There is no other coach for the girls in the entire school now. What are they going to do? Just sit around? Walk from one class to another as their form of exercise?"

"I know," I said, reaching out to touch her arm. "I want you to have your job back. And I think that perhaps if we use this angle, it's a step toward helping cover your pregnancy and delivery. Using the same argument as, say, a sprained ankle," I said, nodding to Edmond. "This is something they can understand. Once they can grasp that concept, then, well," I said. "We can see about pushing it to the next stage."

Edmond reached down to his foot and flexed it, moving it in circles.

"Which is . . . ?" she asked, waiting for a response.

"Congress taking action," I said.

By this point, birds had only begun to fly around Washington with talk of the Pregnancy Discrimination Act, but nothing was happening. The world needed a catalyst like this case, like Alma, to get it passed.

"What do you want to do?" Edmond said to Alma. His voice was deep, but soft. "This is your fight. It's up to you."

Her lips pursed into a slight knot toward the center of her face, as she bit the inside of her cheek. I'd done that a million times to hold my tongue when I knew it wouldn't benefit the conversation. Then, she placed a hand on her husband's shoulder and lightly pressed. A signal, a sign between the two of them. He was supportive of Alma, provided she did all the work, her name was in the lawsuit, and her face would be attached to it. Not his.

This is your fight, he had said.

Of all the words in our two-hour-long conversation together, those four are probably the only ones she took home with her. She must have known then that she would be in it on her own.

"Mama!" we all heard, turning around to find Hector standing behind Alma with a mixture of tears and sand splattered across his cheeks. His eyes were brown and seemed almost too large for his face.

Alma pulled him into her lap and started tickling his stomach, pulling up his shirt to find her way to his belly button.

"You still have this?" she joked. "I thought it was going to go away when you turned one. Let me see about closing it up."

He laughed a low-pitch sort of roll as she bent over and pressed her lips to his belly button, kissing him with affection.

"Ms. Álvarez," I said, smiling, trying to get her attention again. It was nearly noon. If I was going to make Mariana's art show, I needed to leave soon.

"This is how it will work," I added. "I'll draft and file what's called a writ of certiorari, which is essentially an written appeal on your behalf, asking the the Supreme Court to take the case. Based on that, they can decide whether they'll hear the case or not."

She nodded along. She knew exactly how this was going to work. This wasn't her first intro to the law. In fact, this was her second appeal, her last chance. But it would hopefully be both of our first times at the Supreme Court. I'd have the ACLU behind me and Stan and the heft of the organization, but I'd also have the opposition and a century of case law that mentions practically nothing about this, pushing back at me.

"I'll argue two things," I said. "First, that the short-term disability insurance afforded to you and your husband was not applied equally to you both. And second, because of that, the disability insurance should extend to pregnancy, and that the school district should have used that here and not fired you during the time you needed it, both during the pregnancy and after to recover from it."

Her arms were wrapped around Hector, who was still sunny in her warmth.

"What would I have to do?" she asked.

"Nothing, really," I said. "The work is on me. It's on the Seneca Falls Project, which seems as though it was made for this case." I smiled, looking around to reassure her. "And on the ACLU. But you don't have to do much. Because this is an appeal, it's about the law, not purely the facts. There are no witnesses and evidence like in a trial. I will, of course, keep you updated on everything along the way, but I draft the appeal, I file it with the court, and then we wait. If we get a minimum of four justices to agree to hear the case, it will move forward. Then we have what's called an oral argument, where the nine justices will listen to me and opposing counsel for about an hour in person, asking questions about the case and the law. Then, they make a decision."

She nodded. "When would we find out?"

"It can take months or weeks; it's hard to tell. Depends on their schedule."

She licked her lips, and kissed Hector on the cheek.

"Can you give me a minute?" Alma said to Edmond, who picked up Hector, swinging him around to his back, wearing him like a pack.

"Let's go play on the slides," he said, and they went off.

Alma smiled at me nervously.

I didn't want to project my feelings onto the case for her, and I definitely didn't want to pigeonhole her or pluck her from obscurity and make her dance like Jane Roe. But the municipality of Seneca Falls was the perfect location for this case, at least for headlines, and Alma was the perfect plaintiff.

I cleared my throat and smiled back.

"I know this is the right move," she said. "That's why I reached out to you. I'm just nervous. That's all."

"Of course you are," I said. "It's natural. Lawsuits are one of the most stressful parts of life. Lawsuits, divorce, and death."

She laughed and a slight tear fell from her eye.

"You're not going through a divorce, are you?" I said, only sort of joking.

I'd used that line before and it usually worked.

"No!" she said, laughing again through her nervous tears.

"I can tell you're still hesitant," I said. "And I understand."

She looked away. She was silent, nervous, as her husband and son headed back toward us. I took one last chance.

"You know, my mother told me when I was twelve years old that we—women—were close to being the larger group in America. Well, now women *are* the majority, and yet we hold almost no power at all. In some small way, perhaps this is a slight chiseling away at that. And if successful, it's a legacy you can pass on to more than Hector. It's a legacy to pass on to an entire country."

CHAPTER 4

The painting was called *Umständlich*. "Circuitous." In it, a mother holds her baby daughter near her belly, leaning over her as if to protect her from some unknowable outside force. She is as unclothed as the child, who is rippled with fat rolls on her legs and thighs and arms. Their bare skin is dirty, their eyes closed, but gripping each other, they seem sincere and calm, while around them chaos takes shape—orange leaves and black clouds and footprints and fists and rust-colored drops of water. It wasn't on a large canvas—only ten by fifteen inches with the wooden frame, in a small art gallery in Brooklyn. The gallery card was in German, not English. Whereas her abstract floor-to-ceiling pieces were immediately eye-catching—black and whites splashed with every color of the rainbow, jarred with symbols of war and family—this piece, *Circuitous*, was different.

Artistic vision likely comes from more than the actual eye itself, I remembered.

Lessons learned in adolescence stay with you, often longer than they should.

Mariana was surrounded by men with long hair, and women wearing oversize glasses and tiny little braids hidden between long strands. A few wore leather, a few wore white. Mariana still dressed like a model from the forties. Her lips were baked with red, her eyes lined with thick black liner. When she saw me, she acknowledged my presence with a slight dip of her head.

We had become more distant in the past few years, speaking less frequently even though we were in the same city. She spent her time with her friends and Aviva, and she rarely asked about my work. I never quite knew why the change had occurred, but I didn't push.

"I'm glad you like this one," said Mariana, walking up behind me. She draped an arm over my shoulder and held on to me, almost as if I were holding her up.

"I do. Quite a lot. Is it about Aviva?" I asked. "*Your* Aviva?"

"It can be," she said, rubbing her right cheek with her thumb. "I wasn't thinking exclusively about her when I painted it."

"Who were you thinking about, then?" I said, almost nervous to ask.

She dropped her hand and readjusted her position, as if she were drawing attention to her painful leg.

"Can I get you a chair?" I asked.

"I'm fine," she said.

"Maybe you should—"

"I'm fine," she repeated. Her voice was only slightly elevated.

The points in her face deepened and softened and deepened again, inimitable contractions of pain coming and going in waves. She never gave in to them.

"Perhaps, maybe my Aviva," she said, finishing her earlier thought. "*Our* Aviva, too. My own mother. All the others."

I looked at the work on the walls. So many pieces that I couldn't understand, didn't understand, didn't want to understand.

There were fifteen paintings in total, and under each were already little red stickers, including one for *Circuitous*. I reached out to the painting. My fingers hovered near the baby in the image and I wanted to touch it.

"Who purchased this one?" I asked Mariana, pointing to it. She was standing directly beside it, almost protecting it like it was her child.

"I don't know," said Mariana. "I'll be able to find out later."

"I love it," I said, staring. "I can't quite figure out why." I bit my tongue. "I mean, it's speaking to me but I haven't figured out why yet. I feel like I'm reading it in translation."

She rubbed my back and then my exposed neck, where the short hair was starting to get a little shaggy.

"You will one day," she said.

"Congratulations." I turned to her, and then took in the run-down room filled with fluorescent lights and subtle coloring. "On all of this."

"It's no law degree, no exciting job, but——"

"But nothing," I said, swatting away the thought. "Oh," I said, remembering, reaching into my bag. I handed her a gift I'd wrapped in *The Village Voice*. "This is for you."

"You didn't need to," she said.

"All the same. Congratulations!"

She opened it, tearing right through the words with her name, to find a black leather notepad I'd picked up on Fall Street in Seneca Falls a few hours earlier.

"I saw it and it reminded me of the one you were always writing in when I was a kid."

She smiled halfway.

"Thank you, Sylvie." She placed her hands together and softly bowed her head. Then, she placed her hand on my back and led me back to the paintings.

"Look around," Mariana said. "Enjoy yourself. And thank you for being here."

Joe and I took our time in the gallery. Some of the paintings were beautiful, some ugly, some repulsive, I assumed intentionally so, some mesmerizing. Aviva walked around separate from Joe and me, standing in front of each piece with one hand on her chin and the other on her hip as if she were trying to take in art as an adult. Her legs were placed in various ballet positions. She looked adolescent, on the cusp of her Jewish adulthood, and childlike at the same time. What would she be like as she grew up? In her twenties, thirties, forties, or even fifties? Would she wear a suit like me? A smock like Mariana?

A moment later, she glanced at me and Joe and waved, and she was once again twelve, curious, looking for answers in all the places I wished I could provide.

Aviva took her time taking in the art like a critic, and after moving on from each painting, she walked up to Mariana to give her opinion. Mariana put her arm around Aviva as if she were her own daughter, and took her face in her hands, delicately. I felt their intimacy as a stab of envy.

Joe came up behind me. "You like the little one, don't you?" he said to me. "The *German* one."

I turned to him and smiled so that only he could see. Then he kissed me on my temple and wrapped his arm around my body like a blanket.

Mariana brought her hands together, showing public gratitude, which was ridiculous and not like her at all. After her small speech filled with a few thank-yous and I-appreciate-yous from afar, her friends began to disperse. She kissed them on their cheeks, smiled and said goodbye to many of them, while Joe and I waited in the corner like distant guests.

Mariana came over to us after the last person left, exhausted but joyful. Her red lipstick had faded, and strands of hair had fallen out of her bun to frame her face.

"Shall we?" she said to us, placing the notebook I gave her in her handbag. She opened her arm to lead us toward the door and picked up a cane as she followed us out.

"Since when?" I asked, looking at the cane, curious.

"Since always," she said.

"Not *always*," I said.

She smiled at Aviva, who joined us, taking her arm. "You know what I mean."

"Since a while," said Aviva, turtling her neck to make sure I knew that she knew. "You've been so busy with work, Mom, you haven't exactly been by in a while."

"A kind parting gift from Tony," Mariana added. "One of many."

"So you're off again?"

She grinned. "This month."

I hadn't been in the same room alone with Tony in more than ten years, save the occasional holiday dinner, which was so full of people, we never had to connect one-on-one. We hadn't really spoken to each other since that day in his clinic.

"He's seen every single one of these," said Mariana, placing her arm around me. "I painted half of them in his extra exam room at the office."

"Really?" I said.

She nodded, holding the look for an extra second like I was supposed to know something.

"Really," she said, as if it were a secret.

Aviva and Joe walked back to us.

"So the cane?" I said, motioning to it again as she settled it on the ground.

"It helps," she said, her mouth curling upward. "At least for now."

"You know, Congress is going to take up legislation to help protect the disabled," I said. "To help protect them in the workplace and schools."

"Them?" she said, her head lifted high, but shaking, contemplative.

"Disabled people," I said. "People with disabilities. Like—"

"What is this word," she said, without pause. "*Dis*-abled?"

"Disability is becoming a widespread term," I said. "It will be part of civil rights legislation. We are picking up a few cases at the ACLU that should work to provide aid for people who need extra support and—"

She laughed, cutting me off.

"It will," I said, insisting.

"By what? Separating us? By calling us something different, which is apparently a category you now put me in?"

"No, that's not what I mean, Mariana," I said. "It's just a legal term, a word that will be a vehicle of dialogue to hopefully get services and help for those who need it."

"A word?" she said, thinking. "Fine. Let's just say that the law separates people who are, what you say, dis-abled. Then when will the government help them? After the Blacks? After women? After the homosexuals? Or after Jews like us, who were, in fact, already turned away from America while being killed in Germany, like my family? Like *your* family? Who's holding the next number in the butcher's queue? It's certainly not me and this," she said, pointing her cane to her foot. "Whether we want it to or not, things come in an order. *Some* order. You should have spent more time in the deli. Each person pulls a little paper with a number out of this little plastic contraption. Whoever is next gets helped next. You can't slice five different meats at the same time. The machine can only be used once at a time."

Joe massaged my shoulders, but I shrugged his hands away. I didn't want to be touched. Twice that night I pushed him away. Twice. I think about that often.

"You know you could always buy five slicers," I said to her, quietly.

But nobody heard. And nobody had the money.

"How's it feeling now?" asked Aviva, turning to Mariana again.

"Now?" she said, lifting up her foot. "This is nothing. It's a little pain every day. It reminds me of where I came from. What I have now," she said, smiling. From at least ten feet away, I could see that her smile was dark, hollowed out at the back, where teeth were still missing. "Now, I have *you*."

Aviva took her hand and they held each other for what seemed like forever.

"I'm working on a case right now," I said. "It's not a disability case specifically, but rather about pregnancy discrimination."

Mariana looked to me and tilted her head, curious, confused.

"And?" she said, staring at me, laughing. "What exactly are you trying to prove? That the government doesn't want women to work? That's pretty clear to me, and I don't even have a law degree."

Aviva's brows connected at once. "Mom?"

"Veev, it's okay," I said. "The government likes women."

"No, it doesn't," said Mariana, pivoting. "Don't let your mother be a hypocrite. Say one thing but act another way. That's not her intent."

"Mariana, please don't speak about my intent with my daughter."

"I'm right here," said Aviva, looking back and forth between us. "I can actually hear you both."

"I have a new case and I think it has potential, that's all," I told Mariana. "I'm representing a woman who was fired from her job when she got pregnant and was put on bed rest. But now, we have a new line of cases that are suggesting that if we place pregnancy into the bucket of employment insurance benefits, then perhaps we can—"

"Speak to us like we're not your colleagues," Mariana demanded.

Aviva placed a hand on Mariana's shoulders. Mariana quickly shrugged her off, but I noticed it. It lasted no longer than a second, maybe two, but I saw it all—Aviva's attempts to play diplomat, to appease the both of us, as if she thought even then I was doing something wrong. And so I tried to clarify that it was the opposite.

"Mariana, I'm arguing that pregnancy should be included in the disability insurance that employers already provide for their employees, so that their income and jobs are protected while they have a child, while they are out, and especially if something happens during that time. There is no protection now for any women when they get pregnant, paid or otherwise. If we get this, then at least the women who already have this insurance benefit will have some protection. They won't lose their jobs, maybe not their income, their independence, their self-worth, their . . ."

The overhead lights turned on in the gallery, putting an end to the evening, and I lost my words in the process. In the bright room, Mariana looked different, older; not the 1940s model, but someone from a story I knew well. Her hair was nearly all gray at this point, though still wild and wavy. She looked almost exactly like Miss Havisham at the end of the story. Please don't turn into Miss Havisham, I thought. No matter what changed in the past ten years, no matter how much we see each other or don't, or how much I rely on you or don't, please do not leave me, Mariana. Please do not leave Aviva. I don't know how we got here, I don't know what I did to cause you to pull away, but I promise to make the time, to find the time, and get us back on course.

"It's a terrible argument," she said to me without much pause. She led me away from the bright lights, but there were too many stairs to get down to the street and I could see how much she struggled.

I waited a brief moment.

"Thank you for easing into that," I said. "Clearly you don't *like* it, but it's actually a very good *legal* argument. It's all based on Equal Protection of the Fourteenth Amendment. It's a way to get protection for pregnant women, a way to provide equity in economics, which is where it all begins. It's a *step*."

"A step," she said, laughing as she took a physical step away from me. She squeezed her cane and lifted her foot, calmly. "So you're telling me that now you want to conflate a lifelong disability, as you call it, with pregnancy?"

"No," I said, defensive. "I'm not talking about a *lifelong* disability. It's *short-term* disability. For when you have a temporary medical condition and can't work, like a broken ankle or an appendectomy. They are different insurance plans and medical conditions altogether."

"Uh-huh, right," she said, nodding.

"Mari, please don't misunderstand this. Or misconstrue what I'm saying here."

"I didn't realize I didn't understand you."

"No," I said. "I'm not saying you don't understand."

Aviva pulled at my hand and then dropped it, trying to get me to stop. I bit my tongue. I ran my hands through my hair. I licked my lips.

"Mariana, I'm not saying you're not understanding it. I'm just trying to tell you in a way that I hoped you might actually think was a good thing. They already have short-term disability insurance for both men and women, which is a great thing, a necessary thing, but it's not being applied *equally* between the sexes—that's the only issue here."

She nodded slowly. "A *good* thing?"

"I'm not creating this. This already exists."

"Which is what you're now trying to claim pregnancy is," she said. "I see, I understand."

Aviva turned to me, confused, and again her brows came so close together they were nearly one.

"Mariana," said Joe, finally tiptoeing his way into the conversation. "I don't think Sylvia is making a judgment call here. She's using the system to help women. To help mothers. To get them some protection during their time of pregnancy so that they don't get fired from their jobs anymore so that they have agency in their own lives. It's a legal tactic. That's all."

"Oh no, Joe, I understood her," she said, again tilting to me. "I *understand* her."

"It's a first step," I said.

She walked forward slowly.

"Okay. Let's say you win. Then what? What sort of message are you putting out there? That pregnancy in its entirety is a disability? What's next? Motherhood?"

Aviva looked to me and back to Mariana, and back to me.

"No, Sylvie, don't take that road," she said, tensing up, and then turning her attention to Aviva. "You won't like where it winds up."

CHAPTER 5

One evening, two months after I submitted the brief to the Supreme Court, I came home to Joe and Aviva playing chess at the kitchen table. The radio was on but they weren't listening; their laughter rose in waves from the table.

"Who's winning?" I asked, hiding a yawn behind my paper-cut-riddled hands.

"I am," Aviva said, looking up at me with a cocky grin. She was wearing gold hoop earrings that were way too mature for her, a birthday gift from Joe when we'd allowed her to pierce her ears. I hated the earrings and so of course she loved them.

Joe picked up his black knight and moved it near her white rook. Aviva made a fist and banged the table lightly, making Joe smirk. It was a sweet smirk, filled with love and pride, but a smirk nonetheless, and it seemed to be aimed at me. They continued their game in their tightly sealed bubble.

Aviva was three moves out from checkmate. I wasn't sure she or Joe knew it. I sat down at the table beside her and she instinctively moved a few inches away.

"You're almost there," I said, cheering her on.

She and Joe turned to me, annoyed, and then looked back to the board as if I had just ruined the game.

"I know what I'm doing, Mom," she said. "Don't give away my moves. I'm trying to win here."

And that's when I noticed the stack of Hebrew books sitting beneath the chess board, untouched, practically sealed, serving as a riser.

"Are those your Bat Mitzvah books?" I said, hesitant.

She ignored me.

"I said, are those your Bat Mitzvah books?" I repeated, this time louder. "Are you using them as foundation for the chessboard?"

"Stop, Mom," she said to me, hands up to my face. "You're distracting me. I'm close."

"Of course you're close. You just need to move your queen on the diagonal to h5 and then Dad is toast. But seriously, sweetheart, you shouldn't be using these books as a leveler for this game."

"Syl?" said Joe.

"What?"

"Mom, why did you do that?" she said, upset. "I could have figured that out on my own. Why did you have to interfere?"

I don't know whether it had something to do with her or with the chess match or the fact that I could almost see Joe's face moving before me without hearing a sound, but I wanted to scream. The way Aviva carried herself with such outward strength and indifference, she couldn't be more different from my own mother. Or me. How many years does it take to erase the former generation, diluting it until the memory of the first is wholly lost?

"You know what?" I said to Aviva. "You're lucky. It's 1974. Girls are having Bat Mitzvahs now. Girls are not such a rarity in law schools. Girls are doing everything. You still have to fight for it, but you aren't going to be the only person fighting. Don't you realize what that means?"

She stared at me, said nothing, and then looked back to her white rook.

"I don't want to fight, Mom," she said. "With anyone."

But one chess move later, she left, slamming the door to her room, leaving me alone with Joe.

"You could have taken my side in there, you know," I said to Joe.

His eyes narrowed, and he stopped himself a few times before finally speaking. "What's going on with you?" he said.

"You told Aviva she didn't need to have a Bat Mitzvah?" I said, walking into our bedroom, the words sort of dribbling out of my mouth.

"Hold on a minute," he said, following me, his voice pressured. "You've been MIA for weeks now, and suddenly you're upset about something I may or may not have said *weeks* ago?"

"Did you say it?"

He stared at me, looking almost scared.

"Joe," I demanded. "Did you say that to our daughter?"

"What part?"

"What part?" I mocked, staring at him. "That she didn't need to have one or that it was a boy thing?"

"I said that she has to make her own choices," he replied. "It's her choice whether to do this or not. For thousands of years, it *has* been for boys only. And yes, now girls are having Bat Mitzvahs, but if she doesn't want to have one, then it's *her* choice—not yours, not ours. And she doesn't *need* to have one; she's not *required* to. It's far better to have the option to choose, wouldn't you agree?" He sounded just like a damned lawyer. He was good at it. Better than he often let on.

"No, I would not agree. And don't give me that it's-arbitrary-like-everything-else-in-religion bullshit," I said. "It's a rite of passage. It means something."

"It means something to *you* or to her?"

"To everyone," I said. "Don't you want to make sure that she has more opportunities than me? What happened to you?"

"Syl." He reached out for me, traced my nose, my cheekbone, my jaw with his rough index finger. "There's a lot going on right now. I get it. It's overwhelming."

"Please don't patronize me."

"I'm not," he said, cradling my face with his hands. And I know he meant it. But I didn't want his bony hands on me, poking me, prodding me, trying to comfort me when he couldn't, so I pushed him off.

"Let me get you something to eat," he said.

I closed my eyes and pictured the head of the shower raining down on me, warm water, hot steam, solitude. I turned away from him and went into the bathroom. I sat on the toilet for a good five minutes, waiting for my sweat to dry, waiting for my anger to dissipate.

When I came out again, my face washed, my hair brushed, Joe was kneeling on one knee, starting to sing *Carmen*. Goddamn *Carmen* again, like I was three-year-old toddler Aviva.

"*Hi everybody, how are you today?*" he sang. "*I fought a bull. I fought a bull. Yes, she was the meanest bull in town. Syl-vee-ahh, how are you today?*"

I tried not to roll my eyes.

"You're right, Syl," he said, one half of his face falling down, the other smiling. "I'm sorry. We should have spoken first about the Bat Mitzvah thing. You're absolutely right about that. But I stand by what I said. It's her choice. *That* is the whole point, isn't it?"

It was a perfectly good apology. Genuine and authentic, as Joe always was. He placed his hands lightly on my arms, cold as they touched me, before lifting them off fingertip by fingertip, each removal transferring with it heat, confidence, trust, life. He leaned away, clutching his arms to his chest as if he were the one who was hurt. But maybe he was. That's the thing about relationships and pain and longevity and partnership. Spouses, partners, they sometimes take on your pain, your joy, your anger. And then sometimes they don't. In all those years of marriage, I'm almost certain that Joe did more of that for me than I did for him.

"Syl," he said again, standing. "I'm really, really sorry."

CHAPTER 6

"Think back to Boston," Linda said when I answered the phone. I was at the office and she at hers. There was a hint of energy and innocence behind her voice. "1960. What was the single most influential thing that happened to you that year?"

"Hello to you, too," I said, squeezing the phone between my ear and shoulder, wondering where she was going with this. "Getting married, getting pregnant, my internship—"

"The public defender's office—" she burst out.

"Where I worked for a day? That's what you think the single most—"

"Listen," she said. "Remember the name Amy McCartney?"

"How could I forget?"

"Well, apparently, she's been in prison for the last fourteen years and has just been released early. I'm doing a story on her."

I waited, returning to the image that had never faded in my mind. Amy's broken skin, tilted nose, the pictures of her bloody vagina embedded with shards of glass.

"I'd like a quote from you for it."

I sat forward and moved the phone to my other ear.

"From me?" I paused. "Why?"

"A judge in Boston reviewed her case on a writ of habeas corpus. Looked back at the record and claimed it was ineffective assistance of counsel. Also claimed that the evidence had been improperly evaluated. And that newly discovered scientific evidence is showing her injuries as severe and as a direct result of abuse from when she pushed him. So in other words—"

"Everything she did was in self-defense," I said.

"Exactly."

"Which, of course, we already knew."

Linda waited on the other end. I could hear her breathing. I thought about what I would have done differently back then. I thought about how I should have handled it as a twenty-three-year-old student, how I would have handled it now.

"Syl?" said Linda. "I'm on a deadline."

"I wasn't on the case but for ten minutes. Maybe even five. And it wasn't even for *this* case."

"All the same. You have the Seneca Falls Project now, so it may mean something coming from you for that reason. The personal connection is the icing on the cake."

I remembered the flash of my own booking lights. The metal bars. The black ink of my fingerprints.

"All right," I said, putting my thoughts together slowly. "Here's something: Amy McCartney is now out of prison after fourteen years behind bars for defending her body, her life, her freedom, and the lives of her young children. This is something that happened on American soil. This is something that happens all too often to women. And at the end of the day, who suffered the most? Yes, she killed her abusive husband out of self-defense. *That* is a valid defense. She did not intend for him to die, despite the fact that he intended for her to suffer and die over thousands of scrapes and bruises and cuts when counted over her body over the years of abuse she no doubt endured. But what about their children? They had three together, if I remember correctly. Those children—more than likely—were taken to a foster home and/or placed in a system that most certainly does not care about them. And they have no father left either. And when she was unfairly sentenced to life in prison, the government took away their mother, too. So who else suffers here? The children. The motherless children, the fatherless children. Had a woman been in charge of that court in 1960, I'm not convinced the outcome would have been the same, or in fact *should* have been the same."

I let out a breath and took a sip of water. My throat was sore, my face hot.

Linda was quiet, audibly scribbling her notes. Finally, she spoke. "Clearly you haven't given it much thought," she said.

"I haven't, actually," I said.

"Well, that's a good quote." She paused, waiting. "So, are we off the record now?"

"Sure," I said.

"That's bold," she said, and I could almost see her body smiling from afar. "And it makes you look radical, which is good. It works with this whole thing you've got going on with the project and all—"

"But I'm not radical," I said. "I'm not *a* radical."

"Okay," she laughed. "There's more than one way to be radical, Syl."

"Have you spoken with her?"

"Just for a brief minute. I'm hoping to get more out of her. It's going to be a feature for the magazine," she added. "Gloria Steinem is going to help get her a larger profile, too.

"I see," I said. "Gloria Steinem."

"*She* likes to march in the streets," said Linda, and I could almost see her smile. "Not quite like you."

I laughed, sort of. "No, not quite like me." Though maybe Aviva wished I was, I wanted to add.

Before we could finish the conversation, Stan walked into my office, holding a pile of mail. In his hand was a thin envelope from the United States Supreme Court. He handed it to me.

"Syl?" said Linda. "Hello?"

I clicked the top of the pen in my hand and the tip disappeared the way a blade closes inside a pocketknife. Was this it? Was this the answer?

"Are you there?" said Linda.

I stared at the paper in my hand.

"I have to call you back," I said to her, filled with hope and anxiety as the phone dangled from my fingers.

And then I opened the envelope.

CHAPTER 7

I came home late that night with the letter from the Supreme Court in my hands. Aviva was already asleep, and Joe was in bed, watching the news while also reading a book.

"Hey," he said, smiling at me as if it were any other day.

I didn't say anything in return. Instead, I showed him the envelope with the seal of the Supreme Court and my name addressed on the front.

He sat up, his eyes wide, his face melting into joy.

"And . . . ?"

"They granted cert," I said as quietly as I could.

He jumped out of bed, wrapping his arms around me and swinging me in circles like he had when we were younger, like he had with Aviva when she was a child.

"They granted cert?" he shouted. "You did it! You did it, Syl!"

He placed his lips on mine. They were warm and soft and thick and I loved them and wanted them to stay on me forever. He took a strand of my hair and delicately played with it between his thumb and forefinger.

"I haven't done anything yet," I said, but I couldn't hold back a smile.

While it was true that I hadn't won—I hadn't even had a chance to advocate in person—the Supreme Court had decided to hear me out, which on its own felt like a win.

"You will," he said. "Oh my god, I'm so proud of you, Syl," he said, kissing me again.

I could feel a bigger smile coming from within, but I didn't know what to do with it.

"Have you told Alma yet?" he asked.

"Not yet," I said, shaking my head. "I'll call her tomorrow. It was already late in the day when I got word."

He pulled me onto the bed, handcuffing my wrists with his hands. Then he kissed me on one side of my neck and then again on the other side, and it felt so good, I wanted to let everything else go.

"Shhh," I said. "Aviva's so close."

"Aviva's asleep," he said, as I wrapped my arms around him, feeling the weight of his body on top of mine. That feeling of comfort and safety and home. He kissed the space behind my ears and whispered, "Let's give her a sister or a brother."

On instinct, I pushed him away. "Excuse me?" I said, shocked.

He sat up. "What?"

His hair was messy, his eyes open wide, as though he was genuinely confused.

"I think we're pretty much done here." I stood up, buttoned my blouse.

"What the hell? Why are you walking away?" He pulled his pants up and followed me.

"I'm not walking away."

He laughed. "That's literally what you're doing. It's basic physics."

"You're not funny, Joe."

"Come on, Syl. There's a small window left here. Aviva's lonely. She needs a friend, a playmate."

I turned around.

"Giving her a playmate who will be young enough to technically be her daughter is not a playmate."

"Her *daughter*? Let's take a deep breath, okay?" he said. "Let's not get carried away."

"I'm not getting carried away. I just . . . I don't want to have another baby, Joe. Not now. How could you possibly think that me coming home with news of my first case before the Supreme Court—specifically a case for *pregnancy discrimination*—is code for knocking me up?"

He paused, thinking. "Well . . ."

"Well?" I demanded.

"I didn't think about it that way. But that's beside the point. You wanted to get to a place in your career before expanding. You're there. Even if it takes us months, years, we probably need to start pretty soon. It's not like you'd be pregnant by the time you have oral argument."

"Tell that to Macklowe!" I said, nearly shouting, and then I stopped myself.

"*Dean* Macklowe? Judge Macklowe?" said Joe, walking toward me, confused. "What the hell are you talking about?"

I avoided his gaze. The house was organized but filthy. Things were put away neatly, but a film of dust coated them. Trash cans were in their proper places, but full. Sheets were folded, but not evenly.

"Why on earth are you bringing up James Macklowe?"

I touched my clothing where my cesarean scar lay. I wanted to run my fingers along it. I always wanted to do that, to calm myself, but I couldn't get to it. Not that night.

"Never mind," I said.

"Seriously, Syl, why are you talking about Macklowe?" he said, still confused.

"Nothing, Joe," I said. "No reason."

"Fine. Don't tell me," he said, waving his hands in the air, his own white flag, as if he didn't want to push. "Let's just forget about all this and go to bed. Okay?"

"Fine." All I wanted was to lie down, to sleep, to forget this conversation.

But then I thought of my father, who was always "fine." And of Edmond, Alma Álvarez's husband, who had little to say beyond "fine." I thought of James Macklowe dismissing his wife and offering me a drink. *Times are changing. Don't make them harder weighed down with someone like Joe Bernstein.*

He couldn't have been any more wrong. Part of me had always wanted to tell him that.

Joe got into bed and untucked my side, holding the blanket open like an invitation. "Let's get some rest now," he said. "You have a lot ahead of you." I changed quickly and got in beside him, my back facing him. I was not ready to make up.

Then his fingers reached for me, finding my back to touch each vertebra as if feeling for a pearl, and it softened me.

"I'm sorry," he said. "I don't want to fight. Not tonight. Not about this." He let out a long breath that warmed the skin of my back.

I wanted to thank him, but I don't think I did. I don't think the words came out. He kissed the triangle behind my ears, where only an inch of hair covered. It was my favorite spot. It was the spot that would always work. Even through the years of arguments and agreements.

"I'm sorry, too," I said, but I didn't want anything more that night, even though his hand was still on my back, his fingertips softly tapping. I shivered away from his embrace.

"Okay," Joe said, sighing. He sounded sad.

If I could go back to any point in my life, it would be this specific instant, this moment in my life's history, to do something to change the sound of his voice. To try and take away some of the disappointment and remove it from my heart's muscle memory and skin it, scale it, scalp it like a butcher. But I can't. This is my second greatest regret in life.

He coughed a few times—I remember that it was four, specifically—and then sat up again.

"You okay?" I asked.

"Just thirsty. I'm really thirsty. I'm going to get some water," he said, defusing the tension. "You want some?"

"Sure," I said, nodding. "Thank you."

He kissed me on the cheek and disappeared into the kitchen. That was his MO. No matter the argument, no matter what happened, he would always rise and return to himself within minutes, as if the entire ordeal had never happened. It never helped to resolve long-term issues, but it always helped in the immediate moments. It was how we were able to maintain a strong marriage after all these years.

"Ice!" I called out, still annoyed and yet still charmed. "Can you add ice?"

"Sure," he called back after a brief pause.

I didn't even notice it as it happened. I didn't realize it until after the fact. But first, I heard the sound of glass breaking, and next, a heavy thump.

"Joe?" I called.

There was no response.

I didn't need to see to know that Joe was lying unconscious on the floor thirty feet away.

CHAPTER 8

I held Joe's hand as the paramedics took his vitals and placed him on the gurney. I didn't want to get in the way. I needed them to fix him, help him, save him. Right before they rolled him into the back of the ambulance, I squeezed his hand and I think he squeezed it back.

"We'll meet you at the hospital," I said to him. "Stay with us, sweetheart. Stay with us."

As his hand dangled off the side of the moving gurney, alone, I grabbed Aviva and together we hailed a taxi.

At the hospital, Joe was rushed into a trauma room and hooked up to monitors and machines. Doctors tried to stabilize him, revive him. But no sooner had they got a heart rhythm than new sounds took over and a code exploded in beeps. Doctors shouted commands and collectively descended upon him like ants to a crumb, prodding and poking. They mentioned something about seeing what they could do to save his heart. They mentioned something about damage from clogging. A nurse saw Aviva and me standing outside the trauma bay and closed the curtain, blocking our view.

I wasn't ready for it to be over. It wasn't close to being time. We were too young; he was too young. I started counting down—ten, nine, eight, seven—as if they would give me an answer when I got to one. But they never did. So I started over from higher up, squeezing Aviva's hands and counting down again with her until all we could do together was wait. And count. And wait.

It was then that I realized Aviva was the same age I had been when my mother died.

CHAPTER 9

We buried Joe in a Jewish cemetery in New York forty-eight hours later. Aviva was by my side the entire time.

When I replay his funeral in my head, decades later, a few images remain. The first is the identification of his body. Mourners, members of the *Chevra Kadisha*, who had guarded his body every minute of the previous forty-eight hours, said prayers to God for his transference, and to protect his spirit, whatever that meant. His spirit was long protected anyway: in me, in Aviva, in the grandkids he would never meet, in our bed and his clothes and his work and his food and his friendships. But walking into the small identification room next to the sanctuary, I stood above him, and though it seemed his spirit was beside me, there was only a body. Nothing more.

The second image that remains: a sea of black, as far as the eye could see. Linda told me that over two hundred people tried to come to pay their respects. The hall held only 150. Respect collided with curiosity, and confusion with sadness, in standing room only, as whispers spread through the room.

He was so young. What will Sylvia and Aviva do? Half his life still ahead of him . . .

The third image is of the dirt, soil raining from silver shovels into the casket-filled plot. Thousands and thousands of particles of soil dropping to the ground, covering Joe.

The rabbi recited the Mourner's *Kaddish*.

Yitgadal v'yitkadash sh'mei raba.

The minor key hung in the air, unleashing a dissonance of notes. I joined her, as did everyone in my presence. My voice cracked, but my lips didn't stop moving.

B'alma di-v'ra chirutei.

My limbs felt atrophied; my arms lay weak at my sides. Aviva stood to my left, holding on to my right elbow like a leash. Mariana held her, while Linda stood on my right. Dirt fell into the hole, each speck a memory being shoveled into the plot. We four—Aviva, Mariana, Linda, and I—a significant counting of the *minyan*, led by a rabbi whose melodic soprano was just as powerful as that of Maria Callas, even when reciting the prayer without song.

V'yamlich malchutei

b'chayeichon uvyomeichon uvchayei d'chol beit yisrael,

ba'agala uvizman kariv, v'im'ru:

Amen

Aviva stayed with me as Linda and Mariana walked to the car, our hands clenched together before Joe's plot. We waited, wanting, hoping the day would reverse, realizing it couldn't. The tombstone would arrive a year later for the unveiling, but for now, the grave was a blank sheet of darkness, a clean nameplate marking thousands of memories.

Aviva was ready to leave the cemetery as quickly as possible with Linda. Mariana and I stayed with the sea of tombstones a bit longer and made a final stop first on the other edge of the cemetery, the hidden lots, the smaller ones without fanfare. Mariana was limping more than I'd seen before, so I placed my arm around her as we dipped down and picked up a handful of stones hidden in the grass. My parents' headstones were simple, far simpler than Joe's would be. We cleaned off the nameplate with stray tissues from our handbags. The headstone was still fairly clean and untarnished.

"You know that when we first met," said Mariana, "when I first moved here, your mother hated me."

"She didn't *hate* you," I said, trying to smile. "She was afraid of losing me. She was afraid of a lot."

Mariana shook her head, no.

"She knew she was sick when I arrived."

I turned to her slowly, taking it in. "Maybe."

"She knew," said Mariana, with pure confidence. "You don't fear another woman's presence in your home unless you know you're about to be replaced. Instead, you should embrace it, knowing your child will be cared for, protected," she said, thinking. "She didn't know how to combine those feelings, so she mixed them up."

I read the headstone: *beloved daughter, wife, and mother.*

"You didn't replace her," I said.

Mariana held my gaze, tipping her head to the side, and bit her lip so hard, it bled. We both placed our stones beside my parents' names.

An hour later, I sat on the floor in my apartment on a large cushion, surrounded by people in black. My shirt was slashed over my heart as tradition dictates. All the mirrors were draped with sheets and blankets. Aviva sat beside me. She was also silent in her mourning, her face still in the same expression from the night at the hospital when he died, as if her heart had stopped alongside his. No matter what I did, I couldn't bring her back.

Mariana sat beside Aviva, rubbing her back in circles, while Linda took control of the crowd. The faces were so different from twenty-five years earlier when my own mother died. Stan was there, along with other colleagues from the ACLU, and old friends from law school and college and Long Island. I didn't remember seeing them at the funeral or at the grave site. Did they fill the plot with a shovel of dirt, too, or just watch, a mourning voyeur trying to convey support and sympathy from a distance? I saw colleagues from Joe's firm, a few distant family members, and friends of Linda's from the *Times*, until my gaze settled upon the familiar face of a young blond woman in her twenties. I didn't quite recognize her at first.

We gathered in a circle, taking turns telling stories about Joe, again as tradition dictates, circulating their own versions of his life that served a purpose—to memorialize, to remember, to think upon with fondness, to evoke sadness and joy and celebration of a life well lived, or at least half-lived.

Linda was the first to speak. She mentioned meeting Joe at the same time as she met me, saying that there was never any doubt in her mind that we would wind up together. *Bullshit* was all I wanted to say, but I appreciated her revision.

A heated spasm shot through my back and I could feel the anger coming. One by one, Joe's friends from his law firm chose to speak, sharing platitudes and anecdotes like confetti. I could have done without them. I could have done without most of it.

He loved to cook.

My ears shut to the memories.

He loved to eat.

My nose shut to the smells of his favorite foods because I didn't want the memory of his favorite foods. I wanted his cooked food on a plate. I wanted his penne alla vodka. I wanted his hand holding a wooden spoon to my lips, asking me to taste. I wanted his body hanging over mine, heavy, secure, warm.

When he swam, he pretended he was in the ocean.

He rarely swam. At least not with me. That was something he did with Aviva. And apparently his friends.

Fatherhood changed him. He became the person he was supposed to be when Aviva was born. He became the person we all wanted to be when Aviva was born.

That's what everyone said. That's what our friends said. That's what my colleagues said.

Then the young blond woman stood to speak.

"I remember as a kid how much Joe . . ." She stalled, correcting herself. "I mean, Mr. Bernstein, made me smile and laugh. He always brought these little daisies to our house when he came over for my father's research assistant dinners." She paused and looked around until she found us.

"Who's that?" whispered Aviva. And as soon as she asked, I knew. Alexandra Macklowe, now grown. She had followed Joe around years ago, the little girl with the bright yellow bow in her hair.

"I wanted to bring these to you to try and give you a touch of the brightness he brought to me when I was a child," said Alexandra, and then she pulled a handful of daisies from her handbag and walked over to me and Aviva. It looked like she had handpicked them. A white ribbon was tied around the stems. Our hands grazed each other between the petals, and then she stepped back.

"Thank you, Alexandra," I said, looking around. "Is your father here?"

She shook her head, and I can't remember if I was relieved or disappointed.

"He couldn't make it," Alexandra said. "But he wanted me to send his condolences."

I squeezed Aviva's hand again and handed her the daisies, and Alexandra took a seat again.

"My father used to pick me up out of my crib and sing to me," said Aviva, her voice breaking through.

The crowd shifted its eyes to her.

"He would pick me up and swing me around the room, making up song lyrics to old opera arias. It drove my mother crazy."

Everyone laughed.

"It did," I said, nodding for impact.

"But they stuck," she continued. "And even now—especially now—I can hear this stupid song lyric to the tune of that opera, *Carmen*, but with *my name* in it. Thanks, Dad." She smiled, glancing up as if an ethereal conductor had tossed a baton to her, and she began to sing. "*Hi Aviva Bernstein, how are you today?*"

At first there was piercing silence. Dozens of eyes on her, prickling her with discomfort. The silence of the crowd was pure and painful in this moment. Oh, how I hated being the center of attention. I'd thought she'd get that from me, but she was more like Joe in this respect. She seemed okay with it.

"*I fought a bull,*" she sang again, nervous, plaintive, seeking. She was not yet thirteen, but sat beside me with the poise of an adult, so different from me when my mother died. I could feel the eyes on her; I could feel their gaze, concentric and lasered, and I knew she needed me.

"*I fought a bull,*" I sang, joining her, following the next lyric in the song, passing the warmth from hand to hand, forming a unified voice. Aviva squeezed my hand and smiled and I saw Joe in her smile, and I squeezed back.

She looked to the rabbi.

"Would it be all right for us to put on some music?" she asked.

I glanced at the rabbi, who lifted her hands to me, as if to question the very point of the old rule.

"I think it's all right," said the rabbi, smiling.

I put my arm around Aviva. "I think Dad would approve," I said to her, and then I kissed her forehead.

I stood to dust off my turntable from 1960, the same one he bought me in law school. *Carmen* was sitting nearby, right where Joe left it. I inspected the record for scratches. There was already one on the first track, near the end of the overture.

The needle dragged to the record and static slipped into the room. Through the percussion and brass, the bass and strings, Joe's face came back to me as it was when I first saw it: smiling, young, in his early twenties. His nose was a bit crooked and his forehead slightly over-size, just it was when I first saw him up close, the aperture of my memory closing, opening, closing, opening . . .

It's 1960.

I'm studying in a library. I hear someone turn a page in a book, crisp and precise. I don't look over to see what it is. Neither does Joe. We are fixated on each other. He's telling me that he wants to marry someone smarter than himself, someone with whom he can sit and have a conversation at dinner. He's also telling me that he thinks I'm a liar. I'm angry with him. No, not angry. I'm playful with him, in that just-discovered flirtation. I don't realize the power of the flirt. I don't realize what it means until so much later.

He drops his head and says something more. I can't remember the words, or any words after that, but it's the look I remember. The action I recall, as crisp as if it were happening right now. He's leaning into me. His breath is sweet with a slight twinge of sourness, as if he forgot to brush his teeth. I don't mind, though. He was probably too busy talking to stop and give his mouth a wash. I place a bookmark on the page I'm reading and close the textbook. I look up. He's here. And my heart warms like the heat of a fireplace on a snowy day.

The aperture closes.

It's December again, 1974.

I was back in the apartment we'd shared with Aviva for four years, with Mariana beside her, and Linda on my other side. Joe was still dead.

That first night, Aviva stayed with me in my room, sleeping beside me in bed—in Joe's spot—and she held me. She held me as a mother, as a daughter, as a friend. Our hands clasped as they did when she was a baby, and we embraced each other as we had twelve years earlier, her tiny hands tapping around my neck, my shoulders. That was her realm, while my back was Joe's. Late at night, when we found ourselves exhausted, too tired for sex, too tired for conversation, we would strum our fingers across each other's backs, feeling each vertebra like piano keys.

Now Aviva placed her hands on the top of my back and gently moved her fingers down my spine, bone by bone. The last place Joe had touched me. My face began to flood, but I didn't wipe my eyes. The world needed to be a blur.

"Shhhh," she whispered in my ear. I heard her holding back tears while I let mine spill. "It's going to be okay," she said, holding me tighter. "It's going to be okay. It's all going to be okay," she said. "I've got you, Mom."

And in that brief moment, I believed her.

Aviva and I slept in the same bed every night for seven nights, with Mariana next door in Aviva's room. We woke up within thirty minutes of each other, ate breakfast together, and prepared for the *shiva* calls each evening in synchrony. For seven days, people stopped by, dropping food and drinks and well-wishes. A few of Aviva's friends came with their parents, who snooped around our apartment, and there was a consistent rotation of flowers and deli meats and deliveries of bagels and condolence cards. Several different rabbis came by and led *minyan* with the prayers each night. On most nights, we didn't struggle to make ten. On the seventh night—after the last people left, holding food out to me in Tupperware, grasping my wrist with that needless pull: yes, they care, yes, they are sorry, but now it's time for them to leave, there's school the next morning, work to be prepared, a meeting to take—I collapsed onto the sofa.

Linda was part of *shiva* for at least five of the seven nights. She brought Ray Blayne with her for one of them. Even though we had never met, we knew enough about each other that I appreciated the gesture. He didn't look like I'd expected him to. Usually Linda's men were fashionable, overly confident, tall. Ray looked a few years older. His hair had receded over halfway already in a clean hairline separating his head in half. He was wearing a black cardigan sweater over a navy blue button-down, and he wasn't wearing a wedding ring. It was the first I'd met him. I remember thinking his voice was slightly higher-pitched than I'd expected over the years of imagined meetings we might have one day. And that his eyes were a bit watery for paying respects to someone he'd never met. I remember wondering if he had met Joe and I'd just not known, and above all, I wished I'd met him under other circumstances.

Mariana stayed nearly every night, too. I didn't know how to tell her that I needed time on my own with Aviva. Time to plan, to grieve, to cry, to connect about what we were going to do next.

On the last night of *shiva*, Aviva lay next to me in my bed, still in Joe's spot, her hair spread evenly over his pillow. I hadn't washed the sheets yet. Her eyes were half-open and she was trying not to doze. She was facing the window, and I was facing the back of her head, trying to find my way into it. Her hand curled around mine and squeezed like an infant's.

"Ahhh-vee-vahh," I whispered. She turned over to me. I moved her hair from her eyes and traced the circumference of her face with my right forefinger. She grinned with her lips tightly shut.

"I like it when you do that," she said.

"I know," I said, smiling. "You did as a baby, too."

I could see her sweater rise and fall with her breath. She took in the room, much the same as I had for the past several days. How large it now seemed without Joe in it.

"Why didn't you guys have more kids?" she asked. "I mean, I get it, I think, but it would have been nice, I don't know, like, *now*. You know?"

I traced her face again and she flinched momentarily. It was ever so brief, something so slight I might have missed it with a blink, but it was there.

"We had our perfect family," I said. "Just the right size."

She breathed in and out and glanced away at the window again, as if maybe that was enough for her, as if she was trying to convince herself it was. I rubbed my elbows with my hands. They were sandpaper rough, old.

Her silence spilled into tears, and I saw she was crying, her body crumpled beside mine. I held her. *Shiva* was over. We'd have to move forward now as a twosome. I had no idea how to do that. I had never really been part of a twosome, even after my mother died. Mariana was there just in time to bring our two-headed unit to three.

"Are you going back to work tomorrow?" she asked, wiping her tears.

"Yes," I replied, nodding. "And you've got school."

"I don't want to," she said. "Not yet. Can we stay home for another *shiva?* Like, make it a double?"

I smiled. "It doesn't work that way, sweetheart."

"I know," she said. "But we can always make our own rules. Right?"

I felt my airway constricting, slowly, an inverse incineration of air, stopping me from speaking.

"I need you, Mom," I heard her say through her tears.

She'd never said that before, or if she had, I hadn't heard it. I ran my fingers through her long curls, and got stuck in them.

"I need you, too," I said, wrapping my arms around her for another minute.

"Can I take a walk outside?" she asked, releasing herself. "I want some air."

"It's freezing," I said. "Let's stay together right now. There's no-where else I want to be than this exact place. With you."

"It's just with all the people here for the week, I haven't been able to think clearly. I want to walk around the neighborhood by myself. Like Dad used to."

She raised her shoulders, her brows, her hands with such hope, such innocence, such pleading, I couldn't help myself.

"You're too young to be so insightful. And you're also too young to go out on your own."

"I'm nearly thirteen. Practically an adult, right?"

She forced a smile. It was beautiful, but empty. She argued well, though; just like Joe.

"Fine," I said, and then she walked away. "Just for a few minutes, though," I shouted after her.

Mariana walked past her on her way out and joined me in my bedroom.

"May I sit here?" she asked.

I nodded and she sat down in the spot Aviva had just abandoned. Joe's side, Joe's pillow, Joe's night table, Joe's stack of unread books. *One Hundred Years of Solitude. Carrie.* A biography of J. R. R. Tolkien.

I closed my eyes to remember how he looked in life, not in the hospital, not as a middle-aged man with early-onset coronary artery disease who forgot to exercise, but instead to hear his singing and feel his touch, which was at once peaceful and electrifying and wholly mine.

"This is going to be especially hard on her," Mariana said.

"I know," I said. "It's not going to be easy on me, either."

My eye started to itch in the corner in a way it hadn't in years. I needed Mariana to embrace me; I needed her to hug me and tell me it was all going to be okay.

"You know, Aviva just asked me about something she's never brought up before," I said.

"Oh?" Mariana was still sitting upright on the bed, while I was lying down.

"She asked why she doesn't have a sibling. Maybe wanting one, I don't know. I can't tell. I hope she doesn't think that we failed her by not giving her one."

I needed Mariana to embrace me, but she didn't even hug me after my own mother died. It was the *rebbetzin*. Mariana didn't know how.

"You know when Hitler tried to exterminate us, he failed," she said. "*You* had the ability to do more, and you chose against it."

Her face was swollen.

"I know Joe wanted more children," she continued. "You think it wasn't obvious? Every *Pesach*, every *Rosh Hashanah*, he would glance at the table, small as it was, and frown. You still had the chance to have more. You were young enough. You *are* young enough."

"Mariana," I whispered, pleading. My rib cage felt shoved.

"You never told Joe about the second baby," she said. "Did you?"

"What are you talking about?"

I stood up from the bed slowly and walked to the partially opened door, glancing down the hallway to make sure Aviva had left. I turned back to Mariana, my voice escalating into a pressured whisper.

"How did you know about that?"

Her eyes skipped around, refusing to focus.

"Mariana," I said, at once pleading and furious. "Answer me."

But she looked toward the door, as well, and then played with the arthritic knots on her knuckles.

"Tony told you," I said, thinking out loud. "Didn't he?"

"He didn't tell me anything," she said, like whiplash. "I figured it out on my own."

My nose twitched and my eye itched even more. My chest began to sting.

"Why are you bringing this up?" I said, finally finding some words, but keeping my voice down. "Why *now*?"

"It's just a question, Sylvia."

"I don't understand," I said. "I don't want to talk about something that happened over ten years ago. I don't want to talk about what happened a week ago. Right now, I just want to think about Joe."

"But this *is* about him," she insisted quietly. "You were pregnant with a second baby, a miracle, and then you got rid of it without ever even telling Joe about the pregnancy in the first place."

I closed my eyes and played with my ring, trying to picture Joe alive and healthy, but I couldn't see his face; I couldn't grasp his smile. And Mariana was pushing.

"You betrayed Joe," she continued. "You betrayed your family. You're going to need to come to terms with that if you want to have peace. With yourself and Aviva."

"Betrayed?" I said, pushing back, unable to hear my own words. Did I shout it? Whisper it? Even vocalize it at all? "I *just* buried my husband."

"A week ago," she said. "Joe died a week ago. *Shiva's* over now. Life must return."

My nose leaked and my eye wouldn't stop itching. I wanted to ignore her advice for the first time in my entire life and poke my filthy forefinger into my eye and scratch out the pain. But I didn't, because in that moment, that precise moment, I sensed Aviva's presence. My beautiful daughter, standing at the door in her puffy winter coat, hat smooshed over her wild hair, and one lone glove on her hands. She was wearing the large hoop earrings from Joe. And she was staring at me.

"Is that true, Mom?" she said.

I never heard her footsteps. The overpowering metronome of my own telltale heart blasted over them. I never heard my own child unearthing my memories as if they no longer belonged to me.

"Aviva . . ."

Her name was three syllables of bliss, of sweetness, of love. I could say it in my sleep, I could say it in my work, in my absence, in every day of my life.

"Tell me," she insisted. "Did you lie to Dad? To us?"

CHAPTER 11

"Aviva!" I banged on her door.

She didn't answer.

"Please open the door," I said, my voice loud and desperate.

The door opened on its own and I walked inside. Her room was uncharacteristically clean. Her bed made, her books stacked on her night table, her laundry piles hidden inside the hamper instead of spread across the carpet. It hit me how little I entered this room.

"Do you want to talk about what you heard?" I said nervously.

She paced in front of her bed, glancing at me sideways. "What exactly did I hear?"

"What do you think you—"

"Did you have an *abortion*?" she said, whispering the word.

At twelve, I hadn't even fully understood pregnancy. At twelve, I would never have known what it meant to have an abortion, let alone grasp the reasons why someone would get one in the first place. But when Aviva was twelve, I had already spoken to her about choice. *Roe v. Wade* had only just become law.

"Well," I said, "yes."

"When?"

"When you were a baby," I said. "But the factors that went into—"

"Factors? What factors?" she said, jumping on my words. "What does that even mean—factors?"

"It means . . ." I searched for the right words. "It means . . ."

"What does it mean, Mom?"

Breathe in and out, I thought to myself. She's grieving. We're both grieving. This is the time to stay levelheaded, calm, even in mourning.

"I knew your dad wanted more kids," I said, slowly easing into the conversation. "Yes. I knew that. But it's much more complicated than you think."

"How is it complicated? It's pretty obvious to me. You clearly had a child you never wanted in the first place. Why on earth would you have a second?"

"Aviva, that's not true," I said, trying not to raise my voice.

"Isn't it?" She looked at me with fury in her eyes.

I reached out to her, needing her, wanting to run my finger over her nose, through her hair, around her cheek.

"Sweetheart," I said softly.

"Don't *sweetheart* me, Mom."

She turned away.

"Aviva, please. I know you're hurting, but I'm not leaving," I said. "I'm here. I want us to talk about what you just heard."

She folded her hands together and tapped one fingernail against the cushion of the opposite, digging into the lines, making half circles in her flesh. Her breathing was pressured.

"Did you know that at least once a month, Dad would tuck me in and tell me how sorry he was for not giving me a sibling? And I apologized to him, as if I had anything to do with it. As if I wasn't enough."

"I didn't know that."

"Of course you didn't. Because you're not home. You're never home. You don't even know what he wanted. Or worse, you did know, and you didn't care."

"You don't know what you're talking about," I said, defensive. "It's not an either-or."

"You can't speak down to me when it's convenient for you and then like an equal when you want."

"I'm not speaking *down* to you—"

"Dad wanted more," she said, getting louder. "More of a life, more kids, more from you."

"With all due respect to your father, it wasn't about him," I shot back.

"He didn't get a say?" she yelled. "Does anyone get a say in your life or is it all about you?"

I stared at her, filled with a fury I never quite allowed myself. If I had, maybe my life would have turned out differently. Maybe I would have channeled my contempt into something else.

"You're not going to answer?" she said.

"I . . ." I stalled, trying to think clearly, trying not to be impetuous, emotional, as if those were bad things.

"Answer me, Mom," she demanded.

"I'm answering," I said. "I'm here. I'm listening. But I don't understand why you're so upset about something that happened over a decade ago that had nothing to do with you."

"Because it has everything to do with me. Because it had to do with Dad. With us. I'm not allowed to be hurt that Dad died? I can't be angry and shout?"

"Yes," I said. "You can."

"Then I'm angry," she said, starting to raise her voice.

"Be angry, then," I said.

"I am!"

"Me, too," I said, growing angry with her.

"Please, Mom, just get out of my room," she said. "I don't want you here."

"Aviva—"

"Please," she begged. "I can't look at you anymore. I can't look at you because every time I do, I see that the wrong parent died."

It was as if the world stopped in that moment. A bullet flung in my direction, and I stared at it head-on.

The wrong parent died.

It hit directly between the eyes.

"Stop," I said weakly. "Please stop."

"Just admit it," she said, growing louder and more powerful. "You wish you were Aunt Linda. You wish you never had kids!"

Her body was convulsing as she spoke, and her voice shattered.

"That's ridiculous," I said, straightening, defensive. I tried to change my tone, my voice, my contempt for everything coming out of this week.

"What's ridiculous? Having a child that you never wanted? Letting her feel second best to literally everything in your life?"

"Stop, Aviva," I said. Tears were boiling in my eyes and it hurt to look at her.

"I mean, look at your stupid case. The one thing you care about more than us. You're calling me a disability. You're calling me *your* disability. Motherhood is *your* problem. The thing holding you back."

"Aviva . . ." I said, broken.

"You wish I was never born," she sobbed. "You do."

"No."

"Say it, Mom. Stop lying!"

"I'm not lying, Veev."

"I don't know why you can't just be honest with me. Just say it.

Just be honest. Just be honest for once. You wish I was never born," she cried.

"Fine!" I said, yelling. "Yes, I do!"

There was a knock inside my body, a crumbling of the scaffolding, breaking our story in two parts. The look of knowledge before and the look of knowledge after.

She stood back, her eyes widening. We both knew that this would change things forever. It didn't matter that I didn't mean what I had said. I've had so many regrets in life, but this was worse than regret; something so wrong it could only exist outside the bounds of regret, eclipsing it like the moon eclipses the sun. You simply can't look at it because if you do, you will go blind.

Aviva glanced at the floor and then the window. A tree branch was tapping against the glass. I heard footsteps and I saw Mariana, who was suddenly in the doorway.

"Can I come and live with you now?" Aviva said to her. She didn't even wait a breath before continuing, as if she had been waiting to ask this for all her life. "I can't stay here anymore."

CHAPTER 12

Aviva stayed with Mariana in my childhood apartment, in my childhood bed, in a warped form of revisionist history. I slept alone in a bed I once shared with both Aviva and Joe, reciting the Mourner's *Kaddish* into the pillow for weeks. Though *shiva* had long ended, I called Aviva at Mariana's each night to recite the Hebrew words on her answering machine. One night, she answered but didn't say anything. I could hear her breath pushing into the phone, and that's all I needed to fall asleep. I didn't even realize the phone was still off the hook until I awakened to a dial tone hours later. Her words crept into my subconscious like ants crawling everywhere. I developed a feverish chill, hearing her silence and her cry and then her silence again, until the two merged into one.

In silence, though, you can't say anything you regret. In silence, you can rearrange language and rewrite history as if an audience of one is enough. Every once in a while, though, sound comes through, drenched with rancor, and you can hear nothing else.

The wrong parent died.

I heard it everywhere. Four little words, abandoned in the house like stray hairs, scattered. I'd find them on the floor in the bathroom, in the sheets of my bed, stuck to a sweater or shirt when walking to work. I heard the words when I got dressed and left the house to be-gin my new life without Joe. I heard it when I spoke on the phone with Alma, updating her with the good news about the case, that we were granted cert and given a date for oral argument. I heard it when I spoke with colleagues, with Stan. I heard it when I played with my wedding ring, still on my finger, slipping around loose, like a bracelet shifting up and down a skinny wrist. I heard it when I stood on the subway, holding on to the metal pole as it carried me all the way to the cemetery, where I hoped it would stop, where I wished I could jump in and give Aviva exactly what she wanted. Then, maybe, the silence would end.

The wrong parent died.

The truth is, if you hear it enough times, it becomes true.

On one of my first visits to the cemetery to visit Joe, I found a piece of paper hidden in the makeshift cement cracks in the stone, our personal Wailing Wall.

> *Dear Dad,*
>
> *I miss you. I wish you were here. I wish our roles were reversed. I wish so many things were reversed.*
>
> > *Love,*
> >
> > *Veev*

I ran my fingers over her handwriting. The penmanship was per-fect, always had been, even in grade school. I folded it and placed it in my pocket. I called her again when I got home later that day, but to no answer. She was in school or at a friend's house, no doubt. I didn't know. Mariana didn't tell me anything, no matter how hard I tried to get information.

Days passed and then weeks. Then one morning, I wiggled my

toes as if I were coming out of anesthesia and started to move one limb at a time. Another day, I got out of my bed and prepared for oral argument at the Supreme Court for Álvarez. I ended each day by taking the subway to Brooklyn and standing outside the front steps of the deli, looking up, hoping to catch a glimpse of Aviva. Sometimes the lights were on, sometimes not. On Friday nights for nearly two months, I waited outside the door and watched from the windows as the candles lit the room, as the prayers were no doubt spoken, as they ripped apart pieces of challah in their hands together.

Every other day, I went to her school and spied as she walked in and out of class. Once, she saw me. We locked eyes for three, maybe four seconds, until she turned away and walked inside, surrounded by her friends.

But it was in those moments when I saw her, even from afar, that I was momentarily happy. She had people there for her. More people than I'd had when my mother died, and so I left and went back to work.

Stan and I prepared our strategy for the case. It would be my first time stepping foot in the Marble Palace of the Supreme Court, arguing before it—but I'd be doing so without Joe. I focused on the paperwork that had piled up in my absence. I met Alma a few more times, reviewing all the ways the case could go. A majority opinion for us— they could agree with us and we'd win. A majority opinion against us—they could disagree with us and we'd lose. Or a concurring opinion—they could still agree with the outcome, but not for the reasons we put forth.

I would practice and argue and sculpt the clay my mother had described when I was Aviva's age. *You can make the world a different place if you want, but you must do it by learning the rules,* she had told me. *Learn how to work with clay and then sculpt it as you see fit.*

And when I practiced for oral argument with Stan, I imagined Mariana watching in the back of the courtroom twenty years earlier. I argued for Aviva and I cried out for Joe and I bled into my shoes for Linda and Mariana. And no matter where I was, Aviva's words haunted me as I prepared.

You're calling me a disability, I heard her say. *You're calling me* your *disability.*

I couldn't get it out of my head.

Motherhood is your problem. The thing holding you back.

No, I wanted to scream. It's not holding me back. It's society that isn't helping people, pregnant or disabled. It's not the injury or the medical condition or pregnancy or even motherhood that is a disability. It's society that is disabling people by not creating a level playing field. It was only in the shower that the words in my head paused, briefly. I welcomed the water droplets as they rained down on me, pressuring my back and drowning out the sound, gifting me with a new form of silence. I needed the warmth, the fog, the pressure, the reliability every morning cleansing and starting anew. The soap in my hands would spread around my waist, my neck, and across my belly, where my cesarean scar was still visible, a line of skin, still numb after nearly thirteen years. The doctors told me it would heal over time, that I wouldn't even notice it, but they were wrong. This is always the last part of my body that I wash.

CHAPTER 13

A week before oral argument, Stan and I drove down to the Supreme Court, a ritual he insisted on before every major appeal.

"You ready?" he asked. We were sitting in his orange VW, the windows rolled down, looking out at the white columns of the court.

I nodded. I was.

"I just realized that one of the judges on the Second Circuit who ruled against Alma was at Harvard when you were there," said Stan. "Judge James Macklowe. Did you have any classes with him in law school?"

I bit my lip. I hadn't spoken to Macklowe since before graduation, as he'd already left by then to move to New York. Obviously, I'd followed his path, but it wasn't reciprocal. At least I didn't think it was, until his daughter showed up at Joe's *shiva*, as if we were long-lost friends. Alexandra Macklowe may have cared about Joe in the past, but James Macklowe certainly didn't. And I was certain he didn't care about me, either.

"I did," I said. "As you know, Macklowe actually drafted the dissent in favor of Alma," I reminded him. "He disagreed with the majority of the appeals court, which voted against her before she found us."

Perhaps he'd changed his mind, but I remembered Macklowe's rebuke of equal protection for women in his office a few years before Title VII passed in 1964, as if it seemed like such a shocking consideration. I knew then that the same argument wouldn't work for nine men on the high court. Men, or at least those nine men, would need something with which they could sympathize to rule in our favor. And I hoped I had it here, as long as I got the narrative right.

Stan lit a cigarette. The crackle of fire against paper echoed in my ear.

"He was my teacher years ago," I added. "I don't know him anymore. Not personally."

"It's a small world," he said, blowing a ring of smoke out the window. "But it's only going to get smaller the higher you rise."

He ashed out the window and I thought that my world might not get smaller. Perhaps, instead, it would vanish entirely if I got this wrong.

"How are you really feeling about everything?" asked Stan.

"I'm fine," I said. "Really."

"Are you going to be able to do this? I would understand if you couldn't. It's only been two months."

I took the cigarette from him and inhaled slowly. "I have to win this case."

Smoke filled my lungs and I coughed hard.

"Don't ever smoke again," said Stan, grabbing the cigarette from my fingers. "You actually make it look—what's the opposite of cool?"

I laughed. "Shut up."

"Should I bring you to the hospital? Need an IV?"

"You know, Linda likes to be the only person who can properly tease me," I said, turning back to him. "She'll never sleep with you after this."

His cheeks flamed red. "No, don't say that. I have to hold on to hope, somehow."

I liked Stan. I didn't see how he could revel in unrequited love this long, but he was a good guy and deserved some happiness with someone, even though I knew it would never be Linda, no matter how much he seemed to court her from a distance. Linda never wanted to settle down, despite all the people who wanted to with her.

I thought of Ray, and of the future he and Linda had spread out across the ground like a tape measure when they were mere children. He was the only name that stayed consistent over the years. A week earlier, Linda had asked if I wanted to go out to dinner with them when I felt up to it. He'd gotten divorced and they'd reconnected mutually and amicably. She sounded happy, as if the previous fifteen years apart had been necessary.

"Is she with that cardigan guy?" asked Stan. "The doctor she brought to *shiva*?"

"He's an old friend of hers, a dentist," I said, smiling and placing a hand on his shoulder.

"I see," Stan said, sitting back, lost. Perhaps he was envisioning all the years they'd never spend together, or perhaps he was thinking of someone else. It didn't matter. I could think of only one thing.

"I'm thinking of changing part of the argument," I said. I didn't look at him when I said it. "I can't place the artificial label of 'temporary disability' on pregnancy, because it's not. It's something else entirely. Pregnancy is in its own category."

"Sylvia," he started to say, a confused expression on his face.

"There *was* a complete failure to protect Alma's job equally under the law," I continued, "but it has nothing to do with arbitrary insurance labels."

I could hear Mariana at the art gallery ask with confusion, *What is this word . . . dis-abled?*

"But you submitted the briefs on *this* argument," he said. "We practiced. We prepared. You can't change an entire argument at the eleventh hour just because you want to."

"Because I *want to*?" I mimicked.

"Sylvia, you aren't thinking clearly—"

"Don't speak to me that way, Stan. I *am* thinking," I said. "And not just as a lawyer for once. We can look at the law and it makes sense, but life exists outside of case law, and it's interpreted by people differently who don't follow the law the same way. That faulty interpretation will also matter in the long run."

"Not these nine people," he said in a monotone.

I cleared my throat. "You know Aviva moved out," I said.

I looked away from him. I didn't want to see his horror or pity or confusion. I didn't want to explain to him something that I couldn't understand or fix myself.

"I didn't know that," he said. "Before or after?" he asked nervously.

"Right after," I said. "Almost two months ago. Fifty-seven days, to be specific. She told me that she thinks she's my disability. That motherhood is my disability."

"I'm sorry, Syl," he said, and I could tell he meant it, "but you're arguing at the Supreme Court. I'd hardly say that—"

"What if she's right?" I said. "What if people begin to look at women as being unable to work six months after pregnancy, a year after pregnancy, three years after? And even if nobody buys that truth, the reality is that motherhood is an extension of pregnancy in many ways, so when will the distinction end?"

"Because it *is* pretty black-and-white. One is about pregnancy and one is about motherhood."

"And yet they're hardly severable," I said.

"Well," he said, thinking. "If this is a way to help women, let's not opine philosophically here or get bogged down by semantics. Let's return to the legal argument and what's before you for Alma. Thank goodness there is short-term disability insurance. It exists. It is a good thing—a great thing, in fact. It helps people when they need it. It covers you if you have a temporary medical condition that prevents you from doing your job as you normally would. Pregnancy can—and does—reasonably fit under this category."

I dropped my hand to my cesarean scar.

"How you frame an issue is how people will view it," I continued, lowering my voice. "The argument we prepared was framed purely for those nine men on the court."

"But this would be providing *some* protection, Sylvia. And right now, there is none. I get what you're saying, but this is about the law, not policy. You can't create a new category of laws through a single case. That's not our job—that's not the Supreme Court's job either, and they'll be the first to tell you that in public and on the record. Go run for office if you want to focus on policy."

"Policy is an extension of the law. Policy is represented by the law."

I thought back to my internship with Macklowe, when he asked me how I'd defend Amy McCartney. He'd seemed frustrated that I was focused on her narrative. But at the end of the day, the people who write the narrative control the laws, and we all know who has been writing them for the past two hundred years. But in order to rewrite them to include every person, we must dismantle the first draft and revise and rewrite. Just like I'm doing here.

Why else would I be writing this book now?

"Listen to me, Stan," I told him that day, overlooking the Supreme Court. "The women's movement has split many times before now. Did you know that in 1848 when Elizabeth Cady Stanton stood up in Seneca Falls, and said for the first time in history, 'We hold these truths to be self-evident, that all men *and women* are created equal,' she had pushback from both the men and women supporting her? That language was too radical, too much to ask at the time. Almost no one took her seriously."

Stan was listening, but I wasn't sure if he was hearing me.

"There is always going to be a question of whether we are asking for too much just to get the bare minimum because the system can't handle such a powerful overhaul. But we can't keep compromising. We can't keep contorting ourselves to fit the male narrative, to get the male version of what a woman needs. Because that's exactly what this is."

"Sylvia, the briefs have been submitted on this argument. The court granted cert on *this* narrow issue of first impression that *you* have championed all the way. Calling pregnancy a short-term disability for insurance purposes doesn't mean there's a problem with pregnancy. Or disability. Or conflating the two."

"That may be true, Stan, and I get it. I do, but it's the wrong category. It's like trying to fit a twin sheet onto a king-size bed. It may provide *some* protection, which is indeed better than no protection, but it doesn't fit correctly."

"Fine," he said. "For the sake of argument, let's say you're right, and you throw this case because of a technicality, all because of semantics?"

"The battlefields of law are filled with semantic minefields!" I said, raising my voice. "Language matters. Especially here."

His thumbs tapped against each other like they were dueling with themselves. I remember that feeling; I knew that feeling, when my body and mind fought with each other.

"All right, then," he said. "You've made up your mind."

"But that's the thing," I said. "I haven't. I know that no lawyer in her right mind changes her argument right before her oral argument. Believe me, I know that."

"You and I both know that blowing up this opportunity could have serious ramifications. And it will be Alma who suffers. It will be all women you want to help who you are gambling with."

"I know, Stan" I said, nodding. "There has to be another way."

CHAPTER 14

The sixteen Corinthian columns of the Supreme Court stared down at me as I approached the building. At the top in front and in the back were allegorical sculptures of mythological creatures, intellectual idols, and biblical icons that seemed to eye each approaching person with judgment. I tried not to be awed by the majesty of the court from every angle. After all, people built it, not gods. People also wrote the rules on its walls. But its power overwhelmed me nonetheless, as if it were Mount Olympus, still alive and functioning before us.

"Let's do this," Stan said beside me, and we walked in.

Once inside, we made our way through security. We were second on the docket that day, behind a rather large case about South Dakota land rights for Native Americans. Compared with so many other cases that were swimming through the channels in 1974 and 1975, ours wasn't a particularly loud one. Nobody much cared about Alma Álvarez or pregnancy, but that's because they didn't understand what the case really meant. Linda covered *Álvarez* along with a small school of other reporters, but she was one of the few who understood its significance.

Inside, I greeted the other attorneys and opposing counsel, and soon, the court crier opened his mouth and spoke.

"Oyez, oyez, oyez."

The first time I heard those words was in a criminal court in Middlesex County, Massachusetts. Here, they sounded the same, only with a louder echo chamber. Justice is justice, regardless of where it's doled out.

We all stood as the justices slowly walked into the courtroom from behind the red curtain, not in single file, but three by three and all at once, as if they materialized on the spot. There was no grand fanfare, no pomp. One moment they were absent, and then suddenly they were seated before us, high on their pedestals. A sea of black robes, topped with gray and white, with a captive audience before them. It was largely empty in the gallery—a few reporters and spouses and clerks, a handful of tourists. I looked behind me and spotted Linda. In the row in front of her, I saw someone whose face resembled Aviva's, and for a split second before I knew I was wrong, I was happy. I realized then that I want and need that pursuit of happiness, no matter what.

"Counsel for petitioner Álvarez," said the chief justice, calling our case.

I stood and walked to the small podium between the two tables.

"Yes, Your Honors," I said, clearing my throat. My heart beat and I felt its syncopated rhythm in my temples. The metronome. The beat, the *buh-bum* of life continuing on even while I was here and Joe was not.

I had brought two sets of notes with me, and I glanced at them quickly before my time began—would I continue with my oral argument as planned or not?

Each side was given thirty minutes to speak, and if you were lucky, you made it to minute three without interruption and questioning. My hands shook at the podium as they held my notes. The red light came on, signaling my allotted time, and I felt the nine men staring at me, waiting for me to begin. I saw the dirt rain into the plot of land where Joe rested. And when I looked up from my notes, I knew what I had to do.

CHAPTER 15

Several weeks after oral argument, as I awaited the outcome, Mariana stood at my apartment door, carrying a suitcase. I was sitting at my dinner table, surrounded by newspapers and briefs, including Linda's *New York Times* article about the case, with Alma and Hector's photo printed at the bottom of the politics section, when the doorbell rang.

"Mariana," I said. Her name spilled out from me when I opened the door. I wanted to both embrace her and slam the door in her face.

"Sylvie," she said, her voice hoarse.

She hadn't seemed this nervous about approaching me since that first day she walked into my life, when I was twelve.

"How did the case go?" she asked.

"I'm not sure," I said, and it was the truth.

"I am sure you were wonderful, Sylvie. You always argue the right words, get them to see your side. You'll win."

"Are you alone?" I asked, thinking only of Aviva.

She nodded. "Aviva's in school right now, and then she has Hebrew school after."

I put my hand on the chair to steady myself. "Hebrew school?"

"Nothing's changed," she said.

"What do you mean 'nothing's changed'? Everything's changed. She left her home. She left *me*."

"Get over yourself, Sylvie," she said. "Nobody ever said it would be easy."

"I can't do this today, Mariana."

"Today?" she said, at once annoyed and calm. "I'm not under the impression you have a lot of options here."

I couldn't look at her. I didn't want to look at her.

"Why are you here now?" I asked.

She placed the suitcase on the floor.

"To get more clothing for Aviva. It's getting warmer."

"You know, Mariana, I go by the apartment every day after work. I stop by the school every day on my way into the office. I know she sees me there. I could bring her new clothes myself."

"But you don't come in," she said quickly.

"She doesn't *want* me to come in. She's made that abundantly clear."

"She'll be thirteen soon. She'll change."

"Please don't talk to me about my child as if I don't know her."

"But you don't, Sylvie," she said. Her voice didn't crack. She said those words as easily as she said everything else to me. "You think you do. You may want to. But you don't."

I glanced at the floor, at her shoes, at her cane.

"You should know that Aviva is doing really well in school. She's joined the speech and debate team. And an art class. And she's studying hard for her Bat Mitzvah."

No doubt Mariana could see the reactions in my face from her update. An upward turn in my lips so small, it could hardly be detected by the human eye. An extra blinking of my eyes. The tightness of the skin around my cheeks when they started to move.

"She's going through with it?" I asked, plaintive, nervous. My voice climbed as if it wasn't sure. "Really?"

"Not for you, Sylvie. Don't think it's for you. It's for her."

My throat swelled and it became hard to breathe. Mariana noticed, but she didn't say anything.

"The rabbi never told me," I said. "She didn't reach out."

"Aviva also doesn't know I'm here," Mariana said. "She doesn't want you at the Bat Mitzvah, but I thought you should know. I wanted you to know. So if you do come—"

"If?" I cried.

"*When* you come," she continued, "please don't sit in the front. Don't make yourself too obvious."

"You've got to be kidding me," I said.

"I'm not."

"It's my daughter's Bat Mitzvah, Mariana. She just lost her father. She can't have no parents there."

Mariana glared at me without moving a muscle in her face. Not a blink of the eye, not a twitch in her lips, not a snuff of the nose. Nothing. Her silence scalded me.

"Please don't tell her I told you about it," she said, softening.

"I'm her mother. Did she think I wouldn't know? That I wouldn't be there?"

"You didn't know before right now," said Mariana. "But I wanted you to know. You deserve to know."

And with that, she nodded as if any tension between us was over. A slight severance of the past and moving on to the future in a single word.

"Okay?" she said, with an upward lilt. "Now, that's that."

Her face glowed with pride and she stopped moving, stopped rushing, and sat.

"It may not seem so now, but Aviva *will* understand once she realizes what you've accomplished. You just argued a case *at the* Supreme Court. Perhaps one day you'll even be on the court—think of it, a Jewish woman, just like my parents back in Warsaw. How's that for a first?"

"Stop," I said, brushing her off, refusing to allow the prospect to enter my consciousness. Besides, it's hard to dream about something you've never seen.

"You never know."

"Well," I said. "Right now, all I can hear is people saying that I argued this case wrong, as if I'm messing up everything out there, when I know the truth. I'm really messing up *in here*—at home."

"*Sha*, now you stop, Sylvie," she said. "It's just noise. You can work through noise no matter where it comes from."

"But what if the noise is what people hear most of all?" I said.

"Then change the sound. Become the noise," she said, and for a split second, I thought it was Joe speaking to me, reaching around to run his hands down my back. "You've never really cared what people said about you."

"I *don't* care what they say," I said to her. "I do care what Aviva says. And *you*."

And with that single word, she smiled as if I had just given her the biggest compliment of our lives.

"Come," she said, putting an arm around me, awkwardly, like it was something she was used to doing but simply hadn't in a long time. The truth is, she'd only hugged me once before. It wasn't how she mothered. It wasn't how she loved. She ran her fingers through my hair and it felt calming, comforting. She was raking through the years, sorting out my past with her touch.

"It's a lot of pressure, isn't it?" she said. "Being the first *anything*."

My arms draped her in that instant, full-bodied and heavy, the embrace I needed since Joe died, the embrace I needed when my mother died. I know she tried; she just didn't know how. She placed her hands on my back and lightly tapped as if she still didn't know what to do, but that time, at least she tried, and she hugged me back.

"Keep reaching out to Aviva," Mariana whispered in my ear. "Don't give up. For God's sake, isn't that half the battle? Knowing the inevitable rejection, knowing the failure and the love, knowing the battle and the triumph, but engaging anyway? That's what makes you a parent."

CHAPTER 16

Three months later, the Supreme Court made a decision on Alma's case. I stood on the steps of the court with reporters and other attorneys as one of the associate justices read out the announcement. A majority opinion held in a close 5–4 decision against Alma.

News cameras were on outside the courthouse with reporters, Linda among them, waiting for the opinion to run. Also on the steps of the court that day was a twenty-three-year-old Alexandra Macklowe, bra-less, with flowers in her hair—daisies—holding a megaphone. The morning light kissed her face, and it was clear that she was as beautiful as her mother and as commanding and brutal as her father, who was still sitting on the Second Circuit. I noticed her in passing before I walked to the side entrance of the court, which was reserved for attorneys and media. Once inside, I sat in the gallery and listened to the court read out the words everyone was waiting for:

> On its face, it appears that this case could fall into an Equal Protection argument, but this court finds that there was no failure to protect Petitioner Álvarez equally under the law. What's more, covering pregnancy in the category of disability insurance could burden the companies and government

to the point that they may not be able to offer any form of disability protec-
tion to individuals who will need it. Therefore, we find that Respondent did
not discriminate against Petitioner Álvarez as employers have the right to
reasonably include or exclude any condition they choose from a disability
plan. It is so ordered.

Four little words that would forever change the direction of my life, my career, my identity.

It is so ordered.

If it's not clear from this manuscript or from the mountains of articles that have been written about the case and me, I went with my original argument. Only a fool would have shifted her statements before the most important argument of her life. Not then, not now. As my mother told me, *Change the system from inside out if you want it to last.* It would have sealed my fate long-term if I had changed everything at that moment, and more important, it would have foreclosed any possibility of people being protected during pregnancy. The Supreme Court would have been unlikely to grant cert to a similar case for years, citing my erroneous behavior as precedent. So, I stuck with the original argument. I thought clearly, I remembered the judge from the case in Boston when he asked me to answer his questions, and I spoke as expected.

Nobody has known my hesitation about this case until now, instead hailing it as a turning point in protections for women and mothers because of what came next. After all, it's not always the decisions that make history. I was still a woman walking up to a building created and run by men. And as my mother came to me and reminded me so often in my dreams, I wanted to build something that would last forever, not put paint on a canvas that could fade.

Justice Pindgarden dissented in a scathing opinion, and someone on the outside must have heard his words, because despite the ruling, Alma was quickly hired at a nearby high school in Seneca Falls, where she's taught math and coached soccer ever since. Rationale and outcome aren't always the same.

A day after the decision was announced, I was back at the office, pushing forward, as Mariana would have wanted, on a new case. I called Aviva three times and she didn't pick up. Reporters called, Linda called, Stan called, all leaving messages I still have to this day.

"You've reached the residence of Sylvia, Joe, and Aviva Bernstein. Please leave us a message and we'll call you back."

"Syl," I heard. It was Linda's voice. "Please call me. I need to talk to you about something. It's important."

But I didn't answer her. I'm not proud of myself, but I couldn't speak to her, or to anyone else, then. Instead, I sat, drank tea, and let the reality of what was happening rush through me, allowing the phone to ring again and again.

"You've reached the residence of Sylvia, Joe, and Aviva Bernstein. Please leave us a message and we'll call you back."

My ears popped with the beeps of the machine as the symphony of life crescendoed. The vacuum of our upstairs neighbors, children playing outside, the building settling back into place after the subway ran beneath us, Joe's voice on the answering machine. I hadn't changed it yet. I didn't want to. It took another ten years until I finally replaced the message.

"Miss Olin," said a familiar voice. "I've been following your case, and I have to say I'm quite proud. If you're so inclined, would you please give me a call? This is James Macklowe. It would be lovely to catch up."

I rushed to the phone.

"Hello?" I said. It was hot inside, my body sweaty. "Hello? Dean Macklowe?"

But he had already hung up.

A week later, Aviva would stand on the *bima* in a synagogue across the street from the one in which my parents were married, and step into adulthood. When the time came, she wore a *kippah* on her head, clipped back by her curls, and a red silk dress of Mariana's, with the gold hoops from Joe in her ears. Draped in the white tassels of a new *tallis*, which hung around her knees like golden beads, she read from the Torah and sang before a crowd of people for the second time in seven months.

Aviva's friends filled the benches, at least forty of them, trying not to fidget.

I watched from the back of the sanctuary, hoping Aviva wouldn't see me, and yet hoping just as much that she would, as she led the Torah procession on its journey around the congregation and back to the ark.

When she turned the final corner of the room, we locked eyes. I smiled and tilted my head. She nodded back, ever so briefly, and then continued. The rabbi, standing behind her, smiled and sang and followed the procession back to the *bima*, in time for Aviva's speech. I don't know if she was happy or sad that I was there. From the podium, she glanced down at the pages, took a sip of water, and searched the audience for one seat in particular: the first chair in the first row, empty, covered in Joe's *tallis*, the white tassels hanging down. She never moved her eyes from his empty seat. I can only hope his spirit was there, looking up at her, his hands clasped together on his lap, his legs crossed (right over left) so that his foot hung loose and limp, his hair balding and patched with gray. That's how I wanted to remember him; that's how I still remember him today, as if he were sitting in that chair, relaxed and excited, stoic and weepy, with me beside him in the front row. He would turn his head slightly toward me and raise the sides of his mouth in the most intimate of smiles that only I would see. And he'd whisper with relentless pride: *We did this.*

In response to the Álvarez case (and so many others like it that followed), Congress passed the Pregnancy Discrimination Act of 1978, in part using language from Pindgarden's dissenting opinion. Throughout it all, I heard Macklowe's voice about dissents tickling my ear, when we were speaking about *Dred Scott* and *Brown v. Board of Education* back in his office at Harvard. *When in life is the opposition, or the quote-unquote minority opinion, ever given the time of day?* But the court's minority opinion didn't represent the majority of the American people. Women are the real majority. And it took Congress codifying and creating a clear law to correct the court's error in judgment and opinion, yet again.

Nevertheless, pregnancy would become tangled up in disability insurance and the law. And despite the passage of the law, there was little movement toward creating an entirely new category of protection for pregnant people and new mothers in the workplace. I take ownership for that—both the good and the bad. Women were getting to keep their jobs during pregnancy if their employers provided insurance and if they qualified, but they still weren't paid for time off immediately after giving birth.

That was my big compromise, though, wasn't it? Practice for all the compromises I'd face for the next forty years, or perhaps it was a reminder that compromise is complicated. And so is change. Despite the faulty groundwork it laid, I did what I felt was right at the time, to chip away at the old law. It was something—not everything, but *something*. And back then, something was what we needed.

Now something isn't close to enough, and so we begin the process again, seeking change, seeking fairness, seeking equity. Once you hit a goal, the goalpost moves farther away, sometimes based on new progress, and sometimes with unexpected regress.

CHAPTER 17

A week after the Pregnancy Discrimination Act passed, I came home to a package waiting for me just outside my door. It was small, but surprisingly heavy. Inside was the painting *Circuitous*, framed and signed with a single *M* for Mariana, encircled with a bold flourish. I ran my fingers around the frame, staring at the colors of the different brushstrokes, the thickness of the grays and blacks and reds. My cheeks ran wet with tears. The first time I'd seen the painting, Joe and Aviva were with me.

The painting was just as I remembered: weeping and yet filled with joy. What I didn't remember about it, though, were the footprints surrounding the mother and child. Feet, healthy and broken, all in motion, walking in circles.

I opened the thin envelope that was taped to the back of the frame.

"Joe bought this for you when you started working on the case, and he wanted to give it to you when you won," it said in Mariana's handwriting. *"I think now is as good a time as ever for you to have it. You may have lost that first battle, but you're winning the war. Keep going.—M"*

Eventually, Mariana underwent another major surgery on her leg, and this time, she moved in with Dr. Discanti to recover. Aviva came home to me, giving Mariana space to heal on her own. When she was ready, Aviva could have gone back, but by then she had already gotten used to our apartment again, and her room, and its proximity to school. She decided to stay, but it was never the same. We lived together in those final years of high school, rarely speaking about anything beyond groceries or college applications or piano lessons.

By the time I was appointed to become the dean of the Fordham University School of Law, she was a junior in high school, and by the time she was in college, I had moved to DC to become the Solicitor General of the United States. But you know these details already. The external story—the facts, the books, the degrees, the speeches, the branches of the Seneca Falls Project that opened all over the country—that's all public record now, the official story that is told at schools and institutions and will be on repeat at my funeral one day. What's not written down anywhere is that Aviva went on to study anthropology at NYU. She lived on campus and took the train home occasionally for *Shabbat* dinners and to introduce me to her latest boyfriend or to tell me about changing her major from anthropology to culinary arts, to playwriting, and eventually finding education. We spoke from time to time. Birthdays passed, and only occasionally would we speak outside of them. No one was really at fault anymore, and as much as she would probably have me believe it all stemmed from Joe's *shiva*, it didn't. It never does. Estrangement and distance don't come from one thing only. And it wasn't estrangement—not exactly. Nor was it that we fought—or fight, still—but rather that distance is a little bit like death, and this was a gradual distancing, an unspooling of a thread that takes time. Hearing but not listening, watching but not seeing, being but not living, until eventually the silence became routine.

The only way I knew what she was really thinking was when I would visit Joe at the cemetery and find a handful of notes there, gathering dirt under the stones. I would pick up the paper that was the cleanest, the most recent, and hear her voice through the page year after year.

Help me talk to her, Dad, Aviva wrote in one of the notes. *I don't know what to say.*

To this day, those words rush through me, over me, like a lacy wave I can see coming but refuse to duck or jump. But I should have ducked or jumped or moved in some way. I had to make things better. I had to fix this.

The last day I went to visit him, the cemetery was empty, and there was nobody around for what seemed like miles. I sat down in front of Joe's grave, beside him, beside Aviva's note, waiting for the wave to overtake me.

"Aviva," I said, struggling to mouth the only three words I knew she needed to hear. But she wasn't there. How could I make this better? How could I fix this? I needed to fix this. I collapsed onto the damp soil, my eyes sealing shut. "I'm so sorry."

Part Four

WASHINGTON, DC

1986

CHAPTER 1

There are forty-four marble steps leading to the entrance of the United States Supreme Court. At the top are sculptures of turtles—made of bronze, now weathered to a pale lime green—supporting large lampposts framing the side entrances to the court. The heavy bronze on their backs doesn't break them, doesn't crush their shells, but they are struggling to climb out from the weight above them. Frozen in motion, their necks stretch out as if they are trying to go somewhere, anywhere.

Sometimes, when the visitors and journalists are no longer around, I stroll by my favorite island of turtles and touch their heads, easing them to move forward a bit faster. Now, after more than thirty-five years of daily touch, the tops of their heads have smoothed over, like they're wearing tiny yarmulkes. One day when I am gone, the little turtles will still be here, their necks outstretched, their feet seemingly in motion, going somewhere.

I nearly missed them when I first stepped foot in the court in 1975, but when I walked inside the second time, in 1986, I noticed them, and when I looked closely, it seemed almost as if they were inching forward. Now I see them everywhere. The turtles carrying the weight of the world on either side of the court, and scattered throughout the marble. A hidden message from the architect: *Justice is slow and deliberate.*

They must be exhausted by now, but I know one day they will get there.

On a Sunday morning thick with humidity, I watched the funeral on television from my apartment in DC. I could practically hear the procession outside on the streets as it passed, moving toward the court. Standing at the top of the steps were the eight remaining Justices of the United States Supreme Court, wearing black in mourning for Justice Abraham Pindgarden, who had died at the age of 92 after a record-setting thirty-nine years on the bench.

"They're already calling him The First Feminist Judge," said a journalist on TV.

Mariana was visiting for the week from New York, and we were glued to the news. It was true that in his tenure, Pindgarden had voted in favor of women's rights on at least fifteen occasions, and he did move the needle for women more than most men in his position. He had dissented in favor of Alma Álvarez on my case, and later wrote the majority opinion on a few other cases that helped women and other marginalized people, but his words weren't universally lauded. Some people hated him, others thought he was a hypocrite for choosing to help women only when it seemed to help himself, and of course others lived in extreme devotion to his influence—James Macklowe among them.

The procession for Pindgarden was impressive. Senators, congresspeople, even a few celebrities dominated the TV screen. I recognized some of his clerks from over the years, there to pay their respects, including Macklowe, whom I spotted on camera in the background. His head was down, his face forlorn. He looked genuinely sad, like he had lost his mentor—a father figure, perhaps—someone whose career he had clearly wanted for himself.

"Look, Linda's on TV," said Mariana, sounding impressed. Linda was wearing her trademark dark lipstick, only now it was more red, her hair was pulled back into a low bun, as it was every time she went on-screen, and she wore a brown suit with an off-white striped shirt underneath. Linda had covered the legal beat at *The New York Times* for nearly two years. Recently, she'd begun writing a column at the paper and was occasionally tapped for talking points on the news. I was excited for her success; people were starting to recognize her on the street. She was made to be both seen and heard.

"We know the question on everyone's mind," said Linda, speaking into the microphone. "Who will become the next Supreme Court justice?"

I knew she was covering the funeral. And I also knew she was covering what was next for the court, but she wasn't sharing. The vetting process had begun, but we had swerved around the topic in recent conversations. I didn't know where I stood in the queue or if I was even being taken seriously as a candidate.

"Justice Pindgarden will be sorely missed by his colleagues," said Linda. "It should be noted that he wanted to proceed with his replacement quickly, per a note he left for the president, in which he requested that a woman take over his seat; and so we know that the president has already begun to circulate a list of potential replacements, including several women."

The television was a small black box with rabbit ears, fifteen years too old. I walked up to it and turned the volume knob to the right until the sound reverberated inside the apartment.

"Well, several possibilities have floated across the president's desk," said a reporter. "Three circuit court judges who have left a good impression, but with the changing times and the now-famous note left by Pindgarden—"

"It remains to be seen whether Pindgarden's wishes will be honored," Linda said, chiming in.

"Come on, Linda," I mumbled to myself.

Mariana turned to me, confused, and then looked back to the TV with an eyebrow raised.

"We have no way of knowing who the president will actually choose. Will that person be someone like a Judge James Macklowe, who clearly wants to inherit the title of 'Second Feminist Judge,' or an actual female judge? The short list, we are now learning, includes people groomed for this position exactly like Judge Macklowe, who served as Pindgarden's very own law clerk decades ago, as well as Judge Stuart Marchessy, a federal judge in Nevada." She paused. "Another name getting some play is the Solicitor General of the United States, Sylvia Olin Bernstein, who, if nominated, would not only be the first woman, but also the first Jewish woman on the high court."

Mariana turned toward me, stunned. "Sylvie?"

My eye itched and I needed to scratch it.

"Though she's currently solicitor general, Bernstein is most publicly known for being the face of the Seneca Falls Project, one of the early forces behind women's rights," said one of Linda's colleagues, interrupting her. "And that project has grown to become a staple in every law school and every city, serving as a stepping stone for public servants the country over. Before that, Bernstein was a constitutional scholar and a dean at Fordham Law, and before that, an ACLU attorney. An interesting fact that many people may not know is that Bernstein is said to have worked under Judge Macklowe, who is likely to be the favored nominee."

"Sylvie, did you *know*?" said Mariana. I wasn't sure what to tell her, or even if there was anything to tell. Dozens of people are vetted every year. Vetting isn't a nomination. Rumor is not the same as possibility, not even close. But before I had a chance to tell her that I didn't know it would get this far, a reporter muffled me.

"Still, Bernstein does not have the depth of judicial experience— or any judicial experience, for that matter—that someone like Judge Macklowe has, which is essential for this job," added another reporter. "And since this seems to be about gender, James Macklowe has done just as much—if not more—for women's rights as Mrs. Bernstein. Just because he's a man, that shouldn't discount him at this critical time in our nation's history."

"Sylvie," said Mariana, practically yelling in my ear. "Did you know about this? Tell me."

"I will," I said, my eyes focused on the television.

"That may be true," Linda continued. "But we are also at a point in history in which gender representation matters on the bench. This appointment has the chance to be historical, just as it was for Louis Brandeis, the first Jewish justice, in 1916, and Thurgood Marshall, the first Black justice, in 1967."

The phone rang and I ignored it.

"Sylvie?" said Mariana. "The phone."

But I refused to turn away from the TV, where photos of Macklowe, Marchessy, and me were plastered on the screen. I remembered back to the first phone call from the White House several weeks earlier, thinking I was just one of dozens of people being considered— not one of three.

The anchor spoke over our images. "Will this be an appointment about who is right for the job, or an appointment about politics, making firsts?"

"It's entirely possible they are one and the same," added Linda, smiling subtly. Was her smile directed at me? For me? Was that the message she was trying to convey?

"Right," added the anchor. "Playing politics with an appointment, as wrong as it is, does not necessarily mean it's the wrong appointment. Politics alone does not imply poor judgment."

"Nevertheless, these judicial appointments are *designed* to be distinctly apolitical," said Linda, dropping her smile. "Even if they fail to be."

I turned to Mariana, but she was no longer beside me. And the phone had stopped ringing. She had answered it. When I looked over at her, she was cupping her hand over the phone receiver.

"It's the *Times*," she said to me. Her face was ashen. "They want Linda to interview you."

CHAPTER 2

The newspaper proof stared up at me, peeking between a few other mock-ups. In the previous weeks, the list of potential nominees had been whittled to two, and my photo was now side by side with James Macklowe's, as if we were in a political race with each other instead of two names on a short list. Given our history and our relationship, the media played it up. Even the headline read almost like a parody.

**THE PRESIDENT'S SUPREME COURT PICK:
JAMES MACKLOWE, THE PRESUMPTIVE LEGACY,
OR SYLVIA OLIN BERNSTEIN, THE CONTEMPTUOUS S.O.B.?**

My photo beside his looked comical, as if I were his child. The editors had chosen a years-old photo dating from when I first argued before the court with *Álvarez*. In it, I stare directly into the camera, my hair short and tight around my scalp, just as it is today, slicked back from a side part. My wedding ring hangs on a long chain around my neck, dangling low, hitting my rib cage, where it has lived since I took it off twelve years earlier. I'm wearing a black suit, a green blouse, and small opal studs in my ears. The woman in the picture is fierce and

clueless about the future. Her confidence both terrifies and embold-
ens me, even now.

The photograph the *Times* used of Macklowe, however, was his
formal government portrait, taken when he was appointed to the circuit court more than a decade before. At the time, the photo
appeared alongside a small announcement, hidden somewhere in
papers that only lawyers and politicians read. But over the next weeks
or even months, it would be plastered everywhere as he ascended to
the high court instead of me. There was little doubt in my mind.

I picked up the proofs as I waited for Linda in her office. The words
"contempt of court" were all over the article; those three words came
alive in bold letters and seemed to turn into a noose before my eyes.
Then, I read about my pregnancy and temporary expulsion from Harvard because of it, which had been highlighted in the article as a way
to connect Macklowe to me beyond the short list. But all of it was focused on the wrong narrative. The piece wasn't about my qualifica-
tions for the job, or the Seneca Falls Project, the ACLU, or my work in
government at the solicitor general's office, or even how Fordham Law
grew under my leadership. Rather, it was about my missteps and how
they intersected with James Macklowe: my failed oral argument at the
Supreme Court in 1975, the public defender's office, Amy McCartney,
the Macklowe internship, and ultimately, the arrest.

And then that atomic word before my name: *contemptuous.*
Sylvia Olin Bernstein.
S.O.B.
Son of a bitch.
I read on.

*It was then-Dean Macklowe who expelled then-student Olin from law
school purely for becoming pregnant, and this may have, in fact, propelled*

her forward in her legal career in the first place. But looking back on this unique history, what might it mean for a possible Justice Macklowe to reach the highest pinnacle of judicial achievement on the basis of supporting women, when he himself was instrumental in nearly expelling a possible Justice Bernstein because she was a woman? Let's examine both potential justices' histories to see how they might rule on important matters.

My hands started to tremble as the proof crumpled in my fist. I'd read stories about me before, but they were usually about my work, not my personal life, and they were never like this, never looking back, never on this scale. The mock-up fell from my fingers, and the loose pages scattered on the linoleum. Sweat collected under my breasts and I dropped to the floor to gather the pages, when Linda walked in.

"Shit, Syl." She rushed toward me, seeing the pages on the floor. "I wanted to talk to you first before you read it."

"*The Contemptuous S.O.B.,* Linda? Really?"

She sat me down in her chair, calmly.

"We've talked about your name before. Remember? During the Álvarez case? It makes you sound like a powerful and groundbreaking radical. I thought you'd be happy with this."

"Happy? I'm an attorney, not a radical," I said. "And you're a journalist, not a . . . I don't know . . . comedian? What is this? Making up names? In *The New York Times,* no less?"

"My editor really liked it."

"It's a ridiculous name. It doesn't even make sense."

"It makes perfect sense," she said. "Since you've been at the solicitor general's office, that's what people have been calling you. I mean, it's usually in the back of the paper, so you've never really noticed, but it's out there," she said, forcing a disappointed smile.

"Contempt has never exactly been a *positive* descriptor," I said.

"Being radical or being *a* radical, no matter which way you spin it, that's contempt for the status quo," she added. "I'm sorry you don't like it, but it fits. Be proud of it."

I looked at the headline again and then back to Linda. Her lips were pursed and her right eyebrow raised.

"Do you *not* think I should be nominated?" I asked nervously.

She didn't respond. Her lip curled for a second, almost like a tic, and so I filled up the space and walked toward her, away from her desk.

"I can't tell what you're thinking, Linda," I said, frustrated. "You're pitting us as rivals, turning him into some sort of villain. It's not a political race. You know this."

"Stop," she said. Her voice was calm, smooth. "Look beyond the headline, Syl. Actually read the article."

"I did," I said. "It's so focused on the past. What about the future?"

"The past matters, especially here," she pressed. "And your past happens to cross over with Macklowe's. That's interesting and needs to be shared with the public. I didn't write this as your friend. I wrote this as a journalist presenting facts. That's my job."

I touched the skin around my clavicle. I'd gotten into the habit of doing that since Joe died, touching the same area where my shirt was meant to be torn from the first month of mourning. It had been twelve years, and I couldn't stop.

"Linda, I don't care what readers say about me. I care what *you* think," I said, picturing her in the bathroom at Harvard, in our apartment when she tore it apart because she was leaving, when she visited me after Aviva was born, and for a brief moment, I almost didn't recognize her.

But before she could answer, her assistant buzzed over the intercom.

"Ms. Loving," she said. "You have a phone call."

Linda looked away from me.

"Who is it?" she asked.

"It's Aviva Bernstein," said the assistant. "Said she's returning your call."

Linda turned back to me, her face a mix of confession and apology.

Aviva and I hadn't spoken in nearly three months. Linda knew and had never mentioned anything about them speaking during this time. But there wasn't a conversation that didn't go by without us talking about her.

"Tell her I'll call her back," Linda said to her assistant.

"No." I stood and walked toward the door. "You talk to her. I'll leave."

CHAPTER 3

*M*om, *you were arrested?* Aviva said on my answering machine shortly after the article came out. *I wish I had known when I was a kid, I would have been a little less afraid,* she continued. *And congratu—*

But the machine cut off before she could finish.

Her voice sounded positive, but distant.

Afraid?

Aviva wasn't afraid of me, was she? Was she calling me because of the article or her conversation with Linda? I wanted to know what she and Linda talked about, how often they really spoke.

I went to the machine, rewound the tape, and played it again, as if magically the entire message would appear.

Mom, you were arrested? I wish I had known when I was a kid, I would have been a little less afraid. And congratu—

Come on, I said to myself, I know there's more. I thought back to the last time we spoke. I remembered the conversation vividly. Each turn of phrase, each awkward silence, each throat-clearing clarification.

"I can't talk long," she had said. "I have class in an hour." I heard her take a deep breath. She wanted to get off the phone, but maybe a part of her wanted to talk to me. Maybe part of her was ready.

"Of course, of course," I remember saying, hoping to linger a little bit longer. "How is grad school going?"

"I like it," she said quickly. "One more year of student teaching and then I'm done. I'll be a licensed special ed teacher in California."

I remember wiping my eyes, which were wet and warm, but not itchy.

"I'm really so very proud of you," I had said. And I was. I am.

"Thanks," she said, and this time, she sounded happy. I could hear her lingering, running her fingers in and out of the white plastic coil of the phone cord.

Any good lawyer knows when to stop examining someone on the stand. But I wasn't in court this time.

"And then you'll leave Berkeley and come home?" I said, hopeful.

She breathed out with exasperation. Because exasperated was what she was with me—not with Linda, not with Mariana—always me.

"I am home, Mom," she said, the final gavel slam ending our call. "I live here now."

And then she hung up. And one month passed. And another, and another. Which is how it had been for years. A phone call, a brief conversation skating around anything and everything, and a quick goodbye.

But then came the vetting and the article. After my photo was plastered on TV, my machine filled with calls from Stan at the ACLU and Joe's family back in Long Island; calls from Alma Álvarez, who was now a high school principal, and Leo the atheist, who was a social worker at my old high school in Brooklyn; and calls from Ray Blayne and even Alexandra Macklowe. But the only call I wanted was the one from Aviva, and there was no space left for her by the time she did. Was her call because of Linda, or on her own initiative?

I played the message again to hear her voice, but when it failed to move past *congratu*—, I pulled the machine out of the wall, furious, and threw it on the ground.

"Dammit!" I shouted, just as the phone rang again.

"Aviva?" I answered. "Is that you?"

"No," said a voice I recognized. "It's James Macklowe."

This time, though, I didn't hang up. And neither did he.

CHAPTER 4

Macklowe and I hadn't been alone together in nearly twenty-five years. When my assistant let him into my office, my body tensed. He had aged fairly well over the years. His hair was half-white, half-peppery, nothing like the photo Linda had published in the *Times*, where he was portrayed as some sort of warped mentor. When he asked to meet me, I debated whether to accept, but I decided I wanted to know why. It was always the why that got me, or perhaps the why was exactly what I needed to see the world clearly.

"Sylvia Olin . . . *Bernstein*," he said, the corners of his eyes crinkling in a grin. "Thank you for meeting with me."

"James," I said, keeping my face still.

Outside my office were my law clerks, my staff, my paralegals, an entire department of the solicitor general's office depending on me. Without the short list and the news, they might not have known who he was.

"Sit," I said, motioning to a chair on the other side of my desk. With my heels, he now seemed even shorter than I remembered.

"Thank you." He held his weight with the armrests of the chair and slowly sank down into it.

I stood behind my desk, waiting. "It's a busy day, James. This would have been easier over the phone."

"I think our paths have crossed enough over the years that this deserved a conversation in person, not over the phone," he said. "Besides, you know how this works. Let's not leave anything to chance, or the FBI and phone records," he added, chuckling.

"Well," I said, leaning over my desk. "Perhaps it will be neither of us."

"Perhaps. But for the sake of argument, let's say it's you."

He seemed to be baiting me. The corners of his mouth were pinned up like laundry.

"Okay." I sat down, my arms over my chest. "For the sake of argument."

"I'll be honest with you," he said, seeming to relax. "I know how ridiculous it is they called Pindgarden 'the first feminist judge.' Rest assured, I know it's absurd."

"I'm glad to hear it."

He stalled, and I couldn't tell what he was thinking in the moment, but his face seemed to cover fear, pride, joy, and confusion in the course of a single moment.

"I wanted to offer you a bit of advice." He collected his hands together. "I've been vetted before. This isn't my first consideration for a seat."

My surprise must have shown clearly on my face.

He nodded. "It was fairly early in my career and my name was never released because I was quite far down the list. It wasn't newsworthy, not like this," he said, motioning to us. "But it was a brutal process, and I want to prepare you for what's to come."

"I'm sorry?" I folded my arms. "You want to prepare me?"

"They empty out all your drawers, Olin."

"I'm quite aware of that." I glanced at the very office for which I had been vetted, inside which he was sitting.

"This is a different sort of vetting." He looked around my office for the first time, as though measuring whether his was larger.

"They empty *all* your drawers," he emphasized, looking back to me. "Even things you didn't think were possible to uncover."

"The arrest has already come out in a headline. I can handle that and a little wordplay on my name."

"I'm not talking about the arrest, Olin. I want you to be prepared. For all of it."

"If you have something to say, just come out and say it. I don't have time for games and guessing."

He looked at me longer than necessary, as if trying to tell me something. Then, I remembered him standing above me in the women's bathroom, handing me a paper towel after I had just thrown up. It was 1961, before *Roe*, and one of his female students had just thrown up in the middle of the day, unprovoked. He must have suspected that I was pregnant, even before I had known. But his face had been kind. He had been my mentor, but in the months that followed he had also become a kind of inverse mentor—he'd pushed me harder by pushing me away.

Now we were sitting before each other as candidates on a short list, and everything had changed. For the past ten years, we'd lived in fear of *Roe*'s potential overturning. A Supreme Court appointment is for a lifetime. A Supreme Court decision is not.

"We both know I didn't kick you out," Macklowe said, leaning closer. "You were never 'kicked out' or expelled. Moving forward, it's important to be clear about my record—*both* of our records."

"Both of our records?" I laughed.

"I have given many jobs to women, to Blacks, to Jews like you, for decades when other people wouldn't touch you. And look at what you've done with the Seneca Falls Project, your work at the ACLU, what you did with the Álvarez case, what *I* did with the Álvarez case, your tenure here at the solicitor—"

"Stop writing my personal history for me, James." I got to my feet. This time, we were in my office, not his, and I wasn't on the bathroom floor.

"Is this really about the *Times* article?" I asked. "You came down here to talk to me about that?"

"I brought you back in," he said to me. "I helped you. Multiple times."

"You don't get to be rewarded for fixing problems you created," I said calmly. "You do realize that."

"There are more women in the law today because of what I did— what *we* did—twenty-five years ago."

"Why are men always so concerned with their legacies?" I said, exhausted. "You're all so focused on the past, instead of the future. Yes, James, you brought the first women to Harvard Law, but of course you don't take responsibility for all the women you hurt in the process. What about people like Linda? She never became a lawyer. Remember, you expelled her. You didn't bring her back in. You didn't help her out. Perhaps it could have been her standing here, getting lectured about the contents of her drawers instead of me."

The shell of his shoulders flew back. "Who?" he asked.

"Linda Loving. The reporter. The one who wrote the *Times* article. Don't pretend you don't know who I'm talking about."

I could hear his heavy breathing, and I waited for the light to come to his face.

"She was one of your nine, the same year as me. One of the women you are so proud to boast about shepherding into the law."

He let out an inadvertent chuckle.

"What?" I said. "You're laughing?"

"Olin, please," he said, smiling. "Loving didn't want to be a lawyer. Not really."

"Of course she did."

"No, she didn't," he said with as much confidence as he had on that first day of class. "If so, she wouldn't have quit when things got hard."

"Don't tell me what happened twenty-five years ago. I know what happened. I was there. She was kicked out. Without getting the benefit of a second chance like I got."

"You don't know?" he said, surprised, the light passing over his face.

"What?"

"Loving left Harvard *voluntarily*." He shifted his tone, as if I were the one left out of the secret. "I was on the committee. I had to sign off on it. She came to us and asked for help on how to *unenroll*. I always remember those conversations. The ones who couldn't cut it. It's not unique. *She's* not unique, Olin. It's not easy doing this job. I think we both know that."

"This conversation is over," I said.

He raised his brow as he feigned indifference with a shrug. "Funny, from where I see it, she's much better off. Done far better than I could have imagined."

"Except that she wanted to be a lawyer," I said.

"It's never as simple as it seems, Olin."

"It's time for you to leave." I walked around my desk to the door.

"Well," he said, standing, impervious to my words. "Whoever the president chooses, I like what she called you in the papers. *The Contemptuous Son of a Bitch*." He smiled at me again. "Wear it well, on the bench or off."

His words stung in the way he said them, proud and indifferent at the same time. To be both present and invisible, considered and abandoned in a single thought; well, that's something he couldn't possibly understand. There's no word for it. Perhaps in other languages there are, but in English, we have no language for the contradictory experience of being female.

"Goodbye, James," I said, and closed the door behind him.

CHAPTER 5

I took a train up to New York.

"I just saw Macklowe," I said when Linda opened her door.

"When?" she asked. Her face betrayed nothing.

"Earlier today. He wanted me to come to his office as if I was still his goddamn student, but I told him if he wanted to meet he could come to mine."

She stepped aside to let me in.

"I hate how we left things," I said.

"I know," she said. "I hate it, too."

She led me to the living room, where we sat on the couch, our knees touching.

"So what did he want?"

"What made you leave school?" I asked.

Her face changed from warm to cold almost immediately. "I see," she said.

"Will you tell me?"

Linda nodded. I listened as she spoke for what seemed like hours, a geyser of information that, in my blood, I'd known already. God, I had to have known. How could I not have known?

She told me about her relationship with Macklowe, which carried on for two weeks late in the spring term. He tried to engage her in his work with civil rights to "understand the people he wanted to help," she said, quoting him. She had been admitted to the best law school in the country, she knew, but still, she couldn't even vote at that time. It was five years before the Voting Rights Act would pass. She told me that she was skeptical about Macklowe's promises, his values, his proposals, but that she felt like she had no choice but to go with him to his office and to a dinner outside Boston and to his house. And that in the process, she started falling for him, wanting to believe in everything he was doing, saying, and teaching, because, after all, he was one of the good ones. She liked him, even if he slipped into hyperbole and frequently name-dropped all the people he claimed to have met. He cared about her, about her family, her community. She told me that he compared her to his daughter, Alexandra, who he also hoped would "buck the system." She told me that she was starting to have feelings for him, her professor, *our* professor. She couldn't admit this to herself, let alone me, especially when he seemed to be so incredulous in his protestations. And then he said he loved her and removed her clothing from her body, garment by garment, in the backseat of his blue Cadillac, just to show her how much. She told me she couldn't say it back because she didn't understand what it meant to be loved, to be *in love*, after her breakup with Ray. She wasn't sure if she loved him, or even liked him, but she was in awe of him. Though they'd had sex before, she didn't think she wanted it that night. Not there, not then, not like that. She told me that her brain was still and frigid and confused when he ran his fingers around her nipples, her belly button, her thighs, and that it restarted when he slipped them inside her. She told him to stop, to take his hands out of her, but he closed his eyes halfway and started moaning instead of responding.

She told me that he unzipped his pants and moved himself on her, and she cried out in pain when he did that, but he forced himself into her, and pushed and pushed and pushed so hard that she tore and bled. She told me that he came in a burst of high-pitched laughter. She told me that he lay on top of her for the duration of "Everyday" by Buddy Holly, which was on the radio at the time. She told me that it was dark outside, or at least dark inside the car, which was parked in his garage at home while his family was in Cape Cod for the week. She told me that he invited her in for a drink after he was finished. He told her the sex was better than it was with his wife, and he thanked her for it. Then he put her in a taxi to take her back to the apartment and told her he hoped he would see her again. She never did one-on-one again outside of class. A week later, she failed her first exam in his class. Two weeks later, she failed the next, and by the time the summer rolled around, she had failed the entire term.

"Oh, Linda . . ." I said, my voice cracking.

I reached out to her, but she didn't reciprocate, so I waited, listening to the silence, wanting to hear the metronome, and though she was standing in front of me very much alive, I could barely hear it.

"I'm so, so sorry."

"Thank you," she finally said, running her thumb against the edge of her ring finger, thinking, waiting, digging into the skin with the tip of the nail, a silent technique she'd learned long ago to quell her anger in public.

"That was right after my arrest, wasn't it?" I asked. I held my hand out to her.

She nodded and took my hand.

Then, I remembered. I had been completely distracted by my new relationship with Joe and my own failed internship. What if I'd been more attentive? Could I have done anything to stop it, to help her?

339

"After I left school, the first time I saw him again was at your wedding," she added. "He came over to me and kissed my cheek as if I was just an acquaintance."

"Jesus, Linda. And you've been carrying this around with you for decades? This is not right. If I had known—"

"Don't do that," she said, taking back her hand.

"What?"

"Don't make this about you and what you say you remember or not."

I sat back, confused.

"Linda, I didn't know what happened, I swear." I flipped through the pages of my memory to see if there was something there I'd missed. The flirtation at the bar? The redirection away from my conversation about Macklowe? "Maybe in the back of my mind, I thought you two were dating, maybe, or having some sort of an affair. That night at the Cloak Room, it seemed as if something was happening, but you never mentioned anything. Deep down if I think about it, I might have had my suspicions, I suppose?"

"You *suppose*?" she said, looking at me, her upper lip curling. "Don't give me that line, Syl. We've been friends far too long for you to lie to me."

"I'm not," I said. "If I had known I would have gone with you to the administration, to help. To fight this. To fight *him*."

She shook her head, trying not to laugh.

"I would have!"

"Fine. Let's say you did. You want to think *that* would have made a difference? Think about what you're saying."

"What do you mean?"

"Are you really going to make me spell it out for you, Syl? Come on. What do you think I could have said? I told the administration I was being treated unfairly in class and that it was impacting my grades, without telling them why. Macklowe denied it all, of course, and they believed him," she said. "Of course they believed him. They'd still believe him now, wouldn't they?"

"And they kicked you out for that?" I asked. "Or you withdrew?"

She sat back on the couch and bit her bottom lip, shaking her head.

"I may not have graduated from law school, Sylvia, but I went to enough classes to know that they might as well have kicked me out. They did everything in their power to ensure that I would have no option other than to leave. I would have gotten an F in Macklowe's class and every other class—including Legal Writing—which would have caused me to lose my financial support and my summer internship, which I needed for both the money and the résumé. I wouldn't have been able to crawl back from that, to afford tuition or get a job. So they forced me to do it on my own so they wouldn't have to own up to it. I had no choice. They constructively kicked me out."

Constructive expulsion. Pulling the strings on the marionette and placing you in a position that forces you to make the final move. At the end of the day, they can claim clean hands because you're the one who quits, who resigns, who walks out the door.

"And here we thought that it mattered that they offered me admission. They got the headline they wanted back then. That was it."

"The headline," I echoed. I thought for a minute. "Are you upset that they let me back in?"

"Please, stop making this about you," she said, sounding exasperated. "It happened so long ago, it's ancient history at this point. It's one ring in my life's history—not all of them. One."

"But—"

"But . . ." She stopped me and chewed on her bottom lip. I stared at the tiny vein that traveled between her eyes. The little red dot in her left eye. The brush of freckles on her nose.

"Think about it," she continued. "Do you think that if you were in his car, he would have raped you? Do you think if you had gone to the administration after he raped you, they would have listened to you? Because I'm fairly certain they would have. I'm fairly certain you wouldn't have gotten kicked out of Harvard Law School as one of the first women to attend—but not graduate."

"I don't know."

"Of course you do."

"I'm not . . ." I stumbled.

"You were able to redo your classes. You got the job with Macklowe after your one-day internship at the PD. Whether you asked for it or not, you got help not once but twice. How many second chances is that?"

"I don't know," I said again.

But I knew how many second chances I'd had. Exactly two more than Linda.

She cleared her throat. "Sylvia, this relationship isn't what you think it is if we can't confide in each other, can't be honest. Do you wonder why I never told you?"

"I don't know," I said. "Nobody was sharing back then."

"Bullshit, Sylvia. I told people. I didn't tell you."

It was a matter-of-fact statement, not a question. Not about school, but about us and the friendship I thought we had, the friendship I *wished* we had.

"Sylvia," she said. "We need to talk about this. After all these years. With the two of you on the short list, for Christ's sake. One of you will be making important decisions that impact all of us one day. It matters."

I played with Joe's ring around my neck and heard Macklowe's voice.

This kind of thinking gets me excited. Very excited.

Then I saw his face as a younger man and then later, when he was older, lecturing me about his legacy.

"It happened to you, too, didn't it?" she said, trying to hold my gaze.

"Me?" I placed a hand on my chest, at first confused. "It's not about me. You just said that."

The truth is, I wasn't shocked or surprised when she said it, as if I had been waiting my entire life for this conversation.

It happened to you, too, was so many things for so many people, and yet completely different for each. I wish that I had an answer prepared for her then, but I didn't.

"He never touched me like that. He didn't force his body on mine."

I held my hands up on either side of my body. There was nothing to surrender, nothing to say.

"He never laid a single hand on me," I pleaded. "It's not the same. It's not fair to put this in the same category."

"Did you ever talk with Joe about him, though?" she asked.

"No, not exactly," I said, shaking my head. "There was nothing to tell. You said you told someone?"

"I told Ray," she said. "Not when it happened, obviously. Things weren't great between us then, but years later when we were both in New York."

"I see," I said, the history sinking in. "I'm glad you had him to talk to."

"Yeah," she said, looking away. "Me, too."

She moistened her lips as if to speak, but stopped. Her silence was incapacitating.

I tried to piece together my words, unemotionally, judiciously. "Linda, I won't diminish what happened with you by mixing it up with some sort of perverted power struggle."

"I appreciate that, I do," she said, waiting, tapping her fingertips against each other again. "You know, Syl, you always talk about working *within* the system in order to change it. But the truth is that you *can* work within the system because the system is designed to help people like Macklowe, and even people like you."

The trees outside were rustling. The leaves slid across the glass windows like nails on a chalkboard, and I felt them deep inside my body.

"Do you really think that had you been me, that had you been Black, *this* would have turned out the same?"

"But you have a voice now, Linda," I said. "You write for *The New York Times.* You're on TV every single week. People are listening."

"I had a voice then, too. Just nobody cared to hear it!" she said, angry. "Including you."

I felt the heat of her resentment, frustration, and pain of having your so-called best friend reopen your wounds; to be dismembered not once, but twice from the same cut. I did that to her, not Macklowe. All of it was justified. I had wanted us to be in the same boat, to have the same enemy, to change the world as a unit. And yet, it took me nearly my entire life to realize that we were starting from different places.

"Especially me, is what you mean," I said. "I was one of the people who didn't care to hear it."

"I tried to talk to you about it," she said. "Over the years there were a lot of times when I tried."

She had called me and more than once I hadn't returned her calls. She had reached out to me in ways that I hadn't realized, so that the only way she could talk to me, finally, was through the damned article.

"You're right," I said, moving closer to her on the couch. "I'm so sorry."

She nodded and breathed in deeply, a slow melodic sort of breath that lasted a few seconds longer than normal.

"They should have listened," I said. "*I* should have listened. I was wrong."

This is my third great regret in life. I wonder how different things could have been, then and now, if I had been someone else when it counted. If my silence, like in court, had come at a different time, the right time, when she needed someone to listen. But perhaps no one can answer that. Perhaps regret grows larger over time. I know regret is essential—it's taught me everything I know—but it becomes dangerous if you can't learn from it.

Her eyes didn't falter. They were angry and loving and kind and calm at the same time, and absolutely honest. Just as they were when we first met twenty-seven years earlier.

"Now, moving forward, don't you ever speak to Macklowe or anyone else about me again," she said, returning to her best broadcast voice, the same one that would welcome all of America to the nightly news for a decade. "Whether you get to the Supreme Court or not, I will decide what to do about him, and all this, and when. On *my* terms. Is that clear?"

"Yes," I said. I could feel the heat of the women's bathroom back in Boston spread through her apartment, and I wanted to light it on fire all over again. With her. "Yes, of course yes."

And then I finally heard it—the voice, the metronome, back in my heart, loud and fast, and I could hear its methodical rhythm if I just listened for it a little bit more. If I just worked at hearing it a little bit harder. If I changed my tempo to go along with it, instead of forcing it to follow mine.

I waited for her to speak next; I wanted her to yell at me, but she never did. Instead, her eyes filled with water. I looked around at her apartment. I should have foreseen that in two years, she'd become a household name, and five years later, she would become an anchor for *NBC Morning News*. The entryway to her apartment would be decorated like the entrance to a museum, with covers from different magazines in which she was featured as either the face or byline. But in 1986, there were only three frames gracing the empty walls.

I reached out my hand, and she took it. We didn't fully embrace, but it was a start.

"Sylvia," she said, her voice changed, soft and thick, like honey. "I'm not upset that they let you back in. You're exactly where you should be now. And by the way, so am I. Contrary to what you or anyone else may think, I don't actually think I'm a failure because I didn't graduate from Harvard Law School. Maybe I felt like one at the time, but sometimes you need one door to slam to see a better one open. I am genuinely happy with my career, and yours. I'm proud of us. *From the inside out and the outside in,*" she said. "And if you become the nominee and are voted in, I think you will make a fucking brilliant justice. Our country needs you right now more than ever. There is no doubt in my mind about that. So embrace that beautiful contempt, you sonofabitch, and step up to the plate. It's no longer about you. It's about all of us."

I realized at that point that if I did become the nominee, and then a justice, I would never be asked that question again, regardless the source, regardless the reason. I would never have someone look at me and say: Why *didn't* you tell me? I would never look at myself and wonder who I was. No. I would listen. I would be honest; I would tell the truth as if I were always under oath, so help me God. No matter what.

A day later, I got the call from the president. Two weeks after that, I would testify before the Senate Judiciary Committee.

CHAPTER 6

Twenty-one men and one woman sat before me, hidden behind a wooden dais and nameplates. With their varied backgrounds and uniform appearance of silver hair and black-and-white suits, the Senate Judiciary Committee was a tableau of political history. The lights glared down at me. The chair was an uncomfortable old wooden flatbed. My arms rested at the table, where dozens of books and yellow legal pads were spread in case I needed to consult them. We were only halfway through the first day of questioning.

"Good afternoon, General Bernstein," Senator Bloom said in a friendly tone. "You are positioned as one of the youngest people to be on the highest court of the land. We know some of your views and they are radical at best. You are inconsistent in your legal reasoning, making our job a bit harder today trying to figure you out. You are vocal in support of small government, and yet you have never held a position as a judge. I can't place you as a nominee, and quite frankly, I don't want to vote to put you on the court for a lifetime appointment just because you're a woman. So I have some questions for you."

As the senators cleared their throats and the cameras turned on me, I wondered whether Aviva was watching. Could she see me wearing the hoops Joe gave her for her birthday that she left at home when she moved to California? Could she tell that the vein in my temple was pulsing? Were the cameras close enough to spot the heavy makeup that Mariana had suggested, with the red lipstick that Linda had bought for me?

"I'm happy to answer any questions you may have about my record. If you would like a specific question answered, can you please repeat it?" I said. "I would like to make sure I'm responding comprehensively."

The senator nodded. "I need to know, as do the people I represent, that you will follow the law before you. That you will not activate your own judgments as applied to these cases. That you will follow the original intent of the founders."

"The framers of the Constitution lived in a time where the concept of original intent is inconsistent with present-day life," I said. "That's not to say it's not important, but it must be viewed in context."

I could hear Joe's soothing voice in my ears. He was whispering.

Please, Joe, I thought to myself. Stay with me.

"I need to know before I can vote, though, what you really stand for," said the senator. "Because from what I see, it's a travesty you are even here. You stand for shouting, yelling, disagreement—in other words, contempt."

He pulled out a large printout of my mug shot from 1960 and displayed it behind him. In it, my hair is still long and blond and strung around my face.

"You see, General Bernstein, it appears to me that you stand for contempt of our very system of rules."

I smiled slightly, but tried not to let them see. I had long since learned that to smile in deference to another's faulty introduction is to yield power. But I had expected this. I had prepared for it.

"You are holding a picture of me from when I was a law student," I said. "It was 1960 and the first day of my internship with the Middlesex Public Defender's Office, where I worked for one day. As you know, and as I'm sure everyone here knows by now, the judge threw me in jail for contempt for refusing to answer a question. I suspect that at least a few of you have experienced the same."

I glanced at the dais of white hair on white faces and paused, picturing Amy McCartney's broken face and hairline, her torn vagina. I didn't need to close my eyes to imagine it. Since then, I'd seen hundreds of Amy McCartneys.

The senator continued, unmoved. "Perhaps some among us do not believe this to be so serious an offense, but given that this is one of the highest positions of power in our country, not even a small error is permissible, particularly when it reflects upon your character and your judgment," he said. "Personally, I do not believe that we should allow onto the highest court of the land someone who not only has been arrested for not following the law, but for *contempt* of it. Someone who has no respect for the rule of law, who is filled with the type of loud, radical behavior that should never grace our nation's highest levels of justice."

I waited. The room seemed to buzz with hundreds of people, microphones, lightbulbs, and camera flashes going off.

"As you know," I said, "contempt of court is not exclusively for yelling or shouting or being 'radical' as you say. As I stated, I was held in contempt of court for refusing to speak. In fact, for silence."

"And you expect us to believe that your *selective* silence, then, is helpful to the court now? Both demonstrate a failure to act."

"I understand your position, Senator," I said. "But when you think about it, contempt can be inward-looking, too. I suspect that not a soul among us doesn't feel guilt or frustration about certain choices we made in a prior life. But a mark of growth is to learn from our pasts and improve. And that is something everyone in this room has mastered, no doubt, whether or not they care to admit it."

"Let's move on," he said. "I'm reading from an article now in which you're empathizing not with the victim of a heinous crime, but rather the perpetrator of it. In fact, you're even quoted as saying about the convicted killer, Amy McCartney, and I quote, 'At the end of the day, who suffered the most? Yes, she killed her abusive husband out of self-defense. That is a valid defense. She did not intend for him to die. But what about their children? Had a woman been in charge of that court in 1960, I'm not convinced the outcome would have been the same, or should have been the same.'"

He put down the paper and looked at me.

"What did you mean by that—the outcome *should not* have been the same? Are you suggesting we don't lock up violent criminals?"

"Of course not," I said quickly.

"Then what are you trying to say here?"

I expected this question, as well. I had practiced my answer days earlier.

"I suspect you thought I had my eyes on the bench back in 1974 when that article came out, but I assure you, I did not."

A few people laughed.

"Life is perspective, senators. Whoever wears the robe is going to bring her life experience to her analysis. We are human, after all. Representation is the only way that neutrality can be achieved."

I took a sip of water and continued.

"Now, I'm not suggesting what is right or wrong in that particular case, and I'm certainly not suggesting that I would use my personal beliefs as a justice, because my role is to follow precedent and interpret the law as it is written—not to create it and *not ever* to impose my personal opinions and judgments. But to suggest that justices do not bring their lived experiences into their interpretation is naive. Judicial opinions are rendered through an *interpretation* of the law, which in turn is rendered by the collective life experience of the judge. If that wasn't the case, there would never be a split vote, and all decisions would always be 9–0."

He squeezed out a smile and nodded.

"Thank you for your honesty," he said. At the very least, he might vote for my nomination to proceed from the committee to the full Senate, but there was no telling how he would vote once it got there.

The next senator pulled out a binder filled with tabs—law review articles, interviews I'd given over the years, speeches I'd made, the well-circulated Seneca Falls Project pamphlet, and more. He thumbed through to one in particular. I knew what it was instantly.

"I see from this *New York Times* op-ed from the seventies that you are a supporter of abortion."

"I'm a defender and supporter of a woman's right to choose," I said. "If that includes the termination of an unwanted pregnancy, then I support that woman's right to make that choice for her body."

Aside from the op-ed, I mostly stayed away from this topic in public, but I'd given a few statements over the years. And I was proudly quoted in one of Stan's articles a few years back when he was appointed the head of the ACLU.

"I understand your position. I can see it clearly on the page. But I wonder, have you ever had an abortion?"

I looked around at the layers of neoclassical architecture in front of me and replayed the question. *Have you ever had an abortion?* It was not one he could have asked any other nominee before me, though he could certainly have asked if any other nominee paid for or requested one of their partner.

When I didn't answer at first, the senator repeated the question.

Again, hundreds of eyes fell to me.

The aperture of the camera lens widened, the red light still on.

"Senator, I try not to have a label on my back," I said calmly, closing my hands. "I find it looks vaguely reminiscent of a bull's-eye."

A few members of the committee smiled.

"But have you?" the senator asked forcefully. "It hasn't always been legal, so we need to be fully aware of your position. And this speaks to your ability—or inability—to personally follow the law."

The cameras were on. This was not a court of law. This was something entirely different.

"Are you asking me this as a woman or as a lawyer?" I said. "As a professor or as a jurist?"

"I'm asking you as a woman," he said.

I tapped the microphone with my index finger. The only woman on the committee, I had heard, had done the same thing in her first speech on the Senate floor three years earlier. The newspapers had deemed her pushy.

"Please, Mrs. Bernstein, can you answer the question?"

I recrossed my legs in the other direction and removed a wisp of hair that had drifted into my eyes. My face no longer held a forced smile, and I wanted them to see it clearly. I could have answered a million different ways, chosen my words carefully, spoken as a veteran attorney. I heard Linda's voice in my head; I saw Mariana's intensity as she bent over her easel with a paintbrush in hand, Aviva's excitement while taking notes in her graduate school classroom, and my mother coming into my room late at night with a book in her hand, and realized that my version of contempt wasn't through public outrage in the streets, or even silence in a courtroom. It was born from something else entirely, and would have to change moving forward. When

I was twelve years old, I remember telling the rabbi that exemption is also exclusion. I am sick of being both an exception and exemption. I simply want to be the norm.

"Yes, Senator," I said, without hesitation. "I have."

There was no outburst of contempt. Just silence.

Even today, when I look across the bench and question counsel every week, I sometimes feel that we are all merely our actions and reactions. It's taken me a lifetime to try to understand this.

"Thank you for your answer," he said.

Despite what history tells you, I'm not the only woman who could have been in this position. I know it could—or should—have been Linda, but for better or worse, it was me. And I knew that day that if I was going to be this experiment, the person with whom they subverted their rules, the rules needed to change. I sat in that room on behalf of all the women who could have been there instead, and I vowed in that moment never to be blind to them again.

I waited for a follow-up from anyone on the committee.

"Do you have any other questions?" I asked, but there were none.

You don't need to know whether I had a smile on my face at that point. You can look up the video on your own.

CHAPTER 7

When I came home after the final vote, Aviva was waiting for me at the front door to my apartment, sitting on her suitcase. She looked different, somehow. Older, yes, but also like a new person.

"Aviva," I said almost breathlessly. "I didn't expect to see you here."

"I thought I should finally check out this DC apartment after all these years."

I opened the door and she pulled in her suitcase. She was carrying a brown paper bag, which she put down near the door.

"So, you know those scenes at the end of movies where the workaholic dad makes amends before he dies or the movie ends? *It's a Wonderful Life. The Godfather.*"

"Am I supposed to be the dad here?" I laughed, placed my hand over my chest, and felt Joe's hand on top of it.

"You're nobody's dad. Certainly not mine," she said calmly. "But if you were wanting to make amends or whatever, I don't see why I shouldn't let you just because you're a mother. *My* mother."

The light was coming in behind her, shading her. She was tall, her skin almost translucent. I don't know why it took me so long to realize it. Aviva didn't look like her father. Other than her hair, she looked like me. She and I had the same-shaped eyes, the same nose, even the same lines stretched around our necks.

She stopped in front of *Circuitous*, which was hanging on the wall prominently beside the entryway. Everyone who enters my apartment sees it, to this day.

"I see something new every time I look at it," I said to Aviva.

"Me, too," she said, consuming the painting like a drug. "It's crazy to think that a death march is where Mariana's life basically restarted."

"What?" I said after a long pause.

"Mariana said that she painted this because of the death march from Auschwitz, where her leg was injured. Where she escaped," she said.

Mariana had never told me about the death march in any of her stories, and I felt as if I'd been punched in the gut. Perhaps pieces of her stories were disbursed to different people at different times, like a paranoid person hiding money all over the house. It would be hard to put them all together to fully understand what she had experienced. But maybe that was the point.

Then Aviva told me how Mariana and tens of thousands of other Jews marched from one death to the next for over thirty miles in the snow without shoes. Halfway through, one officer struck her in the leg with the neck of a rifle, fracturing the bone in two clear pieces. She tried to continue marching, but couldn't. Aviva said that a friend helped Mariana move forward in order to avoid gunfire and beatings. But when she couldn't walk on it, somehow, she and her friend escaped, peeling off from the group. Mariana told her it was the only miracle she'd ever experienced. Together, they escaped the march, hiding in the countryside. Her friend died of hypothermia while waiting for safety, and Mariana hid with the dead body for another week.

I looked at the painting again and noticed the footprints surrounding the mother and child. Feet, healthy and broken, injured and clean, all in motion, walking in circles.

"I see the footprints everywhere now," I said, examining the painting with new eyes. "They were difficult to capture in the gallery at night, but now in the light, I can't see anything else."

"Apparently, a bony callus formed around the break in her leg, what Tony calls her man-made crevasse, which is basically holding her together. Her leg was so weak, that's why she fell in the subway when you were kids and she sprained her ankle. But that's also the only way she survived. If her leg wasn't broken, she would have marched directly into her death. Nothing, and I mean nothing we've experienced, will ever compare to that. I'm grateful to her. For giving me a history. For giving me perspective. For giving me—"

"A fight," I said, completing her thought.

But Aviva didn't smile back.

"A fight?" she said, echoing me, but with a tone all her own. Disappointment, pure and unadulterated. "It's always a fight for you, Mom. I was going to say a family. For me, a family."

"Is that what you think?" I said. "That it's a fight *or* a family?"

Her lashes, long and smooth, blinked against her skin and then came together again for an extra moment, before continuing.

"Look, Mom, I've wanted to come home for a while, but to be honest, I didn't know where to start. I mean, every time we speak, it's an argument, so it just seemed easier to avoid everything. You know?"

"You speak with everyone but me," I said, laughing awkwardly. "Mariana, Linda, apparently even Tony—"

"Please, Mom, just let me talk," she said. "I need to say this."

"I'm listening," I said.

She flattened her pants with her palms, breathing in and out with deliberate speed.

"I don't want to talk about the dumb abortion. I don't care that you had one. Though I am shocked—no, blown away—that you just told Congress—"

"The world!" I said, shocking myself.

"The world, yes," she added, her eyebrows lifted.

"I probably sealed my fate then," I said, mocking the expected headlines. *"No Women on the Court. Not This Year. Not like Her."*

"Honesty matters, though, regardless of what it reveals," she said.

I wanted to embrace her, touch her. I needed her. And I know she needed me, too.

"I hope you're right," I said. "But you should know that I'm not sorry for what I did."

"I know that," she said, as if it were obvious. "What I care about is that you lied about it and that you lied to Dad about it."

Her words burned. They still burn today. Joe never lied to me, not expressly. Nor did Aviva. I was the liar. I think that's what she wanted me to say. I used to think lies of omission were different, that they carried a different weight. I was wrong.

"You're right. And I'm not lying now," I said. I reached out to her and she hesitated, but still didn't reciprocate. "We both said things we didn't mean back then," I said, reading her face to see if it was okay to continue. "We were in shock, we were grieving. We've both apologized in our own ways. For years."

"Have we, though?" She sounded skeptical. "I haven't, not really. You haven't. Not really."

My hands dropped to my lap and braided together. "I don't know what you want me to say, Veev. I don't know how much more I can apologize. I'll keep trying. But will it ever be enough?"

Her face started to twitch and she turned away from me.

"I've spent years trying to understand," she said. "I don't think I can move on without knowing, really knowing if—"

"If I wanted you?" I said, answering her question before she even asked. "That's your question."

She nodded.

"Aviva, I got pregnant a second time when you were only six months old. I was twenty-five and had been kicked out of law school for getting pregnant the first time. I didn't know if I wanted more kids, and if I had another child *then*, I wouldn't be here today. And neither would you. Please, try to understand. I know your father wanted more kids, but it just never happened again."

"But did you want it to?" she asked, still looking down.

No matter my answer, it would have been wrong. It would have hurt someone.

"I don't know," I finally said. "It was a different—"

"Don't give me that 'it was a different time' bullshit again," she said, looking up at me. "I'm sick of hearing it. It's a different time now than it was then. It will be a different time in thirty years, sixty years, one hundred goddamn years, but women will still get pregnant. Women will still get raped. Women will still be mothers when they want to and when they don't. Just answer the question, Mom," she said.

"At the time, when I got pregnant with you? No, I didn't want children."

I said it without emotion, as though it was a legal statement of fact I'd honed for years.

"But then, once I had you, I wanted you so deeply, so completely, so comprehensively, and I never stopped. It's just that the way the world was set up; it seems like we need to choose what we want, and it's one or the other. But I know that's a lie. I am everything because of you. You were enough. You were always enough."

Her eyes began to water.

"And then after?" I said, thinking. "I wasn't thinking about more children then. I couldn't. I'm sorry I don't have a different answer for you, a better answer, but it's the truth."

"You didn't even give Dad a chance," she said.

"I know," I said, accepting it.

And she didn't question it, as if maybe she understood. Maybe she needed time. Maybe she didn't. But she didn't push back.

"It was really hard when he died. And it didn't help that you suddenly became sort of famous and invisible soon after. Everywhere and nowhere, like smoke. I could see you, but not touch you."

"It wasn't easy on this end, either. I promise you that."

She nodded.

"You are so much like my mother," I said to her. "Smart, beautiful, driven. I wish you could have met her."

"Please don't change the subject," she said. "And please don't lie to me anymore."

She needed to hear that one final thing. And I needed to give it to her. "I promise," I said. "I won't."

She frowned. I took her hand and this time she allowed it, and we squeezed, but didn't embrace.

"Is this like the point in the movie when the son holds the dying father's hand and they decide that everything's okay?" she asked.

I shook my head.

"Then why not?" she added, hopeful but flat. "Why doesn't it feel right?"

"It doesn't work that way because I'm not your father," I said, clearing my throat. "I'm your mother. The rules are just different. And no matter how much we rewrite them, no matter how much we repave the roads, they still lead to different places. And the sooner we can all accept that, the more we will be seen, and the more equal we will finally be."

I watched her face for a reaction. She was listening, so I went on.

"It won't be like the movies, but it *will* be okay. In a different way. A better way."

She cleared her throat.

"*Ah-vee-vah*," I said, reaching my hand out for her face and tracing it around her cheekbones, which, since childhood, had risen like yeast. Her face was now chiseled around her cheeks and jawline like a grown woman. "How can I make it right? How can *we* make it right?"

"Well, I'm home now," she said, finally smiling. "And congratulations. You have work to do."

CHAPTER 8

Mariana once told me that everyone has a feature that reminds them of who they really are, or how they came to be: an accent, a birthmark, the color of their skin, the curl of their hair. It's taken me a lifetime to realize it, but the crescent scar of my cesarean is mine.

"Mom, you okay?" Aviva called on the day of my swearing-in. She knocked on the bathroom door, where the warm water of the shower rained over me in a small thunder.

"I'm fine," I called back. "I'll meet you outside in a few minutes."

I washed my back, my hair, and finally my scar. Then I turned off the shower.

I found her on Joe's side of the bed, a pink robe tied around her waist, her wet hair pasted to her face. She was looking at the stack of books Joe was going to read sitting on the night table. When I moved to DC, I took the stack with me, and set it out in my new bedroom on his side of the bed just as it had been in New York. It still sits there today.

I took the hairbrush from her hands, an old Mason Pearson, black with black bristles and an orange cushioned home, the same brush my mother bought for me as a child. I gave it to Aviva when she was young, but I had never seen her use it. My fingers ran against the old bristles, blanching my skin, leaving white dots all over my fingertips. As the spots faded quickly into pinkness, I dragged the brush downward on her scalp, delicately attempting to untangle the knots in her hair.

"How is this?" I asked.

"Nice," she said, leaning into me. We were both still wet, our hair still moist, drying in the breeze from the open windows.

When I finished brushing, she turned around. "Mom, I have something for you."

She left the room and came back with a small package. Inside was a collar, a jabot, for my judge's robe. I picked it up, the lace spilling between my fingers, and then spread it out on my bed. My first and only jabot.

For more than thirty-five years now, the jabot has hung, unused, in the closet of my judicial chambers like a talisman. The lacy snowflakes swirling in circles and ovals inside a long white collar were supposed to take the place of a man's tie. But I never once wore the jabot. I would never wear anything to embellish the robe. Today, it hangs, pristine in its plastic, a daily reminder that Aviva is always with me.

When I first tried on the black robe that day, only Aviva was with me, and I think I was only beginning to understand what the next thirty-five years would bring. For her, for me, for the country. Aviva walked up behind me and placed her jabot around my collarbone. It was stunning, a work of majesty, of purity. She closed the clasp behind my neck. It was tight at first, the buttons a bit snug and uncomfortable, but it didn't matter. For the first time in fifty years, I was finally able to breathe.

Two weeks later, I was sworn in inside the Supreme Court, beside more hidden turtles that were sculpted into the building inside. Linda was next to me on one side, with Aviva and Mariana on the other.

Joe was also with us. The first chair in the first row beside us was empty, just as it had been at Aviva's Bat Mitzvah. I could almost see the white tassels of his *tallis* waving in a slight breeze. I imagined him sitting with my mother and father, and can only hope their spirits were there, too.

Hundreds of eyes fell on me that day as if they knew what would happen next, as if they knew who I would become. It's not easy being the first anything, I thought. But that day was about every other person in the country who wanted more. Even today, as I write this, after putting in thirty-five years on the bench, and preparing to retire at the age of eighty-four with a new woman to take over my seat, that day was a rebirth.

The president introduced me, and when he finished speaking, he had me walk forward to meet him. In that moment, I saw my future and past as one. I saw Joe holding Aviva in the hospital just after she was born. I saw Linda as a morning news anchor, interrogating Macklowe in a live interview that would go viral twenty years later. I saw Mariana at her very own art gallery, where she began a small school for young artists. I saw my mother and father as they had been when I was a child. I saw friends and colleagues around their kitchen tables, pounding fists and pounding bread. I saw Amy McCartney sitting in jail for killing her husband, and Alma Álvarez cradling her second and third babies while grading papers. I saw women marching in the streets and organizing from their homes. I saw the men they loved and the men they hated, the parents who had abandoned them and the parents who would nourish them. I saw Mariana's twin sister, my daughter's namesake, behind the glass wall, screaming out in pain, and I saw the serum injected into her eyes, and for the first time in my life, I didn't try to scratch away the pain, the discomfort, the irritation. I needed it. And in that exact moment, I was all of those ages, all of those years, frozen in time.

I turned to Aviva and remembered her in the synagogue when she was thirteen, her feet sinking into the velvet carpeted steps. I saw Joe take his final breath as the doctor closed the curtain on us. I saw my mother as she counted out all the checks addressed to her as she placed them on my bed. I felt myself holding Aviva as an infant in my arms and counting down, ten, nine, eight, seven, six, hoping she'd calm down, stop crying, sleep. Why are so many important things set to a countdown? New Year's Eve. Rocket blasts. Anesthesia. It's all backward. Shouldn't we try to count forward instead?

So I did. And she was beside me, returned to me, looking up at the beauty of that day, our eyes open, our heartbeats loud, and we counted.

One.

Two.

Three.

The numbers stayed with me.

Four.

Five.

Six.

I stood beside the stone turtles, beside Aviva and Mariana and Linda . . .

Seven.

Eight.

. . . and beside the president of the United States, and the chief justice, as he opened his mouth and said, "Please raise your right hand."

And,

. . . *Nine.*

A week later, I was on the cover of *Time* magazine with this headline: JUST CALL ME BITCH. I'M NOBODY'S SON!

How easily one line can be misinterpreted. How easily one line can be read and reread a month later, a year later, forty years later, to mean something entirely new. One of my biographers recently wanted to put that quote on the cover of a new book about my life on the bench. I refused.

But then I wasn't writing my own story.

I am now.

Acknowledgments

A book is nothing without its community. Endless gratitude goes out to the following people:

The depth of love and appreciation I have for my agent, Sarah Bowlin, knows no bounds. You are everything a writer could wish for in an agent—thank you for believing in this book, and in me, for years. I am in awe of your dedication, kindness, and brilliance, and am thankful for you every single day. Thanks also to everyone at Aevitas who has helped foster this novel to publication, including Allison Warren, Erin Files, and Vanessa Kerr.

To my editor, Sarah McGrath—to say I'm honored to be edited by you is an understatement. From our first phone call, I was hooked. Thank you for your remarkable insights, inspiring conversations, and mostly for pushing me to places I didn't know were possible. I am indebted to you and Riverhead for bringing this book to life.

Thank you also to Alison Fairbrother, whose kind and intuitive editorial eye helped at every turn. Thanks also to a dream team at a dream imprint, including: Delia Taylor, Rebecca Reisert, Alicia Cooper, Kym Surridge, Amanda Dewey, Bianca Flores, Ashley Sutton, and Viviann Do.

ACKNOWLEDGMENTS

Many thanks also go out to early readers of this manuscript, especially such dear friends and extraordinary novelists, Emma Claire Sweeney and Caeli Wolfson Widger, who each read so many drafts of this novel I've lost count. Thanks also to Natashia Deon, Sari Wilson, Rachel Schwerin, Cassandra Lane, Kaylyn Betts, Janine Kranz, Wendy Bergman, Saul Nadata, and Sarah Jagels for additional reads, for correcting me where I got things wrong, and for reminding my impatient self that writing takes time.

I consulted with several experts on law and religion in the process of writing this book. Many thanks to Rabbis Noah Farkas and Shira Wallach for your insights and expertise on Jewish custom, history, and culture. And thank you to Michael Shenkman, Esq., for the tour of the United States Supreme Court. Though the research was indirect, thanks to the Honorable Paul Womack of the Texas Court of Criminal Appeals, for giving me a job as judicial clerk fresh out of law school so many years ago, and for showing me the inner workings of the judiciary long before I would even begin Sylvia's story.

Thank you to the women who inspired this book, most notably the late Honorable Ruth Bader Ginsburg. Thank you also to Sandra Day O'Connor, Sonia Sotomayor, Elena Kagan, Amy Coney Barrett, and Ketanji Brown Jackson for inspiring generations.

And thank you to my family. To my parents, Charles and Kathi Silver; my mother-in-law, Etty Moldovan; my siblings, Arielle, Sasha, Yael, and Adrian; my nieces and nephew, Leah, Ilana, Daria, and Yossi; and most of all to my children—Avital and Levi, who have been writing their own stories with their own dedication and acknowledgment pages since they could hold a pen. Finally, thank you to Amir, who has believed in this book since before it was written. *Everything that happens to me happens to you.* I love you.